FOR RICHER, FOR POORER

"I have to speak with you, Jonathon."

Surprised at her gravity, Jonathon immediately indicated a chair, which she declined. "Speak away."

"I've come to ask you . . ."

"For another favor?" Jonathon quickly provided at her hesitation.

"In a way," she agreed hastily, grabbing at his words as she would a safety line. "But it would be of benefit to you as well as to me."

"And it is?"

Rebecca paused, struggling for words. "How would you feel about marrying me?"

Struck by her unexpected question, for a moment Jonathon could only gape at her in astonishment. After stammering over several beginnings, he swallowed his surprise and managed to ask, "Are you proposing to me?"

"No, I'm trying to proposition you."

Other Leisure Books by Kim Hansen:

UNTAMED DESIRE

REBECCA McGREGOR

KIM HANSEN

LEISURE BOOKS   NEW YORK CITY

A LEISURE BOOK®

March 1991

Published by

Dorchester Publishing Co., Inc.
276 Fifth Avenue
New York, NY 10001

Printed in the United States of America.

1

The people crowded the decks of the vessel, pushing their way to the railings and straining to see the land beyond the harbor's edge. Most of them had traveled halfway around the world to reach this port, carrying dreams, hopes, and fears with them from their deserted homes.

Now, all these emotions stood out brightly on their faces and were reflected in the high pitch of anxious voices echoing around the decks.

Alone among the chattering mass of passengers stood a man. He was a good head taller than most of the other men on the deck, and his shoulders beneath a travel-stained but well-tailored coat stretched the material with lean strength.

Not listening to the excited talk flowing steadily about him, he surveyed the docks they were approaching with cold and bitter eyes. This was what he had left England for, what he had been forced to leave England for.

His mouth formed in a hard line as the activity on the landing at the water's edge became clearer to the eye and the big ship swallowed the distance between itself and the land. People were waiting there: curious onlookers, relatives, friends, dancing children, laboring seamen, and beggars.

His lips twisted into a smile when he saw the beggars, men and women who depended on the good fortune of others to survive. They had to beg for food, for drink, for life itself. The smile abruptly faded and his blue eyes turned hard with hate.

They had wanted him to beg. They had wanted him, Jonathon Gray, to ask for mercy, to admit his inferiority. But he denied them seeing his humiliation and robbed them of their laughter. Because of his pride, they drove him out, forced him to leave his job, his family, his home.

His eyes lost some of their bitter sheen, and he began to scan the nearing shore. This was his new start, a new beginning away from England. Australia.

Here was a new land, a young land. Here he would find a way to succeed. Here he would find a way to make money, enough money to insure never again being subject to another man's will. When he was ready, when he was secure in money and power, he would return to England—to England and those who had driven him out.

The ship lumbered up to the waiting dock, and an audible murmur ran rapidly through the crowd as a town became visible beyond the waiting planks. Whatever these people had expected, it was not this. None of their dreams materialized into reality with the vision before them.

There were no brick-paved streets, no carefully constructed houses, no flower-lined windowsills or freshly whitewashed fences to greet their hopeful eyes. Instead, waiting for them were raw wooden structures leaning along wheel-rutted, muddy streets; rough wooden planks were thrown before store fronts to serve as boardwalks. There was no paradise here.

Jonathon Gray shifted his eyes from the shore to the people around him. This looked to be a poor place to come to find a fortune, but a fortune was exactly what most of these people were expecting to discover. And they were expecting to discover it by finding gold.

Gold. It was a magic word, a word that made people dream of things that *could* be. No class of civilized man was immune to the effect of the images gold could create, and no class was strong enough to withstand gold's temptation. Wherever it was found, the rich wanted to go there to get richer and the poor went there to attempt to become rich.

Forsaking good homes and solid jobs, men uprooted their families to chase after a dream of gold. Anger and pity burned Jonathon's eyes as he searched the sea of faces about him. Few of these people would catch their dream. Few would ever see the shining metal they all sought. Too many would leave again in a matter of months. Broken hearted and disillusioned, poorer than when they began, they would return to the homes they left behind.

He sighed as the gangplank was lowered and the bustling throng headed down the walk toward the town. People seldom thought of the odds when faced with a chance to become rich. They thought only of what being rich would bring. That was where he and they differed.

He had thought about the odds, about becoming rich. He had thought about this land, its possibilities, its liabilities. Along with its strengths and weaknesses, he had weighed this land against himself. Yes, he differed from those he had traveled with. He was prepared for the worst and ready to make it better. He, unlike they, would not try to get rich. They would try. He would *succeed!*

Separating from the others, his long legs carried him away from his fellow travelers. Jonathon moved down the streets of the hastily erected yet growing town. There was motion everywhere—people walking, voices calling, the very air seeming charged with a life of its own.

Even those who stood idle seemed to be active, their minds carrying them to places built on dreams with the kind of hope their bodies could not attain.

Slowing his pace, Jonathon let the town surround him as its sights and sounds penetrated his senses. Stores lined the streets, each different and yet the same, carrying products of need and want.

Hardware stores stood packed with equipment for digging in the earth; dry-goods stores had shelves lined with food; overcrowded diners served food to the passing; stables rang with the sound of blacksmiths' hammers; and saloons spilled music into the street while

7

immodest women stood waiting for willing men.

Yes, it was a growing town, a thriving one. Opportunity waited here for a man if he would but grab it. Jonathon had no need to mine gold. A man had only to find something worthwhile to sell, something people wanted, needed, and they would bring their gold to you.

Impatience plagued Jonathon Gray as he walked down the busy streets. He had to act. He had to start. He had to begin to work, but hard-earned caution held him back. He had to think before he started. He had to plan before beginning.

He paused on the street, his eyes running mindlessly over the scene before him. Planning meant time. Time meant money. He was not without the latter, but his pockets were far from overflowing. He could afford to wait, but not for long. Time waited for no man, and he must be sure he didn't let it pass idly. Every day, every minute had to work for him.

Turning decisively from the street, he began to look for a place to stay, a hotel, a lodging house, whatever a town such as this offered a man. But no welcoming sign met his eye, and a frown settled over his face. Since coming ashore, he could remember seeing no hotel. Nowhere could he recall seeing a sign advertising rooms instead of material goods.

Pausing to speak to a shopkeeper who was vainly attempting to brush the accumulated mud on his floor back into the street, Jonathon was directed down the street to a sagging building where no sign hung to announce its purpose.

Bending his head to pass through the low doorway, he stopped inside to allow his eyes time to adjust to the darkness within.

Around him, sleeping figures lay sprawled across the floor, filling the "lobby," and hanging on the stairs. To one side stood a bench, a wooden plank serving as a counter for the man waiting behind it.

"You lookin' for a room?" the man demanded, his eyes narrowing as he watched Jonathon approach the counter.

"I am."

"It's fifty pence for a place to lay, a shilling to share a room, two shillings to share a bed, and three shillings for a room to yourself." Insolent eyes lingered on the tailored suit Jonathon wore before rising to meet the piercing blue of Jonathon's gaze. "What'll it be?"

"A room," Jonathon answered coldly, his eyes unwavering under the man's appraisal.

The attendant shoved a book across the counter. "In that case, sign the register."

Dropping three shillings on the counter, Jonathon took up the pen to write his name in bold, clear print across the page.

"Room's upstairs in the back. Number seven," the man instructed, holding out a key and turning the book around to read the name. "Mr. Gray. That right?"

"Jonathon Gray."

An involuntary shudder passed down the attendant's spine as he once again felt the effect of this newcomer's icy blue stare. He nodded a respectful acceptance, and his eyes dropped, rising again to watch Jonathon Gray turn away to mount the stairs. There were men a man just naturally knew to stay clear of. This Jonathon Gray was one of those men.

Upstairs, the key sprang the rusty lock to the room. As Jonathon stepped inside, a strange excitement built in him as he closed the door.

Without stopping to look over the contents of the barren room, he brushed past the wrought-iron bed with its thin mattress and a table with a chipped water basin and pitcher on it to stand at the window.

On the street below were people, people sleeping in alleys or on boardwalks, people sleeping and resting wherever there was room to lay because they couldn't afford to spend what money they had on a hotel, even one of this kind.

There was little difference between this hotel's lobby and the street. Why then should people desperately in need of every penny they had spend precious money on sleeping there when the money could be spent on food

9

and the necessary tools for the digging of gold?

A smile touched Jonathon's lips, a true smile that reached his eyes as well as his mouth. One ramshackle building serving as a hotel for all these people! It was incredible. It was an opportunity. *His* opportunity.

It there were a hotel neater, cleaner, and made affordable for people of every class, with guaranteed *rooms* (no sharing of floors, steps, or bed)—if there were, since people would rather sleep in beds or on mats under a roof . . .

Abruptly, Jonathon spun from the window and began to pace the floor. It was possible. It could be done. There were the lumber and furniture to worry about, of course, and endless details to work out.

He would have to go slowly, build gradually. He had to start with the necessities and let the luxuries be added as they may. Rugs and bedspreads would have to wait. Wood for a solid floor and blankets would have to suffice at first, at least in the beginning. And this was a beginning.

Jonathon stopped pacing. It could be done. It *would* be done. And *he* would do it. He would build a hotel. It would be his first step in obtaining his goal, his first step toward returning to England.

Allan Hendrix had followed Jonathon Gray into the lobby, went into his office and closed the door with a satisfied smile. Four months had passed since his arrival in Australia. In that short time, this hotel had been built, giving him the money to pay off the only debt he had in this new land.

The next day, after a night of planning and organizing details, Jonathon rose and approached Allan Hendrix, the local real-estate agent, with his idea.

Hendrix hesitated at first, knowing the need for a real hotel existed but doubting a plan such as Jonathon's could work. In the end, it was Jonathon's confidence in himself and his idea that swayed Hendrix. Looking about the lobby now and feeling the weight of

Jonathon's gold in his pockets, Hendrix knew he wasn't making a mistake in trusting his visitor.

It was hardly more than a few weeks later when the older man found himself saying, "I never would have believed it possible if I couldn't see it with my own eyes."

Jonathon smiled, his dark brow temporarily free of worry lines and intense determination. Everything was going well for him. With men working day and night, the hotel had gone up in a matter of weeks; the furniture had followed rapidly, it having been obtained in town, ordered from England, or bought from people coming off ships who had no use for such luxuries as chairs and sofas in the wilds of Australia.

The rooms were now full except for the higher-priced suites with the thicker mattresses on beds draped with lace spreads.

"I'm glad you approve, Mr. Hendrix," Jonathon said with a cordial nod to several passing customers.

"Approve?" Hendrix grunted. "You don't need my approval, only my congratulations. I just wish I'd become your partner instead of your banker."

Jonathon's smile broadened as he accepted the man's firm handshake. "I believe the saying is, 'Your loss is my gain.'"

"Yes, indeed," Hendrix quickly agreed as they crossed the cleanly swept and cleaned lobby. "And I've been hearing rumors of your other gains. You have interests in many places."

"Only in the places where it counts."

Hendrix grinned. "Jonathon, a lot of people come here hoping to get rich. The majority of them won't make it; they won't get a penny more out of it than they put in. But you, you, my man, are going to be one of the few—one of the very few—who succeed."

"I intend to."

Hendrix sighed. "Ah, to be so young and so determined. I wish I could share your enthusiasm, but I'm afraid I'm too old and settled in my ways to become ambitious again.'' He patted his balding head to emphasize his point. "But best of luck to you, Jonathon Gray. If it's land you ever become interested in, look me up.''

"I'll do that,'' Jonathon agreed. "And thank you again for your help.''

Hendrix snorted. "I only supplied the money. You made it work.'' He took in the lobby with a sweep of his hand. His gesture stopped abruptly at the door, where a man with a shining mane of silver hair was escorting three young women into the lobby. "Richard Cunningham. First time he's been in town in months.'' He glanced up at Jonathon. "He's hard and stubborn, but he's a good man for an ambitious young gentleman to know.''

"He lives nearby?'' Jonathon asked, watching with interest as the four approached the desk.

"About three full days' ride from here. His business is mostly in sheep, but gold fever has infected him, too. He has a mine on his land, not a very prosperous one from what I hear, but he's trying.''

"And the women? His daughters?''

"Two of them are. The other is Rebecca McGregor, his niece. She came to live with him about two years ago, after her father died here—looking for gold.'' Hendrix nudged Jonathon. "Come, it's *your* hotel. You're a man of importance now and worthy of being introduced to the local gentry.''

2

Rebecca McGregor turned at Allan Hendrix's call, expecting to see the older man's familiar face, but her eyes halted on the man beside him, a big man, broad of shoulder and much taller than most of the men she knew. Despite his unusual height, this man was by no means ungainly or awkward. His movements were fluid and spontaneous, his posture straight but not rigid. While he could not be called handsome, he had about him an attractiveness, a virility and masculinity that commanded attention.

"Mr. Cunningham," Hendrix greeted, nodding a welcome to the women as Richard Cunningham turned from the desk, "might I introduce Jonathon Gray to you, the owner of this hotel?"

Cunningham appraised the young man before him with a quick glance and extended his hand immediately. "Indeed, you may, Mr. Hendrix. It's high time someone built a hotel such as yours, Mr. Gray. It's an honor to meet the man with the initiative to do it. My congratulations on your venture."

Jonathon gripped the older man's hand firmly. "Thank you, sir. I'm pleased my efforts are welcome."

"Let me introduce my family," Cunningham continued, turning to the women. "My two daughters, Alison and Elaine, and my niece, Rebecca McGregor."

Jonathon nodded and bowed to each woman. He was impressed immediately by the differences in appearance among them.

The younger of the two sisters, Alison, was a slender blonde, a young beauty who met his eyes with openly curious interest. Elaine was dark where her sister was light and, while she was shorter and big boned in comparison to the younger daughter's slender outline, she had about her an efficient and competent air. Elaine met his glance with a small smile and a demure drop of her dark eyes.

While Cunningham's daughters dared to meet Jonathon's eyes with bold inquiry, Rebecca McGregor seemed totally indifferent during her introduction to him, honoring Jonathon with only the briefest of nods and a curtsey before looking away. She had startling green eyes and her hair had the telltale reddish glint of the Scots among its burnished gold.

Jonathon felt a spark of irritation at Rebecca's high-handed indifference toward him, but his irritation quickly became speculative curiosity. Her indifference was not caused by snobbery but rather by impatience, a fiery urge hidden behind a cool and beautiful mask.

How did such a proud and spirited young woman get along in a household run by the seemingly mild-mannered Richard Cunningham? "My pleasure," he greeted her respectfully.

"If you have rooms for us, we'll be staying for two nights," Richard Cunningham said, drawing Jonathon's attention back to him.

Jonathon nodded acquiescence and looked meaning-fully at the attendant behind the desk. "Our best rooms for Mr. Cunningham and his family."

"Very good, sir," the boy responded quickly. "With your permission, sir, I'll take them up myself."

"Excellent," Jonathon agreed and turned again to Cunningham. "I hope you'll find everything satis-factory."

"I'm sure we will, Mr. Gray," Alison interceded boldly, holding a gloved hand out to him with a dazzling smile. "It was a pleasure meeting you."

"My pleasure entirely." Jonathon accepted her hand and bowed briefly over it.

Watching the gesture her cousin made with the obvious intent of drawing Jonathon Gray's interest back to her, Rebecca rolled her eyes to the ceiling and stepped away to stand next to Mr. Hendrix. She had more important things on her mind than flirting with a

14

stranger.

"Mr. Hendrix," she said in low tones, leading him a short distance from her family, "would it be possible to see you tonight or tomorrow night in private, without my uncle's knowledge?"

Hendrix smiled, not at all taken aback by Rebecca's unusual request. To know Rebecca McGregor was to expect the unusual. "It would be my pleasure to keep such a date, Becky. Tomorrow would be best. Eight o'clock?"

As Rebecca smiled, lightly etched dimples showed in her cheeks. "Could we not make it ten?"

Hendrix's mouth dropped open in amazement, but he quickly recovered himself and smiled acknowledgement. Obviously, there was something Rebecca wished to discuss with him. This would not be the first time she had come to him to talk, but it would be the first such meeting at such an odd hour. "I'll be waiting."

Rebecca flashed him a quick smile, her green eyes lighting up with pleasure. She squeezed his arm silently and hurried off to join the others as they ascended the stairs to their rooms.

Jonathon watched her go before returning to Hendrix's side. "A clandestine affair?"

Hendrix laughed. "That I should be so lucky! She's a bit too young for an old man like me. But you. She's a spirited Scottish lass, that one. A man would be hard put to maintain control over her, but she'd be worth the battle." He cast an inquiring look at Jonathon. "A man could do well with a wife from that lot—if he was looking for a comfortable setting to live in."

Jonathon raised an eyebrow.

"An ambitious man needs a wife, Jonathon Gray. You don't have a better pick than among those three in the entire territory. All three of them are as different in personality and looks as dawn, noon, and midnight." He clapped Jonathon on the shoulder. "Food for thought, my boy. If that's one of the places where your interests lie."

Jonathon watched Hendrix stride from the hotel without replying. Nonetheless, when the older man disappeared from sight, he turned a thoughtful eye to the stairs the Cunninghams had just passed up.

Upstairs, Alison Cunningham threw herself down on the bed with a loud sigh. "Wasn't he magnificent?" she exclaimed to the other two women. "I don't think I've ever seen a man so tall—and handsome, too."

Elaine smiled solemnly at her sister's words, but Rebecca turned her back on Alison, refusing to let herself be drawn into such a conversation. She had too much on her mind. She had to think, and she didn't want her thoughts interrupted by idle chatter.

"Don't you think so, Elaine?" Alison prodded her older sister. "Isn't he handsome?"

"Yes," Elaine agreed, more subdued in her display of attraction to the man they had just met. She was always more conservative than Alison, always more thoughtful and less impulsive.

"And what of you, Rebecca?" Alison demanded. "What do you think of Jonathon Gray? Don't you think he's handsome?"

Rebecca turned from the closet and the dresses she had hung there to look at her cousin. The young girl's eyes were dancing with excitement. Already, Rebecca could see the glint of scheming reflected in their bright blue depths. "He's an unusual looking man," Rebecca conceded, her tongue rolling over the words with a soft Scottish brogue.

"Unusual?!" Alison exclaimed with a squeal of laughter. "He was that. So tall and dark. And his eyes! Such a pale blue." Alison watched her cousin move across the room toward the window. For the moment, Jonathon Gray slipped from her mind.

Alison had been delighted when Rebecca first came to Australia. She had thought it would be wonderful to have someone closer to her age to talk to. But when Rebecca arrived, Alison was disappointed. Instead of meeting a cool and sophisticated Scotswoman, she found instead a country bumpkin. Raised in the hills of

16

Scotland, Rebecca was, in Alison's eyes, extremely uncultured. They had nothing in common, and the gap between them seemed to grow with time instead of becoming smaller.

Now, feeling slighted by Rebecca's obvious indifference to their discussion of Jonathon Gray, Alison strove to strike back. "Perhaps you find older men more to your liking," she suggested with a cold smile. "You were paying more attention to Allan Hendrix than to our handsome stranger."

"Older men are often more desirable company," Rebecca replied, evading the argument Alison was planning. "But I think your Jonathon Gray is quite old enough."

"Old?" Alison gasped in dismay. "I don't think he's old! How old do you think he is, Elaine?"

Elaine furrowed her brow thoughtfully. "Surely he can't be over thirty."

"Thirty! He can't be over twenty-five!" Alison protested heartily.

Rebecca shut out the conversation with a smile and pushed the curtain aside to look out the window. Below her, the street hummed with activity. How the town had grown in the past two years! Gold did that. It brought people from everywhere. With people came businesses and the need to build homes.

As Rebecca stood looking down at the street, her thoughts were not on the town's growth or on gold. They were on one man, and she searched the boardwalks for him.

Several moments passed while she feared he might not come, but then, there he was. Moving slowly down the walk, he stopped in front of the building across the street from the hotel and lounged idly against the wall.

Rebecca glanced quickly back into the room at her cousins. They were still deep in conversation, completely unaware of her presence. She turned back to the window and waited for the man to find her waiting there.

As his eyes found her, she smiled softly. Then slowly but distinctly, so he could not fail to see, she nodded her head.

3

Returning to the hotel room following dinner, Rebecca forced herself to walk calmly to the window and sit down. It was hard to be calm, hard to be patient. But she must be. She couldn't rush now. If she did, she would ruin everything.

She sighed silently and clenched her hands in her lap as she pretended to look out at the dark street below. Maybe if she thought of something else, if she could occupy her mind with something other than what lay ahead . . .

Jonathon Gray. A strange man but a very ambitious one. They had met him again only moments before in the lobby, standing tall and silent in the midst of the dinner hour rush.

"I say, Gray," Richard Cunningham had called upon seeing the hotel owner, "could you tell me when the restaurant across the street was put up?"

"Shortly after this hotel, Mr. Cunningham," Jonathon replied, easily towering over the older man in dignity as well as height. "People need to eat as well as sleep."

Watching the two men, Rebecca smiled to herself as her uncle hesitated. Richard Cunningham wasn't used to people addressing him as an equal or with such self-assurance.

"Another one of your ventures?" Cunningham queried.

"Another investment, Mr. Cunningham," Jonathon corrected with a smile that did nothing to light up the cool blue of his eyes.

Cunningham grunted and nodded quick approval. "I dare say it will be an investment that will pay off. If we could get more men with your kind of business head in this town, we might turn it into a city."

"Indeed, father," Alison agreed, interrupting before Jonathon could reply. "Mr. Gray may well set a new trend. I cannot help wondering what else interests him besides restaurants and hotels."

"Nothing, I'm afraid, that would interest a lady, Miss Cunningham. I'm not interested in stores or shops."

Alison pouted prettily. "What a shame. It would be nice to have some respectable stores where women could shop."

"Some day, my dear," Richard Cunningham soothed. "Some day."

After dinner, Rebecca gazed out the window at the star-filled sky above. Jonathon Gray. There was more to him than met the eye. He was so polite and proper, always saying the right things while his eyes said something else. She frowned thoughtfully. It made one wonder what he was really thinking. She smiled suddenly. It might not do to know.

What had brought a man like Jonathon Gray to Australia? Abruptly, Rebecca's green eyes hardened. Money. What else? It was what everyone came for. Putting her thoughts aside, she pulled her father's old watch from her skirt pocket. Half an hour had passed. She could go now.

Rebecca rose to her feet and casually walked to the closet to take out her shawl.

"Where are you going?" Alison asked sharply, looking up from the book she was reading.

"Down to the porch for some fresh air," Rebecca replied easily, her face remaining calm but her heart beginning to pound anxiously inside of her. "Would you care to come with me?"

Alison shook her head. "No. I'm too tired."

Rebecca smothered a sigh of relief as her cousin returned to reading her book. It was safe. She could go. Closing the door behind her, Rebecca moved quickly down the hall to the top of the stairs.

Pausing, she scanned the lobby below. She could see

no one but the desk clerk. There was no sign of her uncle. It was almost ten o'clock, and he should have retired by now. She could not afford to be overconfident. If he even suspected what she was about . . .

Satisfied it was safe for her to leave, Rebecca descended the stairs quickly in a manner that did not appear to be hurrying and crossed the lobby without looking right or left. She did not want to invite a conversation with the clerk. However, in keeping her eyes straight ahead, she failed to see Jonathon Gray behind her.

Outside, she hesitated on the porch and stared out into the night. He had to be here. She knew he would be. He never let her down. A movement in the shadows caught her attention as a man stepped out into the moonlight. A smile burst on her lips, and she hurried across the street to meet him.

Jonathon followed Rebecca cautiously to the door, stopping in the dark shadows of the entrance to watch her as she looked carefully about before rushing across the street to meet a man.

Jonathon was not surprised by her action, but he was surprised to see the man she met. He was dirty and unshaven. But Rebecca McGregor paid no mind to the man's appearance as she allowed him to lead her into the blackness of the alley.

Protected by the cover of the building's shadow, Rebecca turned to looked up at the man beside her. "For a moment, I thought you wouldn't be coming, Ben. You gave me a start."

"I just wanted to make sure there was no one else out to see your coming over here."

Rebecca nodded hastily, excitement bubbling up in her. "Oh, Ben, I'm getting impatient, and it won't do. I must stay calm."

"You must do that, Becky, or you'll give yourself away."

She shook her head obediently. "I know that, and I'll be careful." She glanced back anxiously at the empty street. "I'll be meeting with Mr. Hendrix tomorrow night, Ben. He'll sell me the land, I'm certain. If I ask, I don't think he'll give me away to my uncle.''

Ben leaned his slim, muscular body against the building, nodding thoughtfully. "You're sure you can trust him?"

Rebecca nodded. "I'm sure."

"All right, then. When should I come to the house for you?"

"The day after my nineteenth birthday," she answered decisively. "At nineteen, I become of marrying age. When I disappear, they'll think I've run off with a man."

"They won't be too far from the truth," he told her with a grin.

"Aye, but it won't exactly be the way they'll be imagining."

Ben sobered momentarily, the lightness gone from his voice. "I'll meet you behind the stables after midnight."

Rebecca's smile faded. "I'll be there. What of the supplies?"

"I've got most of them up at the cave already, and I've got an extra horse. The cave will make a good camp and a safe place to stay until we can get started."

She grasped his arm impulsively. "Oh, Ben, if only we didn't have to wait. If only we could go right now."

"There's going to be a lot of waiting," he reminded her firmly. "It'll be months before we can make any profits off the land."

"You're not thinking we'll have trouble getting sheep, are you?"

"No. We can buy them from anyone. Once we do buy, we can make it known that the land belongs to me. That'll not only keep squatters off, it'll keep our neighbors from becoming too friendly."

Rebecca began to laugh but quieted herself immediately. "My uncle never did like you much."

"I never much liked him either."

She shrugged. "After next month, it won't matter what he likes because we won't have to see him again."

She looked back across the street to her hotel-room window. Her cousins would be awaiting her return. "I'd best be getting back now. If I'm gone too long, they'll come to look for me." She turned back to Ben. "Will I see you tomorrow night?"

"I'll be around. You be careful."

"I will." Rebecca moved to the edge of the building they were standing beside, cautiously looking up and down the walks and at the hotel windows before hurrying back across the street. Once on the porch, she didn't glance back but walked on through the door straight into Jonathon. "Oh! Mr. Gray! You gave me a start."

Jonathon smiled apologetically. "My fault entirely. I should have been watching where I was going."

Having to raise her head to look at him, Rebecca suddenly felt very small.

"You've been enjoying the fresh air?" Jonathon asked pleasantly, studying her expression with amusement and curiosity.

"Yes. It's a fine night," she replied with a smile. "Perhaps that was where you were going before I abruptly stopped your progress?"

He inclined his head in consent. "People tell me I should enjoy the good weather while I can."

"And so you should," she agreed, her eyes glinting mischievously. "The summers are hot and the winters wet, Mr. Gray. The spring and autumn are the only times you can enjoy a nightly stroll."

"The seasons are strange here."

"Only because you're used to England. Summer is winter here, and winter is summer. You'll become adjusted to it in time."

"And are you adjusted to the change in seasons?" he asked, staring down into her eyes.

"After two years I should be, Mr. Gray," Rebecca retorted, growing tired of playing cat and mouse with him. It was a game she was sure Alison enjoyed playing much more than she. "Now, if you will excuse me, I'll be going in."

Jonathon moved aside and bowed slightly, turning to watch her slip quietly up the stairs with silent grace. At

22

the top, she paused and looked back at him, her eyes filled with suspicious uncertainty. He smiled and inclined his head at her. She immediately lifted her chin in defiance and disappeared from view.

Jonathon remained in the lobby for a moment before striding out to the porch. Narrowing his eyes, he searched the dark street with an air of insolent indifference but could find no movement in the shadows. Then he glanced at the alley where Rebecca McGregor had gone. There was no sign of the man she had met. He was gone, for now.

Jonathon moved to the end of the porch and looked thoughtfully toward the harbor at the end of the street. What was that man to Rebecca McGregor? Whatever he was, it wasn't what Jonathon had first suspected. He wasn't Rebecca McGregor's lover. Her expression when she returned to the hotel was not filled with the all-too-obvious feelings of love that usually accompanied such secret meetings. Her face had been flushed, yes, but more with excitement than love.

He paced slowly down the porch. If not her lover, then what was he? Why else would a beautiful young woman go from her hotel room at ten at night to meet a man?

Moving back into the hotel, Jonathon slowly crossed the lobby to climb the stairs to his room, his thoughts still on Rebecca. Spirited, Hendrix had called her. Beautiful and mischievous as well, Jonathon added with a smile.

He stopped at the top of the stairs and stared down the hallway toward the Cunninghams' rooms. What was she up to? He shrugged emphatically and moved on. Why should it concern him? Why should he care what Rebecca McGregor did? He had too much at stake to allow his thoughts to be occupied by a mere girl.

He hesitated outside his door. Perhaps this diversion would be amusing—and profitable? She was up to something, something unusual. Thrusting his key into the lock, Jonathan was suddenly determined to find out what it was.

23

4

Rebecca was up and out early the next morning, roaming the boardwalks and visiting the shops and stores lining the streets. She had many errands to run before the return to Cunningham House the next day.

For a few hours, her chores freed her from her life with the Cunninghams. For a short time, she could relax and be herself. She could meet and talk to people. She could mingle with those who wore rags and those who sold goods. In Scotland, she had known people like this, simple people, who were unlike her guardian and his family. These people didn't care if someone was born in a hayloft or a castle.

What an adjustment living in Cunningham House had been. From living a busy but carefree life in a modest home, Rebecca had found herself buried in a house on a small estate that was filled with suppression and criticism.

Before Rebecca's arrival, Elaine had done most of the chores in town, as well as those at home. But when Rebecca came, Elaine relieved herself of what she considered to be the more menial chores and passed them on to Rebecca.

Elaine remained in charge of running the house, managing of the servants, and supervising the kitchen activities, while Rebecca did the gardening, the errand running, and most of the sewing. Alison was left to ride, read, or play the piano.

At first, Rebecca had been eager to please, not caring about the chores or the responsibilities she was given. She only wanted to belong. She didn't want to become a burden. Soon, the attitude and reasoning behind the duties she was given became clear, and she came to realize there would be no sharing in her new home—of either work or pleasure.

There were times when she wanted to leave, run away, but her pride stopped her. She was raised and taught to accept life as it came, to wait for opportunities to come when she could find a different path to follow.

As Rebecca was walking down the streets greeting people she knew and stopping at stores to shop, her smile came easier to her lips because she knew her opportunity was coming soon. She would get away from the Cunninghams' selfishness and be on her own. With this knowledge held close to her, all her ordinary worries and cares seemed unimportant and trivial. She was going to be free.

Completing one final task before returning to the hotel, Rebecca stepped from the dry-goods store and met Ben coming down the walk. It was an unexpected confrontation, but she showed no surprise and smiled brightly.

From across the street, Jonathon watched the meeting with interest. Under the glare of the midday sun, it was easy to see an assumption made concerning romance between Rebecca McGregor and this man was impossible. It was hard to imagine any woman maintaining an interest in this man, no less a romantic one. Not only was he dirty and unshaven, but the daylight revealed him to be an older man. His otherwise black hair was streaked with gray, and his face was lined from hours in the sun and wind and from the passing of many years. Neither his appearance nor his age seemed to diminish Rebecca McGregor's friendly attitude toward him.

Jonathon watched her cross the street, her face alight with a bright smile.

"Good day to you, Mr. Gray. Are you still enjoying our Australian air?"

Jonathon's eyes locked with hers as he smiled pleasantly. "One can't get enough of a good thing, Miss McGregor." Her eyes shone, but she didn't respond.

Nodding politely, she continued on through the door. Jonathon followed her but hesitated before going inside.

Across the street, the man Rebecca had met was talking to some miners. Jonathon's eyes fell on Jackson, the man he had hired to keep the lobby and boardwalk clean.

"Jackson, you know everyone in this town. Do you recognize that man across the way?"

Jackson stopped swinging his broom to follow Jonathon's gaze. "Why yes, sir, Mr. Gray. That's Ben Ritter. Fine fellow, though you'd never guess by looking at him. I guess he was about one of the first men to come here to Australia. Done a fair share of mining, but I reckon he's a wanderer by birth."

Jackson went back to sweeping while Jonathon watched Ben Ritter. He then turned, stepped through the door, and crossed the lobby to his office.

The record books were spread across his desk. He had been working on them the previous night just before leaving his office, when he had seen Rebecca slip out. He now sat down to look at them again. The hotel and restaurant were doing well. They were both running at a profit, both earning money for him—but not fast enough.

Shoving the books aside, he stared at the walls in front of him. The wooden planks he saw weren't the restraints he was thinking of. There had to be something else he could do. There must be. But what?

Hendrix had mentioned land. Was land an investment he should consider? Jonathon frowned. Why buy land and hunt for gold when the hotel and restaurant kept him supplied with the precious metal? Would it be worth his time and effort? He had as good a chance as any to find gold. Should he risk money on such an uncertain venture?

He shook his head. There was sheep herding, too. Land could be used for grazing. Somehow, that wasn't what he wanted. He pushed himself to his feet and paced the floor thoughtfully.

He knew he was impatient, impatient to get back to England, impatient to meet once again those who had forced him to leave. But he couldn't be reckless. He had to curb his impulses. There was time. There was plenty of time. A year had not yet passed, and already he was making good profits. He must be patient—and yet.

Shrugging off his sense of inactivity, Jonathon abruptly turned on his heel and left his office. He would walk off some of his frustration, use up some of the time that seemed to pass so slowly.

"Mr. Gray."

Jonathon stopped at the call and turned to watch Alison Cunningham approach. His lips twisted into a speculative smile. "Good afternoon, Miss Cunningham I hope you're enjoying your stay?"

"More than I ever have before, Mr. Gray. Your hotel is beautiful, but," she responded, dropping her eyes from his, "I mustn't interrupt you. You seemed about to go someplace."

"Only outside for some fresh air. Perhaps you'd care to join me?"

A smile immediately brightened Alison's face, and she accepted his arm eagerly. "Thank you. I would."

Once outside, Jonathon turned toward the docks. The port was filled with activity when they arrived. Stopping on the boardwalk, they paused to watch a ship depart, its piercing whistle echoing through the air as it left, bound for some unknown destination.

"Traveling must be so exciting," Alison said staring after the ship with hungry eyes. "Did you come directly from England, Mr. Gray?"

"Yes, London," he replied, his voice hardening on the name of the city he had once called home. But Alison did not notice.

"Tell me, was it the cry of gold that brought you to us?"

"In a way," Jonathon agreed, looking from the ship and down into her upturned face.

"And do you like it here?" she persisted, undaunted by his evasive answer.

"I've been here only a short time."

"Long enough to build a hotel and restaurant." Alison smiled and put her head to one side. "Father says you'll be a very successful man some day."

"I plan to be," he agreed, amused by her attempts to flirt. Jonathon was sure the spoiled and pampered Alison Cunningham was very used to having her own way.

"In only hotels and restaurants? Or are there other interests, ones ladies care nothing about, which will make you a success?"

Jonathon laughed. The sound rang across the water. "Why would you like to know what other interests I have?"

"I'm curious," Alison answered, looking away from him to gesture toward the departing ship. "Could it be shipping, I wonder? Or perhaps you're about to start a hardware store?"

"If I told you my secrets, I'd have none of my own."

"Must a man have secrets?" she pouted, certain he would confide in her.

"He must," Jonathon answered lightly but with no echoing light in his eyes.

Disappointed but not ready to give in yet, Alison turned from looking at the water to the land. "You might be interested in sheep herding like my father. Wool brings a high price on the market."

Frowning slightly, Jonathon followed her gaze to the rugged terrain beyond the shore. "I have considered it."

"But you haven't decided yet?"

Jonathon smiled and shook his head, unwilling to say more. Were her questions products of her own curiosity or encouraged by an aging father who was thinking of his daughter's future and the prospect of obtaining an ambitious son-in-law? "No, I haven't decided yet."

Silence fell between them. Alison scowled as

Jonathon turned to look at the sea. He was so mysterious. He never answered a question directly. "Have you traveled out into the bush since you've come? It's really much more interesting than the water you're staring at."

"I'm sorry," he murmured, facing her once more. "I didn't mean to neglect you."

Alison tossed her head carelessly, a cunning smile touching her mouth. "You have many things on your mind."

"Many," Jonathon agreed, offering his arm to start back toward the hotel. "But to answer your question: No, I haven't had the opportunity to get out into the bush."

"You should go. It's not anything like England."

"Have you been to England then?"

"A few times," she replied. "I was there last about three years ago. I loved all the balls and operas they have in London. We don't have any here." She sighed heavily, her young face reflecting her longing vividly. London's social whirl was a far cry from the lonely wilds of Australia. "We don't have much to entertain us here, but at least we do have horses." She smiled up at him once more. "Do you ride?"

"I do," Jonathon admitted. "I used to ride quite often in England."

"The country here is much different from the rolling green of England. You can ride forever and not see a single soul, or so it seems. But you must be careful if you go out alone," she continued earnestly. "It's very easy to get lost if you don't know the land. My own mother was lost riding. She rode away one day and never came back. They found her two days later, dead from exposure."

"I'm sorry."

Alison smiled gaily, pushing aside vague memories of the mother she had hardly known. "So, you must promise me two things before we part company."

"And they are?"

29

"First, should you go into the bush, you will be extremely careful. It would be a shame for you to be lost when you're so close to becoming a success."

Jonathon laughed lightly. "I promise that," he agreed. "And your second request?"

"Is for when you travel in the bush. When you go out, you must be sure to stop and visit with us. We have a beautiful home, and our cooks are the best in the territory. I'm sure my father would want me to tell you that you are welcome at our house any time."

"Thank you. I will remember your invitation," Jonathan assured her as they reached the hotel.

"I enjoyed our stroll, Mr. Gray," Alison beamed graciously. "Perhaps I'll see you again before we depart tomorrow?"

"I'm certain you will."

Slipping away, Alison reentered the hotel, unable to hide her pleasure as she hurried up the stairs to the hallway beyond. He said she would see him again! Perhaps he was taking an interest in her. She would have to make certain his interest was not lost.

She stopped at a mirror on the wall and critically studied herself. She knew she was beautiful. Men's eyes told her so when she passed them on the street. But the men here held no interest for her. At least not until now.

If only she could invite Jonathon Gray to Cunningham House—if she could meet him on her own ground where she reigned supreme. But she couldn't invite him. It wouldn't be proper.

A smile suddenly burst across her face. *She* couldn't, but her father could. She spun from the mirror to run down the hall to her father's door. There was no doubt in her mind that her father would do as she asked. He always did.

5

Rebecca lay silently in her bed, waiting. They had all retired early after dinner. Their long journey home would begin just past dawn in the morning. The trip stretched out over two days and nights of continuous travel, and her uncle insisted on everyone having a long night's rest before their trek began.

By nine o'clock all of them were in bed. Rebecca lay awake while endless minutes passed. She could hear the low breathing of her cousins in the bed next to hers. They should be asleep by now—she hoped.

Carefully, Rebecca slipped from beneath the covers and crept to the closet. In the dark, she could see the bed where the two sisters lay. There was no movement from there. Only even breathing.

With a heavily pounding heart, Rebecca grasped the handle to the closet door and pulled. It opened silently. A sigh of relief passed her lips as she hastily drew her nightdress over her head and dropped it to the floor. She quickly pulled a dress over the undergarments she had not removed before retiring, and, fastening the buttons, went to the door.

In moments, she was in the hall, hurrying down its deserted length to the top of the stairs. There were only two people in the lobby: Jackson and the boy behind the counter. Taking a deep breath, Rebecca gathered her skirts and descended the stairs, not pausing to speak but smiling briefly at Jackson as she passed through the lobby and out the door.

Darkness covered the street. She hastened on, carefully avoiding the saloons and dark corners where lone men would be lurking. If someone stopped her now, if a disturbance was made, all her plans would amount to nothing. When the land office finally came in sight, she was winded. Though unobserved, a new fear touched her as she raised her hand to knock on the, closed door. The office looked deserted. There was not a light to be seen, and she wondered anxiously if Mr. Hendrix had forgotten their appointment. At the sound of her knock, a door at the back of the office opened and Mr. Hendrix crossed the room to let her in. "Come in, Becky. I've been waiting for you."

"I'm late then?" she asked apologetically as he closed the door behind her.

"On the contrary, you're early," he replied with a smile and gestured toward the open door. "Won't you join me back here? It's not much in the way of a home, but for an old bachelor like me, it serves the purpose."

"I hope you won't mind my coming at such an hour," she said, passing him as he stepped aside to allow her to enter the room before him.

"I don't mind at all," he assured her warmly. "I'm up late most nights."

Rebecca paused to look around the large room. In the glow of the fire, it reminded her of some of the cottages she had seen in Scotland. It held only the necessary furniture, a bed, some chairs, a table, and dresser, but it was designed for comfort. "It's a lovely place you have here, Mr. Hendrix."

He smiled appreciatively and motioned to a chair by the hearth. "Please, make yourself comfortable."

She took a seat and turned a serious face to him. "You must be wondering why I've come to see you, Mr. Hendrix, so I'll not waste words or time. I've come because I'd like to buy some land."

Hendrix nodded solemn acceptance of her statement, and she continued.

"You know better than most the story of my being here in Australia. You know that, when I first arrived, I hated this country, which I blamed for my father's death."

"Yes, I know. We've talked many times."

"It's been two years since I've come here to live with my only surviving relatives. The passing of time has changed the way I feel. I've decided to make Australia my home."

"And you want some land of your own where you can build your home?"

"Yes. A place of me own."

"You're young yet, Becky," he cautioned.

"I'll be nineteen in two week's time, Mr. Hendrix. Although people believe my father left me penniless and without income, I've a legacy to prove that's untrue. He passed the money he had on to me without anyone's knowledge and without the tiresome attachment of a will. I have it in me possession now and have made up me mind what I want to do with it."

Hendrix nodded slowly and rose to go over to a map on the wall. "Did you have a piece of land in mind?"

Rebecca followed him to the map. "Aye, the section that runs to the east of the Cunningham property."

Hendrix smiled broadly. "A fine choice. A river runs through it, and there's good grazing ground for sheep there—if that's your aim."

"Part of it, Mr. Hendrix. Only part, but it's only a beginning."

"But you won't be starting for awhile," he objected mildly.

"Not for awhile," she agreed with a quick and re-assuring smile. "But I do have your word that you won't tell a soul, Mr. Hendrix, of this meeting or its purpose? I don't want to start a fuss with my uncle."

"You have my word."

Across the street from the land office, Jonathon stood in the shadows waiting for Rebecca to leave the building she entered half an hour before. What was she doing in there?

Suddenly, a light appeared and Jonathon watched as Rebecca shook hands with Allan Hendrix at the door and went silently back down the street toward the hotel.

33

She hadn't gone far, however, before Ben Ritter emerged from an alley to join her.

Jonathon remained still as they talked animatedly for several minutes. Then Rebecca once again hurried toward the hotel, and Ben Ritter slipped back into the alley.

Minutes passed before Jonathon stepped forward, detaching himself from the shadows. It was safe to go. Turning to trace Rebecca's steps toward the hotel, his thoughts chased themselves in circles. Allan Hendrix and Rebecca McGregor. Why were they meeting? And why in the middle of the night? Had they spoken about land? Jonathon couldn't believe there was any other reason. Land was the only possible explanation.

But why meet in secret? Had Richard Cunningham's spirited young niece found a pot of gold? Or was she merely running another errand for her uncle, as she had done all morning, while her cousins slept?

Surely, if Cunningham had found such a treasure, he would give himself away. How could a man keep such a secret? Especially a man like Cunningham? The man was shallow enough to read at a glance.

Jonathon paused on the porch of the hotel and looked back down the street to the land office. Allan Hendrix had told him to come see him if he ever developed an interest in land. Jonathon smiled. His interest in land had suddenly increased. Tomorrow, he would become the owner of as much land as he needed.

The next morning, Jonathon was in the lobby when the Cunninghams descended the stairs to depart. "I hope you've enjoyed your stay," he told Richard Cunningham as the older man stopped by the desk.

"Indeed, we have," Cunningham assured him. "Your hotel is much better than the accommodations we used to find in this town."

"Very," Rebecca agreed unexpectedly, drawing a look of disapproval from Alison.

Jonathon nodded his pleasure at their compliments, playing the part of the satisfied proprietor before turning back to Richard Cunningham. "Then I hope to see you again."

Alison cleared her throat, and Richard Cunningham grunted. "As far as seeing us again, perhaps a meeting could be arranged somewhere other than your hotel. Could you come to Cunningham House the weekend after next? My daughters and niece tell me you've not had the opportunity to visit the bush. Such a visit would provide ample opportunity."

"You're very kind," Jonathon answered, intercepting the surprised and amused look Rebecca passed to her uncle and Alison. If there had been discussion in the family regarding Jonathon's visit, it had been only between Cunningham and his youngest daughter.

"Not at all, young man. It's good to get to know the country you're living in. And what better way to learn than with friends?"

"I'm honored, Mr. Cunningham. It will be my pleasure to accept your invitation."

"Good, good. Weekend after next then. You can take the coach. If you prefer to ride, anyone can give you instructions on how to get to our home." He turned abruptly to the women. "Come, we must be going, or we'll miss our coach."

The Cunninghams bustled from the room, but Jonathon waited several moments before leaving the hotel himself. Rebecca had found him too close to stumbling on her once to let coincidence lead them in the same direction twice.

Hendrix looked up from his desk as the door to his office opened and Jonathan entered. "Come to do more business?" he asked with a wide grin.

"Yes."

"Right to the point. That's what I like about you, Jonathon Gray," Hendrix laughed. "What type of business is it?"

"Land," Jonathon replied evenly. "You spoke of it

35

before you left me last time we met, if I remember correctly.''

"Your memory serves you perfectly, for I remember the conversation well.'' He paused to study the tall man before him. "Are you thinking of raising sheep? Or is it gold you're after?''

"Possibly both. One might find the other.''

Hendrix nodded. "In this land, anything is possible.'' He turned to a map much like the one that hung on the wall in his back room. "Do you have any particular area you were interested in?''

"I thought you might recommend one. I know the Cunninghams have a prosperous sheep ranch. Where might they be?'' he asked, watching for a reaction, something to indicate the purpose of Rebecca McGregor's visit the night before. He was not disappointed.

A thoughtful shadow passed over Hendrix's face as he gazed at the map. "They're over here,'' he said, pointing to the location on the map. "And I've just sold the piece to the east of it.'' The reflective look passed away, and he returned his attention to Jonathon.

"I would say that area looks promising if two separate individuals have invested in it, and,'' he continued, "it would probably be best to have neighbors.''

"It would certainly be a benefit. There are a good many miles between one property and the next, with not many people inbetween.''

Jonathon nodded agreement. "Tell me, where does the boundary run on the east side of the property you just sold?''

6

Jonathon raised a hand against the glare of the sun and looked out over the land spread before him. He had left town three days before with his aborigine guide and was now traveling through the Australian bush. He lowered his hand to stroke his horse's neck, but his eyes still clung to the waves of blowing grass that stretched endlessly through occasional groves of gum trees and past bright clusters of blooming flowers.

This was like no land he had ever seen. Dry and wild, the landscape was colored by golds and browns instead of the familiar vivid greens of the English countryside. It was a strange but exhilarating feeling to be sitting astride a horse in such a primitive and growing land.

When his guide moved beside him, urging his mount forward once more, Jonathon followed. He hadn't felt so at ease in a long time. It was as if the land had bewitched him and was lifting away the weight of responsibility and his bitterness. Nothing else seemed to matter but the strange sights, sounds, and smells around him. Jonathon breathed deeply of the fresh air and received a nearly toothless smile from the thin, wiry man serving as his guide who went only by the name of Sam.

Sam had taught him much about the land in the past few days, explaining the seasons, the wildlife, and the hardy plants that belonged only to Australia. Lifting his arm to wipe sweat from his brow, Jonathon wondered again at the difference in the seasons and at the heat of the Australian spring. Summer in England could sometimes compare with the warmth he was feeling now, but he had been warned by Sam and others to expect the temperature to soar before the year was over.

By the time December came, the warm breezes of spring would be gone and the full strength of summer and drought would arrive. How odd it would seem to be wearing only shirtsleeves at the end of the year instead of huddling beneath the protection of an umbrella and a great coat.

"Mr. Gray."

The softly spoken words broke Jonathon's thoughts. He looked up to see Sam motioning to a point beyond the next rise. Jonathon squinted against the midday glare but saw nothing unusual in the indicated direction.

"A rider," Sam added with a wide smile of understanding. His dark eyes were used to the bright blinding light of the sun.

Jonathon shook his head with a resigned grin. It would take time before he would be able to notice all that Sam, as a native of this country, could see at a glance. He didn't see any sign of the rider for several moments more, but he guessed who the rider would be long before Alison Cunningham stopped her horse beside his.

"Welcome to the bush, Mr. Gray," she greeted, her hair blowing about her shoulders. "I see you found yourself a guide to bring you, but I can take over now." She started off without allowing Jonathon the chance to make introductions.

Frowning, Jonathon turned to Sam, but the aborigine shrugged his lean shoulders and grinned at Alison's retreating back. Jonathon followed Sam's gaze with narrowed eyes. She was not only spoiled but ill mannered as well. Irritably, Jonathon urged his horse on, leaving Sam to follow at a distance, but Alison seemed indifferent to his reaction and immune to his silence. She chattered on mindlessly until, mounting a rise, a large, two-story building loomed into sight.

"Your home?"

"My home," Alison agreed with a proud toss of her head. "The most beautiful in this region. You'll find none like it anywhere in Australia."

"It *is* impressive," Jonathon murmured aloud. *But beautiful?* he wondered silently. Perhaps in England, on the streets of London, it would be called so. But here, in these unfamiliar surroundings, it looked strangely out of place.

"My father built our house to please my mother," Alison continued. "He used her childhood home as a model."

"An action she appreciated, no doubt."

"I don't know," Alison answered carelessly. "As I told you before, my mother died when I was quite young. I never really knew her."

"Has your father never considered remarrying? It must have been lonely for him all these years."

"No," she retorted sharply, her chin raised defiantly and anger glinting in her eyes. "Though I barely remember her, no one could ever take my mother's place."

"Surely your father would have enjoyed another woman's companionship and you a mother's love."

"My father is the only parent I've ever known. I don't want or need anyone else. He feels the same for me and Elaine. We are enough."

Jonathon fell silent, following her thoughtfully toward the stables behind the house. Richard Cunningham was either a very lonely man or one foolishly led by the desires of his children. A man left in such a desolate country could hardly have found complete consolation in two small children.

"The groom will take care of our horses, and someone will bring your things in," Alison told Jonathon as she slipped from her saddle.

"And Sam?" Jonathon inquired, dismounting to stand beside her.

"The groom will show him where he can sleep," she answered airily and led the way toward a white picket fence. "Before I take you to your room, let me show you through our garden." She opened the gate and moved inside, confident of having some time alone with him before letting the rest of the family know he had arrived. But her enjoyment was short lived.

As the gate opened and Jonathan walked in, he found his eyes suddenly locked with Rebecca's. Kneeling beside a bed of flowers, she rose to her feet and greeted him.

"Welcome to Cunningham House, Mr. Gray. I hope you'll enjoy your stay with us."

"I plan to," Jonathon replied, smiling at her sharp tone. Even being caught digging in the dirt could not rob her of a silent dignity.

"You must be thirsty," Rebecca continued. "The kitchen is beyond the door at the end of the path. Mrs. Lewis is the Cunningham cook. She'll be happy to serve you some refreshments after your journey." Before Alison could recover her voice, Rebecca added, "I'm sure Alison wouldn't mind showing you the way."

Smothering the urge to laugh as he watched Rebecca walk calmly away, Jonathon unexpectedly remembered Allan Hendrix. Hendrix had called Rebecca spirited. Jonathon would say the word was more like rebellious.

Recovering her voice, Alison smiled at Jonathon. "She's right, of course. I should have thought you'd be thirsty after a long ride. Won't you follow me to the kitchen?"

Dinner was formal. The women dressed in long dresses, and Richard Cunningham appeared to preside over the lavishly set dinner table in an immaculate dress suit.

Jonathon was seated on Richard Cunningham's left, beside Rebecca, while Alison and Elaine sat across from him. Favored with the full benefit of the two sisters' charms and attention, Jonathon was amused and captivated by the contrast between them. Alison flattered him with her warmest smile. She had wrapped herself in a daringly lowcut gown that revealed an intriguing expanse of fair skin. Elaine, however, was not as bold in her approach, in either attire or manner. Dressed in a simply cut, high-necked gown, her dark eyes met Jonathon's with grave and subtle charm lit by only an occasional smile.

"You have a beautiful home, Mr. Cunningham," Jonathon told the older man as the first course of dinner was laid before them.

"Thank you, Gray. I'm quite proud of it. Built it myself for my wife when we came from England. I love this land, you understand, more so than England, but I can't forget I'm English. Building this house was like planting part of my old home in my new one."

"What do you think of Australia, Mr. Gray, now that you've seen the bush? It's quite different from the view you see from town," Alison interceded in an effort to be drawn into the conversation.

"Indeed, it is. And I don't mind saying it's like nothing I've ever seen before," Jonathon answered honestly. "Beautiful, yet there's something mysterious about it."

Cunningham grunted. "Yes, mysterious. A quality that caught my heart and convinced me to stay when I first came here. But tell me, do you think you'll stay? Or are you here only temporarily, for an adventure, a break from the routine of England?"

"I'm not certain," Jonathon responded cautiously, choosing his words carefully and watching Rebecca covertly. "However, I have decided to try the land. I purchased some about a week ago."

"Land!" Alison exclaimed, her eyes blazing with excitement. "Where?"

"Not far from here. I plan on riding over to see it when I leave here. It's just east of a river."

Carrying a forkful of food to her mouth, Rebecca's hand hesitated but quickly continued its path. She did not speak.

"I know the place," Cunningham told Jonathan. "It's a good section of land. But instead of buying the land to the east of it, why not buy the land the river runs on? Water is always of benefit in this land."

"I would have, but someone had apparently bought it already. They took the land from the eastern edge of your boundary to the river."

Rebecca looked up at him with wide, innocent eyes. "When you were buying your land, did Mr. Hendrix perhaps mention who our new neighbors might be?"

"No, and I'm afraid I didn't ask," Jonathon answered, trying to make her meet his eyes. She would have none of him and looked away.

"I imagine we'll be discovering who it is soon enough," Rebecca stated with a shrug.

"No one's identity stays secret for long here, Mr. Gray," Elaine said, speaking for the first time in smooth, even tones. "There aren't many people here, so everyone generally knows their neighbors."

"Very true," Cunningham agreed, sipping his wine. "But might I ask what inspired you to buy land? Was it sheep? Or could it be the gold fever has struck you?"

"I bought on impulse. A look at the land when I leave here might give me an idea of what I can do."

"It's sure to be good grazing land for sheep," Rebecca suggested to Jonathon. "This country suits the likes of the furry beasts."

"But you never know where gold may lie," Alison interjected, throwing her cousin a burning look. "Mr. Gray may be lucky and end up rich."

Rebecca snorted in disgust, rising to her cousin's bait instead of letting her comment pass. "Rich. Everyone thinks that by coming here he'll become rich. Even Uncle Richard has been touched by this craving for wealth. He's been working a mine for years. But what has he to show from it? Rock. No profit, no gold, just rock. But still he digs. No matter that money is lost on such a foolish effort, as long as it's in the quest for gold." She shook her head. "Gold is a vixen, a destroyer of men. She robs them of their common sense and lures them on until she breaks them or kills them."

"You're bitter, my girl," Cunningham protested mildly. "And rightly so. You lost your father while he was mining for gold."

"He never would have mined for it if the idea had not been put in his head. He would have remained in Scotland where he belonged and let the other fools of the world dig for their precious metal."

"Rebecca!" Alison reprimanded her. "You're being rude."

"I'm being truthful. I knew my father. He was no dreamer. We Scots are not so simple minded that we chase through thunderstorms to try to find pots of gold at the end of a rainbow." Abruptly, she stood up. "Excuse me. I don't have much of an appetite tonight."

Silence descended on the table as Rebecca strode from the room. The silence held the seated people in its grip until the door closed behind her to break the spell.

"You must excuse my cousin, Mr. Gray," Alison quickly apologized. "She does not always exhibit proper manners." And turning to her father, "Really, father, you must speak with her. She's becoming more and more moody lately."

"You should be more forgiving," Cunningham admonished with gentle firmness. "You know she doesn't like to speak of gold and such. It reminds her of her father. She believes gold was the cause of her father's death. We cannot blame her for feeling bitter."

Alison was suitably silenced. Dinner progressed without further incident and very little conversation. Each person at the table had been strangely touched by Rebecca's words and her subsequent departure. The atmosphere in the house had become subdued.

Moving into the drawing room following dinner, Jonathon slipped away from the Cunninghams shortly after sharing a glass of brandy with his host. He pleaded fatigue from the long journey across the bush. Despite the truth of his excuse, Jonathon was more restless than tired and did not undress to retire for bed when he reached his room. His mind was alive with questions, thoughts, unmade plans, nagging doubts, and ideas. He was still awake with them when he heard the others in the house begin to prepare for bed.

Many of the questions plaguing Jonathon came over him on his arrival at this house, from the people who lived in it, specifically Rebecca McGregor. She had disappeared after dinner and Jonathon hadn't seen her since her departure from the dining room.

Jonathon walked moodily to the window and stared out at the sky lit with more stars than he had known existed. Until coming to Australia, he had never realized the sky was so big or that it held so many beacons of light. Stretched over the bush's great width, not a corner of the night sky remained dark.

Frowning, his thoughts returned to the Cunninghams. Allan Hendrix had suggested a man might do well by marrying one of the women of this household. Jonathon could see why. Richard Cunningham was far from poor. The house was elaborately furnished, the family members well dressed, and the china and silver were shining new. He shook his head. Rebecca had said Cunningham was losing steadily in his mining investment, but still, Cunningham apparently was rich enough to run the mine at a loss.

What of the family itself?

Richard Cunningham would pass for no more than a pompous old fool in London, impressed with his own importance and social position and lost in a world of his own. The man obviously loved his family—in a detached way. He never seemed to totally commit himself, however, to them or anything else. He was a dreamer.

Alison? She was Cunningham's favorite. Perhaps because she resembled her mother, perhaps because she was the youngest, or it could merely be because she knew how to flatter him with her charm. To say she was spoiled was an understatement. Her thoughts were only for herself. No one else mattered unless she wanted something from them. But she *was* beautiful, and he understood her.

Elaine wasn't as easy to know. She was a strange one.

Quiet and unobtrusive, she was filled with common sense; she was the oldest in several ways. She was also hard to fathom, difficult to read. She kept her opinions and emotions locked inside herself. Yet, despite this, Jonathon had seen her watching him with more than passive interest.

Yes, he might do well to marry one of them. By doing so he would receive a sizable dowery and eventually control the Cunningham House. Jonathon frowned. The logical choice would be Elaine. If he married Alison and Elaine married later, he might lose everything. The oldest girl would inherit by law.

Jonathon turned from the window to pace the room. There was a third choice, as well: Rebecca. By wedding her, he would achieve nothing. She was only a cousin, a poor one at that. She depended on the Cunninghams. He stopped pacing. And what a life she had! She was unhappy at Cunningham House. That was obvious. From what he'd seen, Jonathon could understand why. The poor relation come to stay with the rich family. She was, no doubt, given every menial chore possible and put in the lowest position in the house. She had no voice, no decision-making power. She was used as a pawn—a rebellious one.

Jonathon smiled reflectively as he thought of Rebecca. She was doing an excellent job of covering her Scottish temperament to meet the whims of the Cunninghams. How long could that last? She had too much spirit to be subservient to other people for too long a time. She had been doing it for two years. Would it continue? Or was her meeting with Allan Hendrix part of a plan to get away?

Scowling, Jonathon returned to the window. He could gain nothing by marrying the Cunninghams' cousin. But she still intrigued him. He admired her independence. She was also beautiful.

Yes, the women of this house were of different natures. Each was appealing in her own right. Hendrix had described them as dawn, noon, and midnight. The

description fit them perfectly.

Alison came on like dawn, bright and colorful. Elaine was midnight, dark and often unreadable. And Rebecca, Rebecca was hot like noon, bright like the sun with her Scottish temperament and vitality.

Jonathon looked down at the yard below. He could marry. But should he? Was that the right way? Could he achieve more married than he could by remaining single? If he married into the Cunningham family, wasn't it possible that he, too, would be expected to bow to the old man's will?

He had to be cautious. He had to choose his path carefully. There was time. There was time to think and plan. He must not rush.

Unexpected movement in the yard below caught his attention and scattered his thoughts. Rebecca was coming from behind the stables, walking with an ugly mongrel at her heels. She had probably been outside since dinner, Jonathon speculated, watching her stop and stand a short distance from the stables. The moonlight was shining on the gold and red streaks in her hair. In the silver light, the simple green gown she wore turned into glimmering gauze.

Jonathon smiled as she looked up at the sky. Abruptly, without stopping to think, he turned from the window to the door.

7

Rebecca stopped on a low knoll near the house to look out over the moonlit land. It was a beautiful place, Australia. It had caught her heart the same way her uncle told of how it had captured his. She knew his words to be only part of the truth. He had other reasons for remaining here, but they didn't matter. Not any more. All that mattered was that she was going to be free. She was going to own some of this land and run it as she saw fit. She would no longer bow down to the Cunninghams. She would no longer have to swallow her pride. Five days, that was all. Only five days.

Reaching down, she patted the ugly loyal mongrel at her side. The animal had become attached to her immediately after her arrival in Australia and had followed her everywhere since. Now its ragged gold tail beat the ground at her touch, and she smiled. If only humans could be so simple and easy to please. She glanced at the house and frowned. She had almost gone too far tonight. She had been rude in front of a guest, caused a scene. She had lost her temper. She could not afford to do that. She had to be careful. Mistakes could be costly now.

"You're enjoying the night air again I see," Jonathon said, breaking into her thoughts.

Rebecca jumped and spun around at the unexpected interruption, her heart leaping to her throat. Taking a deep breath, she watched him approach with a reproving glare. "You scared me half out of my wits."

"Not my intention, I assure you."

Rebecca watched him bend down and pat the dog. "The cook said you retired early. What are you doing up and about now?''

"I couldn't sleep."

She smiled mischievously, and her green eyes sparkled merrily in the moonlight. "Couldn't you?" She turned and walked to the fence before facing him once more. "I'm thinking perhaps we're a lot alike, Mr. Gray. We have our goals and we intend to achieve them. But I'd be careful if I were you. I wouldn't make a hasty decision on a subject you're contemplating, the one that is keeping you awake."

"And what subject might that be?"

Rebecca smiled again, looking like a naughty child who had managed to steal a cookie and not get caught. "It might not be a bad thing for a man who wants to get rich in a hurry, or might I say, for a man who thinks he might get rich in a hurry." She met his eyes. "Marrying into the family, I mean."

Jonathon folded his hands across his chest and leaned against the fence, a smile playing with his lips. "You think I'm planning on getting married?"

"I think you're thinking of money, Mr. Gray. And that's why you couldn't sleep. You want to be rich. I sensed it in town, and I see it here. You want money. I don't pretend to know, and I honestly don't care, but it is what you want."

"And you? You said we're alike. Is that what makes us alike? Wanting to be rich?"

Rebecca turned to look out over the bush. "There are other riches to be had besides money, Mr. Gray. There are riches in the land, this land. And there are riches beyond our wildest dreams. This is a new land, a virgin land, one has only to make it grow."

"And you think you can?"

"I know I can, Mr. Gray, and I aim to have my chance. There's a kingdom to be had out there, and I'll have it. It's there for the taking, if one only reaches out for it."

Jonathon listened to her words fade softly into the night, the rolling melody of her tongue on each letter adding a mysterious quality to their meaning. "You're an ambitious young lady."

"Not ambitious, determined—as you are yourself," she retorted, looking up to meet his eyes. "We'll both be getting what we want some day." She pushed herself away from the fence. "I wish you luck, Mr. Gray. We both need all the luck we can get." She turned and walked to the gate. "Oh, and Mr. Gray, remember what I've been saying to you," she continued, waving to the house. "There is more here than meets the eyes of someone standing on the outside looking in."

Jonathon watched her walk into the garden, suddenly unsure of what to say. "Rebecca McGregor." She stopped to face him. "Why are you warning me? Why not let me fall into this pretty trap?"

Rebecca cocked her head and regarded him silently for a moment. "I like you, Mr. Gray, though I cannot say why. Perhaps it's only as I was saying, I understand you. I understand what you're trying to do, because I, too, have a goal. And because of that, I know the road to success is not an easy one to walk on. A gentle push in the right direction is always appreciated. Who knows? One day you might be able to do the same for me." She smiled then, a warm bright smile that broke through Jonathon's defenses. "Sleep well, Mr. Gray."

"And you, Rebecca McGregor," Jonathan replied.

After that night, Jonathon saw little of Rebecca during his short stay at Cunningham House. Instead, he found most of his time efficiently occupied by Alison. She took great pains to see that he was always with her, riding over the Cunningham land, seeing the house, and, at his suggestion, visiting the mine.

The mine was a large one. Located in the side of a high rock face, it stood out black and ugly against the surrounding countryside. Beneath its entrance stood what seemed to Jonathon to be hundreds of tents. These simple canvas structures served as homes for the people who worked in the gaping mine.

Riding through the mass of tents, Jonathon was

49

amazed at the number of women and children working and running around among them. These wives and young ones were the families of men who had left good homes in search of gold. They hadn't found it; or if they had, it hadn't been enough to support them. So, giving up their dream, they were working for someone else, someone who had found gold or who was wealthy enough to pay wages while searching for it. They were a sad-looking lot, but they were alive and happy at still being alive. Jonathon stopped to look back at the tent town when he and Alison dismounted at the mouth of the mine. He wondered if, placed in a similar situation, he would have the courage and stamina to stand up to such a pitiful way of living as did they.

Alison admitted, as they toured the man-made pit, that Rebecca had been right when she had said the mine operated at a loss. "But the people stay on for the steady wage, and father keeps on paying them in hopes of finding gold," she explained.

Following the foreman, Jonathon watched and listened intently as the big man guided them through the cavelike structure. Jonathon had never been inside a mine before, had never seen such a mammoth effort by men and machinery to strip minerals from the earth. Everywhere, hammers rang and men shouted above the noise as iron trolleys rolled over heavy rails to the entrance, where the loads of worthless rock were dumped.

As Jonathan and Alison rode away from the great hole that had been dug, what Jonathon saw inside the mine remained vividly imprinted on his mind. It was not a sight he would soon forget. He stored away the knowledge he had acquired, saving it for a time when the future might require him to remember what he had learned.

At dawn of the third day after his arrival at Cunningham House, Jonathon was making his way through the garden to the stables. He smiled wryly as he remembered the night before and Alison's vain attempts to persuade him to stay another day. She could be charming when she put her mind to it. Voices interrupted his thoughts as he stepped through the garden gate. As he approached the stables, he recognized them as belonging to Rebecca and Sam.

"You're late," Rebecca told him as he rounded the corner.

"You're early," he countered, throwing his bag behind his saddle and tying it securely.

"Not really," Rebecca told him, her eyes shining and her dimples showing as she watched him. "I'm a bit of a country girl, you know. I'm used to early hours."

"Is that so?"

"It is. And it's also true that early morning is the only time I have to ride. During the day, there are other things for me to do."

"Now summer approaches. It is best to ride when the sun is still low on the horizon," Sam added. "The hot weather will be here soon."

Rebecca smiled agreement to Jonathon. Before either man could move to assist her, she leaped agilely into the saddle and sat waiting for them to mount.

"That dog always follow you?" Jonathan asked as they started out, pointing ahead to where the big yellow mongrel ran.

"Not always," Rebecca answered, watching the big dog. "Only outside the garden gate. Alison and Elaine will not have a dog in their house, especially not Dingo."

"Dingo?"

"It's a native word," she told him. "An aborigine word for a cross between the white man's dog and the Australian warrigal."

"And that's a dingo?" Jonathon asked.

"No," Rebecca corrected him. "That *is* Dingo."

Sam smiled at Jonathon's momentary confusion and urged his horse forward to lead the way down a knoll, leaving Rebecca and Jonathon to follow.

"How long are you planning on staying in the bush

before returning to town, Mr. Gray?'' Rebecca inquired.

"Long enough to see the property I've bought. I'd like to get an idea of what it's like.''

"I can tell you what it's like,'' she replied with a wave of her hand at the land around them. "All the land here looks much the same. One man's property is no different than his neighbor's. There are no fences to mark off one man's land from the next.'' She eyed him thoughtfully. "You surprised me by purchasing land. What do you hope to find? Gold?''

"One can always hope,'' Jonathon answered easily, avoiding a direct answer. But the seriousness in her eyes made him ask, "Do you really hate gold so much?''

"I do not hate gold, Mr. Gray. I hate what it does to men. It makes them greedy and selfish. It turns them against friends and drives them from safe and happy homes. They uproot their families just to get a look at the shining stuff.''

"What of your father? You really don't believe he wanted to stay?''

"I know he didn't,'' she answered venomously. "He was planning on coming home. He wrote to tell me so. He was only staying on here to be of help to Uncle Richard.'' She sighed and shook her head regretfully. "He was a kind man, and he felt sorry for my uncle. My father knew Uncle Richard was a lonely man, and he didn't want to be the one to tell the man his mine was worthless.''

"Yes, I can understand how a man could be lonely out here and want to cling to a dream. But loneliness can be cured by marriage. Why did your uncle never remarry after his wife's death?''

"He almost did—once.'' Rebecca frowned and looked away.

"You didn't approve of him doing so?''

She snorted. "It was not I who disapproved of his getting married. It was Alison.'' She met his eyes levelly. My uncle would do anything for Alison.''

52

"Another warning?"

Rebecca smiled, the grave expression fleeing from her face. "No, Mr. Gray, a statement of fact."

Sam sat waiting on the next hill for them. Rebecca pulled her horse up beside his.

"Sam, he's all yours now. Be sure he learns what you tell him, and let him lead the way back to town. It'll be the only way he'll learn how to live in this country."

Sam smiled silently, his few teeth flashing against the weatherbeaten brown of his skin.

"Good day to you, Mr. Gray. Have a safe trip through the bush."

"And you," Jonathon agreed tipping his hat to her. "I'll be seeing you again, soon."

Rebecca hesitated, a small, private smile playing on her lips. "Aye, you'll be seeing me again—some day." And then she was gone, spurring her horse away from him with the big yellow dog following close behind.

8

The night following Jonathon's departure was a busy one for Rebecca. Carefully sifting through her possessions, she put them together in bundles to take down to the stable.

She had no fear of being caught packing, nor did she need worry about someone noticing things were missing from her room. She seldom had visitors. The servants did not come to her room to clean, since she preferred to do it herself, and the Cunninghams came to see her only when it was absolutely necessary.

No, she need not be afraid of being caught in her room, but there was always the chance of being discovered while sneaking her bundles silently down the stairs and outside to the stables. She dared not risk more than one trip per night. By beginning this evening, she knew that when Ben came, she and what little she possessed would be ready to leave Cunningham House forever.

The journey through the dark to the stables was painful for her. Her heart pounded loudly against her ribs, and each small night sound made her nerves leap in anticipation. Her fears were unfounded though, and the night passed into day without anyone noting the difference in her or her room. No one suspected anything was amiss.

Going about her daily chores, Rebecca's body seemed to perform her usual duties automatically while her mind dwelled longingly on the freedom that would soon be within her grasp. The busy preparations taking place in the house around her had no effect on her work or state of mind. A party was being planned, her party. It was her birthday, but she did not care.

When evening came, she knew a lavish meal would be served. A richly decorated cake would be brought forward, and the Cunninghams would put her through the same quiet, impersonal ceremony she had received each year since coming to Cunningham House. The solemn occasions of birthdays in the Cunningham home always made Rebecca long for Scotland and the wild and carefree parties her entire village had celebrated. The gifts given had been simple and inexpensive, sometimes nothing more than a bouquet of wild flowers, but they were treasures given from the heart, and the night was spent in dancing and laughter.

As night descended on the household, Rebecca steeled herself to accept the inevitable and managed to smile graciously at each family member as she received her gifts. It was a grave ceremony that the Cunninghams deeply enjoyed, but Rebecca was glad when the night was over and everyone began to prepare for bed.

"Now you're of marrying age," Alison told Rebecca enviously as she followed her cousin to her bedroom door. "I've two months to wait yet."

"You speak as though you already have someone in mind to marry. Could it be anyone I know?"

Alison flushed angrily and snapped, "Who on earth would I have in mind?"

Rebecca smiled and leaned back against the door. "Who, indeed?" she replied. "I know of only one man who's been turning your head in the past few weeks."

"Do you think he's interested in me?" Alison asked anxiously, her mood changing instantly as she thought of Jonathon Gray.

"Who knows what a man thinks?"

Alison sighed. "Do you think he'll come back?"

Rebecca shrugged. "I wouldn't worry if he didn't," she told her cousin, quickly continuing before Alison could protest. "You're young yet and have plenty of time to find yourself a husband."

Alison laughed bitterly. "There may be time to find a

husband, but there isn't always the husband you want to be found." She glared down through the dim light of the hall. "Sometimes, I wish I lived in England instead of this place. It's so empty."

"Perhaps you should put the question to your father. He may have friends you can stay with there."

The younger girl straightened, her eyes glittering thoughtfully. It was an idea, and it might work. When she asked, she usually received. "Perhaps you're right. Maybe I will ask. Good night, Rebecca."

Rebecca watched her cousin go, the proud young head held high as Alison continued down the hall. Rebecca sighed regretfully and slipped into her room, closing the door softly behind her. Walking to her bed, she dropped her gifts onto the lace cover. Tears unexpectedly brimmed in her eyes. She felt so alone, so empty. How she missed her father and the love he had given her!

She wandered to the window and looked at the sky, blinking back her tears. Clouds were skimming silently across the vastness, hiding the stars as she had hidden her heart since her arrival in this lonely house. She had found nothing but unhappiness in this land. Was she foolish to stay? Should she be running back to Scotland instead of to a cave on a barren plain just over a few hour's ride away? What was there to keep her here? There was no family, or at least none who cared. No friends, no one who loved her, no one who worried about her, no one . . . but there was.

Rebecca's chin lifted. She did have friends. There were people who cared for her. Ben, Mr. Hendrix, and others like them. Shoving her wave of self-pity aside, she turned from the window with a determined smile and began to pull together the rest of her belongings. She was going to make this her home, this Australia. After this night, there would be nothing and no one to stop her from doing it.

There was only one more day to be spent in this house, in his house she had never been able to call home. At the end of that day, covered by night, she would slip away and escape to the freedom she wanted so desperately to find. Carefully folding the men's pants and shirts she had bought for her future life in the cave, she pushed them into her bundle and closed it with a decisive tug. "Just one more night, Rebecca McGregor," she whispered to herself. "Just one more."

The waiting for her final night to come was endless. The hours of the day dragged by with eternal slowness as she wandered idly from chore to chore. Elaine snapped at her several times for daydreaming, but it was difficult to concentrate on anything save the coming night. At last, dinner passed and Rebecca was free to retire to her room. Pacing the floor restlessly, she waited. It would be hours before the others went to bed. Hours. She pressed her fingers to her pounding temples. She must be patient. She must relax. Turning out her lamp, she sank down onto the bed, her hands clenched tightly in her lap.

Minutes passed. Sounds. Footsteps! They were coming upstairs! Rebecca's nails bit into the flesh of her palms as floorboards creaked and movements echoed outside her door. No one must come to her room tonight! No one!

The noises died away. Slowly, silence descended on the house. The family had settled into bed. But Rebecca sat, straining her ears for the sound of a footfall or a tap on her door. Time crept on. Half an hour passed. An hour. Rebecca slid off the bed. Quickly stepping out of her dress, she buttoned herself into a pair of trousers and a rough cotton shirt. She was ready to go.

She moved to the door and listened. She could hear the ticking of the grandfather clock in the hall by the stairs. Minutes dragged by. The clock chimed. Eleven o'clock. An hour to go. Rebecca paced the floor, counting the seconds until she was sure the clock was about to strike once more. Then she hovered near the door with a pounding heart. The hammering beat echoed inside her head until it grew so loud she was sure someone would hear it. But no other sound touched the house. Silence remained.

Finally, the chimes began to ring. One, two . . . she reached for the cloth carpetbag that held the last of her possessions . . . seven, eight . . . she opened the bedroom door . . . ten, eleven . . . she was at the end of the hall, staring down at the bottom of the stairs . . . twelve.

She scurried down the stairs and through the house to the kitchen. Stopping by the back door, she paused breathlessly to listen. No sound came from behind her. No calling voices. No footsteps. Only the sound of the steady ticking of the clock lingered in the air. It was safe.

She lifted the latch free of its catch and opened the door only wide enough to slip through before pulling it shut and starting to run. Racing through the garden, she leaped over the rows of flowers and plants she had kept so carefully for the past two years. Beyond the gate, Dingo sat waiting to follow her rapid steps around the stables and over the knoll into a small gully. Tripping over her feet and unseen obstacles, Rebecca rushed down the incline until, abruptly, hands reached out of the darkness and pulled her to a halt.

"Whoa there!" a voice whispered hoarsely while strong hands steadied her. "You're running like the devil himself was after you."

Rebecca gave a shaky laugh, but her voice was filled with fear. "I wouldn't want to get caught now, Ben. They'd have my head on a silver platter."

Ben gave her shoulders a firm squeeze. "You won't get caught," he reassured her gravely. "Before you go, before we mount up and ride away, be sure you want to do this. There'll be no turning back after tonight."

Rebecca looked back toward the house. Only the roof was visible from the gully. The sight of only a part of the building that had held her like a prison only strengthened her resolve to leave. "I've no doubts. But what about you? I don't want to give you any trouble you don't want."

Ben smiled, a flash of white in the dark. "Doubts? I've got none. It'll give me the greatest pleasure to put one over on those Cunninghams."

Rebecca stared up into his rugged face. "Is that why you're helping me, Ben? Because you dislike the Cunninghams so much?"

Ben shook his head. "It's true I don't like 'em. There's few people hereabouts who do. But while I'd like to see them knocked off their high horse, I'd like to see you happy more."

Rebecca threw her arms around his neck and hugged him impulsively. "You're a good man, Ben Ritter, and a fine friend. There's no doubt in my mind of that."

Ben shifted awkwardly, pushing her away to hide his embarrassment. "Come on. We'd best be going." He helped her into the saddle, taking her bag and tying it behind his horse before leaping astride his own mount. "Ready?"

Rebecca nodded, a feeling of wild exhilaration sweeping through her as she turned her back on Cunningham House. "I'm ready."

9

The door to Jonathon's office flew open and slammed against the wall with a resounding crash. Jonathon started at the unexpected interruption, and Allan Hendrix twisted round in his chair to meet a red-faced Richard Cunningham.

"Where's Rebecca?" Cunningham demanded, his voice bouncing from wall to wall in the small room.

Silence fell in the room. Jonathon rose slowly to his feet to face his visitor, his great height filling the room with authority. His voice was coldly cutting when he finally spoke, "I'm sorry, Mr. Cunningham. What is it you want?"

"My niece! Where's my niece?" Cunningham bellowed.

Jonathon's brow furrowed darkly. "I haven't seen your niece since I left your home six days ago."

"And you?" Cunningham demanded of Hendrix. "Have you seen her?"

Hendrix, also now on his feet, answered the irate man with calm. "I haven't seen Rebecca in almost a month. Why? Has something happened to her?"

"Happened! Happened, you say?" Cunningham echoed dumbly. "Yes, something's happened. She's disappeared."

"Disappeared!" Hendrix exclaimed.

"Yes, three days ago, on the night following her birthday. She didn't come down to breakfast, so I sent a maid to her room. That's when we discovered she was gone."

"Are you sure she ran away?" Jonathon inquired coolly. "She hasn't merely gone out for a ride? Perhaps gotten lost in the bush?"

"No, no! She's not lost," Cunningham insisted, running a hand through his disarranged hair. "Her clothes are gone. Everything's gone. And not even a note. Nothing to tell me where she's gone."

The words echoed hollowly around the room. Hendrix found himself remembering the night she came to him at the land office.

Jonathon was remembering, too. What had she said at their last parting? He turned his mind back to Cunningham. "Have you checked the docks?"

"Yes. I thought she might try to go back to Scotland. But no one there has seen her."

"Are any of the horses from the stable missing?" Jonathon asked.

"No, there are no horses missing," Cunningham muttered forlornly, sinking down into a chair.

"She couldn't have walked away. Someone must have been waiting for her," Jonathon said softly, almost to himself. He didn't add that the someone was probably Ben Ritter.

"She just turned nineteen, didn't she?" Hendrix suggested, trying to ease his own mind as well as Cunningham's. "That's marrying age."

"But she wasn't even interested in anyone!" Cunningham protested.

"Young women have a way of keeping such things secret," Jonathon reflected aloud, his mind lingering on Ben Ritter. He had seen the man shortly before going to Cunningham House and couldn't remember having seen him since. Was it possible he could have been wrong about Rebecca's relationship with and interest in the man?

"But why run off? Why not tell me?" Cunningham asked.

"Perhaps she felt you wouldn't approve of her . . . chosen spouse," Jonathon replied calmly.

Cunningham fell silent, looking totally defeated. "What should I do?"

"The only thing it seems you can do is let it be known

she's gone. Possibly, someone will find her," Hendrix suggested.

Cunningham looked at Jonathon.

"I agree. You can't search the entire country for her. She's bound to turn up sooner or later." Cunningham nodded at his reply, and Jonathon realized the man could not understand why Rebecca would want to run away from his house. Couldn't Cunningham see the way she was treated in his home? Was he so wrapped up in himself and his dreams that he really could not see what was happening around him?

"I think it would be best if you accept a room and rest for awhile," Jonathon said. "You've obviously been under a tremendous strain."

"Yes, yes, I have," Cunningham agreed, allowing himself to be led to the door.

Pausing, Jonathon looked back at Allan Hendrix. Hendrix was scowling, deeply engrossed in his own thoughts. Was it possible he knew something both Jonathon and Cunningham did not?

Jonathon glanced down at Cunningham and ushered him out of the room. If Hendrix did know something and was not speaking, the man was not alone, for Jonathon also knew, or at least suspected, more than he was saying. Why was Hendrix not telling what he knew? And, Jonathon wondered, why was he, himself, not speaking?

Miles away, Rebecca stared off into the distance beyond the opening of the cave, unaware of Richard Cunningham's arrival in town—and uncaring. Her only concern was the present. It seemed to her that it had been going on forever. She could not remember another time in her life when she had sat so long in one place.

She glanced over at Ben, who was sitting against the opposite wall, puffing stolidly on a pipe. They'd been sitting idly doing nothing for what seemed like an eternity. In reality, it had only been a few days. She hated this waste of time, but it was necessary.

There had to be a waiting period. They had to wait until everyone had gotten over the initial shock of discovering she had gone. At first, there would be search parties. Uncle Richard would have people out looking for her. He would insist they continue for a week, perhaps longer. The bush was large, almost unending. Many people had been lost there and never found. The men would know it, and they would also know that, without supplies, no one could live in the bush for long, especially not a nineteen-year-old girl. She wouldn't know how to live in the wilderness. She couldn't possibly survive alone. Eventually, Rebecca McGregor would be assumed to be dead.

In a week, Ben would go into town to listen to the talk. He would wait to see if things had calmed down. Rebecca chewed at her lip apprehensively. She didn't like the idea of Ben going in alone. What if someone asked him about her? What if somehow he gave something away? Everyone knew Ben was her friend. But then, she had many friends in town. Why suspect only Ben? What did it matter if he had left town shortly before her disappearance? People knew Ben was inclined to come and go as he chose.

No, she was being silly. There was no risk for him. There was a risk for her. She wouldn't be able to go to town, not for a long time.

Rebecca sighed and tossed a rock aimlessly down into the depths of the cave. "Have you ever looked down there, Ben?"

Ben looked at the recesses of the cave. "Not all the way. It's one of those endless caverns. Goes on for miles."

"Good," she said rising. "It'll give me something to do then."

"Restless?"

"Some. I always hated waiting."

"Worst part of life, waiting. Makes a man age before his time."

Rebecca nodded as she picked up a lamp. "I believe

that's true. Right now, I feel about fifty.''

Ben grinned and watched her start off, lighting the lantern when she reached the dark edges of the cave. The glow from the lantern bounced off the cold walls that encircled her. There were rocks and boulders of all sizes scattered over the stone floor. It didn't look inviting, but Rebecca pressed on. It would occupy her mind for awhile.

Aimlessly walking through the cavern, she made her way around and over the obstacles the cave set in her path until, rounding a curve in the walls, she found herself facing a boulder flanked by a rock wall. Disappointed, she held the lantern up to glare at the offensive boulder. She wasn't ready to give up. Moving forward carefully, she squeezed around the boulder to examine the wall and let out a small cry of delight as her lantern penetrated the darkness. There was a hole. It was big enough to climb through.

Holding up the lantern, she put her head into the opening to allow the light to reflect into the next room. It looked much the same as what she had already seen. With a shrug of her slim shoulders, she decided to go on. Boosting herself up to slip through the hole, she dropped to the other side. A chill ran down her spine. She held up the lantern once more. This cavern was colder and much damper than the one she had just passed through, because the warmth of fresh air could not easily make its way to these buried walls.

Rebecca began to walk again, but she hadn't gone far when she stopped to listen. Running water? An underground spring? With her curiosity aroused, she pushed on, quickening her steps. No matter how small the stream, if the water was enough to splash on the rocks, there would be enough to drink. Climbing through the caverns had made her thirsty.

Following the sound of the falling water, she made her way through the cavern, watching the floor for signs of the cool liquid. Coming to a boulder, she looked up to step carefully around it and saw the light from the lantern reflect off something on the wall. Certain she had found the water, she began to hurry forward but suddenly froze. It wasn't water. It wasnt! It was . . . it looked like . . . but was it? She stood paralyzed, staring at the wall before her. Could it really be what she thought it was?

Rebecca blinked, squeezing her eyes shut and opening them again. It was still there. *It was still there!* She wasn't dreaming! Her paralysis broke, and she spun round to race back through the cave, yelling at the top of her voice. "Ben! Ben, come quick!"

Ben was on his feet and running before he was conscious of moving. He plunged into the darkness, stumbling and cursing as he ran into rocks and tripped over cracks. Muttering hotly, he stopped and lit a match. "Where are you?"

"Here! Back here!" was her reply, and he cursed again as the flame burned his fingers and he let the match drop to the floor.

More matches led him on until Rebecca's lantern brightened the way before him. "What's the matter?" he demanded, seeing her holding the lamp behind a hole in the wall.

"Come quick," Rebecca replied and disappeared back into the hole.

Having no choice but to follow, Ben squeezed his long frame through the hole and began walking once more. When at last he saw her again, she was standing perfectly still, staring at something beyond a huge boulder. "What . . . ?"

He stopped when he saw her expression and followed her intent gaze toward the wall. At first, he, too, could only stand and stare as she had, numbed to stillness. Finally he moved, striding to the wall to put his fingers against the golden vein that ran through the hard rock.

Holding the lantern high, Rebecca watched him study the gold vein, following his eyes as they searched along its length. "Is it . . . is it?"

"Gold?" he supplied for her, his voice hoarse with

choked-back emotion. "It's one of the finest veins I've ever seen." He looked over the length of the vein again, trying to shake the disbelief from his mind. "And I've seen plenty."

"Is what we see—is this all there is to it?" she asked in an awed whisper.

"Hard to say. It looks like it runs into the wall here. It could be deep, but then on the other hand," he shrugged his shoulders expressively, "could be what they call a splash in the pan."

"How can you tell which one it is?"

"By digging. That's the only way."

Rebecca sank down on a rock and sat staring at the vein. "Am I dreaming, Ben? I don't believe what I see is real."

Ben grinned. "If we're dreaming, I don't want to wake up."

Their eyes locked, and suddenly they were both laughing, their voices echoing through the cavern and back again.

Rebecca sobered and looked anxiously at Ben. "You're sure this is real?"

"I'm sure. It's real, and it's yours."

"Ours," she corrected. "We made a bargain."

"Yup," Ben agreed, shoving his hands in his pockets. "We did. And I remember our bargain very clearly. You wanted a partner. I said no. I told you I'd be your foreman, and you agreed."

"But, Ben, if this is real, you deserve more of it than the ten percent we agreed on."

"No," Ben told her firmly. "No more partnerships for me."

Rebecca felt anxiety fill her as she remembered the partners he had had during his life. One was lost in a mine cave-in, one was killed in a fight over a claim, and the third, the third was a woman, his wife, who ran off with another man. No, there would be no more partners for Ben Ritter. She laid an understanding hand on his arm. "Well, then, what will we do about this?"

"What can we do except dig?"

Rebecca smiled as they turned back to stare at the gold. It was still too unbelievable to be true. As the silence of the cavern fell around them once more, she again became aware of the sound of water and her thirst. Moving away, she followed the echo to the back of a nearby wall, where she found a stream running clear and free through the floor of the cavern. She set her lantern down beside it and motioned to Ben. "May I drink this?"

Ben moved to her side and stared down at the running water. "Is it clear?"

Rebecca knelt and put her hands in the water, examining the liquid in the lamp light. "I think so," she told him, putting her hands back in the water. But Ben grabbed her arm and hauled her backward so that she fell against him. "Ben! What?"

"Your hands! Look at your hands! Hold them up in the light."

Rebecca did as she was told and gasped sharply. Her hands were covered with a fine, golden film.

"That answers your question about how big this vein is."

"How big?"

"That's gold dust."

Rebecca stared at her hands for a moment. "For three days we've been sitting on top of a gold mine and we never knew it?"

Ben grinned and Rebecca started to laugh. This gold had been laying in this hidden cavern for years. How many men had used this cave for shelter over that time? How many men had been just a short walk away from becoming rich?

This was what people came to Australia for. It was what they dreamed of. And they, Rebecca and Ben, who hadn't been looking for the gleaming metal, had found it—a cave filled with it!

Her laughter spent, Rebecca sobered and wagged a warning finger at Ben, who was shaking his head silently. "We need to make plans."

Ben became solemn, swallowing his smile. "Such as?"

Rebecca cocked her head thoughtfully. "We'll be needing equipment, and we'll need help as well as protection. We won't be able to stand guard and mine at the same time."

"Makes sense."

She crossed her legs beneath her and stared into the stream. "We'll have to plan carefully." She fell silent, and several moments passed before she spoke again. "We'll have to mail some letters. One will be to a mining company, and another will go to a security agency in London."

"You want me to go to town?"

"No, it's best I go. You can stay here and guard the mine." She looked down at the baggy shirt and trousers she wore. "If I'm careful, I think no one will recognize me like this. I'll put my hair up under my hat and they'll think I'm a boy."

"How soon will you be going?"

"Right away, if I'm to be there by the time the next ship is due to leave. If I remember correctly, there's one departing in four days."

"Take you at least two days to get there."

"Probably three."

Ben nodded thoughtfully. "How soon do you think before we hear anything?"

"If the letters go out with the next ship, and if they answer straight away, the equipment and men could arrive in three months, maybe less."

"That'll be February, before winter and the rains."

"Perfect timing. It couldn't be better."

Ben rubbed his whiskered jaw reflectively. "Only one thing, Becky. How are we going to know when the ship arrives with the equipment and men? Who's going to let us know?"

Rebecca frowned. "We'll need someone in town." She thought carefully. "I could ask for the men and equipment by another name, tell the men to wait at the

68

hotel until I come for them. The equipment will be held until it's claimed."

"But we can't be sure."

"No, we can't." Her frown deepened. "Perhaps we could wait outside town. We could watch for ships. Or maybe we could go in first and put the gold in the bank."

"Becky, we can't just walk off and leave all this by itself."

"Why not?" she asked reasonably. "The gold's been here for years and no one's found it. Why should someone come and find it now?"

"I hate taking chances."

"Oh, Ben!" she protested, jumping to her feet. "You're throwing stones into the puddle. We'll send the letters now and later we'll worry about what may happen."

10

Jonathon stopped his horse to listen to the land. It had been two days since Richard Cunningham's abrupt appearance in his office. The open air of the bush was relaxing in comparison to the atmosphere he was smothered by back in town. People everywhere were talking about Rebecca McGregor's disappearance. It was impossible to start a conversation without someone bringing up the missing niece of Richard Cunningham. Cunningham reveled in the attention he received.

Jonathon grunted. The old man probably couldn't remember being so popular in the town before. Everyone was concerned with him because they were worried about Rebecca. She had many friends. Jonathon frowned. He didn't feel the need to worry. From what he had seen of Rebecca and from the things she said, no one could convince him her running away hadn't been carefully planned. She was gone because she wanted to be, and she wasn't going to be found until she was ready to come out from wherever she was.

A smile touched Jonathon's mouth. He wondered where she was. No one had any idea. Suddenly, Jonathon stiffened in his saddle and gave himself a mental shake. Wherever she was, it made no difference to him. He had enough to think about without letting himself become involved with some fool slip of a girl who had run away from home. He had come out in the bush to think—but not of her. He had come to make a decision about his land. Irritated with himself for letting his thoughts wander, Jonathon urged his horse on once more.

He and Sam had traveled over his property on the way back from Cunningham House. As Rebecca had said, his land looked much like the rest of Australia. It was wide and rolling and covered by acres of blowing grass. There was no way to tell where his land ended and another man's began except by looking at a map. Jonathon knew he had been foolish to buy so impulsively. But when Rebecca had purchased her land in such a suspicious manner, he was certain she had done so with a purpose. She had bought a place to hide.

It galled him to think it was her actions that prompted him to act so precipitously. He set his jaw grimly. He couldn't afford to spend money on something that would not work for him. But he had spent it, and here he was, left with no one but himself to blame.

Jonathon drank in a great gulp of fresh air to relieve some of the fire burning in his mind. He knew a good deal of his anger at the purchase of this land was due to frustration. He hated being idle, hated the boredom that plagued him as he was obliged to sit and wait for things to happen. He wasn't the type to sit. He wanted to be active, to do something. It was this immobility, coupled with the need to make a decision about his land, that had sent him into the bush once more.

It was peaceful here. He felt at ease with the land and with himself beneath the burning glare of the sun. It made England seem far away. He continued on, taking an unmarked trail into the bush, while his thoughts wandered from Australia to England and back again. He had no idea as he rode away from town into the bush that Rebecca was riding into town only a few miles behind him.

Riding day and night to reach the town as quickly as possible, Rebecca arrived stiff and sore from two and a half days in the saddle. She longed to step off her horse, to rest awhile in the shade of one of the town buildings, but she rode on toward the post. As she passed through the streets, unheeded and unnoticed, she saw many people she knew along the boardwalks and longed to speak to them, but it was impossible. She must maintain her disguise.

Posting the letter took only a few moments. All too soon, she was back on her horse and retracing her steps

71

through town to the bush. Passing the hotel, she thought of Jonathon Gray. Had he been told of her disappearance? What would he think of it? Would he remember what she had said to him before they parted for the last time so many days ago? And what of Allan Hendrix? Had he kept his word to her? Had he remained silent about her purchase of the land? Did he think of telling her uncle? Rebecca hesitated in front of the land office. Should she stop to see him? Should she let him know she was safe, that he had no need to worry?

She shook her head and moved quickly on. She wasn't sure what to do. She would have to wait and trust Hendrix and take things as they came.

Night found Rebecca again longing for the company of Ben or Dingo. Sitting in a dark camp among the shadows of the bush was not only lonely, it set her superstitious Scottish mind running wild as well. She shook off her fears and firmly squeezed her eyes shut. It was natural to be afraid of the unknown, even though she was certain nothing would happen. Nevertheless, she kept the shotgun Ben had given her close at hand.

She passed a restless night, tossing constantly in her blankets. Vague dreams and haunting thoughts plagued her weary mind, bringing the fear of being discovered and recognized close to her consciousness. When morning came, she was still alone and safe from curious eyes. Continuing on, she met no one as the next day and still another night crept by. It was as if she were alone in the world. The thought frightened and consoled her. It made her feel happy and free.

Now, only a day's ride from the cave, she was whistling happily when two men appeared out of a grove of gum trees. Halting in her path, they held heavy guns on her as she jerked her horse to a stop. Rebecca's heart began to pound loudly as she faced them. Fear erupted inside her. These were bush runners, men who lay in wait for travelers and stole whatever their unsuspecting victims were carrying. Sometimes, they killed for what they wanted.

"What you got in them saddlebags, boy?" one of the

men asked, an ugly scar twisting his face as he smiled malevolently at her.

"Food. Enough to get me home," she replied, trying to keep her voice from trembling.

The scar-faced man stared at the saddlebags. "Think he's telling the truth?"

His partner, a thin, wiry man, shrugged his shoulders carelessly. "Maybe, maybe not. I don't see that a little look would hurt none, though."

The scarred man grinned and moved his horse closer. Immediately, Rebecca drew in her reins sharply, and her horse danced backwards.

"You've no need to search. I told you I have nothing but food," she retorted angrily.

The second man laughed, the sound grating on Rebecca's raw nerves. "Sassy little fella, ain't you? Surprising that such a little boy has so much spunk. How old are you?"

"Nineteen, if it's any business of yours."

"Nineteen!" the scarred man repeated with a snort of laughter. "Jimmy, I think this boy's lying to us." He stared hard at Rebecca. "Ain't nice to lie, boy. You better apologize."

Rebecca stared determinedly back at him, her mind racing with possible ways to escape. If she could get clear of them, if she could gain enough distance, she might have a chance of outrunning them. She knew the land. There was a clear stretch just beyond the trees —if she could just reach it.

Her heels dug into her horse's flanks, and the animal leapt forward, but too late. The scar-faced man sensed what she was about to do and swung wildly. Pain seared through Rebecca's shoulder as his fist knocked her from the saddle. She tumbled backward and hit the ground hard. The breath was ripped from her body, and her hat fell free. Both men gasped in astonishment as the tangled mass of golden hair cascaded down about her shoulders.

"No wonder he looked so small!" Jimmy whooped loudly, pointing a crooked finger at her. "He's a she."

An evil grin spread over the scarred face beside Jimmy. "Imagine that," he agreed, looking down at the breathless, thoroughly frightened Rebecca. "Pretty little thing, too, ain't she?" He looked over at Jimmy, the scar twisting his lips as he spoke. "How long's it been since you been with a pretty woman?"

Jimmy chuckled deeply, his eyes turning dark as they ran insolently over Rebecca. "Long time, a real long time."

Rebecca watched the scarred man slowly put his gun back in its holster. She felt dizzy, and her heart was pounding; she felt she would suffocate. She looked for her horse, which had stopped off to her left. Jumping up, she broke free of the terror gripping her and ran for her horse, but the big man was too fast. He was off his own horse in a flurry of motion and reaching for her. His hard hands caught her, and he spun her around.

Rebecca screamed as he threw her roughly to the ground and fell on top of her. Lustful hands tore at her clothes, and she struggled vainly to free herself from his iron grip. Crying and sobbing, she struck at him again and again, while her ears echoed with his heavy breathing and Jimmy's malicious laughter.

Suddenly, her hand found the side of his face, and her nails dug in, tearing the flesh as she dragged them down his cheek. He bellowed loudly and grabbed at his bloody skin. Abruptly free, Rebecca kicked wildly and knocked him off balance. She rolled from beneath him and scrambled to her feet, but the man tackled her, throwing her back into the dirt. As she fell, her hand found something hard. Without thinking, she grasped it tightly and lifted it from the ground.

The rock slammed into the side of the man's head with a sickening thud. He collapsed, temporarily stunned, blood spurting from the wound she had made above his eye. Rebecca blindly ran for her horse, pulling the shotgun free of its boot. She turned as the man came staggering toward her, roaring with rage and pain. She cocked both barrels under her thumb, and the desert silence erupted with the gun's thundering blast.

Rebecca was thrown back against her horse as the lead burst in a cloud of fiery smoke from the gun's barrels. From somewhere in her subconscious, she heard another shot, but she didn't see what effect it had. She only saw the man she had just killed.

She had seen a shotgun work before. She had seen one used. But never had she seen it pointed at a human being, and never had she seen its results at such short range.

The gun became dead weight in her hands. It dropped to the ground as she backed away, shaking her head. With a startled cry, she turned to run away from the bloody sight, but instead she ran into somebody's arms.

The contact with another person stunned her, and she burst into tears. Sobbing hysterically, she clung desperately to the man before her as her body became wracked with spasms. The sobs slowly subsided, and cold shock settled in to numb her reactions and her mind to what she had done.

As she became more conscious of someone holding her tightly, of a protective arm around her, she raised her tear-stained face to see who it was. She gasped as she met the stormy blue eyes, usually so cold and aloof, that were now staring down at her in warm concern.

"Are you all right?" Jonathon asked, holding her trembling body close to him.

Rebecca tried to answer, but she could only nod. Her throat was constricted with emotion.

"Can you ride?"

She nodded again.

He studied the dirt- and tear-stained face turned up to him. The green eyes were now pools of fear and uncertainty. He took her shoulders in his hands and put her gently away from him. "Then get on your horse and ride. Don't look back. Just ride. I'll be right behind you."

Rebecca opened her mouth to speak, to object, to explain, to say something—anything. But no words came.

Jonathon's grip on her shoulders tightened. "Just

go."

Rebecca stared up at him, her eyes growing wild with fear, but his calm reassured her. She turned numbly to go to her horse. Even as she turned, her legs buckled under her, and she started to fall.

Jonathon caught her and swung her limp, unresisting body up into the saddle. He held her until she became steadied and her slender fingers were clasping the saddle horn tightly. Then, taking up the reins, he led the horse a short distance away, he released the reins, and slapped the horse on the rump, sending Rebecca on her way. Enveloped in the soft cushion of shock, Rebecca realized Jonathon had left her. She knew he had stayed behind. Many moments passed before she understood why. Slowly, some of the numbness began to slip away, and cold reality touched her mind.

When she became aware of the clothes that hung tattered and torn on her bruised body, she raised a shaking hand to try to pull the remnants of her shirt together. But her strength had been sapped from her, and her hand fell limply to the saddle.

She squeezed her eyes shut against what was happening, not wanting to think about it. She didn't care about her nakedness. She only wanted to get away from what she had done.

With her head bent, a myriad of emotions shook her, and slow, painful tears began to roll freely down her cheeks. She didn't know what she was crying for—whether for herself or for the man she had killed. She didn't know and didn't care.

At last, Jonathon joined her, holding the shotgun she had left behind. He looked at the bent head and the golden hair falling down about her face that veiled her expression from him, but he knew without seeing that fresh tears were falling. He watched a trembling hand being raised to hold the torn shirt together across her breasts, and silently he untied his jacket from behind his saddle. Moving his horse nearer, he quietly draped the coat over Rebecca's slim shoulders. He knew there was nothing he could say to comfort her. There was nothing he could do. She was beyond immediate help. He could only stay close; the time would come when she would need his strength once more.

11

Rebecca felt tired and drained of strength. She and Jonathon had been riding for some time now. She wasn't sure how long. She wasn't even sure in which direction they were going. Her mind didn't seem to be able to function. She felt empty and strangely helpless.

Jonathon's hand reached out and pulled her horse to a stop. She sat motionless as he dismounted, knowing she should climb down, but she was unable to make her stiffened muscles respond. He lifted her from the saddle and steadied her on her feet before walking her a short distance away and helping her sit on the ground. Rebecca watched as he moved about making camp and felt the coldness that had wrapped itself around her begin to thaw. After unsaddling the horses while a pot of coffee boiled, it wasn't long before Jonathon kneeled before her to press her stiff fingers around a cup of the hot brew.

Rebecca put the cup to her lips and drank deeply, closing her eyes as the liquid slid smoothly down her throat. Its warmth rushed to her tired limbs and sent a chill tingling down her spine. She opened her eyes again and found Jonathon still kneeling silently before her. A warm flush colored her cheeks, and her eyes dropped from his. "Thank you," she murmured, her voice so low he could barely hear her words.

Jonathon put a reassuring hand on her shoulder. She seemed so small, so fragile. Releasing her, he turned abruptly back to the small fire to pour himself a cup of coffee. Staring at his wide shoulders, Rebecca became aware of the jacket hanging about her shoulders and of the ripped clothing it covered. A rush of blood colored her face as she quickly slid her arms into the coat's sleeves and pulled it tightly around her.

Her shock began to wear off, and she felt humiliated and embarrassed at his finding her in such a position. What must he think of her? Returning to her side once more, Jonathon sat down beside her. Rebecca huddled down inside the jacket and waited for him to speak. He remained silent.

Moments of tense quiet passed. He still did not speak. Rebecca could stand the silence no longer. "I've never shot a man before."

"He deserved to be shot," Jonathon replied roughly. "If you hadn't shot him, I would have. I had just drawn my gun when you fired."

Rebecca suddenly remembered the second man. "The other man?"

"Dead. I shot him."

She swallowed hard, wondering how he could accept the fact that he had taken a man's life. She wished fervently that she could be so unaffected.

Jonathon hesitated before speaking again. "I never did believe you had run away."

Rebecca lifted her head proudly. "I left Cunningham House because I wanted to, not because I ran away."

He smiled. His attempt to raise her temper had worked. "I can guess why you might have left, but . . ."

"Would you like me to explain?" He nodded and she smiled, a slow, sad smile. "If you've never lived in a house where you were a poor relation, you could not understand."

"Try me."

Rebecca glanced at him doubtfully but continued with a small sigh. "You know I came to Australia because my father died and the Cunninghams were my only living relations. What you cannot know is the difference between my life here and my life back in Scotland."

Jonathon watched her shake her head sadly.

"We had nothing but a wee cottage back in Scotland.

79

Up in the hills as we were, we didn't have the comforts the Cunninghams know, but we were much happier than they. We had to work hard. And every night, when we went to bed, though we were tired, there was always a smile passed between us.''

She shook her head again. "The Cunninghams don't know the meaning of a smile. They're cold to other people and to each other. They're so impressed with themselves and their social position, that they've left themselves no time to laugh. Can you understand what I'm saying?''

Jonathon nodded gravely. "I understand.''

Rebecca nodded thankfully and continued. "I noticed the difference upon arriving. Elaine was running the house then, managing everything by herself.''

"What of Alison?''

She smiled ruefully. "Alison does what Alison pleases. And work does not please Alison.''

Jonathon grunted. "I can understand that, too, but go on.''

"When I arrived—the poor, woebegotten cousin who was dependent on them to live—I was put to work. At first, Elaine told me it was to keep my mind off my grief. After awhile, I knew I was working to earn my way. I received the tasks she thought demeaning to her character: the gardening, the sewing, doing the errands in town. I don't mind hard work, but I do mind the way the work is apportioned.''

"And your uncle?''

"My dear uncle is blind to all except what he wants to see, and he wants only to see harmony in his house,'' Rebecca retorted, but not bitterly. "Besides, I was raised not to complain, to do as I was told. So I swallowed my pride and my temper and waited for my chance to come. It came, and I left. I was tired of being a servant. I wanted to be my own person.''

Jonathon nodded, knowing only too well how hard it was to swallow one's pride and honor to do another's bidding. "Your uncle came to town looking for you. He stormed into my office and confronted Allan Hendrix and me with your disappearance. He wanted to know if we had seen you."

Rebecca's head came up sharply. "And?"

Jonathon smiled. "Don't worry. Hendrix didn't say anything about your land."

"My land? How do you know about that?"

"I saw you go out that night *and* the night before. I only guessed. Allan never told me."

"Is that why you bought your land? Because of me?"

"I don't really know why I bought the land," he answered after a moment's consideration. "At the time, I thought it was because of you and what I thought you might be up to. Now I don't know whether it wasn't in the back of my mind all along."

Rebecca looked up at him, studying his expression. "You're a strange man, Mr. Gray."

He smiled. "Strange but determined."

"I believe you are—for your own purposes."

He fingered his cup and stared into the black liquid, not yet willing to tell her why and what his purpose was. "What do you plan to do now? Search for your kingdom?"

She smiled as she remembered their conversation that night outside Cunningham House. "I've already found my kingdom, Mr. Gray. I have only to make something of it."

"Alone?"

"I have Ben."

"You need more than Ben. You need a husband to look after you. You can't run a kingdom by yourself."

"Ben's as good as a husband."

Jonathon raised an eyebrow, and Rebecca laughed.

"Not in the way you're thinking. My chastity is safe with Ben. In fact, if it wasn't for Ben, I wouldn't have any chastity to worry about."

"I think you had better explain."

She smiled warmly and drew her knees up to wrap her

81

arms around them. "When I came to Australia, it was June, and I was not yet seventeen. My ship was delayed a week in Scotland, and Elaine, who was waiting for me, had no way of knowing what had happened. After a week passed, she went home, assuming my voyage had been cancelled. So, when I arrived, there was no one to greet me, no one to show me where to go or what to do. I arrived on a Saturday night."

Jonathon's breath drew in sharply. He knew only too well how riotous the town could be on Saturday nights, when all the men came in from digging to work off their frustrations.

"I was alone, it was dark, and I was bewildered and frightened. Not knowing where to go, I wandered down the street, hoping to find a hotel or a place to stay until morning. I didn't find a hotel. I found a group of drunken men instead."

Jonathon saw her brow wrinkle and her green eyes darken.

"It was a nasty scene, but things never went too far. Ben came along, busted several heads, and then hauled me and my baggage to safety." She laughed at the memory. "If the truth were known, Ben was a bit drunk himself. Even so, he found a place to stay and kept guard over me like an old mother hen."

She shook her face in wonder. "The next morning, he gave me a lecture about walking the streets before asking me what I'd been about. When I explained, he just shook his head and rubbed his chin. After a moment of thinking, he told me to stay where I was and left. It was two hours later that he returned." Rebecca looked up into Jonathan's eyes. "You may be interested to know, it was when I was sitting in that old building waiting on Ben that I found Dingo, or rather, he found me. He stayed with me until Ben returned, and he's been with me ever since."

"Where is he now?"

"With Ben. If he had come with me to town, people would have guessed who I am."

"You went to town?"

Rebecca hurriedly looked away from him and bit her lip. She would have to watch her tongue. "Just to have a look around. I wanted to see if anyone was looking for me."

Jonathon accepted her words with a nod. "Go on."

"You'll find June and July are wet months here. The roads are often blocked because of the rain. That year was no exception, but Ben was determined to get me to the Cunninghams. He returned to me with two horses and a pack mule and led me off into the bush. It was ten long days before we reached Cunningham House. We became great friends during the trip."

She sighed. "I expected the Cunninghams to be thankful to Ben for bringing me, to offer him a place to stay for a night or two. As soon as Ben delivered me to them, they sent him away. I was very hurt and worried for him and was thankful when I met him again not long after. He told me he had expected no better than what he had received. It was while listening to him talk that I began to realize what I had gotten into."

Jonathon waited patiently for her moment of reflection to pass.

When it did, she smiled up at him. "Don't be too harsh in your judgment of Ben Ritter. He's a good man, and I trust him. He might not be much to meet the eye, but once you've known him, you won't find a truer friend."

"How did you two manage to meet over the years—as you did in town?"

"Always in secret. My uncle would have locked me in my room for a week if he had ever seen me with him."

"Why did Ben choose to help you run—excuse me, leave?"

"Because he's my friend, and because he loves this country as much as I do." She looked out at the darkening land. "I hated it here when I first came, hated it with all my heart. I suppose I resented the fact of having to leave Scotland. It wasn't long, though, before I began to realize I did not hate it as much as I thought."

"And you've decided to stay?"

"I will."

"Stay and build your kingdom?"

"My kingdom," she echoed. "It's a wild land you've come to, Mr. Gray. So far, you've seen only her good behavior. You haven't seen her wipe out miles of land by fire or bury everything during a flash flood. And you haven't seen her slowly dry up until there's not a drop of water to be found." She looked at him, her eyes dark with grave honesty. "Gold isn't the only vixen in this country. The land itself is also one."

"But you're still going to stay?"

"I am."

"With Ben?"

"With Ben."

Jonathon shook his head and pushed to his feet. "You're going to have to face facts, Rebecca McGregor. What happened today won't be the only thing to occur when Ben's not near. He can't be with you every minute of every day. He's not always going to be there when you most need him."

"I can take care of myself," Rebecca protested.

"Can you?"

"Yes," she retorted hotly, throwing her head back to look up at him. "I can ride, shoot, and hunt. I know how to live in this land, and what I don't know, I can learn—if something happens like today, I can do what must be done." Some of the fire left her eyes as she thought back on the past few hours. "Besides," she continued stubbornly, "what you suggest is impossible. How can I expect to know myself and experience my freedom if I'm tied to someone else and trying to get to know him?"

Jonathon threw his head back and laughed, shaking his head at the picture she made with her wildly flowing hair and sparkling green eyes. "You *are* a hellion."

"It's true," she protested. "I want to find myself, to be free of commitments and selfish people. I want to be myself, not what someone else wants me to be."

"Everyone needs to find himself," Jonathon reasoned. "But just because you have a husband doesn't mean you have to lose yourself. Your husband would be like an extension of yourself."

"Are you speaking from experience?"

Jonathon stammered, his tongue tripping over his words. "No, I'm quoting my mother."

Rebecca smothered her smile at his confusion and casually continued, "Is she waiting for you in England?"

"No. She died three years ago, a year after my father."

"I'm sorry."

Jonathon nodded, his face reflecting the loss he had suffered. "They had a good life, and I still have my brother."

"A brother?"

"Yes. He's two years younger than I am, twenty-one. Perhaps you'd like me to bring him here so you can marry him."

"Don't change the subject."

"I *am* changing the subject, back to what we were discussing. Be sensible," Jonathon demanded. "A husband can protect you in ways Ben can't. Why, he can even protect you when he isn't with you."

"How?"

"By reputation, by being your husband. If you have a husband, then everyone knows, if anything happens to you, they'll have to answer to him."

Rebecca wrinkled her nose doubtfully. "I wouldn't know about that."

"I would."

"If you know so much," she countered defensively, "why aren't you married yourself?"

Her unexpected question stung him deeply, and he turned away. "I almost was once, or at least I had plans to be."

Sensing the hurt and rejection he had suffered,

Rebecca put a gentle hand on his arm. "Is that why you left England?"

Looking down at the slender hand on his arm, Jonathon felt devoid of resentment at her curiosity. Instead, he was almost relieved because of her interest. He could now talk about it. "Part of the reason."

"Tell me about it."

"It seems long ago now," he began, surprised at how detached he felt from events of the past. "I left my home in the country to find a position in London. I was lucky enough to meet an old friend of my father's, and he sent me to work in the bank where he was manager. I was good at my job and successful. Through my work, I met many people, people like Arthur Boyd."

Jonathon moved away to stand by the fire. "Because of a series of meetings, during which we discussed business, I often went to his home with documents and information. It was while I was visiting him that I met his daughter." He smiled ironically as he thought of her. "She was beautiful, and I fancied myself in love with her."

Rebecca held her silence as he thought back on the woman he supposed he had loved.

"I started to court her, believing she was truly interested in me. It wasn't until I asked for her hand in marriage that the trouble began."

"Surely, a proposal of marriage was acceptable and proper?"

"Not from me, not from a country boy with no money. I wasn't rich, as they were. I wasn't of their class." He knelt down by the fire, turning a stick over and over in his hands. "Boyd laughed when I asked for her hand. He actually laughed." The stick snapped. "I couldn't believe I had been used. I confronted his daughter with what I thought of as rightful accusations. She insisted she loved me and calmed me enough to send me away, even promising to elope with me." He laughed. "She didn't elope. She went to her father and told him I was threatening her."

Jonathon looked up at Rebecca, his anger fading from his eyes. "Boyd came to the bank to make a scene and some accusations of his own. He told the manager I was a swindler. There was no basis in fact behind what he said, but gossip had begun. Rumors spread of a bank employee appropriating money for himself out of someone else's funds. I saved my employer the trouble of asking me to leave."

"But certainly he didn't believe . . ."

"No. He knew it wasn't true. But what could he do? Boyd was ruining his reputation and the bank's business."

"So you came here?"

"So I came here."

Rebecca watched him for a moment. Under the rapidly darkening sky, the firelight cast deep shadows over his face, highlighting the pain and humiliation he had suffered. "You want to go back, don't you?"

Jonathon's eyes flashed. "I'm going back, and I'm going back rich. I'm going back to have my revenge."

"Revenge is a bitter thing, Jonathon, and its results are not always what you may be wishing for."

"I'm a bitter man, Rebecca, and I'll get what I want."

Rebecca knelt down beside him and touched the hands still holding the broken stick. She met his stormy eyes. Somehow, he knew she understood. "Why don't you go and wash up?" she told him quietly. "I'll fix us something to eat."

They ate while listening to the birds call to one another and the wind whispering through the bush. It was a quiet time. The soothing sound of the running water from a nearby creek eased away the tensions from their bodies.

When she finished, Rebecca watched Jonathan staring out into the darkness surrounding their camp. "You're trying to hate it, Jonathon. It won't work."

Jonathan turned to her with a raised eyebrow. "Do you read minds as well as moods?"

"No. I'm speaking from experience. Remember, I tried to hate it once, too."

He turned back to the darkness. "I have no choice but to like it. I'm going to be here for awhile."

"You might end up staying."

"Like you?"

She nodded, but he shook his head.

"No. It's not home."

"Home is where you make it."

He turned to face her again, his lips twisting in a smile. "Yes, and you plan to make yours alone."

Rebecca rolled her eyes to the stars. "Are we back to husbands again?"

"Only once more," he told her. "Do you realize you're not of legal age to own land—or a kingdom—without a guardian? If you buy anything before you're twenty-one, your uncle can legally take it from you. He's your guardian."

Rebecca frowned fiercely. "I hadn't thought of that."

"You should. It's another reason to consider taking a husband."

She smiled wickedly. "Are you recommending anyone for the job?"

Jonathon laughed as he met her dancing eyes. "I'm in no rush to get to the altar."

"And here I was thinking . . ."

"You were thinking nothing of the kind."

She grinned and turned to her blankets. "It's late. I think I'll get some rest."

Jonathon watched her roll up in the covers. "You're planning on going on tomorrow—alone?"

"Aye."

"Even after today?"

A shadow passed over her face, but she replied firmly. "We all do what we must, do we not, Jonathon Gray?"

Jonathon smiled and nodded slowly, the firelight reflecting the softness in his eyes as his admiration for her grew. Despite the fear inside her, she was going on, as he had to go on with his plans, no matter what the obstacles. "Yes," he agreed quietly, "what we must."

The next morning, Rebecca washed and changed into fresh clothes by the creek while Jonathon fixed breakfast. She buried her torn clothes, knowing that no mention of what had occurred the day before must be made to Ben. He would only blame himself and worry needlessly the next time she was out of his sight.

When she returned to camp and was seated beside the fire and eating, Jonathan asked, "What now? Back to building your kingdom?"

"Back to building," she agreed with an impish smile. "And what about you?"

"Back to looking, back to trying to find a way home."

Jonathon fell silent as he ate. Rebecca studied him while he wasn't looking. Before falling asleep the night before, an idea had come to her. Ben and she needed someone's help, someone in town. Jonathon would be perfect. Detached and uninterested, surrounded only by his own problems, he wouldn't worry unduly about anything that concerned her. Still, she hesitated. She hated to use him that way. However, if their places were reversed, he undoubtedly would use her. Wouldn't he?

Aye, she decided silently, he would. How to approach the subject? How could she ask for his help without saying too much?

"You know, Ben and I will need supplies from time to time," she began carefully. "We've even sent for some merchandise from abroad, things to build with."

Jonathon looked up from his eating, sensing she was leading up to something. "And?"

"We were thinking it would be hard for us to be in two places at one time."

"And you were wondering if I'd watch for your merchandise for you?"

Unable to meet his yes, she pushed her food around her plate. "I know I've no right to ask. I mean, with your saving my life and all. It should be you who are asking for favors."

Jonathon considered her over his cup of coffee. "I don't know that I didn't return a favor for a favor." At her questioning glance, he shrugged and continued, "After all, you did give me a push in the right direction awhile back."

Rebecca smiled hopefully.

"And it seems to me, if I do you a favor now, you might be able to do me one some day."

With a squeal of delight, Rebecca jumped to her feet and threw her arms around him. "You're a stubborn man, Jonathon Gray, but I like you anyway."

Jonathon laughed and unraveled her arms from around his neck. "Tell me what you're expecting."

"Some equipment in the name of R. McNally. I couldn't very well use my own name."

"Of course not."

She returned to her plate. "And there's something else."

"Oh?"

"Some men we've hired to help us, old friends. When they arrive, they'll probably come to your hotel. I'd like you to give them your best rooms. I'll pay, of course."

"You'd better."

She smiled shyly. "You'll do it?"

"I'll do it. When are you expecting all this and them?"

"Probably in February."

"Their names?"

Rebecca looked away quickly. "I don't know them. Ben does."

Jonathon eyed her suspiciously. He was certain she was holding something back. "All right. I'll take care of them and your equipment."

She flashed him an overbright smile. "Thank you, Jonathon."

Jonathon drank some coffee and without looking up asked, "What are you planning on building with the equipment?"

"A house. I'd have to have a house," Rebecca replied, thinking quickly.

"And have you money for this house and this equipment and these men?"

"Aye," she assured him gravely, still avoiding his eyes. "My father left me a legacy."

"That's how you bought your land?"

She nodded. "Plenty left," she added, choking on her coffee.

He watched her deliberate movements until she stopped them to look at him. "You're a determined woman, Rebecca McGregor."

"I am, Mr. Gray."

"And you're up to something."

Rebecca sputtered.

"Never fear, I shan't press. It's none of my business." He watched her raise her eyes slowly to him. "But I am curious."

"A natural thing, curiosity."

"Natural." She took a sip of coffee, and he smiled. "You aren't going to satisfy mine."

"Curiosity killed the cat."

"But satisfaction brought it back." Rebecca only smiled, but he let out a resigned sigh. "I give up. I'll have to wait and find out."

"I promise you'll be among the first to know."

"Well, that's something." He smiled and rose to his feet. It was time to be on their way.

When the horses were packed and ready to go, Rebecca carried his jacket across the space separating them and handed it to him, her eyes downcast. "Thank you—for the use of your jacket, I mean."

Jonathon smiled. In accepting his jacket, he took her hand. He pulled her to him, and, before she realized what he was about, he tilted her head back and kissed her warmly on the mouth. He released her as quickly as he had taken her and turned to his horse.

Flabbergasted, she put her hands on her hips and stared at his back in bewilderment. "What did ye do that for?" she demanded.

He looked over his shoulder, a smile playing on his

lips. "That's how I learned to say 'you're welcome' to women. Besides, it seemed like the right thing to do." Securing his jacket behind his saddle, he swung up onto his horse. "Are you coming?"

She stared up at him a moment longer, trying to understand him, but she gave up and hurriedly went to her horse.

They traveled only a short distance before she brought her horse to a stop. "I'm going my separate way now."

Jonathon stopped. "And I mine." He glanced off in the direction she would be going. "How will I reach you to tell you of the arrival of your supplies and men?"

"Tell Sam. Tell him to come to the cave. He'll know the way."

Jonathan nodded and looked down at the shotgun, which was now back in her saddle boot. "You'll be careful?"

She followed his eyes to the gun and swallowed with difficulty. When she looked up again, it was to find him watching her.

"I've loaded it again," he told her quietly. "Do you have a long ride?"

"Not quite a full day."

He nodded and again turned his eyes to the direction she was heading. "I'll see you in about two months then." She smiled bravely. "Give my regards to Ben— along with my luck. He has his hands full with you on his side."

Rebecca grinned mishcievously. "I'll tell him. Good- bye for now, Jonathon Gray."

He put a hand to his hat, and she turned her horse to face away. He watched her until he could see her no more, unsure of the emotions running through him.

12

The months for Rebecca were busy following her meeting with Jonathon in the bush. She had little time to think of anything but work. On returning to the cave, she found Ben already digging. His preoccupation with the gold enabled her to slip in only a brief explanation of Jonathon Gray's acceptance to help them. Ben raised a curious eyebrow, but he said nothing. Thankfully, his trust in her allowed her to escape further questioning.

After a day of rest following her return, Rebecca joined Ben in mining the gold. Most of their days were spent digging in the back cavern. Their nights were spent in sound, undisturbed sleep. But work didn't fill every day. At least once a week, they declared time out for relaxation and sat idly at the mouth of the cave, watching the sun pass through the sky. It was on those silent days Rebecca found her mind wandering to thoughts beyond her little world. She thought of Jonathon Gray and smiled. What was he doing? What would he say if he could see her, dressed in men's clothing, dirty, unkempt and digging alongside Ben? He'd probably laugh. What would he do if he knew she had found gold in her kingdom? What would he say then?

Her thoughts of Jonathon were not always so happy, however. She often thought of his goal and wondered if he had come any closer to obtaining it. Would he go home to England soon? She worried about such a trip. It was easy to understand why he was bitter and filled with hate. She could sympathize with his feelings, but she could not agree with his plans. Once he obtained the revenge he wanted, what was left to live for? If a man built his life around achieving one thing and finally reached his objective, what did he do after that?

Rebecca longed to try to convince Jonathon he was wrong, but she knew any attempt by her would make no impression on him. His wound was too fresh, still too raw and sore to be forgotten. She could only hope that, with the passing of time, he would come to see he was wrong and find there was more to live for than what he had been believing in.

Rebecca's work continued through the hot months of summer. Submerged in the cool confines of the cavern, the heat of December and January passed, and Christmas and New Year's with them. The holidays were no more than two days spent in the cave; they slid by rapidly. It was a busy time for her, but a happy one. She and Ben worked together and laughed and paid little attention to the passage of time.

For Jonathon, however, time did not pass as easily as it seemed to for Rebecca. His interest in life had picked up since his return from the bush. He had discovered a new way to make more profits, even though it was not from his land. The land still sat waiting for the future. Instead, Jonathon turned his attention to shipping. Building a good, solid dock, he managed to monopolize the shipping trade for the growing town. Next to the dock he built warehouses to store the supplies that came in for shopkeepers and residents.

Once again he was pleased with his progress. Watching the ships come and go from the harbor, Jonathon had the satisfaction of knowing he controlled a good portion of the town's money. The ships docked at his piers, merchants stored their stock in his warehouses, passengers from abroad stayed in his hotel, and both visitors and residents ate in his restaurant.

Sitting on the porch of the hotel in his shirtsleeves without his hat, Jonathon reflected confidently on the progress he had made. He had come far in a few short months. He was getting to the point where he could sit back and enjoy the luxury of being rich.

Watching the people hurrying down the boardwalks around him, Jonathon sighed. He didn't have to work in the scorching summer heat. It was nice to be able to put his feet up once in a while. With an ill-concealed smile of bliss, he realized he had been doing it quite often of late. Temporarily freed from his problems and the accompanying feelings of anxiety and impatience, Jonathon enjoyed his leisure, staring out into the bush he could see from the hotel.

When he watched the brown grass waving slightly with a hot breeze, he often thought of Rebecca. He couldn't imagine what she was doing with Ben in a barren cave in the bush. He refused to believe she was merely sitting and biding her time. He couldn't picture Rebecca McGregor sitting idle for more than a few hours at a time.

Shortly after his meeting with her in the bush, he had met Allan Hendrix on the boardwalk and invited him to lunch. During the meal, they discussed the growth of the town and of each other's investments. Before rising to leave the table, Jonathon changed the subject from business to Rebecca.

"Have you heard from Rebecca McGregor, Allan?"

Hendrix frowned. His silence, held by his given word, had been rubbing sorely on his conscience during recent weeks. "No, I haven't."

"I wouldn't worry about her. She can take care of herself."

The older man looked across the table as if to deny it.

"I know about the land you sold her," Jonathon confided. "I believe that's where she is. I met her in the bush last week. She's in good health and doing well."

"You what?"

"She asked me to remain silent. I know you've been wondering if you should tell Richard Cunningham what you know. Don't. She's fine and happy and can remain that way only if he's not leaning over her shoulder."

Hendrix was relieved and satisfied to hear the news. Whenever the two men met and talked, neither brought the subject up again.

It was two weeks before Christmas when Jonathon received an invitation to join the Cunninghams for the holidays. He hesitated in accepting it, reluctant to become the rope in a tug-of-war between the two Cunningham women. In the end, he decided to go. Being with congenial people was better than being alone during this season. Already, too many old memories were pressing in as he watched and listened to people preparing for the festive occasion.

Jonathon arrived at Cunningham House a few days before Christmas. The house and family remained unchanged. Once again, because Alison was more bold and daring than her older sister, she managed to take up most of his time.

"What have you been doing with yourself since last we saw you?" Alison inquired as they walked through the Cunningham garden.

"Keeping busy, Miss Cunningham." Jonathon answered her with a tolerant smile, noting as they walked that the garden was not looking as well kept as it had when Rebecca was around. Her labors were obviously missed, but was she? "Tell me, have you heard anything from your cousin Rebecca?"

"No, and none of us cares to either. She's gone and good riddance. No one misses her."

"I had no idea your family felt that way toward her."

"She was a difficult person to live with, Mr. Gray. You saw how rude she could be at dinner your first night with us. She really could be quite moody and withdrawn."

"I had no idea."

"Oh, yes, it's true," Alison insisted, confident he would accept her word. "And to just disappear like that without a word of thanks for all we'd given her! It was very hard on all of us, especially my father. After all, he's her legal guardian and responsible for her."

"He was distraught?"

"We mustn't dwell on unpleasant subjects. Let's speak of happier things."

In all, it was a relaxing few days for Jonathan. The stay had removed him from the rut he had fallen into. Christmas with the Cunninghams in no way compared with the ones he had spent on his parents' farm in

England. The food was delicious and the decorations beautiful, but the atmosphere of the Cunningham home was not of festive gaiety. Its somberness reminded Jonathon of Rebecca's words: a family impressed with its own importance, a family that had no time to laugh.

January saw his return to town. It also brought cooler days. At night, the breezes whispered through the streets, often drawing Jonathon from his rooms to stroll restlessly toward the edge of town. There he sat and listened to the calming sounds from the bush, feeling as if the land surrounded him. He heard Rebecca's voice ringing in his mind: *You're trying to hate it, Jonathon. It won't work.* Was she right? Was he, too, falling in love with this unpredictable country? Recalling her words meant remembering the night she spoke them. The flowing of the creek had echoed through their conversation, and the night had enveloped them as they sat in the firelight. How small and helpless she had looked robed in his jacket.

Such thoughts started him worrying about her. Had she made it safely back to Ben? He had been a fool not to insist on taking her back to their cave. For all he knew, she could be lying out in the bush, mangled by unknown hands. Rage pounded through his veins when he thought of the men who had attacked Rebecca and what they had attempted to do. How small and frightened she had been when he found her! How helpless and lovely as she had tried desperately to maintain control over herself while clutching her ruined clothes to her. How beautiful she had been! In those few moments, he wanted to take her in his arms and hold her forever, to protect her from the cruel blows life could deal out.

Usually, when his thoughts reached this point, Jonathon jumped to his feet and told himself he was a sentimental fool. He would force his mind in another direction, to thinking of England and the humiliation he had suffered there.

Time slipped by for Jonathan until February arrived. On a stormy night, with flashes of lightning and thunder echoing in the sky, Jonathon watched the streaks of light erupt and saw the harbor waves rise and splash heavily over his dock. Tomorrow, a ship was due in. With it might come the equipment and men Rebecca had asked him to supervise.

It had been several weeks since the last ship's arrival in port. Jonathon knew the coming of this one would be a welcome event. Ships always brought the supplies necessary for survival in the small Australian town. With delivery of new merchandise, Jonathon knew his warehouses would be put to good use once more and unclaimed cartons would be brought to his attention. R. McNally's crates would be classified as odd, since no one but he knew who R. McNally was. When he heard news of the ship's docking the next morning, he was prepared for an inquiry from his dock manager and ready to receive Rebecca's men.

Soon after the ship's whistle echoed its presence, a meek knock sounded on the door to Jonathan's office. Jonathon looked up from his writing. "Come in."

"Excuse me, sir," the desk clerk said, poking his head around the door. "There are some men here. Just got off the ship, and they're looking for rooms and an R. McNally. Do you know of the man, sir?"

"I do," Jonathon told him, rising to his feet. "How many are there?"

"Four men, sir."

"Put them in our best rooms."

"Sir?"

"I said the best rooms for our guests, or rather for R. McNally's."

"Yes, sir. That's what I thought you said, sir." The clerk backed out, leaving Jonathon staring at the closed door. His clerks didn't usually question his word. They accepted it as law. Was there something unusual about these men that raised disbelief and uncertainty?

Curiosity bested him, and Jonathan crossed his office in three easy strides. He was just in time to watch the four men climb the stairs to the hallway above. They were not what he had expected. They were big men in continental suits, and didn't look like businessmen. They didn't look like miners either.

Jonathon's glance fell on the clerk who was also watching the men go up the stairs. A smile came to his lips, and Jonathon shook his head. He should have expected the unexpected. One couldn't assume the usual where Rebecca McGregor was concerned. An hour later Jonathon was interrupted by another knock. This time the door opened to admit his dock foreman. "What is it, Peters?"

"The tally for the warehouses, sir, and a question I thought you might be able to answer."

Jonathon accepted the sheets of paper from him and skimmed them rapidly. "What's the question?"

"We've received some crates for an R. McNally. I've asked about the docks, but no one's familiar with the name."

"I know who it is, Peters. I'll take care of it," Jonathon told the man. "Put the crates in the warehouses for now."

"Very good, Mr. Gray," Peters agreed, moving to the door. "Will there be anything else, sir?"

Jonathon started to shake his head but stopped. "Yes, there is. Do you know of the aborigine who lives hereabouts? He goes by the name of Sam."

"Yes, sir. I saw him only a few moments ago as I was coming in."

"Good. Ask Jackson to see if he can get a message to Sam. Tell him I'd like to see him as soon as possible."

"It's February sixth today, Ben," Rebecca told her constant companion as they sat beside a small fire eating the lunch she had cooked. "We should be hearing something soon."

Ben nodded, chewing. "Soon."

Rebecca looked away with contentment. Beyond the mouth of the cave she could see the sun beating down harshly on the hard land. The hot summer season had passed, barely touching them in the cool of the cavern. Looking back over the last two months, the days that had passed seemed like a dream. They had gone so quickly. It was hard for her to accept what was happening as real.

"What did you say?" Ben asked.

Rebecca turned her startled gaze at him. "Did I say something?"

Ben nodded. "Something about something or another being real."

Rebecca smiled sheepishly. "I didn't mean to speak out loud. I was only thinking of how unbelievable all of this is. Who would have guessed we'd find gold in this cave?"

"Life's funny that way, Becky. You never know what it'll bring."

A harsh growl suddenly broke from Dingo's throat as he rose to his feet beside Rebecca and stared out toward the front of the cave.

"Someone's coming," Ben whispered, reaching for his gun. "Get in the back of the cave."

"But Ben!"

"Go on!"

Rebecca scurried away to the darkness beyond the mouth of the cave, dragging the big dog with her. She crouched behind a boulder with an arm around the animal's neck and stared back at the entrance. A long, uneasy moment passed as silence hung thickly in the confined air. Then, a voice came. Someone was speaking. Ben was laughing!

"It's all right, Becky!" Ben called. "Come on out.".

Rebecca hurried out to the front of the cave and gasped when she saw the lanky aborigine guide standing beside Ben. "Sam!"

Sam grinned widely, nodding happily. "Jonathon Gray sent me. He told me where to come. He said you were hiding and not lost."

She squealed with delight and grabbed Ben by the arm. "You know what that means, Ben? It means it's time. It's time!"

13

Jonathon stared gloomily at the wall of his office. Six days had passed since he had sent Sam out for Rebecca. Six days. There was still no word from her. Where was she?

Reading over his foreman's list of crates for R. McNally shortly after Sam had left him, Jonathan had found his interest aroused. They seemed to be an unusual assortment and number to contain material for building a home. Unable to restrain himself, he made a trip to the warehouse. What he found did little to answer his questions. Instead, his visit only served to increase them. The equipment in Rebecca's cartons could not be used to build a house. Its only use was to operate a mine!

What game was she playing? Was it possible she had discovered gold in that cave of hers? Or was she merely hoping to do so? Surely, if she had found gold, she would have said something. Wouldn't she?

Jonathon slowly became aware of the steady hum of talking outside his door. Now what was happening? Striding across the room, he flung open the door in time to hear his desk clerk's astonished exclamation.

"Rebecca McGregor? Here in town?"

Jonathon watched the boy race for the door where Jackson was standing. Jonathon was quick to join them, making his way past them onto the porch.

"It's Rebecca McGregor, Mr. Gray," Jackson told him with a wide grin. "She's alive, and she's coming in with Ben Ritter and Sam."

A commotion down the street to his left drew Jonathon's attention. He saw her as he turned. No longer dressed in men's pants and shirt, she sat side-saddle in a simple dress, looking neither to the left nor to the right as she passed down the street. Jonathon watched in amazement as the trio made their way to the bank, where they stopped. As Rebecca dismounted and made her way inside alone, Ben and Sam lifted heavy saddlebags from their horses.

Immediately, a hushed whisper ran rapidly down the street. Jonathon did not need to listen to know what the saddlebags contained. It was gold. It had to be gold!

Little Rebecca McGregor had tricked him. She had used him, and he had allowed her to. No wonder she had taken the chance of coming into town weeks ago. She would have had to mail some letters to get that equipment and those men. He now understood why she had been so evasive when he questioned her. What really amazed him was that he had believed her. He hadn't doubted a single word she said. Who could have under the circumstances? She had seemed so lost and defenseless, determined to go her way in a big, cruel world. He had admired her spirit, had been more than glad to do her a small favor. It was no wonder she had been frightened and had appeared so meek and forlorn. She had discovered gold and was afraid someone else would find out.

A broad grin spread across Jonathon's usually solemn face and he laughed so loud and so hard that everyone turned to look at him as he made his way back into the hotel. He admired her even more now. Rebecca was no ordinary woman. She had not only beauty, but brains and charm as well. She knew how to use each of them to get what she needed. Yes, he had to admire her. Quite unexpectedly, he also found himself feeling happy for her. Now she could buy all the freedom she wanted.

Jonathon stopped at the desk in the lobby to wait. She would come. Sooner or later, she would come. She had to collect the men she had hired. Jonathon threw a curious glance at the stairs. Who were they? They weren't miners, that was certain. But if they weren't miners, why were they here? What did Rebecca need them for?

A man burst through the door, scattering Jonathon's thoughts with the news of gold. The word spread like wildfire as Jonathon stood listening to the excited talk. In moments the town was alive with word of Rebecca McGregor finding gold. Some claimed she had found so much, the bank didn't have enough money to back up her gold. They were wrong. The bank was more than able and pleased to accept her business.

Rebecca found herself smiling as she sat at the desk of the bank president and listened to him give orders while Ben watched the weighing of the gold with a sharp eye. Papers were quickly drawn up and signed and agreements made. More shipments were arranged for, bigger shipments. Yes, the bank assured Ben gravely, they would be able to handle the money and guard it.

Their business finished, Rebecca led Ben and Sam out of the bank. "I still don't believe this," she said.

"You'd better try," he told her with a wink. "This is only the start. There's a lot more to do after we're finished here."

Rebecca nodded. "We'd best start right away. See about the equipment and the wagons to take it back in."

"I'll take care of that. Why don't you go over to the hotel and round up those men you hired?"

She smiled eagerly. "I'm on my way." To Sam, she said, "Thank you for helping us. If you're looking for a job for awhile, Ben and I will be glad to have you. We'll need help getting our wagons through the bush, and no one knows the bush better than you do."

Sam grinned and nodded. "I will go with Ben."

Rebecca watched them stride away, resisting the urge to pinch herself to insure she was really awake. Giving herself a firm shake, she made her way across the street, with the big yellow dog close on her heels. Jackson pushed the hotel door open as she reached the porch, tipping his battered hat to her and smling a big welcome. Rebecca returned the wordless greeting and stepped inside. However, her smile quickly faded and her heart lurhced unexpectedly as she suddenly found herself staring into the blue depths of Jonathon's eyes.

Meekly, she walked to him, and stopped while he looked down at her with a sober expression. Jonathon gazed at her for a long moment. He watched her cheeks flush with color and her eyes widen in anticipation.

"I believe congratulations are in order."

"Thank you, Jonathon."

"I should have guessed."

"You should have, but you didn't. Your mind was too full of other things to notice what I had in mine."

Jonathon laughed, breaking the tension. "I thank you for your frankness, and I humbly admit you are correct." He took her by the elbow to lead her toward the stairs, away from the eyes and ears of the desk clerk. "It seems you'll have your kingdom, after all."

"And much sooner than I'd thought," she replied. "Ben and I had no idea there was gold in our cave. I can tell you it was no small surprise for the both of us when we discovered it."

"I wish I could believe that."

Rebecca flushed again under his steady stare. "How are things with you, Jonathon? I see you've been building again."

"Yes, I have," he admitted, crossing his arms over his chest. "I built the dock and the warehouses by the harbor. Your equipment is here, by the way."

"Will you ever forgive me for not telling you—for using you as I did?"

"There's nothing to forgive. I would have done the same if I'd been in your position."

"You do understand then?"

"I understand, but I can't say I don't envy you. I wouldn't mind finding a cave of gold. It's what I need. But it's yours and perhaps rightly so."

Perhaps? What was it she saw in his eyes? Regret? Was he beginning to realize that what he was striving for was wrong, that revenge would gain him nothing but bitterness? He seemed not to hear her. After a moment's reflection, he motioned toward the stairs.

"Your men are upstairs, in our best room as you requested. There are four of them, and they're not miners."

"No," she admitted honestly. "They're guards."

"Guards!"

"We'll be needing them. Starting a gold mine is a risky business. There are too many dishonest people lurking about. There would be nothing to stop them from taking what is ours if we don't protect ourselves."

"Is it such a big find?"

"I think so, or rather Ben does. I know nothing about mining."

"So he'll be your manager—or partner?"

"He prefers to be manager, at ten percent."

"He has more willpower than I."

"No, Jonathan, he's experienced more. But now, I must go to the hired men." She held a hand out to him. "I thank you, Jonathon Gray. You know, I'm in *your* debt, now."

Jonathon took her small hand in his and squeezed it gently with a benevolent grin. "I won't forget."

Withdrawing her hand, Rebecca turned to the stairs. It was time to get to work once again. What would these men she had hired be like? Would they listen to a woman? Would they be trustworthy? Coming to a halt before their door, Rebecca drew a deep breath and raised her hand to knock.

A short silence followed before a male voice called out. "Who is it?"

"R. McNally," she replied with more confidence than she felt. The door opened and a tall, barrel-chested man stood before her. His eyes were dark and friendly, but cautious.

"You're R. McNally?" he asked after letting his eyes run doubtfully over her.

"Rebecca McGregor, actually," she answered calmly and moved past him into the room. The three other men were waiting inside. "R. McNally was an alias I've been using for reasons of my own." She turned back to face the big man. "And you?"

"Brown. Jeremiah Brown," he replied, still looking at her with studious eyes. "These men are Francis Miles, Aaron Connors, and Bobby O'Riley."

Rebecca received a nod from each man in turn, but her eyes stopped to linger on Bobby O'Riley, a red-haired, boyish-looking man with a lanky build. "Bobby O'Riley, is it? Scotland perhaps?"

"Aye, miss," he answered shyly.

"You'll find Australia to be a different place from our Scotland. There's not a patch of purple heather to be seen." Bobby O'Riley's smile broadened appreciatively, and she again spoke to Jeremiah Brown. "And you, Mr. Brown. Are you in charge of these men?"

"I am."

"Your credentials, sir. I can't be too careful with the matter on which I'll be employing you."

"Which is?" he asked, handing his papers to her.

"Gold, Mr. Brown. Gold." She read the documents slowly before folding them and returning them to him. "Your papers appear to be in order, gentlemen. So, if you're looking for work, you've found it."

The four men exchanged solemn nods, and Jeremiah Brown smiled at Rebecca. "You have yourself four men."

Rebecca echoed his smile brightly. "Then, may I welcome you to Australia? It's a grand place to be."

Returning to the lobby to pay the bill while the men gathered their belongings, Rebecca was disappointed when she found Jonathon had gone. Her disappointment quickly vanished, however, when the men joined her and they moved outside. Jonathon was standing on the porch.

Jonathon turned as Rebecca stopped beside him. "Good luck, Rebecca."

"Thank you, Jonathon. I wish you the same." He nodded slowly, and she moved away, with Jeremiah Brown falling in beside her. "Tell me, Mr. Brown, have you and your men ever worked at a mine before?"

"Once," he told her, slowing his usual long strides to match her smaller steps. "In Ireland. It didn't last long, though. The mine played out."

" So you move around quite a bit, then."

He nodded. "We seldom stay in one place very long."

"But you still like your job here?"

"As well as any other," he answered with a broad grin. "I'm not an ambitious man. I don't mind working for others, as long as I can feel free to leave at any time. I don't want to be tied down."

"Not even to a wife?" she queried.

"Especially not to a wife."

Rebecca laughed. She liked Jeremiah Brown. Big and strong and happy, he was what her father would have called a free spirit. There were many of his kind who passed through the small village in the hills of Scotland where she had lived. Content with a simple lot, they were happy just to be alive.

"Looks like someone's coming to see you," Jeremiah told her, motioning across the street.

"It's Ben," Rebecca said, stepping forward to meet him. "Is everything ready, Ben?"

"Ready as we'll ever be," he assured her gruffly, glancing back at the four wagons standing behind him. "I've arranged for twenty men to start as soon as they can get to the cave. They're good, and they're honest, and they'll put in a good day's work. Most of them came here chasing gold and haven't found it. They're tired of chasing and are willing to work for someone else."

"Good." She turned to Jeremiah. "Ben, these are our visitors from England. Jeremiah, Bobby, Francis, and Aaron. This is my foreman, Ben Ritter."

Ben shook each man's hand and nodded his approval. "Can you men drive wagons?"

"Can we drive wagons?" Jeremiah asked incredulously. "It's one of our steadier jobs."

Down the street from the wagons, Jonathon remained on the porch and watched as the small cavalcade began to move out. He noted that many other townspeople were also watching, wondering what Rebecca McGregor would do next. She was totally unpredictable. One would never know what to expect from her. Quiet and intelligent, she was clever enough to look ahead, to plan for the future and what she wanted, but also woman enough to be gentle in her approach and kind to the people she dealt with, qualities that would win her loyalty—from friends and employees alike. But what would Richard Cunningham say when he faced this new Rebecca, a young woman who would not bow down to his wishes? What would he do when he was told she was not only alive but rich as well?

Richard Cunningham was bound to find out what had occurred in town. The word of gold being found spread rapidly in this country. With that word would go the name of the person who discovered it. Jonathon guessed, when the slow processes of Cunningham's mind pushed aside his anger at her behavior, he would come to realize her actions were to his benefit. He would remember Rebecca was only nineteen. He would know that her age did not allow her to handle such wealth or responsibility legally.

No, it wouldn't take long for Richard Cunningham to recognize the favorable position he was in. As Rebecca's guardian, he had every right to take—or try to take—her property away from her. Legally, if not ethically, he would be allowed to manage her affairs.

Jonathon frowned. He hoped Rebecca was ready to face Cunningham and the obstacle he represented. In the bush months ago, Jonathon remembered speaking to her of her age and lack of legal control. He hoped she would not forget what he had said. She couldn't afford to forget.

14

The first week of Rebecca's return to the mine was busy. For two days, the sound of dynamite blasting away the layers of rock that isolated the golden vein from the mining equipment echoed over the land.

She watched anxiously as men and machinery tore at the rock, clearing away rubble and laying track for the trolleys. Men seemed to have arrived from everywhere, flocking to the mine looking for work and the pay that would enable them to feed their families. Few were turned away.

With the activity and the going and coming of so many people to and from the mining site, Rebecca did not become aware immediately of being watched. It took time before she realized the guards were not only keeping an eye on the mine but were looking after her as well.

"What are you wasting your time watching me for?" she demanded of Jeremiah when she caught him lounging nearby.

"Don't you know?" he asked with a grin. "You're just as valuable as that gold is. Something could happen to you and . . ." He shrugged.

"Nothing's going to happen to me," she protested. But her exclamations did no good. Wherever she walked or went, one of the guards was never far away.

"I think it's time you talk to the men," Ben told her one morning over breakfast. "You're going to have to put them right on who you are."

"But they already know who I am. I hired them," Rebecca protested.

"They know you're a woman who owns a gold mine. They don't know what type of woman you are."

"What type of . . .?"

"I think what Ben means," Jeremiah interrupted with a quick wink at Ben, "is that you're going to have to put the rules down. Let them know you're in charge."

"Give them hell and fire for breakfast," Ben added, shrugging at the wide-eyed look she gave him.

Not an hour later, holding a shotgun in her hand and backed by Ben, Rebecca found herself perched on a rock inside the cave, facing the men she and Ben had hired.

"I want to have a word with all of you before the work on this mine begins. As you all know, I own this mine. But you don't know how I feel about your working in it. I'll pay you a good day's wage for a good day's work. Anyone who thinks he's in this mine for taking gold instead of working it will find himself keeping company with a barrel of buckshot."

Ben moved up to stand beside her. "The rules in this mine are the same as in any other. You work hard and you'll get paid well. We ain't looking for trouble from no man. But if you bring trouble with you, we'll take care of it and you. It doesn't matter to us if you walk out of this mine dead or alive. It's up to you."

Feeling her stomach flutter at such stern talk, Rebecca quickly switched the emphasis. "I know you'll be having problems in setting up the tent town for your families. If there's anything Ben or I can do to help you or if there are any supplies you need until we can set up the supply store, you have only to mention it to us."

Silence fell throughout the cavern as each man nodded quiet acceptance at what was said.

"Now, if none of you have any questions, I'll give you the day off. Tomorrow, we begin work on the mine. The track is laid and the wagons are ready. Go home for a day of rest with your families before we start to work."

A surprised murmur passed through the group of men. As they turned to go, many of them tipped their hats or nodded shyly at their new boss. A day off was a pleasure most of them had seldom had a chance to enjoy.

When the last man was gone, Rebecca stepped down to stand between Jeremiah and Ben. "Do you think they believed me?"

"They'd be fools if they didn't," Jeremiah replied with a grin, shouldering the rifle he had held during the talk.

"I don't think you need to worry, Becky. These men we've got are a fine group. They'll work hard," Ben assured her as they moved to the mouth of the cave, where Jeremiah stopped to talk to the other guards.

Rebecca led the way to their small campfire and knelt to pour out a cup of coffee for Ben, who eased himself to a seat beside her. "You know, Ben, I've been doing some thinking while you've been working so hard getting the mine ready."

"About what?"

"About the mine and about myself," she answered gravely, looking back on the long hours she had spent pacing outside the cave while the men worked. "Jonathon Gray mentioned something I'd not thought of before." She turned to face him. "I'm only nineteen, Ben. I'm not old enough to have my own property."

Ben's coffee cup halted at his lips, and he stared at her over the brim.

"My uncle could come and take it all away." She sighed heavily and stood. "There's only one thing I can do to stop him."

"And that is?" Ben asked warily.

"Get married. I'm old enough to do that." She fidgeted nervously. "Then the mine would be my own—and my husband's."

Ben rubbed his chin thoughtfully.

Rebecca bit her lip anxiously. "I don't know what to do, Ben. I've been thinking hard, but I don't know."

Ben stared up at her. What could he say? How could he help her?

She kicked at the dirt under her feet. "I've been thinking about Jonathon Gray. I've talked with him often enough, as you know, and I understand him. He's ambitious and determined. He needs money to pay a debt. I thought, that is, I've been wondering if we might make some arrangement."

Ben picked up a stick and stirred the fire.

Rebecca went on, "You know yourself he's done well in town. He's built a hotel and a restaurant, and now he's built himself a dock and some warehouses. He's an intelligent man, Ben. He could help us."

"You've already made up your mind. Haven't you, Becky?" Ben asked quietly.

She shrugged and fell to her knees beside him. "I think I have. But I'm not certain." She slumped down against a rock. "This wasn't a decision I planned on making. I wish I didn't have to make it. But if I don't, if I don't do something, my uncle will come and take this mine away from us."

Ben met her eyes and saw the uncertainty reflected in them. "I can't make the decision for you, Becky. I wish I could. You're the one who will have to live with the man."

"Oh, no, Ben!" she exclaimed, her face turning red. "I mean, it won't be like that. It wouldn't be a real marriage. It would be more like—like a business agreement."

Ben looked at her for a long moment before speaking again. He could see the turmoil boiling inside her and he could hear the uncertainty in her voice. How could he help? Offer to marry her himself? He was twice her age. For all he knew, he was still legally married to a woman who had run from him years ago. "How soon?"

"The sooner the better. My uncle will have heard about my gold by now. It won't take him long to find out where I am."

"Leave tomorrow?"

Rebecca nodded reluctantly. "I'll take one of the guards with me."

Ben touched her shoulder with a reassuring hand. "I'll take care of things here."

"I know you will, Ben." Rebecca slowly rose to her feet. "I'd best find Jeremiah. He'll have to decide who'll come with me tomorrow."

The next morning, Jeremiah walked Rebecca to her horse. Dawn was still bright on the horizon, but Ben and the workers were already inside the mine.

"You'll take care of yourself and Ben?" she asked anxiously, rubbing her hands together in the cool morning air. She had lain awake most of the night, trying to decide how she should approach Jonathon on the subject of marriage. No matter how she planned to say it, nothing sounded right. How did men propose to women? Did they come right out and say it? She didn't know, but she reasoned that approach would be the easiest for her—to come straight out with it—while keeping her fingers crossed.

"Don't you worry about us back here. Ben and I will keep everything under control. Bobby will take care of you," Jeremiah assured her, unable to help noticing her agitation.

Rebecca forced a smile and mounted while he held her horse still. Looking down at him as he handed her the reins, she wondered if she should say something. Should she tell him what she was about to do? Should she explain?

"Something bothering you, Becky?" he finally asked.

"No, I mean . . ." She sighed. "Yes, the reason why I'm going to town."

"You don't have to tell me why you're going."

"I'm knowing that, but I think maybe I should." She looked away from him and down at her hands. "I'd rather you hear it from me than from someone who doesn't know what he's talking about."

"I'm listening."

"Yesterday, I told you I had to go into town on business. That's not the whole truth." Taking a deep

113

breath, she managed to meet his eyes. "I'm going into town to get myself married."

Jeremiah's eyes widened in surprise, but he remained silent.

"You see, Jeremiah, I'm only nineteen. It's not the legal age to be owning all this. I should have a guardian to run it. But my guardian, Richard Cunningham . . ." She hesitated. "I ran away from him and his family months ago, before Ben and I discovered the gold."

"That's why you used the name R. McNally?"

"Yes. That's why I hid away in this cave," Rebecca answered. "Ben helped me to run away. We've been friends since I came to Australia. We were thinking of starting a small place. We never thought we'd find gold."

"Now you're afraid your guardian will try to come and take the mine from you?"

"Aye. There's not a doubt in my mind that he'll do just that. That's why I need a husband. If I have a husband, my uncle can't take this from me."

"But your husband can."

"This husband won't—*if* he accepts my proposition. He's a man of honor, Jeremiah, and I trust him."

"If you trust him, that's good enough for me."

Rebecca smiled gratefully. "Thank you, Jeremiah."

Smiling back, Jeremiah shook his head and gestured beyond them to where Bobby sat waiting. "You'd best be going. Bobby's ready to move." He stepped back and watched her start off, returning her wave. It was too bad he wasn't the marrying kind. Rebecca McGregor was one woman any man wouldn't mind being tied to.

15

"Rebecca! I didn't expect to see you again so soon," Jonathon greeted as he rose from his desk to meet her.

Rebecca, however, could not find words to echo his welcome and instead approached him with a serious face. "I have to speak with you, Jonathon."

Surprised at her gravity, Jonathon immediately indicated a chair, which she declined. "Speak away."

"I've come to ask you . . ."

"For another favor?" Jonathon quickly provided at her hesitation.

"In a way," she agreed hastily, grabbing at his words as she would a safety line. "But it would be of benefit to you as well as to me."

"And it is?"

Rebecca paused, struggling for words. "How would you feel about marrying me?"

Struck by her unexpected question, for a moment Jonathon could only gape at her in astonishment. After stammering over several beginnings, he swallowed his surprise and managed to ask, "Are you proposing to me?"

"No, I'm trying to proposition you. You're the one who warned me about my age. You told me that by being only nineteen I was taking a chance on losing my property, and I've come here hoping you'll help me make sure that won't happen."

Jonathon stared at her intently for a moment. He was totally unprepared for such an event. Not for a moment had he ever considered she would approach him like this. But she was doing it, and she was in dead earnest. He sank back down into the chair behind his desk. "And what, may I ask, is in this proposition for me?"

"Forty percent of my gold mine."

Jonathon's eyebrows shot up as he quickly calculated the figures in his head. Ben had ten, he would have forty. That left fifty shares for Rebecca. "Forty-five."

Rebecca looked stunned. "That gives us equal shares in the mine!"

"I know. After all, marriage is a sharing arrangement. Half and half."

She bit her lip in concentration. She hadn't expected this. She had expected him to agree immediately to her proposal, not thinking she would have to barter. "All right," she agreed. "But only under two conditions."

"They are?"

"First, you join your land with mine, including your land here in town."

He opened his mouth to object.

"You said marraige was a sharing arrangement."

Jonathon shook his head with a smile. "Accepted. The second condition?"

"That you agree to stay with me to help me manage and better my property, sharing equally in the expenses and profits for two years. That'll give me enough time to build my house and become settled, and it will give us time to make a solid profit from the mine."

"Two years?" Jonathon repeated thoughtfully.

"Time enough for you to gain the status, money, and respectability you desire."

"We share everything equally?"

"Everything."

Jonathon smiled slowly, his respect for her rekindled. It was a sound proposition. By sharing all profits and losses on an equal basis, they both stood to benefit more than either of them could separately. However, there was one thing he felt the need to draw to her attention. "You realize that by becoming your husband, all titles and deeds go in my name?"

She met his eyes levelly and nodded. "Yes, but I'll take your word of honor not to cheat me and that you will release my properties back to me when our agreement is finished.''

"You oughtn't to be so trusting, Rebecca McGregor."

"One must trust and believe in others sometimes."

"And you trust me?"

"I do."

Jonathon rose to his feet and walked around his desk to stand beside her. "Then I won't fail you. I'll do as you ask."

"You agree?"

"Yes. I'll be your husband under those conditions."

Rebecca breathed a heartfelt sigh and leaned against his desk. "I'm glad that's over with." The grandfather clock standing in the corner of the room suddenly began to chime and she stiffened, remembering the time. "We must be going."

"Going? Going where?"

"The church. The priest is waiting."

"Waiting?" Jonathon threw his head back and laughed. "You didn't even let me decide, did you? You had it all planned that I would accept. How did you know I would?"

"Because I know you, Jonathon, and because I know myself. I told you once, we are very much alike, and we are. We'll use other people to gain our ends—if we must."

Jonathon nodded agreement. "If we must."

As the campsite and cave came into view, Rebecca watched Jonathon to see his reaction. Their marriage had been quick, with Alan Hendrix and Bobby O'Riley standing as their witnesses. Allan had found two rings for the ceremony. They weren't new and didn't fit properly, but they served the purpose.

Rebecca fingered her gold band nervously. They had left town immediately after the wedding, stopping only long enough to allow Jonathon time to collect what he needed and to put his hotel manager and dock foreman in charge of the business operations during his absence.

Jonathon was silent for most of the trip through the bush. Rebecca wondered if he regretted his decision, but he did not. Jonathon could think of worse situations to be in—much worse. Financially, he had made a substantial gain. As for taking a wife, it wasn't something he had expected to do in Australia. Business proposition or not, he couldn't complain about his new spouse. Rebecca McGregor was far from unpleasant or repulsive. She had beauty, charm, and wit plus an intelligence she knew how to use. They were both determined people, quick but cautious, and ambitious. True, their ambitions were not exactly the same. They wanted money, but not for the same purposes. Nevertheless, he told himself, he had made a good move and a good match.

Riding into camp, Rebecca waved to Jeremiah as they passed his post on a hill overlooking the mouth of the cave. The activity around them was heartening. Rebecca scanned the site to see what progress had been made during her few days away.

"We were staying near the mouth of the cave," Rebecca explained to Jonathon as she led him from the horses toward the mine opening. "Ben had never explored the cave to its end. When I became tired of sitting while the days passed, I decided to walk through it."

Jonathon followed her into the darkness of the cave and listened intently as she continued.

"I found a hole in the wall just when I was thinking the cave had come to an end. It was just big enough for a person to slip through. It was in the cavern behind this section that I found the gold."

"An interesting piece of luck," Jonathon commented, stepping aside as a trolly filled with rock rolled past them toward the mouth of the cave.

"It was," she agreed leading him around the curve where the hole and wall had once been. "Here it is."

Jonathon stopped, again feeling the awe he had experienced when visiting the Cunningham mine at the power of men and machines working together. From where he stood, he couldn't see the vein clearly. There were too many men, too much dust. Movement was everywhere, the mass movement of men and iron against a mountain of stone.

Ben appeared from out of the shadows, striding toward them with a dark frown between his eyes. "Becky, I didn't know you'd come back."

"We've only just arrived," she told him with a tense smile. He was staring at Jonathon. "I don't believe you've ever met Mr. Gray, Ben. This is Jonathon Gray, my husband."

Jonathon offered his hand and Ben took it, meeting the younger man's eyes with hostile speculation. "I hope you know you're a lucky man, Gray. She's a fine lady, business deal or no."

"I know, and I'll do my best to look after her and her property," Jonathon responded frankly. He could well understand the fierceness of Ben Ritter's expression. He had helped Rebecca escape from one tyrant. He was worried if she had fallen into the hands of another.

Ben nodded curtly and abruptly went back to supervising the work. He wasn't sure he liked the idea of Rebecca getting married. He knew she hadn't much of a choice. He growled to himself. It was too late to protest, too late to try to think of another way out. It was done. He could only wait and see if things worked out.

When Ben was gone, Jonathon took Rebecca by the elbow and led her back out of the cavern and into the sunshine. "I think we should talk."

Rebecca felt her heart give a frightened leap, but she answered coolly. "Of course."

He led her a short distance from the mine to a quiet place where they could sit. "I have to know what you expect of me and what your plans are. I'm afraid you haven't told me very much."

"There was no time to tell you," she protested lamely.

"No, but there is now," he said, suppressing a smile

as she fidgeted nervously beside him.

"My plans have never been very complicated," she began. "But then, I never expected to find a gold mine. I thought I'd begin with sheep, raising them until I had enough money to grow and expand." She hesitated. "Eventually, I hoped to build a house. I've already chosen a place. I could show it to you if you like."

"Tomorrow perhaps," he assured her. "Is there anything else?"

Rebecca pushed herself to her feet and walked a short distance away. "You're asking me to put dreams into words, Jonathon. It's not an easy thing to do."

"Try."

She spun back to face him. "You remember I told you what a rich country this is—not only because of its gold?"

"I remember."

"I still believe it's true. There are sheep and a wool market, but there could be more than that. There could be cattle, dairy or beef cows. I couldn't say. I don't know what animals not native to this country could live here, but I do know if we could raise cows, we might open a new market. There could be beef and fresh milk—and not only for the people of Australia. If the market grew large enough, we could sell beef as well as wool to other countries."

"That would take time. Years."

"Jonathon, you can't build a kingdom in a day, and you don't build it only for yourself," she insisted, falling to her knees beside him. "I may not be fond of marriage, at least not now. There's so much to be doing. But some day, I'd like to have children, and I'd like to build something for them to have when they're grown."

"A kingdom?"

"If you like. But I prefer to call it a home, a place of their own. A kingdom is a dream, but a home is real. A home is a place where loved ones can be happy and secure. It can remain long after I'm gone."

Jonathon nodded solemnly. "I can understand that. I

imagine we all have thoughts of leaving something behind." He looked down into her upturned face. "Have you considered farming?"

She shrugged helplessly. "I've never known much about farming. In Scotland, we had flocks and herds and only a wee bit of a garden."

He looked away from her, away from the mine to the land beyond, his imagination churning over new ideas. "It might be possible."

Rebecca watched him stand and stride a few steps away to look at something she could not see.

"The land is extremely dry at times. Then again, they tell me it can be very wet. During dry times you could irrigate—you do have a river. And when the rains come, you could drain."

She moved to stand beside him. "But what crop could you grow here?"

"Wheat, perhaps," Jonathon replied thoughtfully. "Yes, perhaps wheat." He looked down at her. "But to get it to grow, to make it work, we'd need someone with more knowledge than I have."

"Who?"

"My brother."

"From England?"

"Yes. He might leave his farm for a year or so. He has a good man who can run it for him while he's away." Suddenly, Jonathon smiled, and in his excitement he grasped her by the shoulders. "Yes, he very well might come here." He laughed. "We may make something out of this place yet!"

Rebecca beamed up at him happily. "Oh, I'm glad you see it that way."

Jonathon captured her eyes with his own, seeing the warm glow reflected in them. He watched her soft smile slowly fade under his gaze as her face flushed before her eyes dropped from his. "And us, Rebecca? What are your plans for us?"

She shook her head mutely. "I've made no plans." She raised her face to his. "You have your goals and I have mine. For now, they're one and the same. But afterward, when our agreement is over, I can't hold you. Whether you return to England or choose to stay here, the decision is yours. I can have no say in what you do after our two years are up. You will do what you feel has to be done."

He took her chin in his hand, oddly touched by her words. "You're so young and innocent to be going on such a quest. Are you sure you're ready for it?"

"I'm ready," she answered with an uncertain tremor in her voice.

"Then we'll cross our bridges when we come to them." He dropped her chin and took her elbow once more as he led her toward the tents. "You spoke of a house. We'll go to look at your site for it tomorrow morning. But for now, I want you to try to sketch an idea of the house you want. I can make a few drawings myself, too. I'm not particularly handy at it, but I can give you a general idea of some of the houses I've seen or been in."

"Do you think it will be difficult to build here?"

"It will pose its problems, but they're not overwhelming. In that respect, you're lucky to have me. While working in the bank, I dealt with some of the best architects in London. Surely, we can convince one of them to come down to the other end of the world to build you a house."

"It will be for you as well, while you're here. I told you we would share."

"And so we shall."

16

"It's in the center of my land, the ideal location for a home, on solid high ground," Rebecca told Jonathon as they sat the next morning looking out over the plateau she had chosen as the site for her house.

Jonathon nodded. After examining the drawings she had made of the home she had in mind and adding some suggestions and ideas of his own, he could see the location she had chosen would be excellent. "You don't have a map of the area, do you?"

"No. Do you need one?"

"Yes, both your land and mine. We'll have to make extensive plans, decide where everything will be. There will be wells to dig for the sheep and cattle, ranges to map out so that our herds don't mix and wander too far. Then there's the farm land. That'll have to be kept separate from everything else."

A quiver of excitement passed through Rebecca. "It's all so exciting, and yet frightening, too."

"Why frightening?"

"Because it's so big, and because everything is happening so quickly."

"Plans are always made quickly. It's carrying them out and making them real that takes time," he reminded her.

She smiled back, her eyes dancing happily. Even his warnings could not dampen her enthusiasm. "Time won't go fast enough for my liking. I know that already."

Jonathon laughed and turned his horse's head back toward the mine. "Come. Let's go back. I have some letters to write, and then I think I'll go help Ben."

Rebecca turned a glowing look of gratitude on him.

"He'd like that."

"Does he have his doubts about me?"

She nodded reluctantly.

"I guess, because I'm your husband and everything is now lawfully mine, he's worried I might start to think about taking all this away from you just as your uncle would."

"But you won't," she stated confidently.

"Still so sure?"

"Aye. I've not a doubt in my head."

Jonathon's lips once more lifted in a smile. "Then I'd better go convince Ben. There's a lot that has to be done on this land. Even though we own it and all it contains, we shouldn't sit back and let others do all the work."

"You're right."

"Of course, I am."

Jonathon went to work in the mine hours later, and each day after that he rose to join the men every morning to work in the cavern. From dawn to dusk, he labored beside the others, gaining their respect and loyalty. He was a man of decision, with natural leadership ability. When an obstacle was met, he found a way through or around it with the least possible waste of time and effort. Ben was always close at hand to give advice. Jonathon accepted his assistance and guidance willingly. He listened with an attentive ear whenever Ben explained some process of the mining operation, being careful never to let his pride get in the way of his judgment. Slowly, Ben's suspicions about Jonathon lessened, and they became friends.

While Jonathon and Ben worked steadily in the confines of the mine, Rebecca kept busy outside. When the wagon returned from town after delivering the latest shipment of gold, the men brought with them a map of the joint properties. Each day Rebecca rode out, trying her best to accumulate the details necessary to make plans for the future use of the land. At Jonathon's insistence, a guard always accompanied her. At night when she returned and the mining was finished for the day, he sat down with her and went over what she had seen and charted.

It wasn't until the second week of their marriage that their routine was interrupted—by a visit from Richard and Alison Cunningham.

Jonathon was in the mine and Rebecca was working outside with some of the men on the plans for building a supply store when Jeremiah suddenly appeared at her side.

"Two riders coming in, Becky. Never saw them before. A man and a woman."

Rebecca's heart jolted against her ribs. "What color are their horses?"

"The woman's on a white. The man's riding a black."

"It's my uncle." She met his eyes calmly, but he wasn't deceived by her mask of confidence. Her knuckles were white as they clenched the material of her skirt, and her face was also pale. "Would you please get Jonathon for me?"

"Right away."

Jeremiah moved off into the mine, and Rebecca put a trembling hand to her forehead to shade the sunlight from her eyes. She could see them now. They were closer than she had anticipated. She dropped her hand, certain they had already seen her, and pulled herself up proudly to meet them.

Richard Cunningham stopped his horse and waited for her to come up to him and Alison. When she stopped before them, he looked down at her with a grave but tolerant expression. "Rebecca."

"Uncle Richard," Rebecca greeted, ignoring Alison.

Cunningham looked past her to the mine. "Is this what you ran away for?"

"No. I left your house to be free, free from you and free from my cousins."

"Did we treat you so badly?"

"As for you, you treated me with respect," she told him honestly. Turning her eyes on Alison, she con-

125

tinued, "But *they* treated me as a poor relation." She looked back at him. "I may have been poor when I came to your door, but I was your relation. I had no right to expect much, but I expected more than to become another of your servants who did all your menial tasks. I brought nothing but myself when I came to you, and I took nothing but myself when I left. You can't have missed me so very badly then."

"You frightened us," he reproached her.

Rebecca smiled sadly. "I doubt that."

"Don't be rude, Rebecca," Alison snapped haughtily.

"Same spoiled little girl, aren't you, Alison?" Rebecca said without malice. "Still telling me what I should and shouldn't be doing." She looked back at Cunningham, her eyes flashing. "You're on my land now, and you can't tell me what to do here—or anywhere anymore.'

"We may be on your land, but you have no right to it yet," Cunningham replied tersely, aggravated by her confidence in herself. "You're only nineteen. You require a guardian."

"I require no one."

"The law is quite specific."

"So it is." Jonathon's deep voice was unexpected as he came up to stand beside Rebecca. Though his clothes were covered with dirt from the mine and his face was smudged with damp dust, Rebecca thought she had never seen him look so commanding. "The law states that a woman is of marrying age when she reaches nineteen. Rebecca is nineteen and she is married."

"To who?" Alison demanded.

"To me," Jonathon retorted. The color drained from Alison's face. Turning back to Richard Cunningham, Jonathon went on, "That puts her property in my hands. I will manage it and govern what happens on it." He paused. "Am I correct?"

Richard Cunningham glared down at him, his face flushed with suppressed rage. "You are."

"Then the matter is settled. Is there anything else we can do for you?"

"You knew where she was all the time," Cunningham accused, his voice shaking with emotion. "You knew."

"No. When you came to see me, I had no idea where she was," Jonathan replied calmly. "It wasn't until several days later that I happened to meet her while riding in the bush."

"And you married her?" Alison asked in disbelief.

"We married each other," he corrected.

Cunningham looked down at Rebecca. "Have you nothing to say for yourself?"

"I think I've already said it, Uncle Richard. I'm grateful for the shelter you offered me in the two years after my father's death, but I owe you nothing." Rebecca felt her knees tremble as she met his hard eyes, but her voice was strong.

"Your father would severely disapprove of your actions."

"I disagree. My father would be very happy for me, and so should you be, Uncle Richard."

The two Cunninghams stared down at them for a long moment, anger and frustration visible on their faces. Then, in unison, they swung their horses around and rode rapidly away. Rebecca watched them go with relief, sorrow, and frustration. If only they could be made to understand. She looked up and found Jonathon's eyes on her. Smiling feebly, she said, "I'm glad that's over with."

Jonathon put a comforting arm around her shoulders and gave her a reassuring hug. "Yes, it's over." He motioned to the cave behind them. "Should we get on with this business of building a kingdom?"

"Aye," she replied eagerly, her spirits lifting at his words. "Let's." And they turned to walk back to the mine together.

17

Over the next two months, Rebecca watched her dream grow. Progress was slow but steady, and everything ran smoothly.

Work in the mine was going well, with shipments of gold to town being made regularly. No attempts had yet been made by bush runners to seize a train of the precious ore, but Jeremiah and the other guards continued to discourage any such ideas with their advance scouting.

The supply store for the mineworkers was built and began to operate. It was one of Rebecca's many duties to make sure the shelves of the store were stocked at all times and that all the needs of the workers and their families was met.

She also made it a habit to ride through the tent town at least once a day and visit with the wives and children there. The guards were also her responsibility. Constantly checking on their needs, making sure they had everything they wanted, she often spent time talking with the person on watch at the top of the hill above the cave.

When it was Bobby, the two of them talked of Scotland, comparing the life they had enjoyed there with the one they found themselves living in Australia. With Jeremiah and Francis, the talk was of the past and of the far-away places both men had been. When it was solemn and quiet Aaron, Rebecca and he discussed his home and the little sister to whom he sent money regularly. All of the men agreed they liked Australia and enjoyed their work. They all felt as Jeremiah did about being free, save for Bobby who, she discovered, could be very sentimental.

Sam remained a familiar figure about the camp. He came and went often, carrying messages, delivering mail, guiding the wagons through the bush, and watching in town for the ships coming in. Jonathon never spoke of it, but Rebecca knew he was waiting anxiously to hear from his brother, whether by letter or in person. She, too, found herself wondering about this younger version of Jonathon Gray. Would they look alike? Would the younger brother have the same dynamic, commanding personality as Jonathon? She longed to ask Jonathon questions but hesitated. Their lives were united and yet separate. What right did she have to intrude into his private thoughts? Also, the only time she was able to see him was at night. Then he was often too tired to talk and skipped eating, going straight to bed.

One day, Sam returned to camp with the news of a ship coming in. It was two and a half months since the letters to Jonathon's brother and the architect had been sent. Rebecca knew this ship should bring their replies, either as messages or in person. She waited by the fire for Jonathon to join her. He didn't arrive until well after sunset, sitting down heavily across from her. He felt as if every bone in his body was made of lead. It seemed to him, if a man worked at the same job every day, he should get used to the steady labor. But he never did. Each day seemed to take the same toll of his body and mind. He accepted a cup of coffee from Rebecca and drank it gratefully.

She watched him, feeling a warm glow within her for him because she knew he was happy. He had become broader of shoulder and stronger of arm since beginning to work in the mine. The responsibilities he had willingly taken on in addition to the manual labor seemed to her to have made him more masculine than ever. She realized he enjoyed the steady work not only because it gave him the feeling of accomplishment but because it kept his mind occupied as well. He had no time to linger on thoughts of England and the hurt he had suffered there. To leave a wound alone was to let it heal, and silently Rebecca hoped time was erasing his anger.

"Thank you," he sighed after taking several mouthfuls of the hot liquid. "It tastes good."

"Are you hungry?"

"No, not right now. I'm just tired." He leaned back against a saddle that had been left by the fire and stretched his long legs out in front of him. "The work is going well," he said, rubbing a hand across his face. "The men are content and work hard, and there seems to be no end to the gold coming out of that hole."

"Would you want it to stop coming out?"

Jonathon started and shook his head. "No, but I do wish it was easier to reach."

"Perhaps more machinery . . ."

"No," he interrupted with a wave of his hand. "I think not though we've considered blasting through to the other side of the wall."

"Do you mean from the other side of the hill?"

"Yes. Eventually, I think we'll have to do it. But for now," he shrugged, "it's too soon."

"There's no danger of collapse, is there?" she asked anxiously, remembering the stories of falling walls and cracking timbers, of trapped men, and the death of her own father.

"No. No. The rock of that mountain is solid. That's why the work is so slow. We could blast, but it's safer to dig. We don't want to take any chances of weakening the stone structure."

Rebecca nodded, relieved. "I'd rather we went slowly and safely than risk lives by trying to go too quickly."

Jonathon smiled at her. "So would I." He reached for the pot and poured himself another cup of coffee. "And you, how was your day?"

"I was hoping you'd ask," she responded eagerly.

Jonathon raised an eyebrow at the quick answer. "What have you gotten yourself into this time?"

Rebecca stiffened indignantly. "Honestly, Jonathon.

130

Sometimes, I believe you think I'm still a child and not to be trusted to go anywhere or do anything without finding myself in some kind of trouble."

"You have to admit, you've found your fair share: bush runners, uncles, and then that drunken Irishman who almost blew your head off when you went riding through the tent town last month."

"How as I to know he'd been drinking and would think I was a specter out of the past because I was riding a white horse?" she protested.

"What about the child who fell down the cliff? The one you went down after only to find you couldn't get back up? No one knew where you'd gone. By the time we found you, it was past sunset, and both you and the child were half starved and shivering with cold."

"I couldn't very well leave him there."

"You could've gone for help."

"I thought I could get him by myself."

"You couldn't."

"I had to try."

"You had to do nothing of the sort. You should have used some of that intelligence you've packed away in that pretty little head of yours."

Rebecca scowled at him. "Sometimes, I'm sorry I married you, Jonathon Gray. I should have looked for a man who wasn't impossible to please."

Jonathon laughed. "I'm only making fun of your follies, Rebecca, and you do please me—sometimes. You've done much to improve the camp."

"Why thank you, milord. I'm so glad I've been able to do something to satisfy you."

He stared at her across the fire. He had learned to recognize the set expression on her face. Her jaw was set firmly and her eyes avoided his. It told him she was angry but determined to say nothing to provoke an argument. The light of the fire reflected the sparkling green of her eyes. "Now I've got you mad at me."

"I'm not mad."

"You are."

"I'm not."

"What were you going to tell me?" he asked, trying a different approach.

"Nothing."

"You were going to tell me something that happened today."

She looked up at him, a line furrowed between her eyes. "I don't know if I should tell you."

He held out a hand to her. "Come here." She hesitated. Smiling, he put his hand down. "I'm not going to bite you. Come here." She rose slowly and went to him. "Sit down next to me." She did, her body remaining rigid beside him. "Now tell me what happened."

Glancing at him out of the corner of her eye, she decided to give in. "I was speaking with Sam today. He was saying a ship is due in town four days from now." She turned to see Jonathan's eyes light up. "I was thinking I might go in to wait for it. I could check on the hotel and the dock and wait to see if our letters have been answered."

Jonathan sat up straighter and took a long drink of coffee before commenting. "It's about time, isn't it?"

"It is."

"There's been no mail?"

"No. I think perhaps he did not wait to write and is coming instead. If he's anything like you, I'm sure that's what he's done."

Jonathon smiled, happy anticipation shining in his eyes. "Yes, Mark is like me to some extent. You would recognize him if you saw him. He looks much like me—not quite so tall, though, and a bit thinner."

"So Mark is his name."

"Yes. Mark."

"You'll be glad to see him, won't you?"

"Very glad. And you?"

"I should like to meet him. Perhaps he'll be nicer to me than his big brother," she pouted.

Jonathon reached out and pulled her to him so she lay against his chest. "Am I so cruel?"

She looked up at him without raising her head from his chest. "Very."

His grip tightened around her for a moment in a gentle hug; then he leaned back against the saddle once more. "You can leave tomorrow morning. But take someone with you."

"Aye, milord, whatever you say."

He smiled sleepily, weariness invading his mind. As he closed his eyes and felt her start to move away, his arm tightened around her. "No, don't go. Not yet. Stay awhile."

She sat back against him and watched his eyes slowly close once more, remaining still for a long time and listening to his breathing lapse into the deep, rhythmic sound of sleep. Looking at him, she thought how peaceful and contented he looked. He did not have the cold, distant gleam in his eyes that was always there during the first months she knew him. She hoped he was finding peace here, that he would want to stay instead of going back to England. If he did decide to go, she knew she couldn't stop him. She had given her word, but, oh, how badly she wanted him to stay.

The three-day trip to town was uneventful. Cool May breezes played over the bush, making travel comfortable and pleasant.

As the town came into view, Rebecca turned to Jeremiah who was accompanying her. "When we reach town, we can check into the hotel and go our separate ways. You can use the rest, and I'll be busy with the books. There'll be no need for you to stand watch over me like a guardian angel."

A smile tugged at Jeremiah's lips, and he shook his head warningly. "You know how Jonathon feels about that."

"Jonathon can stick his head in a mud puddle. What could possibly happen to me in town to endanger my life?"

"You'd be surprised, Becky. I've seen some of these

133

towns get pretty rough. Got a lot of no-goods hanging around. It's not safe to walk the streets."

"I hope that won't happen here. This will be a fine city some day."

Dismounting at the hotel, Rebecca bent down to pet the big yellow dog that remained her constant companion around the camp. "Dingo, what will you be doing today? Will you stay with me inside as well as out, or will you go roaming?"

Dingo merely wagged his tail and Jeremiah laughed. "Some day he's going to answer you. Then what will you say?"

"I doubt I'd say anything. I'd probably fall down out of the shock." She stepped up to the porch, with Jeremiah following her and Dingo staying behind at the door.

Jackson was just inside, as always, sweeping the lobby. "Howdy, Miss Becky. Haven't seen you around town in awhile."

Rebecca smiled. "Running a mine keeps me away I'm afraid. How have things been here?"

"Quiet but busy, Miss Becky. Business is good."

"Jonathon will be pleased to hear that," she responded, with a quick wink at Jeremiah. "Would you please do me a favor, Jack? Run down to the dock and ask Peters to come see me when he can."

"I'll go right away," Jackson agreed, putting his broom aside.

As Jackson hurried out the door, Rebecca nodded smugly at Jeremiah. "You see? I'll be in the hotel all day, working. I'll be taking care of any problems that have come up and doing the paperwork. So why can't we meet at the restaurant for dinner, say seven o'clock?"

Jeremiah pushed his hat back on his head. "I shouldn't go."

"But you will. What Jonathon doesn't know won't hurt him," she said and turned toward the desk. She paused only long enough to look over her shoulder and say, "Good day, Jeremiah. I'll be seeing you tonight."

Shut in Jonathon's office for the rest of the day, Rebecca pored over the books, checking losses against profits and solving the problems that had arisen during Jonathon's absence. There was broken furniture to be replaced, torn rugs to have repaired, people to be notified of goods awaiting pick up at the warehouses, and the matter of undoing the damage sustained during a small fire on the dock. Most of the problems were easily solved, they being more time consuming than difficult to remedy, and it was as she was finishing the books that a knock sounded on the door and Allan Hendrix looked in.

"May I come in?"

"Of course!" she exclaimed rising to meet him. "I was meaning to come and see you. You've saved me a trip. How have you been?"

"Fine. And yourself and Jonathon?"

"Both fine."

"The mine's going well?"

"Can't you tell by all the shipments coming in?"

"Ah, yes," he said with a sigh. "Tell me, how does it feel to be rich?"

"I'm not sure," she admitted. "I'm not feeling rich. I just feel happy."

"Really?"

"Really," she assured him with a broad smile. "It's like watching a dream come true."

"Good. But tell me," he said indicating the books lying on the desk, "is that what brings you to town?"

"No, I've come to meet somebody—hopefully."

"Anyone I know?"

"Jonathon's brother. He might be arriving on the ship tomorrow, along with a contractor who will build my house."

"A house, is it?"

"Aye, I have to have a house."

"He won't be starting on it now, though, surely? It's late in the season. The rains will be coming soon."

"No, he's not coming to build. He'll be coming to look. Jonathon's promised me that before the rains come, he'll build us a shack so we won't drown in our tents this winter."

Hendrix laughed. "Yes, you'll need protection against the weather. And, speaking of protection, as you're without that formidable husband of yours to-night, do you think you could find the time to have dinner with an old friend?"

"I'd like that, but I'm afraid you won't find me without protection. My husband may not be here, but he sent me a guardian angel in his stead. Jeremiah. I'm to meet him at the restaurant for dinner. But please join us. You know him."

"One of the guards, isn't he?"

"Yes, and a nice man."

"As well as a good one, from what I can see."

"He is that. Without him and his men, we wouldn't be keeping as much gold as we do." She glanced at the clock standing in the corner of the room. "It's about time for dinner now. I need an excuse like that to leave these books. Can you come to dinner right now?"

A few minutes later, Hendrix was sitting across from Rebecca at a table in the restaurant. "Have you seen your uncle since starting the mine, Becky?"

Rebecca nodded grimly, remembering the day he and Alison had come to the mine. "Yes, and Alison, too. They came to the mine sometime back. He didn't know I'd gotten married and believed he was still my guardian."

"I hope Jonathon set him right."

She gave a quick nod and smiled. "Right enough."

Jeremiah appeared as Hendrix was about to speak again, striding to the table in fresh clothes and with a scrubbed face. "Sorry I'm late," he apologized sliding into a chair. "Took awhile to get all the dirt off."

Hendrix snorted and Rebecca laughed. They were still laughing when the waiter came to take their order, and no further mention was made of the Cunninghams that night.

18

Rebecca rose early the next morning to complete her errands in town. She ordered food and supplies for the tent-town store, bought material for dresses and more shirts for Jonathon. She was sure he was unaware that he had worn out almost every shirt he owned. He always noticed if someone else was in need of something, but he never paid any attention to his own needs.

Her last stop was to the bank, where she met with the president to insure that no problems had developed in receipt of the shipments of gold. Done at last, she left the bank with Dingo at her heels. The big dog had followed her all morning, waiting patiently outside each door until she came out again.

Jeremiah was sitting on the porch when she arrived at the hotel, lazily lounging in the chair.

"How long have you been sitting there?" Rebecca demanded suspiciously.

"Ever since you left," Jeremiah admitted with a grin. "I've been watching you go from store to store to store."

"Honestly, Jeremiah, I'm sure even the Queen of England isn't watched as carefully as I am. You'd think . . ." A horn blast from the harbor interrupted her. "The ship! It's come in!"

Dropping her packages in the unsuspecting Jackson's arms, she hurried toward the docks, with Jeremiah and Dingo following close behind.

They stood on the pier and watched the lumbering ship drift in, dropping anchor and throwing its lines ashore. It was a while before the gangplank was dropped and more minutes until the passengers were allowed to go ashore. Rebecca watched every face anxiously, completely forgetting about the architect she was expecting and concentrating on locating a miniature Jonathon Gray.

"Jonathon said his brother looks much like him, only shorter and a bit thinner," she told Jeremiah.

"If he's here, we'll find him," Jeremiah assured her.

It seemed to Rebecca the ship would never empty of people. The flow of passengers continued on and on until at last it dwindled to a few lone stragglers. Rebecca examined each one carefully. It was when she was beginning to fear Mark Gray had not come after all that she saw him. "There! There he is!"

Jeremiah quickly moved forward, making his way through the people lingering on the docks, toward the young man stepping from the plank. "Might you be Mark Gray?"

"I am," he answered decisively.

"Jeremiah Brown. I work for your brother," Jeremiah told him, extending his hand.

"Glad to meet you," Mark greeted, heartily returning Jeremiah's firm shake.

"Jonathon couldn't come," Jeremiah continued. "But he sent his wife. I'll introduce you."

"I'd know you anywhere," Mark began before Jeremiah could speak when they reached Rebecca. "Jonathon told me to look for the prettiest girl on the dock, and that would be his wife."

Rebecca flushed with pleasure. "I'm glad to meet you, Mark, but I'll have you know I don't believe a word of it. Jonathon probably told you to look for the girl standing next to the big, ugly yellow dog."

Mark laughed, and bent to pet Dingo. "He's a fine-looking mongrel, all right, just as dirty and ugly as he ought to be."

Rebecca watched him, amazed at the likeness between the man before her and her husband. Slightly shorter and a bit thinner than his brother, Mark had the same blue eyes and proud bearing Jonathon had, but his expression lacked Jonathon's bitterness. "Come, we'll take you to the hotel where we'll be staying the night," she told him accepting his arm. "You can see the whole of our big town through your window."

"I've never been to a boom town before," Mark grinned at her, looking around as they walked along the boardwalk with undisguised interest. "It's like nothing I've ever seen before. It looks like a bunch of barns thrown up on a dirt lane."

Rebecca burst out laughing, and Jeremiah smothered a grin. "A perfect description, though I must admit I've never thought of it quite in that way." Still smiling, she led the way into the hotel lobby, stopping when the desk clerk called her name.

"Mrs. Gray, excuse me. This gentleman here is looking for your husband. Perhaps you could help him."

Rebecca turned to see a derbied, well-dressed man standing beside the desk. He quickly took off his hat at her approach and nodded politely.

"Mrs. Gray? My name's Thomas Pickering. Your husband wrote me a letter some two months back."

"My house! You must be the man who's come to build my house," she exclaimed brightly, extending a hand to him gracefully. "I'm glad to see you. You'll be rescuing us from living in tents."

Pickering laughed good naturedly at her enthusiasm. "I'll do what I can. But tell me, how is Jonathon? It's been a good many months since I've seen him. I had no idea he went to Australia."

"He's fine," she answered, turning to Mark and Jeremiah. "This is his brother, Mark Gray. You've been aboard the same ship with him and didn't know it. And this is one of our friends, Jeremiah Brown."

The men shook hands and exchanged quick greetings.

"Jonathon couldn't be here, I'm afraid. He's out at the mine and has sent me in his stead," she continued. "But since it's lunch time, and I'm sure you're hungry, would you care to go to your rooms to freshen up a bit before eating? The restaurant is only across the street, and I could meet you there in an hour."

139

"I'll admit I could use a good lunch," Mark agreed with a grin.

"You probably have your brother's appetite, too," Rebecca responded shaking her head. "I swear, he could eat a whole hog by himself."

Everyone laughed and parted to meet again at the restaurant in an hour. Mark was early, sliding into his seat beside Rebecca with a wide smile.

"What do you think of your brother's hotel, Mark?" Rebecca inquired, finding herself liking him more each time she saw him. "It was the first thing he built when he arrived here."

"It's quite a place," Mark answered. "He's done well."

Said as a statement, Rebecca could hear the question in his voice. "He's done *very* well."

Mark sobered and nodded, looking at her with deeply concerned eyes. "How is Jonathon? Really?"

"He's fine, really," she assured him, placing a gentle hand on his arm. "As big and healthy as you remember him."

He sighed, relief reflecting on his face. "I've been worried about him. This was the first letter I received from him since he left England."

"The first letter!" she objected. "But he's been here for months!"

Mark nodded sadly. "I know. He's bitter, and I don't blame him for feeling the way he does. I only wish he had stayed in touch."

"He's been a busy man, Mark," Rebecca offered in consolation. "He's been building and expanding ever since he arrived. The hotel, this restaurant, the dock your ship dropped anchor at—they're all his."

"He mentioned some of that," Mark admitted with a fleeting smile, knowing her words were only an excuse and not the reason for Jonathon's long silence. "He wrote a short but fairly detailed letter saying he'd tell me all about it when I arrived—if I chose to come."

"I'm glad you did. He's looking forward to seeing

you. I'll have you know you gave me a fright when you came off the ship so late. I was thinking I'd have to go back and tell Jonathon you hadn't come."

Mark smiled brightly, the gay light returning to his eyes. "You won't have to do that, Rebecca. I'm here now, and everything's going to be all right."

The three-day trip back through the bush to the mine was a happy one for Rebecca. She and Mark spent the hours laughing and remembering times gone by. She revealed her youth spent in the Scottish hills and he his memories of the farm in England he and Jonathon had grown up on. Their conversation was free and light. Rebecca enjoyed listening to tales of Jonathon as a boy, learning how he had grown, the things he had done, and the mischief he had gotten into. It was easy to speak to Mark. Mark idolized his older brother, but she hesitated to say anything that might damage Mark's view of the man he so admired. She also avoided discussing her uncle and cousins and skipped lightly over the details of their marriage. If Jonathon wanted his brother to know how things had been arranged between them, she felt it must be he who told Mark. It would not be right coming from her.

Thomas Pickering was amazed at the wilderness they passed through on the way to the camp, but he was more amazed when he saw the tent town. "People *live* there?" he asked in disbelief. "Day and night?"

"Week upon week," Rebecca replied with a solemn nod. "It may not be much to you or me, but it's all they have and they're glad to have it. They're simple but happy folk."

"What a shame. If only . . ." He shook his head.

"I know," she agreed with an understanding smile. "There are many things in the world that are a shame to see, but we must make the most of what we have, and they do. They're happy," she assured him. "And they're proud."

It was lunch when they arrived at the cave. A throng

of men stood or sat eating their lunches around the entrance and surrounding area. Rebecca tried to find Jonathon among the group, but it was impossible to spot him quickly. As they dismounted, she heard a thundering yell and turned in time to see Jonathon embrace his younger brother.

She watched them in happy silence, smiling at Jeremiah as the two brothers stood staring at each other, grinning broadly until Rebecca interrupted. "I see the two of you have met."

Both men laughed, and Jonathon put an arm around her shoulders, hugging her tightly. "Thank you, Rebecca, for bringing him to me. What else have you brought?"

"The word is who," she told him, holding a hand out toward Thomas Pickering.

Jonathon shook Pickering's hand warmly. "Thomas Pickering. How are you?"

Rebecca didn't hear the return greeting. She only saw the white bandage wrapped securely around Jonathon's free hand. "Jonathon! What have you done to yourself?"

He waved the hand carelessly. "We had a small rock slide in the mine when we started drilling."

"A rock slide!"

"Just a small one. No one was hurt."

"No one but you!" she retorted hotly. "I thought you told me the mine was safe!"

"It is," he assured her. "Just a slight crack in the rock is all."

Ben picked that moment to join the group, limping and favoring his left leg. "Hi, Becky. This must be Mark, Jonathon's brother. Welcome to . . ."

"Ben! Your leg!"

"It's nothing," he said with a shrug. "A small rock slide. Nothing serious."

"Nothing serious. Just a slight crack in the rock," she echoed the two men, putting her hands on her hips and glaring at Jonathon. "You told me it was safe. You told me there was no chance of anyone getting hurt."

"Whoa there!" Jonathon laughed, putting an arm around her. "Cool that Scot temper of yours and calm down. I've got something to show you."

Rebecca didn't see the wink that passed between Jonathon and Ben as she reluctantly allowed herself to be led away from the other men and around a group of trees across the open stretch opposite the mine.

She stopped as they rounded the trees, staring across the open ground. "Jonathon!" she exclaimed turning to face him.

"Do you like it?"

"I ... " She shook her head and spun back to look at the small wooden structure standing a short distance from the trees. Small and unfinished, it stood alone in the open space. But it didn't matter how it looked. It was what it meant: No more sleeping in tents. No more huddling in covers while laying on the hard ground trying to keep out the wind. No more early-morning sun shining in her eyes. No more rain leaking under the flaps or draining through the roof to saturate her and her bedding. And, no more stumbling and stooping to avoid banging her head on the support poles.

"It's not done yet," Jonathon continued. "And, of course, we have no furniture, but . . ."

Rebecca silenced him by throwing her arms around his neck and kissing him soundly on the cheek. "I don't care. It's beautiful. Thank you, Jonathon."

He smiled down at her, aware of the other men who had come to stand behind them. "Why don't you go take a look at it?"

They watched her turn and run, her skirts flying out behind her, until she disappeared through the door of the small cabin.

Jeremiah grinned and readjusted his hat with a small jerk of his hand. "Guess I'll get back to work now."

"Me, too," Ben agreed with a sigh.

Jonathon nodded at Pickering as the older man stopped beside him. Jonathon pointed to the shack.

"It's not what I had in mind for you to build for us when I asked you to come. It's only four rooms and a sitting area by a fire, but do you think you can finish it up for me? You're better at this sort of thing than Ben and I are."

"She told me something about your building a hut for her before the rains started, but she wasn't sure you'd have the time," Pickering replied agreeably. "She's a fine woman, and you've made her day. I'd be glad to finish it up for you, so I'd best go have a look."

Jonathon and Mark watched him go before turning to each other once more. Clapping each other on the shoulder, they turned away to walk to the tents where Jonathon, Rebecca, and Ben had slept just north of the cave's mouth.

"She's nice. I like her," Mark told his older brother. "Where did you find her?"

"At the hotel," Jonathon replied. "At least, that's where I met her. It's a long story. We'll have time to discuss the past tonight. Right now, I want to show you what I brought you halfway around the world for."

19

While lying in her tent after supper, Rebecca could not remember being so happy. Outside, she could hear the steady drone of the men's voices by the campfire. They would probably be up talking a good part of the night.

She looked at the canvas hanging above her and smiled. She would soon have a roof over her head again, even though it might be a small roof. The cabin wasn't much, but it was more than she had hoped for. Jonathon was so busy of late, she had been afraid he wouldn't be able to take the time out to build it. But he had. He had built her a cabin. She closed her eyes, a soft smile on her lips. Jonathon had come to mean so much to her. She couldn't imagine life without him. Still smiling, she fell asleep.

Outside her tent, Thomas Pickering lingered for only a short time by the fire discussing plans with Jonathon and Mark before going to his tent for the night. It had been a long day, and he was wise enough to understand the two brothers had much to talk about after such a long separation.

"So, little brother, what do you think of Australia?" Jonathon asked, stretching his legs out toward the fire.

"I told Becky it's nothing like I've ever seen before. So wild and free. It bears absolutely no resemblance to England. Our meager fields could never compare with this bush country."

"No, it's not like England," Jonathon agreed solemnly, gazing into the fire. The coming of his brother had brought back many memories, many things he had almost forgotten. But he hadn't forgotten, and he never would.

Mark watched Jonathon's face for a moment, seeing there the pain his brother suffered, the disillusion and disgrace. "Tell me what's happened since you arrived here, John. Your letter didn't tell me much."

Jonathon grinned apologetically. "I'm sorry, Mark. I meant to write but somehow . . ." He shrugged.

"I know. I can understand how you've felt. I only wish I could've helped you."

"You're helping me now by being here."

Mark smiled, a warm smile that covered more than words could say.

"But, to answer your question," Jonathon continued, "how much did Rebecca tell you?"

"She told me that when you arrived you started the hotel, and from there you built a restaurant. She apologized for not being able to tell me much, but she said she hadn't met you until after you'd been here for some time."

The older brother nodded. "I didn't meet Rebecca until four months after I'd arrived. By then, the hotel was already built, as was the restaurant. I was very busy in those first few months."

Mark grinned. "So it appears. But how did you get your idea? Why a hotel? Why not something else?"

"Because, when I came here, there was one of something else wherever I looked. But there wasn't a hotel. The only place you could stay at was a run-down building that offered a choice of sleeping on the floor or sharing a room or sharing a bed or having your own room for an outlandish price."

"You're joking, surely?" Mark laughed.

"No, I'm quite serious. I started to build my hotel the day after I arrived. I arranged a loan with Allan Hendrix, who runs our land office here, and began from there. Thirty men worked day and night." Jonathon shook his head in remembrance. "It was hard work, but it paid off quickly."

"And the restaurant went up right afterward?"

Jonathon grinned and shrugged. "I was lucky."

"Lucky. You're always lucky. Everything you do you do well, and you always pass it off with saying you're lucky."

Jonathon smiled ironically, remembering London. He hadn't been lucky there. "I met Rebecca when she came to the hotel with her uncle and cousins, the Cunninghams."

Mark shifted uneasily. "Why is it, whenever either of you mention that name, I get the impression something's wrong? It's as though it's not a subject you care to talk about. Is there something wrong with Rebecca's family?"

Jonathon shook his head and sat up to poke more life into the fire. "I'd better explain from the beginning. It's the only way any of this will make sense, and you can ask your questions when I finish."

Quickly and quietly, Jonathon told of the events from his first meeting with the Cunninghams to Rebecca's disappearance. He explained the difference between her life in Scotland and the one she had in Australia, the difference that had caused her to take flight. He told of how he had found her in the bush and of discovering her at the mercy of two bush runners. From there, he went on to describe the discovery of the gold mine and Rebecca's realization that, without a husband, she would lose everything she had to her uncle.

Mark remained silent as his brother explained the proposition Rebecca had put to him, and of his acceptance and their marriage, recognizing the impact each event probably had on Jonathon. Jonathon fell silent, letting the quiet of the night come between himself and Mark as his younger brother absorbed and considered everything he had heard.

Mark was troubled by Jonathan's relationship with Rebecca. He had hoped Jonathon had found happiness here, away from England. Mark had hoped Jonathon's marriage meant he had forgotten what was behind him, that he had put aside the past. But a business proposition instead of a proposal?

Mark studied his brother across the fire. Rebecca and Jonathon seemed to get along so well together; they seemed to belong to each other. "You do like each other, though?" he asked.

Jonathon smiled, an amused expression of contentment. "We have our moments. But we also both have our own lives to live."

"And they can't be lived together?" Mark questioned. "After all, you are married, and two years is a long time. Things change, people change. Once the house is built and everything is running smoothly, when that's done, when you've finished all this, all this that you're working so hard for, are you really going to return to England and leave her behind?"

Jonathon gestured impatiently. It was something he did not want to think of yet. "I don't know, Mark. Neither of us does. We agreed we would both be free at the end of those two years, free to do what we want, regardless of what the other feels." He rose to his feet. "We'll cross that bridge when we come to it."

"Why don't you burn the bridges behind you first?"

Jonathon stared incredulously at his brother. "Do you know what you're saying? Do you know?" he demanded. "Are you telling me to forget—forget what they did to me?"

"Jonathon, for God's sake, think!" Mark exclaimed, jumping to his feet. "You've got a beautiful wife, a gold mine, a kingdom to build. You have everything here, everything a man could ever dream of. What will it prove to go back and show them you're just as rich as they are? Answer me that."

"England's my home. I've a right to go there, a right to live there."

"You didn't answer my question."

"Because I don't have one. Does that satisfy you?" Jonathon snapped. "It's something I have to do, something I have to prove to myself."

"Don't you mean prove to them?" Mark countered. "Prove you're just as good as they are?" He laughed. "Isn't that something to be proud of! You're becoming the very thing you've always detested, the very thing *they* are. And if you've become no better than that . . ."

Mark stopped, glared at his brother in anger and disbelief, and walked away.

"Mark!"

Mark stopped, but only after a moment did he turn slowly to face his brother once more.

"Mark," Jonathon pleaded, "can't you understand?"

"I can, but I don't want to. I don't want to because it's wrong. Do you hear me, Jonathon? It's wrong."

Jonathon gestured helplessly. "All right, it's wrong. Yes, it's wrong. But it's something I have to do. It's not something I can ignore. It's gone too far now. It's like something eating inside of me, and I have to do it my way." He shook his head and turned away.

Mark felt his heart wrench inside of him at the sight of his brother. Once so tall, so proud, now his shoulders slumped and his head was bent. It was as if he were carrying a burden too great for him to bear.

Understanding began to seep through Mark. Yes, Jonathon was carrying a burden, and it was a burden only he could rid himself of. No words, no arguments, no logic could sway him. He had hated too hard and too long. He had become obsessed with an idea, an idea that had driven him on and on. Hate and anger had become his motivation. Whenever he had a setback, whenever he couldn't achieve something he wanted, he had only to think of his hate and anger to drive himself forward again. These feelings had become part of him, part of his life, and revenge had become his goal. There was nothing Mark could do to change Jonathon's feelings. Jonathon had to realize the truth himself. He had to come to understand revenge was no substitute for life.

Mark walked back to stand beside Jonathon, putting a hand on his brother's shoulder. "We'll go take a look at that river tomorrow," he told him. "I'll help you build Becky's kingdom."

The next morning, Jonathon and Rebecca rode out with Mark and Thomas Pickering. The sun was barely up as they started out. A fresh, crisp breeze was sweeping over the land. The birds called across the

149

grass, and the scurrying of other animals could be heard around them.

It was the kind of morning Rebecca loved most in the bush. Everything was peaceful and calm. Riding with friends only made the glow within her burn brighter. Her mood was picked up by the men, and light-hearted chatter passed between them. On reaching the plateau, they all rode out to its center, showing Pickering and Mark where the house was to stand.

Pickering scanned the area, his trained eye measuring distances, studying the solidity of the ground. At last he nodded. "It's a fine site for a house," he assured them. "What size house were you thinking of?"

Jonathon motioned to Rebecca. "You'll have to get the details from Rebecca. She's been dreaming about this house for so long, she can probably tell you where she wants every beam and step placed."

Rebecca smiled shyly at Jonathon's teasing grin and Pickering's inquiring look. "I want a big house, Tom, but not too big. Two floors will be more than enough. I don't want it to be one of those towering mansions you see in England."

"You want it wider than it will be tall," Pickering agreed. "And you'll want a stable?"

"Of course," she replied, looking past the architect at Jonathon for assistance.

"I think we can discuss the details of the rooms and other buildings tonight. Don't you, Tom?" Jonathon suggested. "Perhaps you and Rebecca can talk more about what is wanted while we show Mark the river."

"Certainly," Pickering quickly agreed. "By all means, let's move on. We can show Mark the river, and at lunch or dinner we can straighten out the questions."

Mark urged his horse next to Jonathon's as they fell in ahead of Rebecca and Pickering. "She's quite excited about that house. She told me she grew up in a village in Scotland and has always dreamed of living in a large house. She used to go for long walks down the country lanes, just to look at all the estates of the local gentry."

"I had no idea the dream was so deeply rooted,"

Jonathon answered. "I thought she started thinking of it only when she arrived here."

"I think we all have dreams we carry from childhood," the younger of the two brothers said thoughtfully. "I can remember dreaming about a farm, the biggest farm in the whole of England. I used to think it would be so big, people would come from miles around just to see it."

Jonathon laughed, a gentle booming sound. "And, tell me, have you achieved this dream?"

Mark smiled shyly. "No, but I'm working on it."

Jonathon reached out and clapped Mark on the shoulder. "If anyone can do it, you can. I remember Mother saying you could make a dead seed grow. You were always much better at farming than I. You used to enjoy those long hours in the field behind the plow and hoe."

"And you? You didn't enjoy it?"

"I enjoyed it. For some reason I've never been able to understand, I've always enjoyed hard work. It gives a man satisfaction. But," he said with a smile, "unlike you, I've always dreamed of going out, of becoming somebody, and of building something."

Mark nodded thoughtfully. "You are out, and I do believe you've become somebody. Everyone in town knows who Jonathon Gray is. I'll wager the shipping lines are spreading the word back to England about the man who's built the finest dock in all of Australia."

"I think your dreams of me are much more glamorous than my own," Jonathon laughed.

"No. Seriously," the younger man insisted, "you talk of being someone and of building something. Look around you, Jon. Look. It's a big land and barren right now. With determination and the proper tools, someone could build something out of it, make it big."

"You sound like Rebecca," Jonathon replied lightly, but he felt a sudden stab of pain. Of jealousy?

"She's right. It's a great land. If the plans you've told me about look as good on the land as they do on paper, you'll indeed be the master of a kingdom."

151

Jonathon did not reply or give any indication of agreeing with his younger brother's words. Inside, something stirred, a feeling of pride, a sense of accomplishment. He *had* started something, something' big. Rebecca's dreams had become part of his life, almost his own, and he wanted to see them turned into reality. Australia was a betwitching land. Sometimes, Jonathon felt he had always been in its vast wilderness all his life and had always been working for the goals he was now reaching for. At other times, when the lonely wind howled over the barren land in a mournful lament, he thought of England and longed for home—and his revenge. Hurt and humiliation were still in his heart, even if they no longer stung so fiercely.

The river came into view, and Jonathon brought his thoughts back to the present. He led the way up a hill, the highest piece of ground in the area, and they stopped to look around. Mark studied the terrain for a long time before speaking. His words were cautious, yet confident.

"It could be done, Jon. At least, I think it can be. Does the river run all year round? You mentioned droughts."

"I've heard it can dry up in an extremely hot summer, but it's been full as long as I've been here."

"Aye, this year the river has been full," Rebecca agreed. "And the year before it ran low but never dry. But the first year I was living here," she shook her head, "it was a bad year. The water was so low you could find strips of sand in the high parts of the riverbed."

Mark nodded thoughtfully, staring out at the land around the river. "You could build yourself a dam."

"A dam," Rebecca echoed. "Is the land fit for such a thing?"

"It could be," Mark answered, pointing toward the river. "See the area where the river widens? The land all around it is fairly flat. You'd have to build the dam as high as you can get it for irrigation purposes. From there, you could plant crops on either side and channel the water out."

Jonathon agreed. "I was thinking much the same thing, but I wasn't sure it would work."

"What of the rains?" Rebecca asked. "They're heavy. Wouldn't there be a chance of the dam's overflowing?"

"You'd have to keep the water low," Mark explained. "You could open a channel directly to the river to run off any excess water."

Rebecca studied the river dubiously. "We'd have to wait until next year to build the dam, then. Wouldn't we?"

Jonathon met Mark's eyes. "What do you think? The rains usually start in June."

"Reversing the seasons," Mark said to himself. "That would mean planting in September and harvesting in May. To answer your question, yes, I think it could be done this year. We'd have to work fast, though. Can you spare the men?"

"We'll hire more," Jonathon told him decisively. "Miners won't know anything about irrigation ditches. There must be some farmers around."

"Tools are also needed to build the dam, and later there will be fertilizer, and much more."

"We'll get them. You make up a list, and we'll send to town for what you need tomorrow with the next gold shipment."

At the mention of gold, Mark flushed guiltily. "I hope you don't mind my spending your money."

"It's what we put it in the bank for," Jonathon responded, smiling at Rebecca, "to draw it out when we need it."

Mark grinned at Rebecca and then at Jonathon. "Then I'll feel free to spend what I need to get what I need." He turned again to the river, a glow of excitement shining in his eyes. "I do believe I'm going to enjoy my stay here, Jonathon. Very much."

Jonathon grasped his brother's shoulder firmly. "You keep that attitude, Mark. It'll give me motivation to keep going myself."

"As if you need my help for that."

The rest of the morning and a good part of the afternoon was spent riding over the land, searching for places suited for absorbing water and therefore likely spots to drill a well. Wells would be needed along with the dam to water livestock during the long summer months.

It wasn't until late afternoon that they arrived back at the camp to pore over maps of the land and make the final divisions where stock and crops were to be kept. Evening fell before they were done, and they sat huddled around the glowing fire, still discussing their ideas.

"I'll do some sketching tomorrow on designs for the house," Pickering said, sipping coffee as he nodded to Rebecca and Jonathon. "The two of you can give me your approval and make any changes you might want."

"And tomorrow," Mark said, "I'm going to ride back to the river to check its flow and to plan out the size of the dam. I'll have to stake out places where water runs off naturally so we can dig drainage ditches."

Rebecca and Jonathon lingered by the fire after the two men had gone, content to sit quietly and think over the day.

"Ben'll be going into town tomorrow," Rebecca said. "I meant to tell you sooner, but I forgot."

"He mentioned he wanted to go in before the rains come," Jonathon answered quietly. "It'll do him good to go into town and relax for awhile."

"And you? You haven't been to town since you came. Why don't you go with him?"

"There's no need for me to go. Someone will have to supervise the work in the mine while he's gone."

Rebecca fell silent. She wished he would go, wished he would give himself the same chance to relax Ben would have. "I haven't told you about the business in town."

"Anything wrong?"

"Small problems. Broken furniture and windows, a small fire in the warehouse, and one of the cooks quit. Nothing serious."

"The books?"

"They show nothing but profit. The warehouse foreman tells me there's been some trouble with the people who are storing their property. He says it's difficult to collect from the store owners who are not doing well. Then there are others who forget to pick up what they've stored when their contracts end."

Jonathon frowned. "Sometimes, I believe those warehouses were a bad investment."

"Oh, no," Rebecca hurriedly reassured him. "As the town grows, they'll be much more important and prosperous."

Jonathon smiled. "Always looking ahead, aren't you?"

"We have to," she answered honestly. "I think we should plan for our cattle and sheep now, too. We should start our herds after winter has passed."

He shook his head. "It's early yet, Rebecca. We have time to consider. We can't rush into everything at once. We have the house, the dam, the planting, and the wells to consider. I know you're anxious to have it all done and finished, but these things take time. As you once told me, kingdoms are not built in a day."

She sighed, but not unhappily. "You're right, I know. But, do you think November, perhaps?"

"We'll see," he told her rising. "For now, you'd best get some sleep. You've had a long day." he held out a hand and pulled her to her feet. "Are you happy, Rebecca?"

Rebecca stared up at him, feeling her heart begin to pound rapidly at his closeness. "Aye, Jonathon. I'm happy." Her eyes dropped before his, and she clasped her hands tightly together. "You've been very good to me."

Jonathon cupped her chin in his hand and raised her face to him. He stared down into her eyes for a long moment, as if searching for an answer there. Then, lowering his head, he kissed her lightly on the mouth. He felt a tremor run through her at his touch and again wondered at how such a small, innocent young woman

155

could be the motivating force behind such a massive amount of effort. Slowly, he raised his head from hers. "Good night, Rebecca."

Rebecca felt unaccountably weak as he turned and walked from her. Why was it she felt so defenseless in his presence? Was it her overwhelming gratitude that made her feel that way? Or was it because he was the man who had come to her rescue when she had been more helpless and terrified than she had ever been in her life? Or was it merely his size? He was so tall and broad. When she stood beside him, she felt so small. She shook her head and moved quietly away to her tent. She could find no answer.

Across the camp, Jonathon stopped beside the wagon where the gold lay packed and ready to be taken to town. Ben was sitting by its wheel, smoking a pipe. "Ready for tomorrow, Ben?"

"Ready. Two of the guards will be coming along. They're good men. We'll get there safely."

"I'm sure of that," Jonathon agreed, easing his long frame down beside the older man. "Are you planning on spending some of your ten percent in town?"

Ben echoed the smile on Jonathon's lips. "I'll be lucky if I don't spend it all. I've been thinking I might get myself a bath and a shave. I might even buy myself a nice suit. Then I'm going to find myself a pretty lady to keep me company, drink some champagne, and in a few days I'll be back."

Jonathon nodded appreciatively. He could remember times back in England when he and his friends had done much the same thing. "I wonder if you would do me a favor while you're there."

"Name it."

"See if you can't find some furniture for the cabin. A couple of beds, some chairs, a stove."

Ben nodded soberly. "I'll do that."

"You know, once we move into that cabin, one of those rooms is yours."

Ben blew a cloud of smoke into the air. "I reckon I might use it when the rains come, but I always did like sleeping under the stars. I'm kind of used to it now."

"Just the same, it's there if you want it."

Ben grunted amiable consent and changed the subject. "I shouldn't be away much more than a week. I don't imagine you'll have any trouble while I'm gone."

"I don't imagine so either. Have a good trip."

Ben grinned as he shook Jonathon's hand. "I plan to."

20

Activity was high in the camp during the week Ben was gone. Mark and Rebecca were out at the dam almost every day, checking the flow of the river, marking points of drainage, and planning the layout of the dam. In a matter of days, they were joined by the first group of farmers who had heard of the building of the dam upon Ben's arrival in town. They came to work, and Mark welcomed them enthusiastically.

Jonathon stayed in the mine, supervising the men, while outside the dark confines of the cavern Thomas Pickering put the finishing touches on the drawings for the house and completed the building of the cabin.

The weather was steadily growing cooler, and black clouds began to pass over the land as warning of what winter would bring. Rebecca watched the clouds silently, worrying at their number and frequency. She feared an early season might be coming, and for Mark's sake she hoped she was wrong. He was working feverishly on the dam and ditches and had great hopes for success. If the rains came, she knew his work would have to cease, whether the dam was finished or not. Mark would be bitterly disappointed if it were the latter.

Pausing for lunch one day late in the week, Jonathon called Rebecca and Jeremiah to him. With the coming of the winter season, final plans had to be made before the rains came and blocked them in for weeks on end.

"Jeremiah, I've been thinking about the gold we've mined since Ben's left," Jonathon began, warming his hands on a cup of coffee. "It might be wise to ship what gold we have into town instead of holding it along with what we mine during the winter here."

"I agree," Jeremiah quickly responded. "It's not a good idea to leave gold laying around, no matter how little. I don't think it would be a wasted trip."

"If you're going in, I'd like to come with you," Rebecca interjected. "The supplies for the tent-town store haven't been arriving, and we can't take the chance on running out."

Jonathon nodded. "You can see Tom off then, too. He's finished the cabin and drawings. We'll have to get him back to town so he can leave on the next ship. He tells me he'll be back in early September with the supplies needed. He also said he'll ship some of them. While you're there, tell Peters to be ready for the crates, to keep them stored until we can get in to pick them up."

"Aye," Rebecca agreed. "Do you need anything from town for yourself?"

"No, not now. Are you sure you feel up to the trip? You haven't gotten much rest in the past few days with all this activity."

"I'm feeling fine," she assured him with a smile.

"All right, then," Jonathon said looking at Jeremiah, "choose who's to go with the shipment."

"Just tell me when, and we'll be ready," Jeremiah replied. He drained his coffee cup and turned to join Bobby, who was standing guard by the mine.

Jonathon stared up at the darkening sky, a frown touching his mouth. "Ben's due back today. With the weather looking as it does, it would probably be best if you left tomorrow."

Rebecca nodded, following his gaze. "I'm afraid we might be having an early season. I hope I'm wrong."

"You sound worried."

"I am—for Mark. He wants so much to please you, Jonathon. If the rains start early, there will be no dam. He'll be heartbroken if he thinks he's failed you."

"He can't help the weather," Jonathon objected, but he knew she was right. Mark was working harder than Jonathon had ever seen him do before.

Watching a group of miners walk past them into the mine, Rebecca suddenly grasped Jonathon's arm. "Jonathon, couldn't you use some of the miners to help? You could send them over in a wagon every morning and bring them back at night. The gold they're mining now will go nowhere till the spring."

Jonathon stared down into her concerned face. "Perhaps you're right. We'll need the winter rains to fill the dam for the crops this summer. The dam is more important now." He rose to his feet. "I'll start taking men out tomorrow."

Rebecca forced a smile and looked up at the clouds once more. "I only hope you'll be in time."

He smiled encouragingly, trying to drive the lines of worry from her face. "Don't worry. We'll manage, no matter what happens."

She echoed his smile. "I'd best be going, to tell Tom of our plans for leaving. He'll have to get his things together."

"And I'll tell Jeremiah and the men." Parting to go their separate ways, neither of them noticed a wagon coming across the range to the camp.

Jeremiah witnessed Ben's arrival and watched the team of horses plunge up the incline toward the mine, hauling a wagonful of furniture and a boisterously singing Ben Ritter.

"Whoa up there, Ben!" Jeremiah called in greeting, a smile bursting across his face. "What you hauling?"

Pulling the lathered team to an abrupt halt, Ben rose from his seat and swept his hat off in a gallant gesture. "I have here some gifts for the lady of the mine. Where might she be?"

"Over yonder at the cabin. Pickering finished it yesterday."

"Then I'm just in time." Ben let loose a rumbling yell, and the team was off once more, rushing away in a flurry of dust and rock toward the cabin. Once there, the wagon jolted to a halt, and Ben yelled. "Rebecca! Rebecca McGregor! If you're in there, come on out!

160

I've got something to show you!"

Inside the cabin, Rebecca stopped in mid-sentence to stare at Thomas Pickering in surprise. "It's Ben!"

"Rebecca! If you don't come out here right this minute, I'll take it all back!"

Looking helplessly from Pickering to the door, she gathered her skirts and ran out into the sunlight to find Ben standing on top of the wagon seat. "Ben Ritter! Are you out of your mind? What are you yelling like that for?"

Ben jumped to the ground, landing agilely on his feet. "No, I haven't lost my mind, and I'm yelling because I want your attention."

Rebecca put her hands on her hips, finding it hard to suppress a smile. "Ben Ritter, I do believe you're drunk."

"Not hardly, kind lady," he said approaching her. "But I do feel mighty fine." With that, he swooped Rebecca up into his arms and deposited her on top of one of the wheels. "Look there and see what I've brought you."

She gasped at the array of furniture: Chairs, tables, mattresses, beds, and a stove. "Ben! You shouldn't have!"

Ben jumped on top of the other wheel on the same side of the wagon. "But I did."

"Thank you, Ben."

"You ought not be thanking me. It's your husband who ordered it."

"Jonathon?"

Ben nodded, sitting on the wagon's edge and crossing his arms across his chest. "He's a good man, Becky."

Rebecca felt a warm glow flow through her, and she smiled. "I know," she agreed softly. "He's a very good man."

"We can sure tell you've come back," Jonathon's voice unexpectedly called from a distance. "We could hear you yelling all the way down in the cavern."

Rebecca turned to watch him approach and felt the

sudden realization of love sweep over her. Her heart began to pound as she stared at the tall man before her. She was in love, in love with this man she had propositioned into marriage.

Jonathon saw the softness of her eyes but mistakenly placed the reason on something else. He smiled at Ben. "So you've told her, have you?"

"That I did," Ben answered, jumping down from the wheel. "And if she'll kindly step down from that wheel, we'll get on with unloading these items of furniture."

Jonathon stepped forward and reached up to her, taking her by the waist and swinging her down to stand in front of him. "Move aside, Rebecca. We're about to furnish your house."

He did not see the loving look she gave him as he turned away. His back was turned. But Mark, just arriving from the dam site did, and his heart ached for her. She began to walk away from the wagon and was startled into meeting Mark's eyes. She flushed hotly and quickly hurried away, knowing the emotion she felt was surely reflected on her face.

Mark watched her go before joining the men in unloading the wagonload of furniture. Was Jonathon really blind to Rebecca's feelings, or did he simply choose not to notice them? Mark wondered further as he stood alongside his brother: Was it really only one sided? Could any man who came in contact with the spirited Scots girl Jonathon had married not love her? Forcing his words back, Mark kept his silence. There was nothing he could say to Rebecca or Jonathon to change the situation. They had to change it themselves.

Later that night, after Mark and Thomas Pickering retired to their rooms in the cabin, and after Jonathon went to the mine to see Ben, Rebecca slipped away from her new home to be by herself. She had to get away. She had to think. She loved Jonathon Gray. There was nothing she could say or do to deny it. It was true. Somewhere, at some unknown time, she had fallen in love with the man she had bargained into marriage.

What was she to do? He didn't love her. To him, she was only a means to an end, a way to get back to England, back to his home, and to the woman he loved.

She stared up at the dark sky and sighed, shuddering against the pain inside her. He must still love her, this daughter of Arthur Boyd. And here he was, married to a woman he didn't even know! How he must hate their mockery of a marriage and being trapped with her in a land that was not his own!

Rebecca sighed and pulled her shawl closer about her. She was in love with him, in love with a man who didn't love her and who was with her only because she provided a fast and easy way to return to another woman, the one he loved. She sank down onto a rock from where she was hidden from view of the camp and could look out over the land she had chosen to make her home. What was to become of her when the two years of their agreement was over? What would she do in this land and in her big house all by herself when he was gone? She couldn't imagine living without Jonathon. She couldn't believe that, some day, she would wake up and he would no longer be there. But it would happen. He would leave. He wouldn't stay, couldn't stay because of the feelings inside of him. And she could not make him stay.

A lone tear formed slowly and started a path down her cheek. *Oh, Rebecca McGregor. What have you gotten yourself into?*

Jonathon was coming from the mine when he saw Rebecca walking away, followed by the big yellow dog who was never far from her side. Assuming she was restless and would come back to the cabin soon, he continued toward the cabin door. Once there, he hesitated, feeling an inexplicable yearning to go after her. For a moment, he fought the longing but with an impatient gesture he gave in and went after her.

She disappeared behind a ridge, and when he saw her again, she was sitting on a rock with Dingo lying on the ground beside her. Her head was bent and the red highlights of her hair shone brightly under the light of the half moon above.

Jonathon stood silent, drinking in the picture of loveliness she made, until he suddenly realized she was crying. Hurrying forward, he dropped down to kneel beside her.

Rebecca started violently as Jonathon touched her. She jumped to her feet and rubbed vigorously at her eyes. "I didn't hear you come up," she managed to stammer.

Jonathon stood and reached out to take her by the shoulders. "What's wrong? You're crying."

Rebecca shook her head and forced a smile. "Nothing," she said, feeling perilously close to a fresh storm of tears. He was so close to her, and yet so far away!

He took her chin in his hand and tilted her head back. Her tears were large pools of green, swelling rapidly fuller with tears. "Rebecca?"

Suddenly, she was against him, and his arms were around her, holding her tightly as she sobbed against his chest. Jonathon stood completely bewildered, unable to think of what to do. He had never seen her cry like this before. What had upset her? If something had happened, if something was wrong, why hadn't she told him?

Rebecca clung tightly to him, feeling the strength of his arms around her and the hardness of his chest against her face and hands. It hurt to have him hold her. It hurt to know he didn't care.

Gritting her teeth against the lonely chills shaking her body, she tried to be still. She knew she mustn't tell him of her feelings. He mustn't even guess. It would only make him uncomfortable and embarrassed. No, she could not force her feelings on him. She must maintain her silence—at all costs.

The crying ebbed and Jonathon put her gently away from him. "Rebecca, what is it? Has somebody done something to upset you?"

She shook her head in quick denial. He must not think she was crying because of someone else. But he had to be told something. What? "No. No one's done anything."

"Then what?" He shook his head helplessly. "I don't understand."

"It's nothing, Jonathon," she said lightly, her smile trembling on her lips. "Nothing. You know how silly women can be. I'm just—just happy." Before he could say more, she pulled free of him and ran back to the safety of her little room in the cabin, a room she believed she would never share with her husband.

A baffled and stricken Jonathon stood by the rock and watched her go, with the big yellow dog following at her heels.

21

"Remember, Jonathon," Pickering told Jonathon as he sat on the wagon seat beside the driver, "immediately after the rains, go out and check the land to see where the rain runs and forms pools. It will be those spots that will be best for drilling well."

"I'll remember," Jonathon promised. "And you'll be back in September?"

"God willing," Pickering agreed. "But I'll begin sending materials to your warehouse as soon as I can arrange for the supplies I'll need."

"I've already told Rebecca to warn my dock foreman of their coming. He'll store them until we can get them out here." Jonathon shook Pickering's hand and swung to face Jeremiah and Bobby, who sat astride horses near the wagon. "I'll see you men in a week."

"That you will," Jeremiah agreed, looking past him when he saw Rebecca coming. "Ah, here comes Becky. We can be on our way now."

Rebecca rode slowly up to the wagon. She hoped, by being late in arriving, Jonathon would be gone and she would not have to face him. But he was there, watching and waiting for her.

Jonathon frowned slightly as she came to a halt beside him. She looked tired, as if she hadn't slept well. If she was happy, why couldn't she sleep? "Are you sure you feel up to this trip?"

She nodded and smiled quickly. "I'm feeling fine. I'll come back in a week with the supplies for the workers. Tell them not to worry."

"I will, and they won't." He stared up at her for a moment longer before stepping away. Should he say something more? "Have a safe trip."

Rebecca smiled vaguely and turned her horse away, urging it forward as the wagon driver cracked his whip and the small procession started out. Jonathon remained behind watching it go, a frown standing darkly on his face.

During the trip to town, Rebecca tried desperately to keep her mind occupied. Laughing and talking with the men, she forced herself not to think of Jonathon. Her feelings must be forgotten, pushed aside. They would do her no good. Dwelling on her love, a love that was not returned, would only make matters worse. Immediately upon arriving in town, she went to work, hurrying to the store where the supplies for the tent town were ordered. She wanted to know why the supplies for the winter and the past month had not been received. The store keeper wasn't answering questions; he evaded the issue until Rebecca lost her temper.

"Mr. Cooper, when we started our agreement, you promised timely delivery each month. Now, are you going to keep your promise and send those supplies immediately, or are you going to return every cent we paid you for your services?"

Cooper shifted uneasily. "I wish I could send the supplies, Mrs. Gray, but the honest truth is I can't. I don't have any supplies to send."

"None to send? What's this? You told me you would have constant access to good supplies, that I never need worry about the shelves of our store being empty."

He looked away and fidgeted nervously. "I lost a good deal of money in a gambling game last week, Mrs. Gray. Not being able to pay my debts in cash, I had to pay them with goods."

"And those goods were mine?"

"Yes, ma'am."

Rebecca let out her breath in a slow, angry sigh. "Mr. Cooper, I have only this to say. Either you find those supplies—every single item I've ordered—and have them packed in wagons to go to our camp by tomorrow, or pack yourself up and get out of this store. Because unless those supplies are delivered, I'll take over your store and every item in it."

The man flinched, and the color drained from his face.

"Now," she continued, glaring at him for one final moment, "I'll bid you good day, Mr. Cooper. I expect to hear from you tomorrow."

She stormed away, passing up going into the bank. In her present mood, she didn't feel like solving any other problems. She felt more like creating them. Going straight to the hotel, she accepted the key from the desk clerk and turned to find Alison Cunningham waiting for her.

"Why, Rebecca, what a surprise."

Rebecca stiffened at the sweet greeting. "I've no time to play games, Alison, nor am I in the mood for them. So, if you'll excuse me."

"Where is Jonathon?" Alison inquired as her cousin began to move away, taking no notice of Rebecca's attempt to avoid the conversation.

"He's at the mine, if it's any concern of yours," Rebecca answered, facing her cousin once more.

"Does he always let you come to town alone with all those men?"

"All those men happen to be my employees, Alison. They work for me."

"They're still men, aren't they?"

Rebecca smiled at the ugly insinuation, aware of the wide-eyed clerk and Jeremiah, who were standing by the door after following her from the store. "I give my attentions only to men I'm interested in, Alison. The only man who is of interest to me is my husband. He trusts me and I him, and the men who work for us respect us both. Even though the men are not unattractive, they really don't interest me, though I know they do you. I think you would enjoy their attentions much more than I. Your own attentions are given so easily, you really should be traveling in my place."

Alison stood, stunned, gaping after Rebecca as, with quiet dignity, Rebecca ascended the stairs to leave her cousin behind. Later that night, Rebecca sat alone on the porch of the hotel, gazing out at the sky beyond the town and listening to its sounds. She had retired to her room after dinner, telling Jeremiah and Bobby to do as they pleased and invited them to show Thomas Pickering the town he had not yet had an opportunity to see. On checking at the desk some two hours later, Rebecca smiled when the clerk told her the men had gone out right after dining. It would do them good to relax, and it would give her a chance to be alone.

A quiet breeze whistled down the street, carrying the scents of the bush and harbor. Rebecca sighed sadly and reached down to pat Dingo, who lay stretched at her feet. She couldn't stop her thoughts from wandering back to the mine and Jonathon. Did he miss her at all? She shook her head silently. It was hopeless. She stood up and walked to the edge of the porch, looking down the street. To her right she could see the lights of the saloons and hear the laughter inside them. To her left lay the harbor. She stared at the strange glow from the dock. What scent was the wind carrying? Smoke! A fire!

She ran to the door and called to the clerk behind the desk. "Fire! There's a fire on the dock! Get help!" Not waiting for a reply, she turned and ran, lifting her skirts as she rushed across the boardwalk.

At the dock she stopped to stare at the awesome scene before her. A blaze was burning in one of the warehouses. Already there were flames coming out of most of the lower windows. Men were running across the dock. Among them she saw Peters. "What happened?" she called above the noise of the blaze.

He shook his head. "I don't know. I smelled smoke minutes ago and came out of my cabin to find this." He motioned toward the fire. "You best get out of the way, Mrs. Gray. This is going to get worse before it gets any better."

Rebecca watched him go, frozen into immobility as she stared at the flames licking their way up the sides of the building. Jeremiah and Bobby suddenly appeared at her side, and she shook herself into action. "Jeremiah. Bobby. We've got to try to stop this before it spreads over the entire dock."

People appeared out of the night and formed a line for a bucket brigade. Rebecca hurriedly joined them as Jeremiah and Bobby made their way to the warehouse. Peters was trying to remove what goods he could before the building was completely engulfed by fire.

Bucket after bucket of water was poured on the raging blaze, but there was no stopping it. It spread rapidly upward. Soon, the roof was burning fiercely, lighting up the sky for miles around. Everything glowed red. The heat and smoke began to take its toll on the bailers, who continued to pass buckets down the line.

Rebecca's eyes burned and watered. Her hands ached as the rough handles of the buckets dug into her palms again and again. She watched helplessly as the fire continued to burn, fearing for the men she could see through the smoke who were running in and out of the flaming structure. She recognized Jeremiah, Bobby, and Peters among them. She wished they would stop. They were risking their lives. The blaze was growing steadily worse. Talk of the roof collapsing had begun to buzz around her. Even as the words were spoken, the roaring crack of breaking timber echoed loudly, and the roof began to cave in. Rebecca turned terrified eyes to the door from which a man ran. It was Jeremiah.

Staring above him, he started to run. As Rebecca followed his gaze, she screamed his name. Roofing had broken free and was flaming a path to the ground where he stood.

Rebecca broke from the line to run forward, screaming again as she saw some of the burning material strike Jeremiah. He fell to the ground as flames tore at his back. She was beside him in a moment, beating at the flames and throwing dirt on the burning embers. He

170

rolled over to look up at her, his face blackened by soot.

"Are you all right?" she cried above the rapidly loudening noise.

Jeremiah began to speak but stopped as another timber cracked and embers were shot into the air. The building began to collapse. He jumped to his feet and grabbed her hand. "Come on! We've got to get out of here!"

Bobby appeared beside them as they started to run. He grasped hold of Rebecca's other hand to help propel her along.

Suddenly, a deafening roar tore across the dock and screams echoed around them as the warehouse's sides ripped apart. Cracking timber showered the area with flaming debris. The bucket brigade broke its line, and pandemonium erupted as people ran for shelter. The dock glowed with eerie red light. People fell and tripped over each other in their panic to escape.

Rebecca, Jeremiah, and Bobby ran on with the crowd. Everyone on the dock was thrown off balance as the flaming inferno exploded. Burning wood cascaded into the air, hurtling across the sky. The water hissed and steamed, coming to life as the timbers hit. The dock echoed with the sound of thudding and people's screams.

Rebecca heard a man cry out behind her and jerked free from Jeremiah and Bobby to turn to help him. As she stopped, something hit her. A searing pain ripped through her body, as though a bolt of lightning had struck her squarely in the back. Then, she fell. Someone tried to grab her. As her knees struck the ground, she heard and felt no more.

22

Tossing and turning in fitful unconsciousness, four days passed before Rebecca managed to overcome the fever that had invaded her mind and body. Struggling past the last barriers of coma to the waking world, she opened her eyes to a sweet greeting from beside her bed.

"Welcome back, princess."

She blinked groggily up at Jeremiah, trying to force her vision to focus. "Where am I?"

"Your room at the hotel," he told her quietly. "We brought you here after the fire. You got hit by a piece of flying timber. The doctor says the burn's not bad, but you're going to have to take it easy for awhile. You bruised your back."

Rebecca nodded, remembering the fire and the sudden pain. "What day is it? Have I been here long?"

"It's Thursday. You've been unconscious for four days."

"Four days!"

Jeremiah leaned forward to touch her arm in reassurance. "Don't get upset. Everything's fine. Peters told me there wasn't much lost in the fire except the building. He's already begun to clear away the wreckage to build another warehouse. A few people were hurt, but no one was killed, and no other fires started."

Rebecca put a hand gingerly to her head. There was a bandage over one eye, and her head was throbbing dully.

Jeremiah flushed. "That one's sort of my fault. When you went down, Bobby went down with you. He got hit in the head. I couldn't catch both of you."

"Bobby?"

"He's fine now. Doctor made him stay in bed for a day or two, but he's up now."

"And you?"

Jeremiah grinned. "I'm not one to lie around in bed."

"Nor am I," she agreed, trying to sit up. Immediately she felt a stabbing pain.

Jeremiah put a hand forward to hold her down. "You're not going to get up for awhile. The doctor said you'll be in bed for no less than a week. Probably two."

"But I can't stay here," she protested weakly, her head swimming from the unexpected pain. "The mine. I have to go."

"There's no need for you to rush back."

"But Jonathon will wonder what's happened. And the supplies. I forgot about the supplies." She tried to move, but Jeremiah held her down firmly.

"The supplies have been sent with a message to Jonathon," Jeremiah told her. "That Cooper fellow came over here the day after the fire looking for you. Said he'd gotten everything together and wanted me to tell you he was sorry for his error, and that it wouldn't happen again."

Rebecca sighed and leaned back against the pillows, too weak to fight. Her head throbbed and her back hurt. A crack of thunder made her eyes fly open once more. "The rains. Have they started?"

Jeremiah rose and walked to the window. The sky was black with the warning of an oncoming storm. "Looks like they're about to."

Rebecca stared at the clouds in panic. Stranded! They would be stranded in town for months! "Jeremiah, you've got to listen to me. If we stay here another week, we'll be here all winter. Once the rains begin, there's no getting to the mine. The roads will be washed out, and we'll be caught here for months!"

Jeremiah frowned and hurried to the bed to try to calm her. "You might be wrong. The rains might not . . . "

"No, Jeremiah. I'm not wrong. You've got to listen to me."

"All right. I believe you. I'll talk to the doctor. I'll see if you can be moved."

Rebecca smiled and sank back against the pillows. He believed her. They wouldn't have to stay.

"You get some rest now," he told her gently. "I'll send someone for the doctor."

She silently obeyed, letting herself drift, but suddenly she remembered Thomas Pickering. "Jeremiah," she called out, her eyes blinking open once more. "Tom . . ."

"Left early this morning. His ship came in two days ago. He told me to tell you he'd see you in September."

Rebecca relaxed again, her mind at ease. Sleep enveloped her slowly, taking away consciousness once more until she woke to the sound of voices.

"She shouldn't be moved yet," a man's voice was insisting.

"What if we rigged a wagon up into a bed?" Jeremiah suggested. "We could cover it with canvas to protect her against the rain. With enough padding, she wouldn't feel a bump."

Rebecca opened her eyes to see the town doctor rubbing his chin.

"It might work," he admitted. "But I'm warning you, her injuries aren't to be taken lightly. She may appear strong in bed, but she's weak. She slept four days with little or nothing to eat. She'll have pain in her back and headaches from that knock on her head."

Jeremiah hung his head and stuffed his hands in his pockets. "I should've sent her back to the hotel as soon as the fire started."

"Won't do any good to regret past actions," the doctor told him. "And it won't hurt to wait a couple more days."

"No," Rebecca retorted from the bed, pushing herself up to a half sitting position.

Both men turned and hurried to her side. "Young

lady," the doctor admonished, "don't you go exerting yourself, or you'll stay here for more than a couple of days."

Rebecca set her jaw firmly against the pain and steeled herself to face him. "I'm going home, Dr. Clayton. You can tell me I'm not, but I am."

Clayton made a sour face. He'd had clashes with her strong will in the past. "You shouldn't go, and you know it. Being stubborn isn't going to help you this time."

"Dr. Clayton, I'm going home with or without your blessing. Now are you going to help me or not?"

"A fire? When?" Jonathon demanded of the driver who had just arrived at the camp.

"Saturday night, Mr. Gray. It was a big one, too," the man responded, quickly explaining what had happened.

Jonathon was frowning when he finished. "Was anyone hurt?" he asked, assuming Rebecca had stayed behind to help Peters straighten matters out.

"That's one of the reasons they sent me, Mr. Gray. It's your wife. She was hurt pretty bad. Got hit by some flying timber. I reckon she's all right now, but she was still unconscious when I left."

"Unconscious? Rebecca! What happened?"

Stammering under Jonathon's scrutinizing stare, the man attempted to describe what had happened to Rebecca. "The men who came to town with her got burned some, too," he concluded. "But they're all right."

"But they're all right," Jonathon echoed sarcastically, pacing a few steps away before pacing back again. "Is there anything else you're supposed to tell me?"

"Just that you're not to worry. They said they'd be back as soon as they could."

"Not to worry!" Jonathon glared down at the man, his fury drawing him up to his full height. He looked at

175

Ben and Mark and turned back to the man. He was beyond words as he strode off toward the cabin.

Mark and Ben followed him, sinking slowly into chairs by the fire while Jonathon paced the floor. They remained quiet, watching the tall figure, who dominated the room, stride back and forth.

At last, able to remain still no longer, Ben cleared his throat. Jonathon stopped to stare at him, his blue eyes dark with helpless anger. "Seems to me you're going to wear a path in the floor if you don't sit down," Ben suggested.

"He's right, Jon," Mark agreed when his brother turned to look at him. "Sit down. Pacing the floor isn't going to help."

Jonathon gave up and dropped into a chair. "If I only knew what was going on."

"The man said she'd be all right," Mark said, watching his brother closely.

"That idiot didn't know the time of day, much less the condition of my wife!" Jonathon exclaimed angrily, leaping to his feet once more.

Ben raised an eyebrow at Mark as Jonathon began to pace again. "If you want," Ben said after a moment, "I can ride into town and see how she is."

Jonathon stopped, his back to the two other men. A moment passed. He began to pace again, only to stop seconds later. "No. No, you stay here. I'll go. I'll leave tomorrow morning."

Ben and Mark watched him go to the door and close it firmly behind him. They stared at the wooden barrier for several minutes before turning to smile at one another.

"That man may not know it yet," Ben said rocking back in his chair, "but he's in love."

Jonathon left at dawn the next morning, traveling for two days before he saw a covered wagon making its way across the muddy wastelands of the bush. He pulled his horse up to watch it come steadily through the drizzling rain studying the two men who accompanied it.

One man rode beside the wagon; the other drove it. Two spare horses trailed behind it. Jonathon recognized one of them. It was Rebecca's.

Jeremiah was riding next to the wagon when he saw a lone man approaching. He drew his gun cautiously but quickly holstered it when he recognized Jonathon.

"Didn't figure on seeing you for a couple days yet," he greeted him with a smile.

Jonathon nodded tersely, glancing at the covered wagon that continued to move slowly on. "Becky?"

"Sleeping last time I looked."

"Can you tell me what happened?"

Jeremiah nodded. Without wasted words or undue pauses, he explained what had occurred on the night of the fire and the extent of Rebecca's injuries. "The doctor said she shouldn't be moved, but she insisted on coming back. She won."

Jonathon smiled wryly. "And you two?"

"Fully recovered," Jeremiah replied, tossing a grin at Bobby. "That knock on the head Bobby got didn't hurt nothing."

Bobby smiled back, a wide, boyish grin. "There's not so much as a rattle when I shake me head."

The men let silence envelop them as they drove on through the drizzle, carefully picking the smoothest route. When darkness paled the landscape, they had to stop to make camp on high ground. It was only then that Jonathon moved to the back of the wagon to look in. Expecting to see Rebecca, his lips twisted into a surprised smile when he found Dingo staring at him. The big dog was stretched out beside his mistress, guarding her as she slept. Dingo made way as Jonathon climbed in and eased his long frame down next to Rebecca. Leaning on one elbow to support himself under the low canvas covering, Jonathon looked down at her.

Securely wrapped in a bandage, her head lay nestled in the softness of several pillows. Her face was pale, except for a feverish flush on her cheeks, and her lashes were dark against her skin. Her arms lay on top of the blankets. He could see the unusual pinkness of her fingers that had been burned when putting out the fire on Jeremiah's back.

Alarm beat fearfully in his chest as Jonathon touched one of her hands. She was so small to carry such a burden of pain. His own body ached for her. If only he'd been there! He reached up to brush some hair from her face, and she stirred slightly under his touch. Her eyes blinked open to stare up at him uncertainly in the dim light of the wagon. "Are we home already?" she asked groggily.

Jonathon smiled and took one of her hands carefully in his. "No. We're about two days' ride away yet. It's slow going with the wagon. The land is covered with mud."

Rebecca closed her eyes again. She couldn't seem to keep them open. Suddenly remembering Mark, she stared worriedly up at Jonathon. "The dam. Did you finish the dam?"

"Almost," he replied quietly. "It'll be done before the heavy rains come."

Dingo whined at the sound of her voice and edged forward to poke her hand with his nose. She smiled weakly and patted the golden head. "Hello, Dingo." The big dog licked her hand, and she looked up at Jonathon once more. "He keeps me company."

"So he does," Jonathon agreed lightly, brushing the hair away from her face again. "How do you feel?" he asked, watching her fight to stay awake.

"Sleepy. Dr. Clayton gave me some pills. They're making me sleep all the time."

"It's just as well. We've a long way to go yet." He studied her closely. She didn't seem to be in any pain. "Do you hurt at all, Becky?"

"Only when I move."

He stroked her hair lightly and planted a light kiss on her forehead. "You sleep. It will be some time before our supper is ready."

She sighed softly and obediently closed her eyes. She was safe now. Jonathon was with her.

He stayed with her. That night, Jonathon traded places with Dingo. Dingo slept under the wagon with Jeremiah and Bobby, and Jonathon crawled in beside the sleeping Rebecca. He stayed awake for a long time, watching as she slept. She looked so weak and vulnerable. But he felt an overwhelming sense of relief to see her, knowing she was safe.

Jonathon listened to Rebecca's quiet, steady breathing and breathed easier himself. He wouldn't have been able to bear waiting for her to be brought to him. It would have driven him mad with worry. Most of the night passed before he finally laid down. Then, stretching his long body out beside hers, he put a protective arm firmly but gently around her, closed his eyes, and fell asleep.

23

The month of June passed slowly for Rebecca, because she was bedridden and handicapped by her injuries. Though she tried to return to her daily routine, she did not have the strength or the ability to ignore the pain that stayed with her. Used to constant activity, she found it frustrating to be so helpless and unable to do what she wished. Her one consolation became sewing. A woman sat with her each day. One of the worker's wives, she was quiet, soft spoken, and a great comfort to the disabled Rebecca. Bringing some sewing with her one day, she suggested Rebecca try it to keep her mind occupied.

Rebecca began to take up most of her days in creating curtains for the windows of the cabin, mending the men's clothes, and darning socks. It wasn't easy to find satisfaction in such an "idle" task, at first, but it gave Rebecca a purpose. Jonathon looked in on her as often as he could, but work at the dam made it impossible to do it very often. Downpours soaked the ground, and the mud slowed their progress, creating more obstacles to overcome.

Each day Jonathon and Mark left early in the morning, coming back at night soaked to the skin and covered with mud. Rebecca listened as they told her of the poor working conditions. She worried over the number of men who had contracted colds and were forced to stay in bed. Her concern was not limited to the men who worked with Jonathon and Mark. It was for the two brothers as well. They, too, had caught colds, Jonathon's being the worst with its hacking cough. Most nights, he came home and went to bed without eating. Rebecca tried to convince him to stay home for just one day to give himself a chance to rest and regain his strength, but he refused. No amount of persuasion could keep him from the work. He insisted he was as strong as he'd ever been.

Despite Jonathon's confidence in himself, Rebecca continued to fear for his health. His cough grew steadily worse until, one day, her fears became fulfilled. Jonathon collapsed in the field and had to be carried home—on the very day the dam was completed.

The cabin door banged open and Mark staggered inside, carrying Jonathon. Rebecca struggled to her feet and rushed to him. Mark carried Jonathon to his bed, and Rebecca and Ben hurriedly peeled the wet clothing from him, rubbing his feverish skin to circulate his blood and bring back warmth to his body.

Rebecca sat with her husband through the afternoon, fear running rampant beneath the calm exterior she showed to those around her. Jonathon was pale and his breathing was shallow. What if he stopped breathing? What if he should die?

When night fell, Mark returned again from the dam site, where he was checking on the final details of the building, and found Rebecca sitting diligently by the bed. "How is he?" he asked, worry etched deeply in his face. He choked on his words, a cough wracking his body.

Rebecca rose slowly to face him. A scowl shadowed her face and her Scots temper flared. "You and your brother *deserve* to be sick. Both of you knew you were near to catching pneumonia. But, no, you had to keep on working on the dam. You couldn't pay attention to something as valuable as your health. So now Jonathon is bedridden and you are coughing. Go to your room and get into bed. I don't want to see you out of it until you're better. I can't nurse both of you at the same time."

Mark cowered under her rage. There was nothing he could say. She was right. He knew she was right. He humbly backed out of the room, went to his bed, and stayed there until his cough disappeared.

Rebecca fed Mark whenever she brought Jonathon his food, staying long enough with Mark to tell him of Jonathon's condition, which wasn't good. As the days passed, Mark was up and about once more, but Jonathon remained ill. Mark prowled the cabin restlessly, condemning himself for his brother's poor health. If only there was something he could do. But there wasn't. He could only wait and watch Rebecca try to keep Jonathon alive.

Suddenly Mark was needed. Rebecca called for his help. Jonathon was delirious. It took all Mark's strength to hold his brother down as Jonathon tossed and turned, kicking off the blankets and swinging wildly at anyone who came near him. Within hours, this stage passed. Jonathon became so quiet it was hard to tell if he was still breathing. Rebecca frequently pressed her hand to his chest to assure herself her husband's heart was still beating. She and Mark almost wished Jonathon had continued with his wild behavior.

He was so quiet and slept so heavily, they feared that Jonathon would never wake up. The fever was still raging inside him. Ben and Mark volunteered to sit with Jonathon as the fever burned on, but Rebecca refused to be moved. She was determined to stay with her man. Nothing they could say made her leave the room.

More days passed. Trapped inside the cabin because of the rain, Ben and Mark began to worry about Rebecca's health as well as Jonathon's. She had become thinner and paler; her eyes were ringed with dark shadows from sleepless nights. They knew the pain on her face was not over Jonathon alone. Endless hours of bending over a bed had affected the recently bruised bones and muscles in her back. Her own aches followed her everywhere, but she didn't complain. She continued her vigil.

Two weeks after his collapse at the dam, Jonathon's temperature soared. From what she had seen in Scotland, Rebecca knew that the waiting was almost over. The fever would either break or Jonathon would die.

It was a long night. Locking Ben and Mark from the room, Rebecca sat at Jonathon's side constantly, keeping cool cloths pressed against his hot forehead and holding his hand while biting her lip to hold back tears of fear. Outside the closed door, Mark and Ben sat or paced the room. They, too, knew tonight should tell whether Jonathon would survive, and they both dreaded the worst. Jonathon was a strong man, but he had been badly weakened by days of endless work and the ensuing days of prolonged fever.

Dawn came slowly. Mark finally stopped his pacing to face the bedroom door. "Ben, we've got to do something. She's been in there all night, and there hasn't been a sound out of her. What if she's collapsed as well?"

"Becky hasn't collapsed," Ben replied quietly, remaining steadfastly in his chair. "She won't collapse until the fight's over. She'll let us know."

Mark searched the older man's face anxiously. He could see the dark fear in the brown eyes, see the lines of worry shadowed deeply in his expression. But Ben remained calm, and Mark forced himself to imitate him. He sat down and continued to wait, but the waiting didn't last much longer.

The door to Jonathon's room opened. Rebecca emerged, leaning wearily against the wall. "The fever's broken. I think he'll be all right."

Mark hurried forward to take her hands in his. "Is there anything I can do, Becky?"

She nodded slowly. "Yes. You could sit with him for a bit. I'd like to try to get some rest now."

Mark entered the room to stay with his brother but remained at his side for the next week instead of a short while. Rebecca was completely exhausted, too weak and tired to move from her bed. As the days passed, Jonathon began to rally, fighting his way back from the oblivion that had surrounded him. When he had progressed and gained enough strength to speak, Rebecca was still unable to leave her room.

"It's about time you woke up," Mark told his brother with a grin.

Jonathon echoed the smile weakly. "How long have I been here?"

"Going on three weeks. You've been sick with fever. It broke only a few days ago, and you've been conscious on and off ever since." Mark studied his brother solemnly as he spoke. Some color had returned to Jonathon's face, and his eyes no longer burned brightly with fever. "Becky nursed you through it. She was with you day and night."

"How is Becky? Is she better? Her back?"

Mark shook his head. "She's in bed herself, Jon."

"She's not ill?"

"No. Just tired. She wore herself out looking after you. She wouldn't let anyone help her. It wasn't until the fever broke that she gave in and let me take over. She hasn't moved from her bed since." Mark saw Jonathon's eyes darken, and he hastened to reassure him. "She's all right, Jon. She's weak is all. Your sickness coming on so soon after her own, it was just too much for her. She wasn't ready for it yet. She'll be up again in a week, probably sooner than you."

The older brother nodded reluctantly. He knew Rebecca's strength had not been returned completely before his illness had come on. He knew she had only been acting when making a great show of feeling no pain and being healthy again. "The dam. How is it holding up?" Jonathon asked.

"Last time I was able to check, it was swallowing water as we knew it would. The drainage ditches are working perfectly. We'll be planting in September. With good luck, we'll have the finest wheat fields you ever saw by the time harvest comes."

When Jonathon woke again later that day, he found Rebecca sitting beside his bed. "You're better," he told

184

her, his voice filled with relief.

She flushed slightly and nodded. "You, too."

Jonathon pushed himself to a sitting position and studied her in critical concern. She was still thinner than she had been before her accident, but there was a healthy flush to her cheeks and a soft glow in her eyes. He held a hand out to her. "Come here, Becky."

Rebecca rose and moved to sit on the bed, sinking against his chest as his arms surrounded her. She felt secure and safe again. It was good to feel his strength and hear his voice. She closed her eyes and whispered a silent prayer of thanks.

Jonathon held her for a long time, feeling the softness of her body pressed against his. A tender wave of warmth washed through him at her closeness, and he finally allowed himself to recognize the love he had denied for so long. He had grown to love this woman, and he could no longer avoid the feeling. A decision had to be made. He reached down and took her head in his hands.

Gazing into her eyes, he found love growing inside him. "Becky, I have to ask you a question."

"What is it?"

"I want to know if you'll marry me, if you'll be my wife."

Rebecca stared up at him, stunned. Her heart pounded hard within her. She could see the tenderness reflected in his eyes. She could see his love for her. Tears spilled down her cheeks, and she threw her arms around his neck with a small cry. "Aye, Jonathon, I will. I will."

24

"Do you want to go to town tomorrow with the first shipment, Jonathon?" Rebecca asked as he and Mark sat in front of the fire in the cabin, warming themselves after their trip into the bush.

Almost a week before, they had gone out to check on the dam and map out possible locations for wells. It was late August, and the rains had stopped. The land was beginning to dry up, and regular work was starting again at the mine.

During the two long months of winter, work at the mine had been erratic. Foul weather and waterlogged land had kept the men away, locked in their tents on the hill. Work was continuing now, and the shipments had to start once more.

"I think so," Jonathon answered, turning to his younger brother. "Mark? We can go in and check on that seed of yours."

Mark grinned brightly. "I might be talked into it. When do we leave?"

"First thing in the morning," Jonathon answered.

He was the first one up in the morning to help to make the wagon ready to roll. The going was slow once they started out, and the trip took longer than usual. The wagon became bogged down several times in the mud that covered the roads, sucked at the wheels, and pulled at the animals' hooves. Five days passed before they came in sight of the town.

Jonathon lifted Rebecca down from her horse, his hands lingering on her waist. "I'll be going down to the docks to see Peters. Do you feel up to going to the bank with the gold?" Though he knew she was fully recovered from her injuries, the trip had been long and uncomfortable, and no one had gotten much rest.

"Aye," she assured him softly. "I'm well enough to do that. Aren't you anxious to discover how rich you've become?"

"Richer than I'd ever imagined," he responded, his hands tightening meaningfully on her waist. He watched her cheeks flush before he hurried her on her way, waiting until she had safely crossed the street before turning down the boardwalk toward the docks. All signs of the fire had been removed. Where the old warehouse had stood Jonathon found a newer and bigger one in its place.

"The business is going well, Mr. Gray," Peters told Jonathon after accepting congratulations from Jonathon. "The warehouses are close to overflowing, but not because of people failing to pick up their goods. The fire cured most of them of that."

"No other problems?"

"None at all," was the confident reply. "But I imagine you've come to check on your crates as well as the business. They've been coming in regularly, most of them from England. I've got them stored in the main building."

"Good. We'll take them off your hands soon. We're expecting our building contractor to return shortly from England. He'll soon be using all this to build my wife her house."

"Would he be the same man who left the first week of June?"

"The same."

"Nice fellow. He came down to tell me I'd be receiving these crates after Mrs. Gray was injured during the fire," Peters explained. "Is she feeling all right now? We were all worried about her."

"Yes, she's fine now, thank you. When will the next ship be coming in? Our man might be on it."

Peters consulted a schedule. "Three days. First of September I'd say. If you're expecting him soon and he's planning on following the material we just received, he'll be arriving then.''

Jonathon accepted the schedule and nodded agreement. ''We'll wait for the ship on the chance he's on it. But I think we'll send this equipment out right away. It's going to take some time to get it across that mud out there.''

When Jonathon returned to the hotel a short while later, Rebecca was waiting for him in the lobby. She handed him a bank statement and smiled mischievously as he read it. ''The Bank of England tells us we're nearly millionaires.''

Jonathon shook his head in disbelief. 'Have you taken out Ben's ten percent?''

''I just arranged for it. The bank is preparing the wages for our workers and the guards. We'll have to take the cash back with us.''

''Good, but we won't be going back for about three days,'' he told her, putting an arm around her shoulders and leading her toward the office. ''There's a ship coming in this week. I think Tom Pickering might be on it. His equipment and the seed for our planting are already here. I've made arrangements to have the goods sent to the mine tomorrow. Perhaps we can send Jeremiah and Francis back with the wagons and the wages tomorrow, too. Do you know where they are?''

Rebecca flushed and bit her lip. ''I think I know where they *might* be. But if they're there, we'd best wait until dinner to tell them.''

Jonathon was about to ask her what she meant when he looked down to see the color flooding her face. ''You mean?''

She nodded. She had seen the two men entering a saloon shortly after the gold had been safely deposited in the bank.

Jonathon laughed. ''Becky, you have a way with words.''

By the end of the week, Rebecca and Jonathon were back at the mine with Thomas Pickering, his men, and his equipment. By the end of the month, the foundation for their house had been laid.

Mark and the farmers he had hired were working on planting, plowing, and fertilizing the land before sowing the precious seeds that had come from England.

Rebecca watched all the activity with enthusiasm. What had begun as a dream was fast turning into reality. Each day seemed brighter than the last. She could not remember ever having a happier time in her life.

Continuing her visits to the tent town, she spent her days helping the families there or riding to see the farmers' wives who had made a new encampment not far from the dam site where their husbands were working in the fields.

It was on returning from the tent town one day that she saw Sam approach and she stopped to greet him. "Sam, we haven't seen you in awhile."

Sam slipped from his horse to the ground. "I've been in town. I brought some letters for your husband. The man at the hotel said they were sitting for several days. He was afraid they might contain important messages."

Rebecca frowned and accepted the letters. "I don't know what they might be. Jonathon is working with Ben in the mine. They're planning on blasting their way through from the other side."

Sam looked doubtfully at the mouth of the cave.

"I agree, Sam," she told him, following his gaze. "I'm not sure they should do such a thing, but they insist it's safe and necessary. The gold will be easier to reach from the other side."

San grunted and shook his head.

Rebecca smiled at him. The man was content to wander through the wilderness, needing to be free from ties of any kinds, a man who accepted all things as they were and didn't attempt to change them. "Thanks for bringing the letters, Sam. I'll give them to Jonathon as soon as I'm able."

Sam nodded and walked to the campfire, where hot coffee was always boiling in a pot.

Rebecca went to Jeremiah in the cave. "Do you know where Jonathon might be in there?"

Jeremiah shook his head. "I only know he's with Ben, making plans for blowing the wall out tomorrow. Why? Something wrong?"

"No. Sam brought me these letters, and I don't know if I should open them or not. They might be important."

"They should be coming out soon," Jeremiah told her, looking up at the sun. "Nightfall's about due, and they'll have to call it a day."

Rebecca squinted up at the setting sun. "You're right. They can wait awhile longer." But when Jonathon walked through the door of the cabin an hour later, Rebecca put the letters in his hand before he even sat down. "Sam brought them today, Jonathon. What might they be?"

"Probably bills," Jonathon answered with a shrug, turning the letters over in his hands.

"Are you sure?" she asked. "They don't look like bills."

"How can you expect me to know when I haven't even read them yet?"

Rebecca sighed impatiently. "You must have *some* idea."

"Maybe so, maybe not," he replied, walking away from her and winking at Mark, who was already sitting by the fireplace.

Unable to make her husband give her a satisfactory reply, Rebecca returned to the stove to stir their dinner, watching him while he read the letters with what seemed to her deliberate slowness.

The door banged open and Ben came in, beating dust off his clothes. "Dirty work, mining."

"Just because it's dirty where you work doesn't mean it has to be dirty where you live," Rebecca admonished him.

"Sure can tell she's become a wife," Ben grumbled, hanging his hat on one of the pegs on the wall. He and

Mark had said nothing when Rebecca moved from her room into Jonathon's weeks before. Neither man could have been happier about the change.

Jonathon rattled the paper in his hands to get Rebecca's attention. "I suppose you ought to see these, Becky. They concern your birthday."

"My birthday?" she repeated, stopping her stirring to stare at him. "It's only November third. My birthday's not until the twentieth."

Jonathon held out the papers and watched her put aside her spoon to come to him, wiping her hands on her apron. As she took them and read, Jonathon glanced at Mark and Ben with amusement in his eyes.

A variety of expressions passed over Rebecca's face as she read, scanning the lines before her with disbelief. When she stopped, she lowered the letters to look at Jonathon with wide-eyed surprise. "You did it! You did it, and you didn't tell me."

"There," Jonathon told the two other men. "That's gratitude."

Rebecca laughed and threw her arms around his neck as she slid into his lap. "Thank you, Jonathon. I should have known you would do it."

Jonathon smiled and shook his head, his eyes saying more to her than words could.

She looked away and turned to the other men. "Both of you knew about it? You knew he arranged for the purchase of cattle and sheep?"

Mark flashed her his usual wide grin. "I've known for a little while, at least—since he wrote the letters."

Ben shrugged and rubbed his ear. "No one around here ever tells me nothing," he retorted, but his dark eyes were glowing.

A week later, Rebecca went into town with Jeremiah to meet the ship bringing in the cattle and sheep. Jonathon and Ben remained behind to continue clearing the rubble from the successful blasting in the mine.

When they arrived at the hotel, Rebecca waited for an opportunity to slip away when Jeremiah wasn't looking.

There was a place she had to go—alone.

Hoping to discourage Jeremiah, she went to the hotel office, shut herself in, and stood listening at the door. It wasn't long before she heard him tell the clerk he was going to his room for a moment. In that moment, Rebecca made her escape. Hurrying down the boardwalk, trying to avoid anyone she knew and speaking to no one, she made it to Dr. Clayton's office.

The examination didn't take long. When she came out of the dressing room, she seated herself anxiously on the edge of a chair. Dr. Clayton looked up from his desk and folded his hands in front of him. "I think you already know what I'm going to tell you, or at least you've guessed. Otherwise, you wouldn't be here."

Unable to stand the suspense that had been building inside, Rebecca blurted, "Dr. Clayton, please, am I . . ."

"Going to have a baby? Yes. I'd say about late April."

Rebecca squealed with delight. "You mustn't tell anyone. I want to tell Jonathon first."

"I won't tell a soul if you don't want me to," Dr. Clayton granted. "You just be sure to remember to take things a little easier from now on. Don't overdo anything, and come back and see me as often as you can."

"I will," Rebecca promised eagerly, humming to herself as she left the doctor's office to return to the hotel. After all the times she and Jonathon had made and shared love and after all the wonderful things he had given her, she was finally going to give him something. She was going to give him a child.

The next morning, Rebecca and Jeremiah sat on the dock watching the men drive the cattle and sheep from the ship. There were only thirty heads of cattle and a small flock of sheep.

As they started off from town, Jeremiah regarded them with a skeptical eye. "They're not much," he commented to Rebecca.

"No," she agreed, turning to watch the animals behind her. Dingo and two sheep dogs were keeping the furry animals in line while the men guided the herd of cattle along. "But they'll be a start, perhaps a start of a new market for this country. If we can make these cows fat, if we can make them breed, and if they survive the droughts and floods, it might be possible."

"Those are a lot of ifs."

Rebecca smiled. "Life itself is a question, is it not?"

Jeremiah grinned and nodded. "I reckon so," he responded, again amazed at how Rebecca could always seem to find the bright side. But then, she was unusually happy today. Things had been going exceptionally well for her and Jonathon. As the journey continued and her mood remained high, he began to wonder. Rebecca seemed to glow, and Jeremiah began to have suspicions. Keeping his speculations to himself, he counted back in time. She hadn't been this happy on leaving the camp, nor had she been this happy when they arrived in town. It was afterward, after she disappeared for almost an hour that this mood had come over her. Jeremiah smiled as he drew the obvious conclusion. The sun was setting behind the tent town on the last day of their journey when he turned to speak to her.

"Becky," he began. "You've been beaming like a full moon all the way home this trip. As a matter of fact, I'd say you were outshining the sun."

Rebecca smiled and flushed happily. "Jeremiah, are you flattering me?"

"Nope. It's the truth." He watched her silently for a moment until she met his eyes. Then he grinned.

She blushed hotly. "Jeremiah! How did you know?"

"Just guessed."

"You won't ruin my surprise, will you? Jonathon doesn't know yet."

"I wouldn't dream of it," he assured her. "I only wish I could see his face when you tell him."

Rebecca's eyes darkened apprehensively. "Do you think he'll be happy?"

"Happy? You'll be lucky if he doesn't blow the top off that hill to celebrate."

She smiled thankfully and they continued up the road

silently, uneasiness touching them both as the unusual quiet around them penetrated their thoughts.

"Jeremiah," Rebecca finally whispered. "Where is everybody? I don't see anyone."

Jeremiah scanned the area around them. "Damned if I know, Becky. You stay here. I'll go have a look."

The unnatural silence was suddenly broken by a joint yell as people came running out of the grove of trees, the mouth of the cave, and the tents behind them. They swarmed around the horses and yelled, "Happy birthday, Becky!"

Rebecca and Jeremiah gasped in surprise as they tried to hold their horses still.

Jonathon strode through the group, making his way to Rebecca. He stopped there and swung up behind her, taking the reins from her hands. "The celebration starts when the sun goes down," he called to the workers around them.

Another joint cry went up and the people broke away from the crowd to rush off in separate directions.

"Jonathon Gray, you're crazy!" Rebecca declared.

"No, I'm not," he grinned at Jeremiah. "*They* are. They wanted to do something to surprise you."

"They surprised her all right," Jeremiah agreed, shaking his head. "Almost scared her to death."

Jonathon laughed and urged the horse on to the cabin, where they dismounted to watch the celebration begin.

Fireworks began the evening as the sun set in a myriad of colors behind the horizon. Those workers who knew how to play instruments provided music. Bonfires were lit throughout the camp and everyone sang and danced in between helping themselves to the food from the long table the wives had set up.

Rebecca lost count of the number of men she danced with, laughing and singing with all of them. Most of her time was spent with Jonathon though. She longed to tell him about her visit to Dr. Clayton, but she kept the secret to herself until she could find the right moment.

Ben hauled out his stores of liquor for a small party

194

that included Mark, Jeremiah, Bobby, and Tom Pickering. It wasn't long before the five men were singing at the tops of their lungs and leading a wild dance, with Ben and Mark playing the parts of flirtatious females. Everyone stood aside while they swung around, roaring with laughter as they collapsed on the ground to continue drinking and singing.

All too soon, the star-studded sky became stained with dawn, and people began to leave for their beds. Rebecca sat beside Jonathon watching them go. It was a noisy and happy group. All called their best wishes to her, with thanks to Jonathon for giving them a day of rest. When most of them were gone, Jonathon stirred and motioned across the way to where Ben and his group were sitting. Tom Pickering had managed to stagger to bed earlier, but Mark was sprawled alongside a snoring Bobby, and Ben and Jeremiah were the only two still awake. "It looks as if I'll have to put my little brother to bed."

Rebecca smiled at the group. "Ben doesn't look too steady, either."

Jonathon stood, giving her a hand. "You get ready for bed. I'll join you as soon as I can get those two put away."

Rebecca nodded, kissing him quickly before hurrying toward the cabin. She undressed and slipped into her night dress preferring to wait for him. It wasn't long before she heard the cabin door bang open and Ben's loud, boisterous voice. Staggering footsteps echoed, and a chair clattered to the floor before one set of footsteps made their way across the room and Jonathon opened the door.

"What a day," he sighed, stretching his long body before unbuttoning his shirt. "And a night," he added, turning to look at Rebecca as she sat brushing out her hair. "Did you have a good time?"

She nodded as she tried to force herself to speak. "Jonathon."

"Hmm?" He did not look up as he pulled his boots off.

195

"I've something to tell you."

He let his boots drop to the floor and looked up to meet her eyes.

"I'm going to have a baby."

Jonathon continued looking at her, not moving. "What did you say?"

Rebecca took a deep breath and repeated the words slowly. "I'm going to have a baby."

"A baby? You? You're going to have a baby?"

Rebecca nodded.

A triumphant yell escaped from Jonathon. He leaped from the chair and strode to her side. Grasping her waist, he swung her squealing from the bed into the air.

"Jonathon! Put me down, you crazy man!"

Jonathon laughed, shaking her gently before setting her on her feet. "You're really going to have a baby?" he asked softly.

She nodded. "Dr. Clayton says it will be late April."

"Dr. Clayton? You went to see him?"

"When I was in town."

"What did he say? I mean, what are you supposed to do?"

"I don't have to do anything. I only have to watch myself and be careful not to exert myself too much."

Jonathon winced and grasped her shoulders tightly. "All that dancing and hopping around. Are you all right?"

Rebecca laughed at his stricken look. "Aye, I'm fine."

"You're sure?"

"I'm sure."

He sighed with relief, and his eyes suddenly lit up with an idea. "Mark and Ben. I've got to go tell them."

Rebecca reached out and grabbed his hand as he started to turn away. "No, you don't. For one, you'll never be able to wake them up. And for another, I don't want you to go anywhere. I want you to stay here with me."

Jonathon reached for her and crushed her against him. England was the farthest thing from his mind.

25

December came, and with it came the heat of summer. For the first time, Mark began to understand Rebecca's and Jonathon's concern over irrigation for the crops. Slowly but surely, the ground began to dry up. Creeks ran dry and the river fell. The wildlife continued to thrive, despite the scorching onslaught, but the wheat had to be watched carefully to insure the ground never became too dry.

The sheep and cattle also had to be closely guarded. Jonathon made regular trips to check on the newly drilled wells.

Rebecca was out every day to meet with Tom Pickering at the house. The work was going slowly because of the small crew he had brought, but progress was steady, and the house was beginning to take shape. He assured her it would be completed no later than March, when she would be able to begin decorating.

All work halted on Jonathon's orders on Christmas Eve. Everyone was given the day off to spend to prepare for the celebration he was planning. The meal Rebecca and he arranged was enormous, complete with wild turkey and pig. Women from the tent town donated their favorite dishes, bringing them to the long trestle table Jonathon set up.

By six o'clock, the preparations were complete. Rebecca donned a light-green summer dress with short puffed sleeves and a high waist and arranged her hair to hang in soft ringlets. When she was done, she joined Jonathon in the main room of the cabin.

"How do I look?" she asked, spinning in a circle before him.

"Beautiful," he told her, taking her hands in his and drawing her to him. He stared down into her eyes. "Are you happy, Becky?"

"More happy than ever."

He smiled and bent his head to kiss her gently. "We'd best get outside and join the others."

As Jonathon led Rebecca outside, he felt detached from his surroundings. He couldn't concentrate on the gaiety around him. His mind was on other Christmas days, on winters in England. Time and again, he tried to draw his thoughts to the present, but he couldn't. He knew he should be happy. He had everything a man could want: a beautiful wife who was about to have his child, property and money, a new house being built, growing crops, and livestock that was doing well. But he couldn't be content.

Something in him kept demanding that he remember, demanding he think of England, of Arthur Boyd, of Arthur Boyd's face when he would see Jonathon return to England rich. The sting had gone from the wound, but the desire to strike back was still strong. Jonathon had to go back. He had to show Arthur Boyd what a fool he had been to refuse to give his daughter's hand in marriage to a man as worthy as Jonathon Gray.

After the celebration was over, and everyone had sung Christmas carols, and after they had all eaten and drunk their fill and everyone had gone home, Jonathon lay beside Rebecca in bed, watching her sleep. What would happen in another year? He had given his word to stay that long, but what then? Would he leave her, never to return? Could he leave her?

He brushed the hair from her face and looked down at the gentle swelling of her abdomen. How could he leave her behind? Her and their child? He knew he would never be able to convince her to come with him, to leave all this behind—her kingdom, her home. What was he to do? He had to leave, but how could he do that to her? He clenched his hand into a fist and rolled on his back to stare up at the ceiling. Why couldn't he forget?

Still unable to sleep when dawn came, Jonathon rose early and slipped out of the room. Ben and Mark were up, too, sitting at the table covered with presents.

Among them, Jonathon recognized the ones he had given Mark to hide.

"Coffee's hot," Mark told his brother. He watched Jonathon pour himself a cup before pulling up a chair to join them. Jonathon took a long sip and then sat back with a sigh.

Mark frowned. "Didn't you sleep well?"

Jonathon shook his head, forcing a smile he didn't feel. "Too much celebrating."

Ben grinned back at Mark. "Me and Mark sure slept good."

Jonathon opened his mouth to comment but stopped when he heard a noise outside the door. "What was that?"

Ben and Mark shook their heads.

Jonathon rose to his feet and moved quietly to the door. He opened it, about to step out, but stopped to stare in amazement at the sight before him. Packages of every size were scattered over the doorstep.

"Will you look at that?" Ben declared, puffing on his pipe as he stared past Jonathon.

Mark bent down to see one of the packages. None of the gifts was elaborately wrapped. "I think you'd better get Becky, Jon. She'll want to see this. I imagine the majority of them are for her, anyway."

Jonathon nodded agreement and crossed to the room where Rebecca still slept. He sat on the bed's edge, reaching out to brush Rebecca's face gently.

"Becky?" She stirred but did not wake. "Becky," he whispered again, repeating the caress.

She moved again, turning her head and stretching as her eyes blinked open. Seeing him above her, she tried to focus her sleep-blurred gaze on him as she felt him lean nearer to kiss her gently. She put her hands out to touch his face and asked sleepily, "Is it morning already?"

Jonathon nodded and gently pulled her to a sitting position. "You've got to get up now. I have something to show you."

She brushed the hair from her eyes and looked at the

199

window where the light was beginning to shine through. "What time is it?"

"Come and see."

She put her feet reluctantly on the cool, wooden floor and stood slowly, her balance still unsteady. "I can't go anywhere like this," she protested as he led her toward the door. Jonathon smiled as she indicated her thin cotton night dress and reached for her dressing gown as she sank back down on the bed again to lean against the bedpost.

"Come on, sleepy head. Wake up."

"I don't want to," she retorted as he slipped the gown over. "I'm sleepy. What time is it?"

"Early. The sun's just come up."

"Jonathon, it's Christmas," she objected as he pulled her to her feet and tied the sash around her.

"I know it's Christmas. That's why you have to get up."

Rebecca followed him slowly as he led her by the hand from their room and across the cabin to the door where Ben and Mark stood aside.

Jonathon planted her firmly in the doorway before releasing her. "Now look."

Rebecca's forehead wrinkled as she looked down at the ground. "What might all this be?"

"Presents from the workers and their families, I suspect," Ben answered, puffing heartily on his pipe.

She knelt down to look closer at the packages. "Oh, Ben, they shouldn't have! They need the money for their own families."

"They wanted to," he replied. "Besides, Jonathon here gave them all a nice Christmas bonus."

A small, pig-tailed girl suddenly appeared, coming shyly toward Rebecca. "My Mommy told me to bring this to your cabin, Missus Gray."

Rebecca accepted the bag and smiled at the little girl. "Thank your Mommy for me and wish her a Merry Christmas."

The little girl nodded brightly and hurried off, her pigtails flying out behind her as she went.

Tears burned Rebecca's eyes as she watched the little girl go. She didn't know what to say.

Jonathon smiled at her. "We'll bring the gifts in."

The rest of the morning was spent unwrapping presents. Rebecca's eyes burned with tears as she opened them. The ones the workers had sent were mostly clothes the women had sewn or knitted for the expected baby, and her heart ached with joy.

She knew how difficult it was for many of the men to makes ends meet, even though they were paid a good wage. Many of them had as many as four children and a wife to support. That these families should take the time and money to make something for someone else's baby touched her deeply.

Ben received nothing but liquor, even from Jonathon and Mark, who had each bought him the best bottles they could find. Ben was not disappointed. Jonathon and Mark both received practical gifts, like handsewn shirts and belts, all carefully chosen tokens of appreciation.

After all the presents were opened, Mark and Ben cleaned up while Rebecca led Jonathon back to the bedroom.

"I've something for you," she told him, going to the closet and taking out a large box. "You've been saying you needed these."

Jonathon took the box, his curiosity making short work of the wrapping paper around it. He opened the lid and smiled at the new pair of black boots inside.

"I hope they fit," she told him anxiously. "You're not a practical man, Jonathon Gray, when it comes to clothing. You'd never get around to buying them yourself until you were left with nothing to wear.

He laughed and hugged her as he sat down on the bed. "I've got something for you, too. Shut your eyes."

"Jonathon!"

"Shut them." As she did, he reached in his pocket and extracted a small jeweler's box. He opened it to reveal a shining gold ring. "You can open your eyes now."

201

Rebecca gasped when she saw the band. "Jonathon! It's beautiful!"

He took her left hand in his and drew off the ring that had been used to wed them. It came off easily. Then he removed the delicate, engraved ring from its box and slid it onto her finger. "Does it fit?"

"Perfectly."

"A perfect fit for a perfect wife, Mrs. Gray."

Rebecca laughed and threw her arms around her husband's neck as he bent his head to kiss her.

It was two weeks later that a lone rider appeared on the road. Standing guard on the hill, Jeremiah called out to Bobby who was near the mouth of the cave. "Rider coming in, Bobby. A woman. Better go tell Becky."

Bobby waved and hurried off toward the cabin. "There's a rider coming in, Becky," he told her when she opened the door. "Jeremiah says it's a lady."

"A lady?" Rebecca repeated watching Mark ride in and dismount by the railing in front of the cabin. "I wonder who it might be."

"What's up?" Mark inquired, nodding a greeting to Bobby.

"We have a visitor, Bobby tells me. A lady," Rebecca answered.

"A lady, is it?" Mark asked. "I think I'll come along."

Rebecca accepted his arm with a good-natured shake of her head, going with him a short distance from the cabin to wait for the rider's approach. It wasn't until the woman had almost reached them that Rebecca recognized her.

"What is it?" Mark demanded in alarm.

"It's my cousin, Alison Cunningham."

Alison stopped in front of them, astride a newly purchased black mare and attired in a fashionable riding habit. The sun was to her back. She looked down with a maliciously pleasant smile as Rebecca squinted up at her. "Hello, Rebecca."

"Good day, Alison," Rebecca returned. "Won't you step down?"

Alison slipped from the saddle, and Bobby quickly stepped forward to take her animal's reins. Calmly pulling the riding gloves from her hands, Alison came to stand before Rebecca, staring blatantly at Rebecca's protruding stomach. "I heard the news in town a few weeks ago. I thought I should come over and congratulate you," she said in clipped tones. "I'm sure Jonathon's happy."

"Very," Rebecca agreed coolly and turned to Mark, who was watching Alison with ill-concealed interest. "This is Jonathon's brother, Mark. Mark, my cousin Alison."

Mark smiled his boyish grin and nodded as he removed his hat. "Pleased to meet you, Alison."

Alison regarded him with narrowed eyes. "I'm sure," she replied with a tight smile. "You look much like your brother."

"So people say," Mark rejoined pleasantly.

"If you're planning on staying, Alison," Rebecca interrupted pointedly, "why not come into the cabin?"

"Why not indeed?" Alison agreed and led the way inside.

Rebecca hesitated, watching her go, before looking at Bobby who was holding her horse. "Tether him to the rail, Bobby."

"Aye, Becky. I'll do that for you," he responded politely, his eyes grave as he watched Alison disappear into the cabin.

Rebecca smiled, and Mark took her arm as she started to follow Alison. "She's beautiful," he told her.

"Yes, Mark, beautiful," Rebecca said sadly. "But she knows she's beautiful, she knows she's rich, and she's very spoiled. She's very used to having her own way."

Mark stopped her. "You don't have to say any more. Jonathon told me all about the Cunninghams."

"That's not to say you should worry about them or about us because of them. You're not involved in this.

It's Jonathon and me they hate."

"Just the same," he told her with a wink, "I think I had best watch my step. She looks as if she may be out for blood."

Rebecca glanced at the cabin door hesitantly. "One thing you might not know, because Jonathon couldn't tell you, Alison was planning on marrying him when she turned nineteen last year. It wasn't that Jonathon encouraged her, but she's a lonely girl, and Jonathon is an attractive man. When I married him instead, it only worsened matters between us. It's one of the reasons she hates me so."

"That's past, Mrs. Gray. She can't hurt you now. Not anymore. So why don't we go meet the lioness in our den?"

When Rebecca stepped inside with Mark behind her, Alison was surveying the cabin with critical eyes. "It's not very impressive, Rebecca. I thought, being as rich as you are, you'd have a much finer house."

"The house you're referring to is in the process of being built," Rebecca replied. "A good house takes time to build, and mine won't be finished until March. In the meantime, we had to have a roof over our heads."

Alison received the rebuff by dropping into a chair. She looked up at Mark, who was watching her with curiosity. "And you, Mark Gray, what are you doing in Australia? Have you come to share your brother's wealth?"

"No, I've come to make him more wealthy," he replied, sliding into a chair across from her. "I've come to help Jonathon grow wheat."

"Wheat!" Alison laughed. "Wheat will never grow here, not with the weather in Australia."

Mark leaned back in his chair and folded his arms over his chest. "I beg to differ with you. I think we'll have a fine crop come May. It's growing nicely and has survived the heat very well so far. The irrigation ditches are working splendidly."

"Irrigation ditches?"

"Yes. We dug them just before the rains came last year," Mark replied.

"Those and a dam," Rebecca put in.

"A dam?" Alison scoffed. "I don't believe you."

Mark raised an eyebrow. "How unfortunate that you can't believe people when they speak the truth."

Rebecca smothered a smile, looking the other way. Alison jumped to her feet, outraged. "What are you trying to say to me?"

Mark rose slowly to face her. "I'm saying you shouldn't come to someone's house and accept their hospitality unless you're prepared to be hospitable yourself."

Alison glared at him, determined to make him drop his gaze before she did, but she didn't succeed. So she turned to Rebecca, her face flushed with anger and frustration, and said, "I'd have to see such a thing to believe it."

"Then come with me," Mark retorted. "I'll show you."

Alison stared after him as he strode out the door. "Is he serious?"

"I believe so," Rebecca replied, still refraining from smiling. "Why don't you go with him to see the fields and the house? I'm sure you'd enjoy the ride. You can go home later and tell Uncle Richard what you've seen."

Alison shot her a stinging look and followed Mark outside.

At the dinner table that night, Rebecca smothered a smile as she glanced at Jonathon, who was seated on her right. The dark lines on his face told her he was both irritated and embarrassed by Mark's tale of Alison's visit. "I'm sure Jonathon accepted her congratulations graciously."

"I did," Jonathon put in before Mark could comment, giving his younger brother a sardonic look.

"But you have to admit, Jon," Mark insisted, "you were caught off guard."

Jonathon took a drink of water before answering. "I'll admit I was taken aback when I saw Alison Cunningham at your side. Considering the circumstances surrounding our past relationship with the Cunninghams, you can hardly call my surprise unjustified."

"No," Mark conceded with a grin. "It's not often I see you speechless." Ben choked on his food, and Mark hurried on. "She said she's planning on coming here again, by the way."

"Oh?" Jonathon queried with a raised eyebrow.

"Yes," Mark explained. "She said she wants to come back to see if the crops fail."

Ben snorted but did not comment. Jonathon merely shrugged and returned to his meal. Rebecca, however, sighed lightly. She sincerely regretted the bad relations between the Cunninghams and themselves, but she could see no way to make amends.

Mark mistook her sigh as a resigned protest. "You don't mind, do you, Becky? If you do, I'll make sure she doesn't come your way."

"No, it's not that I don't want or approve of Alison being here. It's only that we don't get on well. We never have."

"I don't imagine Alison gets on well with many people," Mark observed. "She's too impressed with herself and expects others to be also."

"An understatement if I ever heard one," Ben retorted, wiping his mouth on his napkin. "What she needs is a man to take her over his knee once in awhile to show her who's boss."

"I'll remember that advice should I ever run into an overbearing female," Jonathon commented, continuing to eat without looking up.

Ben snickered and Mark grinned while Rebecca shot Jonathon a disgruntled look.

26

In the month following her first visit, Alison came to see the fields often—as well as Mark. Rebecca never saw her cousin, but Mark kept her informed of Alison's doings. He seemed to enjoy the verbal battles he and Alison had when they met. Although Alison always seemed to come out on the losing end, she always came back. Mark was amused by this and Rebecca was amazed.

Alison had never been defeated before, but this time she returned again and again for the same treatment. Rebecca realized that Alison was lonely. Mark was a diversion. Rebecca could not help but think that Mark was a good influence on her cousin. Though he was a bit more carefree than Jonathon, Mark was as level headed and serious as his older brother—and as determined.

Jonathon paid little attention to Mark's involvement with Alison. The trust between the two brothers was an unbreakable bond. Jonathon simply shrugged the matter off, knowing Mark would not allow Alison to interfere with the work Mark was doing with the crops. Both men were satisfied with the way the wheat was taking to the land. The irrigation was working well, and Jonathon was pleased to see the stalks growing taller when he rode out with Mark.

Jonathon was also a frequent visitor to Thomas Pickering. Despite the heat and working with only a handful of men, the architect was steadily erecting a fine-looking home. He continued insisting the building would be completed no later than March first.

Jonathon seldom had time to work in the mine anymore, but he managed to be with Ben and the other men several times a week. The cave had become more of a tunnel since the blasting of the inner wall, and trolley tracks burrowed through the hill from one side to the other. The mine echoed constantly with the sounds of men and machinery, and the gold kept coming from the cavern depths. The ore was more difficult to reach, since the gold on or near the surface had long since been cleared away. Regular digging often gave way to blasting and drilling, but the work continued to go well. Both Jonathon and Ben were satisfied with the mine's progress.

England seemed very far away to Jonathon as he immersed himself in the activity surrounding him. When he did look back at what he had left behind, he was surprisingly indifferent to it. His apathy was due to being too occupied with the present and his commitment to stay on in Australia for another year. There was no time to brood with so much to be done. Jonathon was content to let time pass, feeling confident in himself and his abilities. There was nothing to worry him, no task he could undertake and not succeed in accomplishing.

One night, when he returned to the cabin, Jonathon discovered he could not control everything that happened to him and his family. Dismounting by their makeshift stable, Jonathon led his mount into the shelter to find Ben waiting for him, puffing harshly on his pipe.

Jonathon could see lines of worry on the older man's face. "Did something happen at the mine?"

"Not at the mine," Ben answered with a grunt. "Here, with Becky."

"Becky?"

"She told me not to tell you, but I think you should know. She fainted today while she was fetching water from the stream."

Jonathon removed his horse's saddle and stopped to stare at Ben.

"I don't think it's anything to worry about. It's the heat and her being so heavy with the baby."

"Where is she now?"

"I finally convinced her to lay down after dinner was prepared, but she didn't go willingly."

"She wasn't hurt?"

"No, just shook up a bit," Ben replied, taking up a brush to help Jonathon rub the horse down. "But we got another problem."

"What is it?"

"Your Mr. Pickering. He came busting in here right after she lay down to tell her the house is ready."

Jonathon frowned. "And she wants to go see it."

"She put him off until tomorrow, but I thought maybe you could get her to wait a day or two. This heat can't last much longer. March'll be here soon."

As Jonathon began to brush the horse again, his frown deepened. "I'll see what I can do. But she has that damnable Scotch temper."

Inside the cabin, Rebecca lay staring up at the ceiling. It had been a miserable day. After a nearly sleepless night, she had risen to another scorching morning. She became ill just after the men went off to work which was when she fainted. She cursed the heat that had been plaguing her the past two months. It kept her from doing things that needed to be done. She hated being idle. She also didn't want to take chances either. Dr. Clayton had warned her not to overexert herself, but the heat kept her from exerting herself at all! If only she hadn't fainted, and if only Ben hadn't found out about it. She frowned. She asked Ben not to tell Jonathon. What would Jonathon say when he came home to find her in bed? What could she tell him?

She had come close to fainting before and had been sick any number of times. Jonathon knew nothing about that. She hadn't told him. He had enough to worry about without her making a nuisance of herself. She sighed and put a hand up to brush away the hair clinging to her damp face. What could she tell him? The truth? It was the heat—he would understand that. As long as Ben didn't tell him about her fainting, he would assume she was resting.

The door opened. Rebecca turned her head to watch Jonathon enter. He came quietly across the darkened room and sat beside her on the bed.

"You're home," she said with a smile as he took her hand in his.

Jonathon nodded and brushed her cheek with his hand. "Ben told me you were lying down."

"It's the heat. I wish March would come."

"Maybe you should stay in bed for a day or two until the heat dies down."

"And miss seeing my house? Or hasn't Tom told you yet?"

"Yes, he did. The house will be there the day after tomorrow."

Rebecca frowned. "Ben told you, didn't he?"

"Ben didn't have to tell me anything for me to know something was wrong," Jonathon answered quietly. "You're not the type of person who lays down if there are things to be done."

She scowled and looked away. "I asked him not to tell you."

"Don't scowl. It will give you wrinkles."

"He shouldn't have told you," she protested.

"I'm glad he did, even though I would have guessed anyway."

She looked up at him, her jaw set stubbornly. "I want to see my house."

"You will. But does it matter if it's tomorrow or the day after?" He put a gentle hand on her abdomen. "We do have someone else to think of, you know."

"He's fine," she assured him, putting her hand on top of his.

"How do you know it's a he?"

"Because I want him to be. I want to give you a son."

"I'd be happy with a pretty daughter—as long as she's not as sassy and hot tempered as you." He watched her smile, and bent to kiss her lightly on the forehead. "Will you wait a day or two? Will you do that for me?"

Rebecca hesitated, studying his face closely. "If you want me to."

He reached out and gathered her carefully into his arms. "I want you to."

Rebecca leaned against him, taking comfort in his nearness but worried by something. "Are you happy, Jonathon?"

"Whatever makes you ask that?" he questioned.

"I don't know. It's only . . . sometimes I get to feeling you're not."

"We can't look as if we're happy all the time. Everyone has bad days." He hated himself for lying, for not admitting there were times when England was very much on his mind.

"Of course, you're right," she agreed amiably. "We all do."

He ran his fingers through her hair, feeling its shining softness. "And you, Becky? Are you happy?"

She hugged him and rested her head against the strength of his shoulder. "Of course, I am."

"Good," he said, tightening his arms around her, "because I want you to be happy, Becky. I want you to be happy." His words became lost as he buried his face in her hair.

Jonathon took Rebecca out to the house two days later.

Rebecca gasped and clutched his arm tightly. "It's just as I dreamed it would be!"

"Tom will be glad to hear that," he answered.

Pickering helped Rebecca up the porch. "You'll have to remember what it will look like when you furnish it."

"It already looks the way I want it to," Rebecca said. "It's a lovely home, Tom."

"Nevertheless, I've taken the liberty of writing to a friend of mine in London. He'll send some samples of material and a catalog of furniture to help give you some ideas."

Jonathon watched as Rebecca stared at the great hallway. A staircase stood off to the right, sweeping up to the second floor, while beyond the entrance stood doors leading to rooms and hallways on the first floor. Exclaiming with delight she hurried off as the two men watched. Tom Pickering nodded at her many compliments, and Jonathon smiled happily.

"It's a fine piece of work, Tom," Jonathon told him as they moved to follow her to the back of the house. "You've done yourself proud."

"I'm happy I was able to please her."

"Obviously, you have."

"The kitchen doesn't look like much now," Tom told Rebecca as he moved forward to guide her there. "There's no stove yet and the cupboards are bare, but it should make any cook very happy."

"Indeed," she agreed heartily, opening the door that led to a storage cellar. "It's a cook's dream. Mrs. O'Brien would go mad with pleasure here."

"Mrs. O'Brien?" Jonathon inquired.

"She used to cook for my father and I when I was little. The two of us used to dream of kitchens like this."

"Hello in the house!" a voice called from the front hall.

"Back here, Mark!" Jonathon responded. "We're coming your way." He offered Rebecca his arm and guided her to the door.

Mark was waiting for them when they reached the hall once more, but he wasn't alone. Alison was with him. "I was coming over to see the house," Mark told them as they approached, "when I met Alison. It looks magnificent, Tom."

"Thank you, Mark."

"You said it would be finished about this time," Alison told Rebecca. "So I thought I'd come over to see it."

"You should have brought Elaine with you," Rebecca replied. She was determined to allow nothing to ruin her day. "She would have enjoyed the tour."

Alison was not to be put off. She quickly slid between

212

Rebecca and Jonathon as they moved toward the stairs.

Mark pulled Jonathon back. "Let them go. Becky can handle it, and Alison needs to be put in her place once in awhile."

"Really, Rebecca," Alison said as they ascended the curved staircase. "Do you think you ought to be running around like this in your condition?"

"There is nothing wrong with my condition, Alison," Rebecca replied. "Women have been walking about in this state for years."

The three men followed the two women at a distance as they roamed through the rooms. Alison maintained a sullen silence most of the time, taking in the big rooms and intricately designed windowseats and shelving without a word. As they started back toward the stairs, she felt forced to speak.

"You appear to have done quite well for yourself."

"Tom has done a wonderful job, Alison," Rebecca said, turning to Pickering. "It's beautiful, Tom. How can I ever thank you?"

"By paying the bill, I suspect," Mark answered, and everyone laughed—except Alison. She stomped down the stairs by herself and was gone by the time the rest of them reached the porch.

27

Mark carried a trunk into the room and set it down on the bed in front of Rebecca. "Here you go, Becky. Another trunk to fill. What do you have for this one?"

Two weeks had passed since the house's completion, and at last Jonathon was prepared to let them move in. Since they didn't have much furniture, Jonathon had sent to his hotel for some of the items they needed. Rebecca had objected, but he was adamant.

"The hotel is our property," he'd insisted. "We can do anything we want to with it or with what's in it."

Now the waiting was over. They were moving into their new home!

"Anyone home?"

Rebecca straightened at the call from the cabin door. "I wonder who that might be."

"I'll go see," Mark offered, stepping from the bedroom to find a gray-haired, bespectacled man standing in the main room. "Can I help you, sir?"

"I hope so. I've come to see Mrs. Gray. I'm Dr. Clayton."

"Dr. Clayton," Rebecca echoed, coming to the bedroom door. "How nice of you to come by."

"I thought I'd better see you, because you didn't come see me," he answered pointedly.

Rebecca made hurried introductions. "Dr. Clayton, this is Mark Gray, Jonathon's brother."

The doctor shook Mark's hand firmly, glancing about the cabin at the litter of boxes. "You folks moving somewhere?"

"Into our new house," Rebecca answered brightly. "You'll have to come with us to see it."

He eyed her over his wire-rimmed spectacles. "Here

or there, makes no difference to me."

She glanced anxiously at Mark, who was beginning to look embarrassed himself. "Dr. Clayton, I'm feeling fine."

"Feeling fine doesn't mean a thing. It's your first baby, and I must assure myself by seeing for myself."

Rebecca looked to Mark for aid, but he quickly went about collecting trunks and carrying them outside to the wagon.

"Can I get you something to drink after your long ride?" Rebecca asked.

"Nothing to drink, Mrs. Gray, but I would like to wash up."

"I'll put some water on to boil," she told him.

"The hotter the better," he responded and sat down to wait.

Mark continued to move in and out, finishing as the water began to boil. "I'll take this over to the house, Becky. I'll send Jonathon back to fetch you."

"Good idea," Clayton agreed before Rebecca could speak.

She watched Mark go, almost wishing he would stay to help calm the sudden fears growing inside of her. She shook off her hesitancy and took the pot from the stove. It was silly to be afraid. There was nothing to be afraid of. "You can wash in here, Dr. Clayton," she said, leading him to the extra room.

Mark met Jonathon a distance away from the cabin and drew his team up beside his brother's wagon. "Clayton cornered her all right. He's an old bear, and Rebecca wasn't much of a match for him."

"I don't care what his bedside manner is like," Jonathon replied, "as long as he's a good doctor." He cracked the whip without another word and sent the horses racing over the road toward the cabin. When he arrived, he found the doctor sitting alone at the table. Jonathon glanced at the closed bedroom door.

"She's all right," Clayton said. "I'm Dr. Clayton, and I've no doubt you're Jonathon Clay. We've never

215

met, but I've seen you in town often enough."

Jonathon shook the man's hand and allowed the doctor to lead him outside. "How is Becky?"

"As I said, she's fine. She's healthy and strong, and the baby should be born the same way."

Jonathon was not consoled. "Are you worried about something?"

"I'm just thinking that this will be her first child. The first birth is usually the hardest. After the first time, women don't let the small things scare them so much."

"Small things?"

"The pains and sickness and such. Has she had any problems?"

"She hasn't mentioned any," Jonathan replied, "but she fainted once during the summer heat."

Clayton nodded. "Heat's hard on a woman in her condition. Has she been sick at all?"

Jonathon shrugged. "Not that I know of."

"It's usually in the morning."

"She always gets up before us to fix our breakfast. After we leave, she's by herself."

Clayton sighed heavily. "That's a stubborn young woman you're married to."

Jonathon smiled weakly. "I know."

Clayton stopped walking and faced Jonathon. "You'd do well to find a midwife in that tent town of yours and have her stay with your wife. Try to find an older woman, one who's helped deliver children. I can't stay here a month waiting for the child to be born."

"You think it will be within the month then?"

"It should be," the doctor replied. "I can't give an exact date. I wish I could. It would make my job a lot easier."

Jonathon nodded, calculating the days in his mind. "Is there anything I can do to help her?"

"Stay with her as much as you can. But don't make it too obvious. It'll frighten her if she thinks you're worried. These women give themselves enough frights without their men adding to them. Stay fairly close.

Drop in once in awhile, or purposely forget something you need and tell her you're more excited than she is. But don't ever let her see you worrying. She's a strong young woman. There's no need to worry. She should have many strong, healthy babies."

Jonathon saw Rebecca emerge from the cabin and turned to shake the doctor's hand. "I'll take care of her."

Clayton nodded and walked back toward Rebecca. "You two decided on a name for the youngster yet?"

"I think Becky's got the names picked out," Jonathon replied, slipping an arm around her shoulders.

"They usually do," Clayton responded. Untying his horse from the rail, he swung himself into the saddle. "As long as I'm here, I'd best pass on through the tent town to see if there's anything I can do for the folks there. You take it easy, young lady, and keep an eye on your husband. See that he doesn't blow his foot off celebrating when the day comes."

Rebecca humbly nodded and watched him ride away. When he was out of sight, she turned to look up at Jonathon with worried eyes, wondering what Dr. Clayton had told him.

"Ready to go to your new house?" Jonathon asked with a reassuring smile.

Rebecca forced a smile to her lips and buried her face against his chest to hide her fear. There had been no fear during the first few months, only happiness. Then the sickness came, the dizzy spells, the weakness, and the pain. She had endured it all silently, longing for the day to come. Now that her time was near, she was beginning to worry. There was no doctor here in the bush and no other woman she knew well enough to go to for help. She was alone. Dr. Clayton's unexpected appearance made her realize how frightened she was.

Jonathon wrapped his arms around her and held her tightly, recognizing her fear. He had never realized how alone she was. She was the only woman among so many men. She had absorbed and handled alone all the small worries and fears Dr. Clayton spoke of, never complaining and never letting him guess what was in her mind. He gently turned her toward the cabin, knowing he loved the woman beside him for her determined silence.

In the days following Dr. Clayton's visit, Jonathon found he had ample opportunity to stay near the house because of the work Thomas Pickering was doing on the stables. He purposely remained to help with the last details, leaving only once in search of a companion for Rebecca. He found her in Sarah Mallory. The mother of six, she had lived in the country most of her life, having her children and aiding others during their deliveries without the aid of a doctor. She was a quiet woman, a good cook, and an excellent influence on Rebecca. Her husband was one of the farmers who worked closely with Mark. Sarah quickly persuaded Rebecca to let her do most of the household chores while Sarah entertained the younger woman with stories of her childhood in England.

Rebecca was enchanted with Sarah's country charm and frank honesty. Looking ahead, Jonathon knew they would not only be needing a cook in the future but a replacement for Mark when his younger brother returned to England. After a brief discussion, Mark agreed with Jonathon's plans to speak to Frank Mallory about taking over the management of the field. Rebecca was thrilled with the prospect of always having another woman in the house with her. The decision made, Jonathon had only to ask the Mallorys if they would accept. They did, and with some of his future problems solved, Jonathon returned his attention to the present.

The mine walls had begun to weaken under the constant blasting. Ben had to call a halt to the operation until supports could be brought in to brace the rock. It was not a difficult job, but was time consuming. With one problem solved, another was quick to emerge, bringing Jeremiah to the house at the end of the week.

Two head of cattle were missing. He had followed one to a dry gulch, where it had become trapped; the other was found butchered and partially cooked over a camp fire.

Jonathon knew that if he allowed the butchering of a cow to go unpunished, it would happen again. The ones responsible had to be stopped, or they would feel free to kill the livestock whenever they wanted a meal.

"We should be back no later than nightfall," Jonathon told Rebecca the next day as she walked him to the porch. "If we're late, don't worry. We may end up sleeping out for the night."

"Be careful," she implored. If the culprits were bush runners, she knew only too well how dangerous they could be.

"I'll be careful," he assured her. "And I won't be far away." He kissed her gently on the mouth and strode down the stairs to leave her watching from the porch.

She remained there, waving, as they rode out across the plateau with the big yellow dog running beside them. She smiled as she watched Dingo run. Since she had been unable to ride for several months, the mongrel had taken to wandering alone or following Jonathon wherever he went, always returning to her after awhile. Sneaking in through the kitchen when Sarah wasn't looking, Dingo would sprawl across Rebecca's feet or find himself a spot close to the warmth of the fire.

"Good morning, pretty lady," Mark greeted as he came out of the house to find her standing by the railing.

Rebecca smiled at him. "Where are you off to?"

"To check on your flourishing crops."

"Will you start harvesting next month?"

"That's right."

"Then you had best be going, to insure that nothing happens to it in the meantime."

He kissed her on the cheek and went to his horse, which was tethered to the hitching rail in front of the house. "I shouldn't be long. I'll probably be back in time to join you for lunch.''

She smiled and waved as he rode away, going back into the house to search for Sarah. She would be glad when she was free to ride again. She missed her daily runs through the bush.

Rebecca found Sarah in the kitchen, cleaning up the breakfast dishes. "Would you like to help me make a decision when you're finished there?"

"Concerning what?"

"The rugs for the upstairs rooms. I can't make up my mind on the colors. I want to send the order back with Tom when he leaves this weekend."

"Going back to England, is he?" Sarah inquired, wiping her hands on her apron.

"Aye. He'll put the finishing touches on the stables, and then he'll be off."

"Lucky man," the older woman sighed, remembering her home across the sea. "But now's not the time to be reminiscing. Let's collect his books and go out to the porch. It's a nice day for being outside."

The morning passed quickly as the two women sat flipping through the pages of Tom Pickering's sample books, debating what color would look best in which room. They laughed as they talked, enjoying the cool April breeze. It wasn't until almost noon that Sarah gave a little cry of alarm.

"Look at the time. I must be preparing lunch. The men will be coming any minute, and I don't have a thing ready," Sarah declared, rising and putting the books aside. "Would you like anything?"

"Perhaps a light snack," Rebecca replied, shifting in her chair.

Sarah eyed her cautiously for a moment. "You're feeling all right?"

"Just shifting him around a bit, Sarah. He's getting to be a mite heavy."

Sarah nodded with a small smile of understanding and left for the kitchen.

Rebecca shut her eyes when the woman was gone and

shifted again. A nagging pain had begun in her back. It occasionally twisted to a sharp ache in her side. There seemed to be nothing she could do to rid herself of it.

Taking a deep breath, she opened her eyes and stood, carefully making her way around Dingo, who had rejoined her only a short time before. She felt the sudden need to lie down. Step by step she moved up the stairs, gripping the railing tightly. By the time she reached the second-floor landing, the pain had become so intense she could no longer walk upright.

Breathing roughly, Rebecca stopped to rest a moment, trying to regain her strength. When she took the next step, instead of taking her forward, it brought her crashing to her knees. Blackness swept around her and a dizzy ringing filled her ears. She grasped desperately at the big dog, who had followed her, clutching his coat of mangled fur so tightly he whined.

The blackness finally lifted and she pushed the dog away, gasping for air. "Help, Dingo. Get help." She watched as the dog clattered down the stairs. Instead of going to the kitchen for Sarah, he ran back out the front door.

She groaned and leaned her head against the post. A dark moment passed and the pain seemed to recede, but she was not so foolhardy as to believe it wouldn't come back. She raised herself up, and, as loudly as she could, she called, "Sarah!"

In the meantime, Dingo was racing across the plateau toward the man he had come to recognize as important to his mistress. He understood Rebecca needed help, and he was going to someone he knew could provide it.

Mark returned to the house shortly after the dog disappeared from view, stopping on the porch to glance at the books sitting on the chairs. He smiled, remembering the conversations Rebecca and he had enjoyed. They sometimes differed in their tastes, and each took delight in arguing.

He moved into the hallway and removed his hat,

dropping it on the table beside the door. "Anyone home?" he called. To his surprise, his only answer was the echo of his own voice.

Stepping toward the kitchen, he stopped when he heard a noise on the landing. Sarah was standing there.

"Mark, put some water on the stove. Boil it and bring it up soon as it's ready. Becky's having her baby."

He hesitated only a moment before turning to run for the kitchen.

Some distance from the house, Jonathon was leaning down, examining tracks in the dirt with Jeremiah when Dingo came bounding up to his side. Before he could put the animal off, the big dog had hold of his jacket sleeve and was pulling him away.

"What on earth is the matter with this dog?" Jonathon exclaimed angrily, trying to shake himself free. As Dingo continued to hold on, Jonathon stopped fighting. The urgency of the dog's motions registered. Once before he had seen Dingo act this way. It was during his first months at the mine when Rebecca had gone down the cliff after the child who had slipped over the edge.

"My God!" he exclaimed as the dog released his sleeve to race off in the direction of the house. "It must be Becky!"

Jumping onto his horse, he whipped the animal into a gallop, thundering away before Jeremiah had a chance to mount.

Mark carried the steaming basin of water up the stairs and hesitantly entered the bedroom. Being a farmer with a small stable of animals, he had often been involved in the delivery of a calf or foal, but he had never before helped with the delivery of a baby.

Rebecca was lying on the bed as he came in with Sarah sitting beside her. "Put the basin over there," Sarah instructed.

Mark placed the basin on the dresser Sarah indicated and hesitated once more before stepping forward to stand beside Sarah. His eyes were filled with worry as he looked down at Rebecca who was breathing heavily. "Is she going to be all right?''

"She'll be fine," Sarah replied, patting Rebecca's hand.

Rebecca heard the words but could not take in their meaning. She was aware only of Sarah's and Mark's presence and the support it provided. Her thoughts were only on her baby.

"What do we do now?" Mark asked.

"We wait until she's ready."

"How will we know she is?"

"She'll let us know."

It was a long ride, even running the horse at full speed. Jonathon arrived at the house in what seemed to him like hours later with a pounding heart and a lathered mount. Leaping from the saddle, he took the porch steps in two long-legged bounds and strode through the doorway into the hall.

Pausing there, he was uncertain what to do when the unnatural silence was broken by the loud wail of a baby's crying. He stood paralyzed, unable to move. The baby had arrived!

He hurtled the stairs three and four at a time. The bedroom door was ajar when he stopped outside it, and he hesitated only briefly before pushing it aside.

Rebecca was lying white and pale on the bed, but she was smiling as Sarah bent over to place a crying baby beside her. Mark was standing to the side, watching the scene dumbfounded. Jonathon looked from one to the other, unsure of what he should do or what he should say. There was so much he could do, so much he could or should say. Words and reason had evaded him. He felt lost, almost afraid, until Sarah turned to face him.

"Mr. Gray," she said with a warm, satisfied smile, "come and see your son."

It was on April 16th, shortly after noon, that Jonathon Matthew Gray II was born.

28

By the time the harvesting began, Rebecca was up and about. She wanted to go to the fields with Mark to watch the reaping, but Jonathon would not allow it. He insisted she stay home with their son and help Sarah.

"There'll be other harvests for you to see," Jonathon told her. "For now, your health and our son are more important."

Mark was at his best in the fields. He and the farmers worked side by side, singing happily as they reaped the wheat to help the time pass. During the month, he often saw Alison sitting astride her horse watching the harvesting. It amused him to see her on the hill and know she found it hard to believe the wheat had actually survived through the summer.

Alison's disbelief was accompanied by pleasure. She was glad Mark had succeeded, glad he was accomplishing what he set out to do. When she was able to speak with him, she admitted her feelings to him. Surprised and pleased by her confession, Mark invited her to the house for dinner to celebrate their success and to see the new addition to the Gray family.

"He's so tiny," Alison told Rebecca, her snobbishness abandoned as she looked at the baby lying peacefully in his crib.

"Tiny he may be," Rebecca agreed with a smile, "but there's nothing tiny about his voice. He can wake the entire house with one wail."

When Alison saw the soft glow in Rebecca's eyes, the jealousy she had felt for her cousin melted away. "I'm very happy for you, Rebecca."

"Thank you, Alison." Looping her arm through the other girl's arm, Rebecca led her to the door. "I think it's time we joined the men for dinner. They won't wait for us, I can assure you. When they come home from the fields, there's only one thing they want: food."

Rebecca felt totally satisfied with life as they made their way to the staircase. It had brought her many wonderful things: Jonathon, her son, their land, friends, and so much more. Sometimes, she felt there were too many blessings to count.

On reaching the bottom of the stairs, Rebecca saw Jonathon through the open door, standing on the porch with Jeremiah. Motioning Alison on to the dining room where Mark stood patiently at the door, she stopped to wait for Jonathon to come in.

When he did, his expression was a deep frown.

"Jonathon, what is it? Is something wrong?"

He looked at her and smiled briefly, slipping an arm around her shoulders. "It's another cow," he replied in low tones. "Butchered like the last."

"What are you going to do?"

"I'm going to put an end to it," he answered grimly. "Tomorrow morning, Jeremiah, Bobby, and I are going out to track the men who did it. This time we won't stop until we find what we're after."

The anger in his voice frightened her. Rebecca clutched his hand tightly. "Do you have any idea who is doing it?"

"Probably some bush runners who feel free to help themselves to a side of beef when they need one."

"Will you be able to find them?"

"We'll find them. And we'll make short work of them."

"Jonathon!"

"Rebecca, it has to be stopped. If one man gets away with it, the next will think he can, too. We'll end up providing a free meal to anyone who passes over our range." He took her firmly by the shoulders. "Now don't start your worrying. No harm will come to any of us."

She stared up into the hard blue of his eyes and

nodded. "I won't worry."

"Good girl," he said, hugging her warmly. "Now, let's go eat."

Early the next morning, before Rebecca awoke, Jonathon crept silently from the room to meet Jeremiah and Bobby in the light of predawn. Riding first to check on the herd to make sure that no more cows were missing, they followed Jeremiah to the site of the last slaughtered cow.

"If they kill a cow, you think they'd at least take the extra meat with them," Jeremiah said disgustedly. Since taking on the responsibility of patrolling the herd regularly, he had also begun to take pride in the health and well being of the animals. This idle slaughtering rankled him deeply.

"You said there was more than one man. Are you sure?" Jonathon inquired, standing to look around the area.

"Positive," Jeremiah answered, pointing toward a lone gum tree. "They tied their horses over there."

"How far did you follow the tracks yesterday?"

"About three miles."

"Do you remember where you stopped?"

"I do."

"Then we'll start there."

Picking up the trail where Jeremiah had halted the day before, they began tracking the two men over the rugged terrain. It was a slow, meticulous process, and time wore on their nerves. They often lost the trail and had to split up to find the tracks once more. Few words were ever spoken as they continued doggedly on.

The men they tracked were moving at an easy pace. Their clear tracks and aimless trail showed they were obviously unconcerned at the prospect of being followed. Midday came and passed without the trio meeting the men they sought. Afternoon saw the sun move steadily across the sky toward the west, but the three did not falter in their pursuit. They followed the trail in silent determination, riding over rocks and grassland, through groves of trees and dry river beds. Nothing could deter them from their course.

Jeremiah and Bobby took turns dismounting as the tracks became fresher. Tension strung the three men tightly together. They would meet their adversaries any time now.

Bobby pulled up to slide from his horse, bending over the tracks before him with a frown. "There's something wrong here, Jeremiah."

A blast shook the air, and Bobby was thrown backward by the power of the bullet that struck him. The horses panicked at the sudden crash of weapons. Jonathon and Jeremiah fought to control their mounts as they were caught in crossfire from the two men who were hiding behind some rocks. Forced to seek cover, they dove from their saddles, carrying their rifles with them. Bullets followed them to the ground, thudding into the dirt and whistling by their heads.

Returning the fire blindly, they staggered into positions where they could protect each other. The shooting became fast and furious. Rifles spit out flaming lead, and the men dodged wildly to avoid the deadly missiles. Pinpointing one man's fire, Jeremiah pulled his trigger. A voice cried out, and a man tumbled from behind a rock to sprawl face down in the dirt. Jeremiah turned to aid Jonathon, but there was no need.

The remaining attacker jumped to his feet when his partner went down, making himself an easy target for Jonathon's bullet. He fell in midstride.

The air cracked with tension. No sound could be heard as the smoke from the guns slowly cleared away. Jonathon and Jeremiah sat huddled, waiting for what seemed an eternity before daring to move. They came out cautiously, standing up to look at the two bodies lying on the ground.

Still alert for danger, Jeremiah stepped forward and Jonathon attempted to follow him. But his leg gave way under his weight and he fell as a sharp pain shot upward through his body.

Jeremiah ran to kneel beside him. "You've been hit."

Jonathon stared down at the red stain spreading over his pants leg. When had he been hit? He didn't remember. "It's not bad. I'm all right. See about Bobby."

Jeremiah scampered away to stoop over Bobby's still form. He turned the young man over slowly, his eyes darkening as he examined the hole the bullet had made in Bobby's chest. "He's alive," Jeremiah called back to Jonathon. "But he's hurt bad. He's losing a lot of blood."

Jonathon struggled to his feet, holding one hand over his wound as he limped forward. "I'll watch him. See if you can find our horses so we can get him back to the house. If you can't find them, look for theirs," he said, indicating the dead men. "They probably staked them nearby."

"Right," Jeremiah agreed and hastened off into the bush.

Rebecca watched Mark come out of the house to bend over the crib where Baby Matt lay. Mark was as fond of the child as Jonathon. He spent a good deal of his free time amusing the baby.

The sound of a running horse echoed across the plateau, and Rebecca glanced up to see who was coming. The horse was riderless, and she jumped to her feet. "Mark!" She watched it come, her heart pounding. "It's Jonathon's!"

Mark leaped from the porch, waving his arms to slow the animal down as it plunged on toward the stable. Dingo bounded off after Mark, helping to stop the frightened horse while Mark grabbed the reins.

Rebecca ran up to stop beside him. "Do you think Jonathon was thrown?"

"If he was, Jeremiah and Bobby are with him."

She looked up as Mark stopped speaking, following his eyes to the saddle. Blood! "Mark!"

"I'll saddle my horse. You get some bandages and supplies I can take with me."

"Saddle my horse, too."

"No, Becky!"

"Saddle my horse, Mark. No power on earth is going to stop me from going to my husband."

Starting where the men had left at dawn, Rebecca and Mark followed the trail with Dingo in the lead. Their progress was slow and frustrating. As the light grew dim and night fell, it left them dependent on the big yellow dog.

Rebecca was forced to call the dog back time and again as they lost him in the dark. Anxious tears burned her eyes. She brushed them angrily away and surged on. She said nothing to Mark, nor did he to her. Talking wouldn't get them to the men any faster. Each knew the other couldn't answer the questions uppermost in their minds.

Time dragged on and they continued to grope through the blackness, depending on Dingo for guidance until at last Rebecca looked up to see a fire lit up ahead.

"Mark! A fire! It must be them!"

Mark didn't wait to reply but spurred his horse forward. Crashing up to the camp, he was off his horse and running to Jonathon before the animal stopped. "Are you all right?"

Jonathon ignored the question as he limped forward to meet him. "Did you bring any bandages with you?"

"Yes," Mark answered as Rebecca ran up to throw her arms around Jonathon with tear-filled eyes.

He pushed her from him. "Hurry with the bandages. It's Bobby. He's hurt."

Rebecca didn't stop to ask questions but ran back for the saddlebags. "How is he?" she asked, looking down at Bobby's pale face.

"Not good. He took a bullet in the chest," Jeremiah told her. "We tried to get him back to the house, but," he shrugged helplessly, "he's been unconscious off and on. I don't think he's going to make it."

Rebecca met his eyes. They were filled with pain. She swallowed the lump in her throat and slowly turned to put a cool hand on Bobby's forehead. He stirred under her touch, and she smiled at him as his eyes blinked open. "It's all right, Bobby. Stay still."

Bobby groaned and moved his head. "Becky? Are you here?"

"I'm here," she told him, taking his big hand in hers. "You're going to be fine."

He blinked at her, trying to smile. He knew her words were meant to calm him. He also knew she didn't speak the truth. He had seen too many shot men not to know what a wound like his meant. "I don't mind dying so much now that you're here."

Rebecca squeezed his hand. "Don't talk like that. You'll be up and around in no time."

"Wish I could see you better," he told her, ignoring her words. "You're one of the prettiest sights I ever saw."

She frowned. Bobby had always been more sentimental and gentle than the men from England, but never had she heard him speak like this.

"You're a pretty lass, Becky. Your mother did Scotland proud when she had you."

"Hush, Bobby. Don't try to talk," she told him, putting her fingers over his lips.

"No. Have to," he gasped. "Have to tell you."

"Tell me what?" she asked gently.

He smiled slowly, a shadow of his usual, big hearted grin. "I love you, Becky. I think I loved you right from the beginning. The first day when you came to the hotel room, so fit and proper you were. You set Jeremiah right back on his heels, you did. Remember?"

Rebecca stared down at him in disbelief. Bobby loved her? "Aye," she managed, the word sounding strangled. "I remember."

"And the time we rode to town to fetch Jonathon? Remember?"

She nodded, hot tears starting slowly down her cheeks. "I remember."

"I enjoyed our talks. Did you?"

She could only shake her head. Words wouldn't pass through her lips. She pressed her hand to her mouth, trying to calm the fluttering beat of her heart. "Bobby, Bobby, I didn't know."

"You weren't supposed to," he choked. A coughing spasm shook his body violently.

Rebecca glanced quickly at Jeremiah, but he didn't look back. There was nothing they could do.

The spasm passed, leaving Bobby wheezing for breath. "Becky?"

"I'm here," she told him through trembling lips. "I'm still here." Her voice broke.

"You're not crying, are you?" Rebecca couldn't answer. "You shouldn't cry for me. You've got a fine man and a wee boy to care for."

Rebecca turned her head away to wipe the tears from her face. How could she have worked and talked with a man so often and never guess how he felt? Was it her own love for Jonathon that made her so blind to the feelings of others? "I'm sorry, Bobby."

He squeezed her hand as a shudder passed through his body. When it passed, he was still.

"Bobby?" she called.

A hand reached out to touch her arm. Jeremiah shook his head. "He's gone, Becky."

Rebecca stared at Bobby, his eyes closed, never to open again. Why had this happened? Why had she never known? Why did Bobby have to die?

She staggered to her feet and fell into Jonathon's arms. But she didn't want to be touched. She had to be alone. She broke away.

Jonathon started to go after her, but Mark put a restraining hand out. "Let her go, Jon. Let her go and cry it out."

Jonathon nodded, glancing down at Bobby's still form before allowing Mark to lead him away to the fire to bandage his leg. It wasn't a bad wound, but the bullet was still lodged in his leg. It would have to remain there until they reached the house. They sat staring into the fire, thinking their separate thoughts.

Many long, uncounted minutes passed before Rebecca returned to camp. Her face was tearstained, and she looked tired and worn, but she said nothing. Sitting down beside Jonathon, she merely curled close to him, patting Dingo absently when the big dog crawled from the fire where it lay to put its head on her lap.

29

In the two weeks following Bobby's death, Jonathon was forced to spend his time in bed while Mark finished the harvesting. Jeremiah looked after the stock, and Ben ran the mine. He even had to stay there when a short service was held for Bobby O'Riley. Everyone accepted it except him. He kept hearing Bobby's dying words, his confession to Rebecca. The words haunted him—and their meaning.

If one other man loved Rebecca, wasn't it possible there was another, or more than one who admired her from a distance? She was a beautiful woman. He could never doubt her faithfulness to him, but the fact remained. Someone else could be in love with her.

Rebecca never mentioned Bobby's death or the deaths of the two men who killed the young Scot. It was as if it had never happened. Life around him was continuing as if these deaths had never happened, but they had. Endless doubts and questions ran through Jonathon's mind. Shouldn't it have been him instead of Bobby? Would it have been better that way? The man who was planning on leaving his wife to go to England should have died so that the man who loved her and would never leave her could live.

Two people had come together to join in a union, a union that would protect one person and give the other his objective. They had committed themselves to each other for two years, putting aside their separate lives to share the achievements life would bring. The arrangement had worked perfectly for awhile. Both people had obtained what they desired. Somewhere, during the time the agreement was shared, the two separate lives had become entwined more deeply than their pact had provided for. The feelings of both had grown more than what had been intended.

Now there was love and a child. Jonathon had a woman, a beautiful wife. He knew Rebecca would have to face the proposal she had put to him many months before. They would both have to face it, face what had to be done.

Alone in his room, Jonathon was brooding on the subject when Rebecca brought Matt in to see him one morning. Not willing to avoid discussing the subject any longer, Jonathon confronted her with it. "Rebecca, have you thought about Bobby's death?"

Rebecca frowned and did not look at him as she set the baby down on the bed. "Aye."

"Becky," he continued, taking her hand as she straightened from the bed, "have you thought of what he said, of what his confession meant?"

She stared down at his hand holding hers. "What are you trying to say, Jonathon?"

"Becky, if one man who worked for you loved you, there could be others."

Rebecca pulled her hand away and stepped back sharply. "What are you accusing me of?"

"I'm not accusing you of anything. I'm stating a possible fact," Jonathon answered earnestly. "You're a beautiful woman, Becky, someone who many men admire and would love if you let them."

She stared at him, her eyes wide with bewilderment and hurt.

"Haven't you ever thought you made a mistake by marrying me? Haven't you ever wondered if you could have found a better husband? One who wasn't planning on returning to England?"

Rebecca looked away, saying nothing. It was a subject she had been avoiding. She had hoped that the passing of time had changed his mind. He hadn't spoken of it in a long while.

"Becky," Jonathon said quietly. "We made an agreement."

"And you want to know if I'm going to break it, if I'm going to try to make you stay."

"It's something I have to do," he stated flatly. "When I leave, you can find yourself another husband."

"You're my husband, Jonathon. No one else."

"You can do better than me. You *deserve* better."

"I deserve nothing except what I asked for," she declared, raising her eyes to meet his. "And I asked for you."

"But I won't be here much longer."

Rebecca walked to the window. "Jonathon, why must we talk of this now? There is time yet."

"We must talk because it's necessary. Because you have to think of your future and Matt's."

She looked at the bed where the small baby lay beside his father. "Matt will stay with me."

"I'm not asking whether he will go or stay, Becky," he answered quietly. "There is no question of where he will spend his future. I could never take him from you. Becky, what will you do when I leave? You can't stay here alone with Matt."

"I have Ben and Jeremiah."

"They're not your husbands."

"No. You're my husband."

"Was that meant as a rebuke?"

Rebecca ran to him, falling on her knees by the bed. "Please, Jonathon, let's not argue. You told me we would cross the bridges when we came to them. The bridge is far away yet."

Jonathon stared down at her pleading face. His heart hurt. Why was he doing this to her? Why did he have to leave? Why couldn't he just forget his hate and stay with his love? He covered her hand with his. "There is something we must consider."

"What?" she asked hopefully.

"If we continue to share the same bed, there could be another child."

Rebecca flushed, but she did not look away from

him,. "Then we shall have a second child."

"It doesn't matter to you that the children we have may not have a father?"

"If you leave or if you die as Bobby O'Riley did, what would be the difference? You'd still be gone—by will or by accident."

"And would that be what you tell them? That I left of my own free will? Or would you tell them I died?"

She clamped her hands over her ears and rose. "I'll not listen to any more, Jonathon. If you don't want me in your bed, say so. It's for you to say, because it's your decision to make. You're my husband, and I'll bear your children, but if you don't want . . ."

"Becky! Stop it!" he snapped, trying to reach for her.

"It has to be said, Jonathon. I want it clearly understood that I have no decision to make. I'm your wife as long as you want me." Her back was stiff as she walked toward the door.

Jonathon threw back the covers and got to his feet, ignoring the pain in his leg as he hurried to grasp Rebecca before she reached the door.

"Oh, Becky!" he cried, holding her so tightly she could barely breathe. "I'm sorry," he murmured against her hair, feeling her cling to him. "I don't want to hurt you, but it has to be said. You know the day will come when I have to leave."

"You shouldn't be out of bed," was all she said.

"Becky," he whispered, "do you love me?"

"You know I do," she told him.

"Then, by God, we'll find a way. We'll find a way."

Rebecca was still with him an hour later when there was a knock at the door. Rising, she crossed the room.

"Alison!" she exclaimed, finding her cousin standing in the hall.

"I hope I'm not intruding," Alison apologized. "But I was out riding and met Mark. He told me what happened. I thought I'd come by to see how Jonathon is. Your housekeeper sent me up here."

"Why don't you come in and see for yourself?" Rebecca opened the door wider and moved into the room.

Alison hesitated, and Jonathon called from the bed. "Come in, Alison. I've got Matt here. You can see him while you're visiting me. He's a good deal bigger than when you last saw him."

Rebecca watched Alison move to the bed and felt pain twist her heart as she thought how handsome Jonathon looked and how, even in bed, he could command whatever went on around him. Tears burned her eyes as she watched him show Matt to Alison. How proud he was of his son! She blinked back the tears and walked to the bed, trying not to think of the future, of when she would be without this man.

"He *has* gotten big!" Alison cried happily. "And I think he's going to look just like you."

"Of course," Jonathon agreed.

Alison turned to look at Rebecca. "How can you stand it, having two of them to look after?"

"It's hard," Rebecca admitted. "But I think I can manage."

"You said you met Mark," Jonathon said, changing the subject. "Where was it?"

"In the fields, as usual," Alison answered. "He was checking on the dam and drainage ditches for the winter rains."

Jonathon nodded approvingly, and Alison rose to go. "I don't want to keep you up. You need your rest."

"I'll see you out, Alison," Rebecca told her.

"Oh, you don't have to."

"It's no trouble. It's time to feed the little one before he begins crying." Rebecca took the baby from Jonathon's arms.

"You'll come back later?" Jonathon inquired, putting a hand out to detain his wife.

"For dinner," she agreed.

Alison closed the door, following Rebecca into the hall before stammering out a question. "Would you mind if I stayed?''

"For the feeding?''

Alison shook her head. "I was hoping we could talk.''

Rebecca smiled. "Of course. Come to the other bedroom.'' She led the way and prepared to nurse the child.

"It's remarkable how different and yet how alike Mark and Jonathon are,'' Alison began.

"Aye, I've noticed their likeness often.''

"Jonathon seems much more reserved.''

"Aye,'' Rebecca agreed thoughtfully. "He is, but then he's experienced much more of life. He's been through things Mark has never had to face. It made him hard in many ways.''

"You're suited to him in that way. I mean, not that you're hard, but that you're both so determined to reach for and get whatever you want.''

Rebecca thought back on that day's conversation with Jonathon. The London wound had healed but the scar remained. He was obsessed with the idea of seeking revenge for it.

"And you always seem to get it.''

"We try to,'' she replied.

Alison watched the baby nurse. "Do you know if Mark will be staying on, now that the crop is in?''

"There hasn't been any mention of his leaving,'' she answered. "I've become so used to having him with us, I can't imagine being here without him.''

"I know.''

Rebecca glanced quickly over at her cousin before returning her attention to the baby. "I don't think he'll stay on much longer, though. He does have his own farm in England to worry about.''

"I thought he had a man looking after it.''

"He does. But the man can't be expected to watch it forever.''

A wistful expression touched Alison's face.

"Does Uncle Richard know you come here?'' Rebecca inquired.

Alison shifted uneasily in her chair. "I haven't mentioned it to him lately. I did at first because he was interested."

"But he's not now?"

"I think he's interested," Alison answered. "It's just that, well, you're so successful."

Rebecca nodded. "He wanted to find gold so badly."

"Yes, but he's losing money steadily now. There hasn't been any gold coming out of the mine in a long time."

"Perhaps he should try somewhere else on the land."

"I've tried to suggest that to him, but you know father. He won't listen to anyone. He's determined to find gold in that mine."

They were suddenly interrupted by a man's call. "Hello in the house!"

"That will be Mark," Rebecca said, watching her cousin's face light up at the sound of his voice.

"Don't get up," Alison told her. "I'll go down and tell him where you are."

"That's good of you, Alison. Good-bye for now. Come again."

"Thank you, Rebecca. It's been nice talking with you."

Alison left, and Rebecca sat alone. Alison was in love with Mark. The thought amused and pleased Rebecca. Alison had changed considerably in the past year. Rebecca wondered if it was Mark who had changed the spoiled and selfish girl into a thoughtful woman.

What of Mark? Could Alison be the reason he hadn't mentioned leaving yet? He had taken the crop into town and could have gone then. He could have remained at the hotel and caught the next ship out, but he had not. Rebecca thought Mark remained because of Jonathon's injury. Perhaps she was wrong.

30

When winter arrived, it brought cold, gusty winds and torrents of rain. June brought rain every day but two, and July began with no sign of a break in the weather. The land was becoming flooded; water was turning the ground into muddy bogs. Traveling was almost impossible, making communication between the mine and the house nearly nonexistent.

Jonathon called everyone into his study. "As you know, the rain has all but paralyzed us," he began. "And there's no sign of this weather letting up." He paced the floor restlessly. "Jeremiah, I think we'll have no choice but to bring the livestock to the plateau. We have hay and feed for them at the stables. Close to the house and in the protection of the buildings, they won't stray into the bush and be lost."

"I agree," Jeremiah said gravely. "They're starting to get bogged down out there, and grass is scarce."

Jonathon nodded, turning to Ben. "What about the mine, Ben? Can you keep it operating?"

"I don't see why not," Ben answered, puffing on his pipe. "We've had some mud slides off the top of the hill, but there's been no weakening in the walls."

"Just the same, you'll keep a careful eye out, won't you, Ben?" Rebecca asked. "We don't want to endanger you and the men."

Ben shook his head reassuringly. "I'll be watching. And believe me, at the first sign of trouble, we'll get out."

Jonathon stopped behind Rebecca's chair and put a strong hand on her shoulder. Both he and Ben understood her fear of cave-ins. She had lost her father in one and wasn't able to let the memory pass from her mind.

"Mark, the fields?"

Mark shook his head doubtfully. "It's not the fields I'm worried about, Jon. It's the dam. It's filling up fast. There's no place to let the water drain. The ditches are full, and a good section of the fields are flooded. There's no place for more water to go."

"What if the dam breaks?" Jonathon asked.

"If it breaks," Mark shrugged, "we'll have to start over again. If it doesn't, with as much water as the land has absorbed, it'll be weeks before we can put a plow to it once spring comes."

Jonathon moved to the window and watched the rain beat down on the pane. "There's nothing we can do for the dam. Ben, I'm going to have to rely on you to keep a sharp lookout on the mine. It won't be getting any easier to make the trip back and forth across this mud, but I'll be over as soon as I can." Ben nodded and Jonathon continued. "Right now, our first concern is the stock. Jeremiah, tomorrow we'll have to go out and bring them in."

The next morning, Ben started back to the mine while Rebecca and Sarah began packing provisions for Jonathon, Mark, and Jeremiah. There was no telling how long they would be gone while gathering the stock. Enough was packed to hold the three of them for at least one week.

Rebecca waited in the kitchen for the men, giving the bundles of food to Jeremiah and Mark as they left for the stables. "Where's Jonathon?"

"Should be coming any minute," Mark answered.

"Please be careful."

Without answering, both men went out into the steady drizzle. There was nothing they could say to reassure her. They could only do what needed to be done and come back as quickly as possible.

She watched them go before leaving the kitchen to search for Jonathon. He was upstairs in the bedroom, packing his saddlebags. "I wish you'd let me come," she told him. "None of you know the bush as I do."

"We discussed that last night before we went to bed," he replied.

"But Jonathon!"

"No. We'll be gone for two or three days at the most. I won't have you out there in these conditions."

"But you could get lost."

"We won't. To make you feel better, we'll take Dingo."

"Jonathon, so many men have gone out there and never come back."

"I'm not so many men," he told her.

"I know."

He kissed her long and hard, pressing her body close to his. When he raised his head, it was to press his lips against her forehead. "You take care of Matt for me. I'll be back in a few days to see both of you."

Rebecca nodded. She followed him down the stairs and watched him join the other two men from the kitchen window. In a few minutes, they were gone, disappearing into the dull gray of the morning with the big yellow dog trailing behind them.

It took the better part of the day to reach the herd and scattered flock. The men led or rode their struggling mounts across the drowning countryside. Heaving and plunging, the horses battled for balance as they floundered past lakes of water and lurched up hills of mud. It was hard on both the men and the animals.

The animals they came to save were a pitiful sight. Huddled together in a group, they stood against the wind, covered with mud and soaked through their coats of fur and wool.

"I'll see how many of the animals are here and if they're able to travel," Jeremiah volunteered, stepping out into the slime. "Some of them could have been injured fighting through this."

Watching Jeremiah go, Mark made his way around his horse to stand beside Jonathon. "It's going to be rough getting them back. Making it through with three horses was bad enough. How are we going to manage with a herd of cattle and a flock of sheep?''

Jonathon looked out at the flooded land. No, it wouldn't be easy. Somehow, it had to be done. Out in the open, the stock was at the mercy of the elements, and their probability of survival was low. If the animals could be driven to the stables, they'd have a chance.

Jeremiah waded back to Jonathon and Mark. ''Two cows are missing and at least five sheep.''

Jonathon looked up at the sky. The rain continued to come down. It would be impossible to search for the animals under these conditions. ''It can't be helped. We'll take what we can. The horses should rest awhile longer before we begin to move the stock. We won't get far today, but we can at least start back.''

He knew they would be lucky to cover a few miles per day. His thoughts slipped to Rebecca. He had told her they would return in two or three days. It would be much longer than that before they saw the house again.

Rebecca sent Sarah home the same day the men left. There was no need to keep Sarah at the house when she could be spending time with her own family.

Rebecca tried to keep herself busy through the long days by sewing and cleaning and watching Matt, but no matter how she tried to occupy her mind with other things, her thoughts wandered to Jonathon, Mark, and Jeremiah. It was easy to get lost out in the bush, even during good weather. The land was deceptive in appearance. No matter which direction a person turned, the terrain looked much the same. Without the sun for guidance, the men would have to rely entirely on their scanty knowledge of the area.

Five days passed, along with five endless nights, and there was still no sign of the men's return. The rain continued to fall. Unable to concentrate on work, Rebecca went to her son's room to console herself. Picking the boy up from his crib, she walked to the window to stare out at the bleak scene. ''We must be strong, Matthew,'' she told the baby. ''We must not give up hope.''

Refusing to give in to her fears, Rebecca returned the baby to his bed and made her way downstairs. She had to keep busy. She couldn't leave herself time to think. Going to the kitchen, she put more water on to boil. If the men returned, they would be cold and need coffee and a hot bath. She checked on the stew she had prepared. It would provide a filling and hearty meal for her three wanderers.

She turned to the sink to begin redoing the tasks she had already done and redone during the past five days. Suddenly, the door flew open, banging loudly against the wall behind it. She spun with a stifled scream in her throat to face a tall, unshaven man. His clothes were wet and covered with mud. For an ominous moment, he stood staring at her.

Then, slowly, he smiled, and Rebecca gave a startled cry as she recognized him under the grime. Throwing aside her towel, she ran to him, wrapping her arms around him.

Jonathon pushed her away with a gruff laugh. "You're getting yourself all wet."

"I was so worried," she told him, ignoring the wetness of his clothes. Warm tears coarsed down her cheeks. "Are you all right?"

"Of course. And so are the others."

"Where are they?" she asked, looking out the door.

"Right behind me. I came on ahead to make sure there's some coffee."

"There's better than coffee," she answered, taking his hat and throwing it on the table. "There'll be a hot bath for all of you and hot stew to eat. Now get out of those clothes and tell the others to do the same. I'll fetch blankets and towels and some dry things for you to wear."

It wasn't until two hours later that Rebecca managed to get Jonathon to bed. He insisted on letting the other two men take their hot baths first while he ate and Rebecca rubbed his cold skin until it returned to its normal color and temperature.

She couldn't understand how he could be so cold and not feel it, and he couldn't explain how the cold had seemed to become a part of their bones. It had crept in at first, touching their skin and making them shiver as they pulled, pushed, and dragged the stock through the mud. After awhile they no longer noticed the cold. It was merely always there with them, a part of them.

Jonathon also did not explain their delay due to a loss of direction. It would do no good to tell her how they had staggered over countless miles before Dingo's insistent barking convinced them they were going the wrong way. How terrifying it had been, not knowing where they were, almost not caring as the wet and cold numbed their bodies and minds.

"You must get some rest now," Rebecca told him, pulling the blankets up tightly under his chin.

"That's one order of yours I will gladly obey."

She brushed his freshly washed hair from his forehead. "You call when you wake up. I'll bring you something to eat again."

He took her hand, kissed it, and, with her gentle kiss pressing warmly against his forehead, fell into heavy, dreamless slumber.

31

When Rebecca rose the next day, the rain had stopped. The sun had begun to shine, and beams of light were breaking through a haze of gray clouds. The men slept on as she began her daily chores of feeding Matt and preparing a meal. It was shortly after noon when Mark wandered into the kitchen, stifling a yawn.

"If I didn't need to eat, I think I'd sleep for a week straight," he told Rebecca, lifting the cover off a pot to see what was inside.

Rebecca slapped his hand and sent him to the table. "You needn't have gotten up to eat, Mark. I would have brought the food to your room."

"He wouldn't have been able to wait that long," Jonathon said, entering the room. "As soon as he smells food, he's off and running."

Rebecca smiled as he planted a kiss on the back of her neck. He looked much better this morning. His color had returned after a night's sleep.

"I smelled the food all the way upstairs," Jeremiah announced, striding through the door and rubbing his hands together. "Couldn't wait to get some."

"See," Mark declared, winking at Rebecca. "I'm not the only one."

Jonathon stopped to look out the window before seating himself at the table. "How long has it been since the rain stopped?"

"Since last night," Rebecca answered, carrying two plates of hot food to the table.

"But how long will it stay stopped?" Mark asked.

"It looks as if it might be clear for a day or so," Rebecca replied, glancing through the curtains.

"Maybe we could go check on the dam," Mark suggested to Jonathon.

"No," Rebecca retorted sharply. "I'll not have the men of this house forever traipsing around in this mud. None of you will go anywhere until you've had a chance to rest and regain your strength."

"But I feel as strong as an ox," Mark protested.

"If you're as strong as the oxen I see standing by the stable, you're not saying much," she flared.

Mark turned to Jonathon for support, but Jonathon merely smiled and looked the other way. "But Becky," Mark continued, "we have to go today. It might start raining again tomorrow."

"Then let it rain," she told him, returning to the table with a plate of food for Jonathon.

"But . . .'

"Give it up, little brother," Jonathon interrupted, putting a fork to the food. "It's no use arguing with a stubborn Scot."

Mark looked from one man to the other, trying to find someone to back him up. There was no one. He was forced to wait until the next day, when all three men rode out to check on the flooded fields and weakening dam. The trip became a daily one. Jonathon and Mark found the dam's structure was badly in need of fresh support. Clouds continued to linger overhead as the farmers came out in a desperate attempt to strengthen the dam's foundation. Rebecca watched the men ride out every day. She waited with Sarah for night to come, when the men would return home, tired and hungry. She knew Jonathon was worried about the mine. It was on the men's fourth morning out that Rebecca decided to ride over to see Ben.

"I don't think I'll be long," she told Sarah as she pulled her riding gloves on. "If you look after Matt for me until nightfall, I should be back by then."

"Are you sure you should go?" Sarah asked. "It's hard going, even for the short distance I come to get here."

"I'll take the high ground as often as I can, and I'll be

careful," Rebecca assured the older woman. "I've got to go before Jonathon decides *he* must. He's too busy, but the time will come when he feels he should go. This weather can't last forever."

Sarah nodded. "I'll expect you for dinner then."

"I'll be here."

Rebecca began to doubt her own words after riding a short distance. Her horse had difficulty getting through the mud. The going was much slower than she had anticipated. But she continued on, determined to save Jonathon the long journey. He had been working outside all through the winter months while she had remained indoors. It was time she began to help with this kind of work again.

Four hours passed before Rebecca reached the mine, and it was a dismal sight. The mud slides Ben spoke of had littered the ground with dirt and rock. It was a miracle that the entrance had remained free of the clutter. Dismounting, she looked up at the hill concealing the mine and wondered at how a good portion more of it had not come down. The constant battering of the wind and the large amount of rain the ground had been forced to absorb had been too much for the hill to withstand. She only hoped the badly beaten rise could hold the rest of the winter.

"Is Ben in the cave?" she asked Aaron, who came forward to take her horse.

"He's been there since dawn."

"Is there trouble?"

"None so far. He says the walls are holding up."

"Let's hope they continue to," she told him and moved off into the cave. Men were hard at work along the tunnel, but she didn't find Ben until she reached the deepest part. "Ben!"

Ben turned at her call and a grin broke over his dirty, unshaven face. "Taking advantage of the good weather to come see me?"

"You didn't think I'd miss the chance, did you? Have there been any problems?"

"Nope, or at least none to mention. We stopped the only problem as soon as it started." He took her elbow and led her a short distance further into the cavern before pointing to the ceiling. "See that crack? It started a week ago. It split open some, stopped, and hasn't done anything since."

Rebecca stared up at the gap in the rock. "You don't think there's any danger, do you?"

"No, but we put up some extra beams like these," he answered, indicating the long blocks of wood standing against the wall and braced across the ceiling above them. "Just in case."

Suddenly, the ground began to tremble. No one moved at first. They stood still, listening. Then someone yelled, and men started to run.

Ben grabbed Rebecca's arm, jerking her away from the crack as the rock began to split, spewing dirt and stone onto the cave floor. Lumber broke. Rocks fell. The cavern echoed with noise as the floor shook and the mud on top of the hill cascaded down its sides.

Rebecca never saw what made her trip. Her ankle twisted as she stepped on something, and her hand was torn from Ben's as he was carried on by his own momentum and fear.

Stunned, with her ankle throbbing, she sat on the floor looking around her. Confusion. Panic. Men were running, dirt was falling. Lanterns were crashing from their hooks on the walls to shatter on the rumbling ground.

Rebecca's mind froze, trying to grasp what was happening. From somewhere, Ben called her name. She opened her mouth to cry out, but a shower of dust and rock hit her from above. Ducking, she tried to protect her face, looking up just in time to see the beam overhead start to fall.

She lunged away, but the beam caught her shoulder. The blow sent her sprawling on her back, leaving her dazed and helpless as the brace holding the cross beam in place above her snapped and released a landslide of rock. Searing pain shot through Rebecca as the rock thundered down on top of her, choking her with its dust and pinning her to the floor with its weight. The supporting beam broke and shattered, bouncing violently on the floor before thudding to an abrupt halt on the slide of rock—and on Rebecca.

Agony ripped through her mind as the beam came to rest. Unconsciousness flooded over her as another spray of dirt fell across her face.

"Becky! Becky!" The voice echoed in her head and through the darkness around her. Rebecca stirred, crying out at the sharp pains that were ripping through her limbs.

She lay for a moment, gasping for breath, the pain sharpening her numbed mind. The mine. A cave-in. She squeezed her eyes tightly shut, trying to remember, trying to think.

Around her was darkness filled with sounds: Men moaning, the scratching of dirt and rock as it slid down walls and across the floor. She opened her eyes again to try to see something, anything, but blinked as dust blinded her and clogged her throat.

She coughed. A weight on her chest choked her. She tried to lift a hand to brush the dirt from her face but stopped as a burning pain leaped to life in her bruised body.

"Becky!"

Ben. It was Ben. She choked and coughed, calling out hoarsely. "Ben!"

"Keep talking," he responded, his voice echoing through the cavern.

"Here, Ben," she managed to call. "Here. I'm caught under something. I can't move." She coughed again. Her gasps brought more pain and breathlessness as the weight of the beam bore down on her ribcage.

The sounds of someone came near and suddenly Ben appeared, a dark shadow out of the blackness. "You here?"

"Aye, it's me."

He fumbled in his pocket and came out with a match. He struck it, blinking against the light. Rebecca lay before him. A slide of dirt and rock partially covered her and a section of beam lay across her chest. Her left arm was completely buried, probably broken.

Ben reached out to brush some of the dirt from her face. "You've got yourself pinned good, Becky. I'm going to see if I can find someone to help me get you out. I can't do it myself."

"How many are there here?"

"Don't know, but you can hear them shuffling around. They won't be hard to find. We'll have to get together to start digging. It'll take time." He put out the match. "Lay as still as you can. Don't try to move. We don't want this beam to shift any more of its weight on you. I'll go get some men and try to find lanterns that aren't broken."

Rebecca listened to him scramble away. She had to keep still. She shut her eyes, trying to close out the pain. Her whole left side ached, especially her arm. Her head swam dizzily. Why had this happened? What had happened? She had to get back to the house. Jonathon would be waiting for her.

Time passed without her knowing, slipping by until someone came toward her once more. A light filtered through the darkness. Ben. It was Ben. He was coming back.

Ben set the lantern down a short distance away from her and came to kneel by her side. "How you feel?"

She shook her head vaguely, forcing herself to speak. "Numb. I feel numb."

"Any pain?"

"My arm."

He put a reassuring hand on her shoulder. "You just lie still. We'll get you out from under there."

Jonathon stood on the porch, staring out into the night. Rebecca wasn't back yet. He frowned. When he returned from the dam earlier in the evening, Sarah told

251

him Rebecca had gone to the mine. It didn't surprise him. He knew she was as worried about the mine as he was.

Dinner passed. Rebecca told Sarah she would be back for dinner. Jonathon turned as Mark came out to stand beside him.

"Maybe it took longer to ride over there than she thought," Mark suggested.

"Maybe," Jonathon agreed, bending to pat Dingo, who had followed him out onto the porch. He smiled at the mongrel. Dingo was as lost without Rebecca as he was. When they returned from the dam, the big dog ran through the house trying to find Rebecca. He had searched the house twice since.

Mark looked up to the dark sky, where only an occasional star could be seen as masses of clouds moved overhead. "You don't think she'll try to come back in the dark, do you?"

Jonathon followed Mark's gaze upward. "No. She knows better than that." As he said the words, doubt stabbed through him. If it wasn't for Matt, Jonathon believed she would stay at the mine. Rebecca was a new mother, and Jonathon feared her desire to be with her son would overrule caution.

"Jon, look!" Mark said, pointing across the plateau.

Relief flooded through Jonathon. A light was coming toward them, a light tied to a saddle.

Mark grinned. "There she is now. We've been worrying for nothing."

The two brothers' feelings of elation quickly subsided. It wasn't Rebecca who dismounted from the horse at the rail. It was a man. Aaron.

Jonathon hurried down the steps. "What is it?"

"The mine. There's been a cave-in."

"A cave-in!" Mark exclaimed. "Becky?"

"She's trapped inside with about twenty others," Aaron replied. "They've been working on the entrance since it happened, trying to break through. But when I left . . ." He shook his head.

"Do they know what caused it?" Jonathon demanded.

"They think it was the weight of the water the hill absorbed. They say it finally gave in."

Jonathon looked across to the plateau. "Mark, saddle my horse. I'm going over there."

"I'm coming, too," Mark said.

"No, you stay here," Jonathon snapped. "There's work to be done on the dam. I'll go alone. Aaron, you stay here. Get some rest."

Ben cupped the water from the underground spring in his hands and splashed it lightly on Rebecca's face. She stirred from her semi-conscious stupor and blinked up at him as he smoothed the water across her forehead.

It had taken a long time to work Rebecca out from under the beam and the rock. She had slipped into the oblivion of unconsciousness during the digging and had remained that way until after they freed and moved her to a spot by the spring. Since then she had awakened often, staying alert only minutes at a time before slipping back into a daze. Her forehead was hot under Ben's hand. Fever. He frowned. He wanted to stay with her, but knew his presence meant nothing to her. Not anymore. She no longer realized when he was with her or when he wasn't. He could do her more good by staying with the men.

Gathering together the men who were still able to dig, Ben set them to work. They had to try to break through to the outside. They needed fresh air.

The work was slow and hard. Rock slides continued to interrupt their progress, but the men pressed on, pounding at the rock that had cut off their escape. They took breaks between shifts of what they judged to be a quarter of an hour. No one had a watch to time it exactly, and Ben was glad. Without a watch, no one would know how long they were trapped. No one could keep track of how much longer they would remain locked inside, or how much time was left before the air became too heavy to breathe.

Outside, Jonathon looked down at his watch. Hours had passed since the cave-in. Though the digging had been continuous, there was still no sign of breaking through the barrier. He shoved the timepiece back in his pocket and warmed his hands on a cup of coffee. When he arrived, men were working on both entrances of the mine at the same time. He had stopped the double effort and started the men digging on one side in half-hour shifts.

Jonathon had only just finished working his shift. During his time with a pick, there was a strong hope of breaking in, but the half-hour ended, and still the wall of rock stood between them and those trapped inside.

How many were alive? Had anyone been killed? Was Rebecca safe? Was Ben? What was happening inside the cavern? Questions buzzed around his head, and Jonathon drained his coffee. There were no answers for him or for the others huddled around the fires. They all had to wait to discover the fate of family and friends.

To worsen matters, the rain had begun again. It was a light drizzle that slowly soaked through their clothes to touch their skin with freezing fingers. Above the campfires, heavy clouds rolled in, a terrifying sign. At any moment, another torrent of water might be released and end all hope of getting through to the people trapped in the mine. New rains would loosen more mud, send down more rock slides, and obliterate what had already been dug away.

Jonathon put his cup down. It was time for his shift to work again. They had to get through this time. He strode to the wall, accepting a pick from a mud-spattered, weary man.

Tools changed hands. As the shifts changed, an echoing sound was heard. Everyone held his breath.

Inside. The noise was coming from inside.

The echo of a pick falling behind the wall rang again. With a wild yell, the men outside dove to the barrier, their picks flying into action to pry it away.

Inside, the men heard the battering onslaught of picks and fell back to stare as the wall before them opened up. Piece by piece, the wall crumbled away, and they held their breath in case what they saw was not real. It was real! With weary cries, they embraced the men who charged through the opening.

Jonathon was among them, fighting his way through the rock in a frenzy until he was grasping Ben by the shoulders. "Are you all right?"

"I'm fine. I'm fine," Ben answered. Tears of relief burned the backs of his eyes. "But Becky," he said, "she's hurt bad. We've got to get her out of here."

Jonathon followed Ben back into the cavern, falling to his knees beside Rebecca. He spoke her name softly, but she did not respond.

"Her arm's broken, and maybe some ribs," Ben said. "But the fever's the worst thing."

"See that a way is cleared up ahead, Ben. I'll carry her out," Jonathon told him, picking Rebecca carefully up in his arms.

Outside, men and women were shouting and crying, clinging to each other. Families were united, friends clasped each other. The men had survived the cave-in. They were alive.

Jonathon carried Rebecca through the jubilant crowd, making his way to the cabin they had lived in only months before. He put her down on a bed, and, with one of the tent town women who had followed him, he went to work. Rebecca's arm was set, and her bruises and wounds were washed and bandaged. Lying in a fevered state, she was covered with blankets and forced to drink broth while cool compresses were placed on her forehead.

Hours turned into days and days stretched into a week as she tossed in delirium. Jonathon stayed by her side, moving another bed into the room with her to be with her even when Ben took over while he rested.

Ben recovered after only a day's rest. Work on the mine was suspended until further notice, leaving him free to stay with Rebecca and Jonathon. Neither man spoke much as they sat beside Rebecca, listening to her harsh breathing and to the rain pelting the sodden earth outside. The storm seemed to increase with Rebecca's fever. As it kicked up force and turned into a whirling downpour, Rebecca's fever peaked.

Jonathon fought the fever with her, staying at her side until, at last, her restless stirrings stopped and she fell into a deep, peaceful sleep. Throughout the next day, he sat anxiously by the bed, smoothing her hair away from her pale face and watching her even breathing.

The wild wind outside died down to a gentle breeze, and Rebecca opened her eyes. It was the beginning of recovery, a time of healing that would pass slowly. Jonathon thought ahead, of returning her to their home and the comforts there. But it would be several days before she could be moved and several more before she was strong enough to be on her feet again.

32

"It hasn't rained in over a week," Mark told Rebecca as she lay in her own bed. A month had passed since the cave-in, but she was still weak and slept most of the time.

"And the dam?" she asked.

"It's still standing," Mark answered with a proud grin. "If we hadn't been able to reach it during that break in the rain, it never would have made it. There would have been too much pressure on the walls."

The door opened and Jonathon entered, carrying Matt. "Your son has come to see you," he told Rebecca, sitting down on the bed and holding the baby while she put out her free hand to stroke the child's soft skin.

"Hello, Matthew," she murmured, letting the nearly four-month-old boy grasp hold of her finger.

Mark leaned over Jonathon's shoulder. "You know, I think he's going to look like me."

Rebecca laughed. "You could hardly call that surprising when you and your brother look so much alike."

"I know, but it's not just looks. It's personality. He's always smiling and happy, content with his lot," Mark said. "Not at all like his father—grumpy, hard to get along with, never satisfied."

"When did you say you were going back to England?" Jonathon asked.

Mark smiled but said nothing. That evening, sitting in the study with Jonathon, he broached the subject of his return. "I didn't want to mention anything in front of Becky earlier today, Jon, but I've been giving thought to returning to England. Much as I like it here, I can't stay on indefinitely. I've got my farm to think of.''

Jonathon sat back and nodded. "We'll be sorry to see you go, Mark, but we understand you have your own life to lead. However, don't feel the need to rush off. We'll have you as long as you care to stay.''

"It's not that I feel I'm unwanted," Mark reassured him. "Though I have to get back, I can't make up my mind exactly when I should go.''

Jonathon's eyebrow raised as he studied his brother. "Is there a reason for your indecision, aside from the fields, perhaps?''

The younger brother flushed and ran a hand quickly through his hair. "Yes, there is. It's Alison.''

Jonathon smiled and put his fingertips together.

"Why are you smiling?" Mark demanded.

"Because Rebecca told me this would happen months ago.''

"Rebecca? But how?''

"Don't ask me," Jonathon replied, shrugging. "Women seem to know about such things without being told.''

"You don't object?" Mark asked.

"Should I?''

"When I arrived here . . .''

"When you arrived here, Alison Cunningham was a very different young lady," Jonathon interrupted. "I don't know what's passed between the two of you, but whatever has taken place made her into a new woman. She's matured, grown up.''

"She has changed some," Mark admitted.

"As have you.''

"Me? How do you mean?''

"Nothing definable. Let's just say you've become a better man in this past year. Coming to Australia has given you a broader outlook on life. You've seen others suffer. You've built something out of nothing, and you've worked to save it. All you've experienced has opened your eyes wider.''

"I can see some truth in that, but it doesn't help me. I

still don't know what to do."

"Do you love her?"

"I think I do."

"And she you?"

"I don't know."

"Haven't you asked her yet?"

"No."

"No!? What have you been discussing these past months if not love?"

Mark colored. "At first, it was a battle of wits. Later, it became more friendly. We talked about England and of each other and our hopes and dreams."

"And it was then you discovered you liked her?"

"I think I've always liked her, but now, I feel, I've grown to love her."

"And you don't know what to do?"

The younger brother shook his head.

"Why don't you ask her to marry you?"

Mark looked doubtful. "I don't know. She might not like being married to a farmer."

"You won't know unless you ask."

"But she might say yes."

Jonathon laughed. "Isn't yes what you want her to say?"

"Yes—and no."

"Why no?"

"Because she's so different, so, I can't explain it." Mark began to pace the floor. "It seems to me that she'd rather live in the city than in the country."

"With the balls and dances and high society."

"Yes."

Jonathon tapped his fingers thoughtfully. "I do owe you something that might help."

"Such as?"

"Money."

"Money?"

"A salary. You've worked hard for us, giving all your time and effort to the growing of our crops. In order to do that, you had to leave your own farm in England in the hands of another man. You're paying him a good deal of money, aren't you? You too should be paid."

"But I don't want your money."

"Nevertheless, you shall have it. You've earned it, and I'll hear no arguments otherwise." Jonathon rose and walked to the window. "You'll be reimbursed for the amount you've paid your friend who is watching your farm. You'll also be paid for the cost of the crops you would have harvested in England, and you'll receive a substantial wage for all the work you've done for us. With that, you ought to be able to return and purchase more land."

"More land?"

"Or you could invest it in something else."

"I don't understand."

"If you're worried about Alison being happy on a farm, you should take steps to insure you'll be able to take her on a holiday at least once a year. That will take money. With a larger yield from your crops, or with an additional source of income, you could afford such an expense."

"It sounds reasonable."

"Of course, it does," Jonathon retorted, turning to face his brother once more.

"But what if she says no?" Mark asked.

"You won't be the first man to be turned down. Others have suffered that fate and lived on."

"Jonathon, I'm sorry."

Jonathon held up a hand. "The love I had for Arthur Boyd's daughter was nothing compared to my love for Rebecca. I was a fool to ever fall for such an empty shell of a woman."

"You have grown to love Becky, then. That means you won't be returning to England."

"For now."

"Jonathon?"

"I'm going, Mark," Jonathon stated firmly. "I have to."

Mark's face grew unusually sober. "Jon, in the end,

if you do go, be sure. Be sure it's what you want to do. Once you go, there'll be no turning back. Once you've done what you feel you must, it will be over, finished. If you regret your actions later, you won't be able to change what you've done—any more than Arthur Boyd can change what he did to you."

Jonathon turned from his brother, but he continued to listen.

"You spoke earlier of changing. Haven't you changed? And for the better? Instead of hating Arthur Boyd, you might consider being thankful to him. He forced you to be what you are now. Because of him, you obtained what you now own."

Mark strode forward to stand beside his brother.

"Look out there, Jon. Do you see anything to hate? I don't. You've got more here than most men dream of. It started as a dream, but you made it real, because you were forced to come here by a man you hate. Don't throw it all away, Jon. Don't give up what you've got to complete a worthless action that can only bring destruction and more pain to you."

33

"The weather in this country is nothing like I've ever seen before," Mark declared as he made ready with the other men to leave the house. "The sky holds nothing but rain for months, then it clears up and there's nothing but sunshine. What comes next?"

"Let's hope nothing," Jonathon answered, turning as they reached the front door to watch Rebecca and Sarah ascend the staircase. Rebecca's arm was still in a sling, but she was stronger now, able to be up and about.

The men had taken the first gold shipment of the spring into town the week before, making their way across the bush under skies that had been clear for over a month. When they returned, it was with two wagon-loads of furniture. Rebecca was now busy arranging the house. Jonathon had no fear of her straining herself. Sarah kept a close watch on her.

Jonathon smiled and returned his attention to the men. "What do you think, Ben? Are we going to make it through the mine today?"

Ben snorted and went down the steps toward the horses. "I'm beginning to think there's more rock on the inside than out," he answered shaking his head. "It sure will be nice when we can start digging gold again. It just isn't the same when you're digging dirt."

Jonathon laughed and waved to Jeremiah, who was over by the stables near the sheep. It was shearing time, and Jeremiah had thrown himself into the work greedily. Coming home from the mine the night before, Jonathon had stopped to talk with him.

Jonathon waved to his younger brother as he swung into his saddle. "See you for dinner tonight, Mark."

"You will that," Mark agreed with a wide smile. "After a day in the fields, there's nothing to keep me from Becky's and Sarah's cooking."

The men laughed and parted, striking out across the plateau in their separate directions to begin another day of work. Ben fell in beside Jonathon. The two men rode quietly along for some distance, enjoying the crisp morning air, until Ben motioned to the horizon.

"Rider coming," Ben said. "Who do you suppose it might be at this hour?"

Jonathon drew up his horse, waiting before speaking. "It's Alison."

"I reckon young Mark will be glad to hear that," Ben commented dryly, rubbing a hand over his unshaven jaw. "I was talking to Bill Mallory last night. He says Mark's been keeping an eye on the hills by the fields almost as much as he's been keeping an eye on the plowing."

Jonathon nodded. He had noticed Mark wandering about the house with a wistful expression on his face.

Alison greeted them. "Good morning."

"Good morning, Alison," Jonathon greeted, tipping his hat. "Out for a ride?"

"My first in months," she agreed. "We've been under water at Cunningham House all winter."

"Mark thought the rain might be the reason he hasn't seen you lately."

Alison's face lit up. "He's still here then?"

"Of course," Jonathon answered. "He's in the fields right now. You might want to stop by and see him."

"I will," she agreed eagerly. "I think I'll go right away."

Ben watched her move off, urging her horse into a gallop. "I wonder who's going to be more happy to see who?"

Jonathon grinned. "I expect I'll be able to judge that question tonight."

Shortly after dinner, Mark appeared in Jonathon's

study.

"Can I come in, Jonathon?"

Jonathon put his pen down and pushed the books aside. "Please do, little brother. I can use a break."

"What are you working on?" Mark inquired.

"The books. Checking our profits against our losses. I'm glad to say we are very much in the black."

Mark smiled, but his mind was elsewhere.

"I'm sure you didn't come to discuss balancing our books."

"No," Mark agreed quickly. "Actually, I—I came to talk to you."

Jonathon smiled. "So she found you."

Mark started. "You knew she came today?"

"Yes. Ben and I met her on our way to the mine this morning," Jonathon replied. "But tell me, did you ask her?"

"I did. And she said yes. But she wants me to talk with her father."

"That is standard procedure. Does Richard Cunningham know Alison has been seeing you?"

Mark frowned. "No, he doesn't. As a matter of fact, he told her to stay away from us. Now she's worried about how he's going to take the news."

"So he still holds a grudge against Rebecca and me."

"Obviously," Mark agreed. "What other reason would he have for denying Alison the right to come here?" He paced the floor anxiously. "Surely, he can't include me in his grudge. I wasn't even here."

Jonathon looked down at the papers before him. "I should think not," he replied with more confidence than he felt. "When are you going to see Richard Cunningham?"

"Tomorrow night. Alison told me she would soften him up a bit before I got there."

Jonathon wished him luck. Later, when he retired to his room for the night, he expressed his doubts to Rebecca. "I don't know how Richard Cunningham will accept Mark. Certainly not with the open arms he and Alison seem to expect."

Rebecca pulled a brush through her long hair as she sat at the dressing table. "Alison usually gets what she wants from him, Jonathon."

"Even when she's disobeyed his wishes for over a year by coming to see us?" Jonathon shook his head. "No father appreciates disobedience in his children, no matter how much he loves them."

"He can be a hard man," Rebecca admitted, stopping the motions of her brush. "Oh, Jonathon, I hate to think that what I did will interfere with Mark and Alison's plans."

Jonathon put a reassuring hand on her shoulder. "It wasn't you alone. I had a hand in it, too."

"But it was I who began the trouble. If I hadn't run away . . ."

"If you hadn't run away, you wouldn't be sitting in your own house now, and Mark and Alison never would have met." He shook his head decisively. "No. You were not wrong. Richard Cunningham has no right to hold a grudge against people who try to make a life of their own, any more than he has a right to stand in Mark and Alison's way if they wish to marry."

She sighed. "I hope you're right, Jonathon. I hope my uncle will think the same."

"I hope so, too," he told her, drawing her to her feet. "Perhaps I should go to see your uncle to speak with him first. I might be able to ease the way for Mark."

Rebecca shook her head doubtfully. "I think not, Jonathon. Or at least not yet. Let Mark go see him. Maybe we're wrong in our judgment. Maybe we're being too critical of my uncle. He might not object."

"But if he does?"

Rebecca dropped her eyes. "We will have to wait and see."

Wait they did, sitting together in Jonathon's study the next night when Mark left to go to Cunningham House. They sat and allowed their minds to wander over the year behind them, over what they had gained, learned, and experienced.

They reconsidered their positions, wondering idly

what would have happened and where they would be if their paths had not crossed, if they had not married. It was useless wondering. They *had* met, they *had* married, and through no fault or wish of Jonathon's or Rebecca's, they had fallen in love. Their love had enabled them to accomplish many things. These things had affected other people as well as themselves. They were only just beginning to understand how much their actions could influence others. Their fears for the results of that influence affected Mark and Alison.

The minutes dragged by with eternal slowness, but neither spoke. The longer Mark was away, the better were his chances.

Suddenly, the front door opened and was firmly slammed back into place. Jonathon's and Rebecca's eyes met. Their hearts and minds told them what they feared. The study door was flung open, and Jonathon rose to face Mark.

"He threw me out!" Mark exclaimed. "He actually threw me out. He told me I wasn't good enough for his daughter—that no Gray was. He told me if I ever attempted to see her again . . ."

Rebecca rose from her chair. "And Alison? Was she there?"

"He sent her to her room. He said she'd get over it, that what she felt for me was mere infatuation."

Jonathon fought to control the anger seething inside him. "Start from the beginning."

Mark ran a hand through his hair and dropped down into a chair. "I went to Cunningham House and met Alison outside on the front porch. She told me her father was expecting a visitor whom she wanted him to meet, a visitor who was interested in asking for her hand in marriage."

"She didn't tell him who you were?" Jonathon inquired.

"No. He didn't know until I walked into the room."

Rebecca drew her breath in sharply. What a shock it must have been for her uncle to see Jonathon's brother walk into his house!

266

"And then?" Jonathon prodded.

Mark shook his head. "He turned white as a sheet and blew up. He was red with rage. I never had a chance to try to explain, nor did Alison. He sent her to her room as soon as he saw me."

"Did you try to talk to him?"

"I couldn't get a word in."

"So you left?"

Mark nodded. "I wasn't looking for a fight. To tell the truth, I wasn't ready for one."

Rebecca watched Jonathon turn from the window. She didn't know what he was thinking. Fearing he would say something he would regret later, she hurried to speak first. "Mark, you must realize what a shock it would have been for Uncle Richard to see you walk in," she told him. "You know how he feels about me and Jonathon. You also know he forbid Alison to come here. He was probably hurt and confused."

"But what am I going to do?" he pleaded.

"Wait," she answered firmly. "You must wait. Give him a few days. Let him think it over. Give him a chance to go over in his mind what has happened, and let him talk to Alison. This is all very sudden and unexpected for him. He was caught unprepared. Perhaps, with a little time, he may change his mind."

"Do you really think so?" Mark asked.

"I think it's a possibility you shouldn't overlook," she answered. "Now why don't you go to bed? Try to get some rest." Mark looked doubtful. She squeezed his arm and smiled encouragement. "My father always told me how dark it is before the dawn. Things could not get worse, so they have to get better."

Mark stood slowly and looked at her before impulsively kissing her cheek. Her words were consoling, a safety line thrown to a drowning man. "Thank you, Becky." He turned to look at Jonathon but left without saying anything to his brother.

"You don't believe a word of that," Jonathon said as soon as the door was closed behind Mark.

"Don't I? How do you know that what I said isn't

true?''

"How do you know it is?'' Jonathon demanded angrily. "You shouldn't build up his hopes and dreams when you can't make them come true.''

"Maybe I can.''

"How?''

"I can go to see my uncle. I'm the one he's angry with, not you or your brother. Perhaps I can persuade him to reconsider Mark's proposal, to look at things differently.

"Highly unlikely.''

"I can try.''

"Yes, you can try. You can try offering him the moon, too, if you like.''

Rebecca hesitated as a new thought struck her. "Maybe not the moon, Jonathon. But there is gold.''

Jonathon stared at her. "What did you say?''

"My uncle has always wanted to find gold. The mine has been stripped of most of its worth, but I could offer him a part of my own share.''

"I can't believe what I'm hearing!'' Jonathon exclaimed. "Do you think you can buy people the way you buy cattle and sheep? Who do you think you are? A princess with a real kingdom at her command?''

Rebecca's temper flared. "I bought you, Jonathon Gray, didn't I?'' she stormed. "You certainly came cheap enough. Forty-five percent of a gold mine and half a share in all the earnings. Yet you're not unhappy. You have everything a man could want: money, property, and a woman to share your bed—all that for being my husband and giving me your name.'' She laughed. "And you say I'm acting like a princess! Are you any better than I am? You sold your name in order to achieve your own vicious goals, goals which will only destroy you instead of bringing you happiness!''

Jonathon pulled himself up to his full height, his blue eyes blazing with unleashed fury. "Are you through?''

"No, I'm not,'' she retorted. "If it wasn't for Mark, I'd send you back right now. I'd tell you to take your share and get out of my life, get out of my life and go back to the sweet little daughter of your Arthur Boyd in England. I'd tell you to go back to her and impress her with your great deeds. Just think, Jonathon, you can prove to her what a great man you are by telling her how you married, had a son just so you could come back to her!"

Jonathon slapped Rebecca. The force of his slap knocked her back against a chair.

Rebecca caught herself, and held a hand up to her burning mouth. Trembling, she drew herself up. "You can beat me if you like. You can beat me until I die. It's your right as my husband. If you don't do that, if you don't kill me, I'm going to Cunningham House and I'll try to persuade my uncle to change his mind. If I can't, maybe I'll offer him gold. Maybe I won't. But I'm going—for Mark and for Alison. I only hope their marriage will be better than this mockery we're living."

Jonathon watched her as she went out the door. His hands clenched as the door closed, and he brought his fists crashing down on his desk.

The time had come, the time when Rebecca and he would cross swords about his going to England. He hadn't expected it to be so soon. But here it was.

He didn't know Rebecca believed him to still be in love with Melissa Boyd. He didn't know she believed he still wanted to go back to England for Melissa, believed he wanted to prove to Arthur Boyd's daughter how important he had become. How the thought must eat at her, and how it must hurt her!

Jonathon paced the room for an hour after Rebecca left, mulling over his thoughts. He would have to make it up to her somehow. He had to prove to her that he loved *her* and not Melissa Boyd. He could not let her believe he would use her that way. It pained him to think she could believe such a thing of him.

When he climbed the stairs to their room, his eyes were filled with confused pain. He had to explain. He had to try to make Rebecca understand why he must go.

He hesitated outside the door but forced himself to go inside. Rebecca wasn't there. She was gone. She had left their room and gone to their son's.

34

Rebecca waited until she was certain Jonathon had left the house before she unlocked her door and returned to their room the next morning. She dressed quickly and quietly in her riding outfit, slipping down the stairs and out the kitchen door, nodding a brief good morning to Sarah and telling her she was going for a ride. At the stable, Sarah's oldest son, who was their livery man, saddled her horse. Soon, she was on her way across the plateau toward Cunningham House.

She forced her thoughts away from the scene with Jonathon the night before. It was enough that she had spent the remaining hours of the night and the early hours of the morning thinking about what had been said. Now it was time to think of Mark and Alison. It would be strange to walk back into the house she had sworn never to enter again, but it must be done. However, she would not beg for what she asked. She would never again throw herself on the mercy of Richard Cunningham. He would want her to beg, want her to confess and admit she had been wrong. Rebecca was determined not to let her uncle know how she felt. He must never know what a grave mistake she had made.

Tears stung her eyes as she admitted to herself, what a fool she had been to ever propose to Jonathon Gray. She should have known no good would come of it. He had had his plans and she had hers, and they were never meant to be mixed together. She would have been better off remaining single and fighting for her rights instead of entrapping herself in a gigantic lie. How could she ever have let herself believe Jonathon loved her? He didn't love her, at least not as she loved him. His true love was *in* England—and *for* England.

He would never settle in Australia, as she had begun to hope he might. He would never leave behind the country he was born in, never leave it and all it held for him. She had been foolish to believe he could or would want to. How could she have thought time would change his mind and his feelings?

Cunningham House loomed before her. Rebecca strengthened her resolve. Richard Cunningham would never know. He would never know Rebecca McGregor regretted any part of what she had done.

The house looked dark and forbidding as she rode toward it, but Rebecca urged her horse on. A flash of yellow caught her eye. She turned her head to see Dingo running along beside her. She smiled sadly. They were both returning for one last time. Dismounting, she climbed the steps, with Dingo following her to the door where, from long experience, he lay down on the porch to wait. The big dog had never entered Cunningham House. Rebecca envied the mongrel that.

She raised her hand to the knocker and let the metal knob fall. It was several minutes before she heard footsteps. When the door opened, Elaine stood before her.

"Good day, Elaine," Rebecca greeted coolly. "I've come to see Uncle Richard if he's in."

Elaine hesitated, eyeing her cousin before stepping back from the door. "He's in his study," she told Rebecca curtly. "When you're through, you can let yourself out."

Rebecca nodded, biting back the retort on her tongue and walking to the study door. She knocked and heard her uncle answer, bidding her come in. Taking a deep breath, she swept the door open, entering the room to find him bent over some paperwork. "Good morning, Uncle Richard."

Cunningham looked up with a start and jumped to his feet. "So you've come back."

"Not to stay. Only to talk."

"Talk? About what?"

"About Alison and Mark Gray."

"There is nothing to be said."

"I disagree."

Richard Cunningham glared at her. "Who are you to disagree in the matters of this house?"

She ignored his retort and plunged on. "Listen to me, Uncle Richard. They love each other very much. Would you stand in the way of their happiness just because of what I've done?"

He laughed. "What you and Jonathon Gray have done, you mean. You took what should have been rightfully mine."

"Rightfully yours?" Rebecca repeated. "Since when did anything I own rightfully belong to you?"

"Since your father left you in my charge."

"Yes, he left me in your charge, but he did not give me to you or your family to do with as you see fit." Cunningham's face reddened, but she continued. "Why must you force your own unhappiness on others? Why must your coming to Australia against your will be used against others?"

Cunningham stiffened. "I don't know what you're saying."

"Then I'll explain," she reasoned. "You're the second son of a wealthy man, Uncle Richard. The truth is, when he died, your father left you nothing. So you came to Australia to hide, to escape the humiliation of having others of your class see you work for a living. But before you left, you had to collect some things.

"It was then you met my aunt. You loved her and brought her here. For her sake, you tried to make something of yourself. You tried to become a wealthy man to prove to her and yourself that you didn't need your father's money." Rebecca met her uncle's eyes. "You failed miserably at becoming wealthy by English standards, but you found enough here to make you a respectable member of Australian society."

"Enough!" Cunningham cried, pounding his fist on his desk.

"No, it's not enough," Rebecca stormed. "I can

understand your bitterness at never achieving your goal, but I cannot understand why you're putting your feelings before your own daughter's happiness."

"I said enough!" he thundered. "I will not listen to such insolence from you. You have no right to speak to me in such tones, especially after I've given you a home and a place to live. You should be grateful."

"You gave me a place to live, but this never was a home to me. I was a slave who did your daughters' bidding. You know what it's like to have to shove your pride aside, so you should understand why I had to leave. Can I help it if, when I left, I stumbled onto a gold mine? Can you hold a bit of luck against me?"

"You made a fool of me in front of the whole town. Everyone knows you ran off and married Jonathon Gray."

"I did not run off and marry him. I married him after I found my gold, months after."

"But he went along with you. He helped you."

Rebecca set her jaw firmly but said nothing. She would not tell her uncle of their marriage, of their working agreement.

"There, by your silence, you admit it."

"I admit nothing. Jonathon helped me because he's my husband," Rebecca countered. "Are you afraid Mark Gray might be as fortunate as Jonathon, afraid he might be able to give your daughter what you were never able to? Is that why you're willing to stand in the way of their marriage?"

"There will be no marriage," Cunningham declared. "She is young and stubborn. She doesn't know what she wants. In time, she'll come to know it was right that I stopped this nonsense. She'll learn with time that she was not in love. She is only infatuated."

Rebecca shook her head sadly. "If you believe that, then you're more of a fool than I thought."

Cunningham flushed. "Get out."

Rebecca remained completely unruffled. "It will be my pleasure to leave this house. But before I go, a word of advice. If I were you, Uncle Richard, I would reconsider my decision concerning Alison and Mark.''

She moved to the door without looking back, closing it behind her with a finality that told her she would never again return.

The hall was empty. For a moment, she hesitated before the stairs leading to the bedrooms. She would like to have seen Alison, but she dared not try. Not only was there nothing she could say to her cousin to console her, she had worn out her welcome.

Once outside, she mounted her horse and turned away from Cunningham House. Dingo ran on ahead of her. She had tried. The decision was now up to Richard Cunningham. If he steadfastly refused, there was no predicting what Mark might do. He was enough like his brother to take what he wanted. Rebecca feared for him.

During the next two weeks, Rebecca moved from the master bedroom to the one beside Matthew's and succeeded in keeping herself as distant from Jonathon as possible. She saw him at meals and at other times during the day, but she always avoided being alone when he was in the house unless she was locked securely in her room.

For the first few days, Jonathon made an effort to see Rebecca alone, but she made it clear that she wanted no part of him and maintained her distance. Given no choice, he was forced to relent. Instead, he decided to wait for an opportunity. She couldn't keep him at arm's length forever.

As their separation continued, Jonathon often received anxious looks from Mark and the other members of the household, but he kept his silence. Mark in particular was worried about the rift between his brother and wife. He feared their parting was due to him. Despite his anxiety over Jonathon and Rebecca, he found his thoughts more occupied by Alison than with the tension in the house. He had accepted Rebecca's advice to wait, but how long could he be expected to remain immobilized? He hadn't seen Alison since the night he went to Cunningham House. Was her father punishing her? Would Richard Cunningham attempt to send his daughter away so Mark could no longer see her? Mark was tormented. He didn't know what to do, but he knew he wouldn't be able to sit still much longer.

Another week slid by without event. Even with the high emotionality surrounding them, they continued with their work. The mine was back in operation, the crops were planted and fertilized, and the stock was back on grazing land. Rebecca was glad Mark had the fields to keep his mind occupied, because she knew he was worrying about Alison. She longed to try to comfort him, but there was nothing she could do or say to help. Like him, she found herself wondering what punishment her uncle would inflict on Alison. She couldn't believe he would abuse the young girl physically, but the mental anguish the man could cause his own daughter was unlimited.

Facing another week of the standoff, Rebecca considered going to Cunningham House to try to see Alison. Her plans were halted abruptly when Sarah opened the bedroom door and showed Alison in.

"Alison!" Rebecca cried, jumping to her feet.

Alison ran to her with tears in her eyes. "Rebecca! Oh, Rebecca, what am I going to do?"

Rebecca held the sobbing girl for a moment, quieting her and leading her to a chair. "Before we try to decide what must be done," she told Alison, "you must tell me what happened and how you came to be here."

"Elaine has been watching me closely ever since Mark came," Alison answered, wiping the tears away. "I haven't had a moment's peace, and I haven't been able to leave the house. Today, I made up an excuse to go to the stables. When I was there, I saddled a horse and rode straight to you."

Rebecca grimmaced. "Uncle Richard won't like that."

"I don't care! I had to do it. I couldn't stay there any longer!"

Rebecca nodded. "I know," she said, squeezing Alison's hand in reassurance. "You can stay here if you like. We won't make you go back." Alison clasped Rebecca's hand thankfully, but Rebecca waved a warning finger. "But if you choose to stay, you'll have to make a decision."

"About what?"

"About you and Mark. You have to decide whether you love him enough to elope with him, go back to England, and live with him."

"I do love him," Alison answered emphatically.

"But do you love him enough?" Rebecca queried. "It will mean disobeying your father, leaving your home and the only country you've ever known. You'll have to live an entirely different life. I've lived in the country, Alison. It's not easy, and it's nothing like what you're used to."

"Mark and I talked about it."

"And?"

Alison swallowed hard. "I don't want to disobey father, Rebecca, but I do love Mark. I know I can be a good wife to him."

"Are you sure, Alison? Are you absolutely sure?"

"Yes. I'm sure."

Rebecca smiled. "Then I think you ought to tell him. Tell him to come back here and get ready to go to town. You're going to be married immediately, before Uncle Richard discovers you're gone and tries to stop you."

"You're right. I'll go right away."

Rebecca followed Alison down the stairs. Sarah joined her as Alison raced off. "It's all right, Sarah," Rebecca assured her. "They're going to be married."

"Praise the Lord," Sarah declared, clasping her hands together. "I'm so glad. They're good for each other."

"Aye, they are. I only hope they'll be able to reach town in time."

"In time to be married?"

"They'll have to do it before my uncle gets there."

"If they're only going to town just to be married, they don't have to go at all." Rebecca turned to look at Sarah in surprise. "The parson is out at the tent town right now. He arrived yesterday and is planning to stay through Sunday to be with the people and hold a service."

Rebecca burst into laughter, laughing as she hadn't in weeks. "Then they will go to the mine and be wed without delay."

"Should I send my son on to tell the parson they're coming?"

"Perhaps you should. It would be better if he's prepared."

Three hours later, Rebecca, Mark, and Alison rode up to the mine to find not only the parson waiting but Jonathon and Ben as well. None of them wasted time, turning immediately to the parson to have the ceremony begin. It was done quickly, as Rebecca's and Jonathon's had been. When it was over, Mark was smiling but concerned. "What now, Jon? Where should we go?"

"For now, back to the house," Jonathon replied. "We're going to have to face Richard Cunningham sooner or later. I'd rather be on our own ground when we do it."

"How soon do you think he'll come?" Alison asked as they mounted again, happiness radiating from her despite her worries.

"It's difficult to say," Jonathon told her. "Was he home when you left?"

"No, he was at the mine."

"We have time then," he commented. "But don't worry. No matter when he comes, we'll deal with him. Nothing will happen to pull you two apart."

Rebecca took Alison to Mark's room as soon as they reached the house. "We'll have to send someone to collect your clothes. Will Elaine pack them?"

"I think so," Alison answered hesitantly. "She

wasn't very pleased with the announcement of Mark's proposal, but I don't think she would begrudge me having my clothing.''

"Good. For now, you'll have to make do with what you have on and some of mine. You're a bit taller and thinner than I, but we'll manage.''

Alison grasped her cousin's hands shyly. "Rebecca, how can I ever thank you and Jonathon?''

"You have nothing to thank us for. We only want you to be happy.''

"I will be.''

The door opened and Mark came in, awkward embarrassment coloring his face. "Jonathon sent me up. He thinks it best for both Alison and me to remain up here for now. He said he'll send dinner up. I hope you don't mind.''

"Not at all,'' Rebecca answered, walking to his side. "Sarah will have dinner ready soon. I'll send it up then.''

Leaving Mark and Alison alone, Rebecca closed the door and walked down the hall, her thoughts wandering to the night ahead. She descended the stairs slowly. What would the next few hours bring? She was so engrossed with her thoughts that she didn't see Jonathon until she was almost upon him. She stopped immediately.

Jonathon watched closely as the shock of meeting him changed her expression.

"What are your plans, Jonathon?'' she managed to ask.

"I have none,'' he replied easily. "I'm merely going to wait and take things as they come.''

Rebecca nodded, her nervousness forgotten as her thoughts returned to Mark and Alison. "I suppose there's nothing we can do except wait.''

"Nothing.''

She looked at him again and felt his eyes lock with hers. For a moment she stood uncertain, but she finally broke the gaze and started to move away. "I have to tell

278

Sarah about the trays for Mark and Alison."

"I've already done it."

"Then I'll go help her prepare them." She continued to move away, but his voice arrested her.

"Becky." He watched her stop and turn hesitantly to face him. "Becky, we have to talk."

"Dinner's ready," Sarah called, coming from the kitchen. "As soon as I get you two settled, I'll take those trays up to our newlyweds." She turned toward the dining room, continuing to talk over her shoulder. "It sure is going to be strange serving just the two of you, with Ben back at the mine and Jeremiah sleeping out in the bush most of the time. But I guess I'll get used to it."

Rebecca stared at Jonathon a moment longer before following Sarah to the dining room. She had just reached it with Jonathon behind her when the front hall exploded with the violence of someone pounding on the door.

Rebecca froze. "It must be him."

Jonathon raised an eyebrow. "Yes, it must." He moved without hesitation back down the hall. Rebecca followed, slowly, watching his long, purposeful strides carry him rapidly to the big door and open it.

Richard Cunningham stormed past Jonathon into the house. "Where is she?" he demanded, his voice echoing through the hall.

"Do come in," Jonathon replied, closing the door softly.

Ignoring him, Richard Cunningham strode toward Rebecca. "Where is she? What have you done with her?"

"Done with whom?" Jonathon asked from behind him, looking magnificently tall and authoritative.

"My daughter Alison," Cunningham retorted. "As if you didn't know. You can stop playing games. I know she's here."

Jonathon descended the step to the main hall floor. "Playing games has never been one of my favorite

279

pastimes, Cunningham.''

''Then answer my question.''

''If you ask it civilly, perhaps we would,'' Rebecca objected, finding her voice. ''We're not accustomed to people storming into our home and making accusations.''

Cunningham flushed with anger. ''Alison is gone. This is the only place she would come to. Where is she?''

''She's with her husband, I presume,'' Jonathon replied.

''Her husband! You mean . . . Where is she? I'm taking her home immediately. I will not have her swept away in such a devious manner. I'll have the marriage annulled.''

''You can try to,'' Jonathon answered calmly, ''but there are few churches that will annul a marriage after it's been consummated.'' He watched the color drain from Cunningham's face. ''If you really want to see her, you can go to their bedroom. That is where newly-weds usually spend their first wedding night.''

Cunningham sputtered, trying to find the words to express his anger. ''You can't do this,'' he protested. ''You can't!''

''I haven't done anything except give your daughter the refuge she asked for. She came to us pleading for help, and we gave it to her. She made up her own mind to be married as soon as possible. No one forced her into it, except perhaps you.''

''Me?!''

''Yes, you. If you hadn't refused to give your consent, she wouldn't have run away. You let your own resentment stand in the way of your better judgment, and now you've not only lost a niece but a daughter as well.''

Cunningham glared at Jonathon. Then he turned to Rebecca. ''You, you're the cause of all this. You and your high-handed ways. Your running off set the example for her. She followed in your lead. You're a usurper. You've always been; you always will be. You came and ruined the harmony in my home, and now you've taken my daughter from me. You're a curse, Rebecca McGregor. You plague everyone you meet.''

''I think you had best leave, Cunningham,'' Jonathon thundered, ''before I throw you out.''

Cunningham turned to him. ''I'm leaving, but you haven't heard the last of this.''

''I believe I have,'' Jonathon replied. ''Now, shall I escort you to the door?'' He followed Cunningham out onto the porch, waiting there until he saw the man's horse disappear into the night. Then, he reentered the house, closed the door, and looked over his shoulder to speak to Rebecca. She was no longer there.

Rebecca ran to her room as soon as Richard Cunningham was out the door. She covered her burning ears and sank onto the window seat until her heart ceased pounding. Matters grew worse and worse. Would there be no end to the complex tangle she had created? First an irate husband and now an irate uncle. Who was next? Mark? Alison? Ben? Jeremiah? Perhaps even Sarah? Who would be her next foe? Her uncle was right. She was a curse, a plague to everyone. Her uncle, Jonathon, Mark and Alison, Bobby O'Riley. A cold chill of loneliness ran through her. Would she be forever alone?

Rebecca stood and walked quickly into Matt's room. She went to the crib and picked the sleeping child up, holding him tightly to her. ''What are we to do, Matthew? What are we to do?''

281

35

The months of October and November passed with only two brief showers. The land was rapidly beginning to dry up under the cloudless sky; the summer heat was only beginning.

Mark and Alison decided to stay through December and Christmas before returning to England to live. Mark kept diligent watch over the wheat stalks and the much-needed water in the dam.

Alison stayed at the house while Mark worked, trying her best to learn about cooking and sewing. She knew she would need to know the fundamentals of both if she were to take care of Mark and herself in England, and Rebecca was a willing teacher. Alison was a quick learner once she discovered she liked the tasks she had always thought were downgrading.

Rebecca filled their hours with the learning of household chores, keeping her own mind as busy as possible to avoid thinking about Jonathon. She longed to ask him when he was leaving, but in reality she was glad she did not know. It saved her from counting the time until he left, from wanting to savor each hour of every day. Even though they no longer shared their lives, and she saw him only from a distance, at least he was still with her. She could see him, watch him, admire and love him while he was in reach.

Jonathon had not had another opportunity to approach her since Richard Cunningham's visit. Rebecca made certain the occasion for such a meeting did not arise. She didn't want to find herself alone in the same room, listening while he explained his plans. Hearing the words would only cause her added pain.

When Rebecca even thought of his leaving, she ached

inside. She often awakened during the night, crying out his name, reaching for him when he wasn't there. She couldn't imagine living without him. It hurt her deeply to know he could live without her, that he could go back to another woman with no thought of her or their son.

Matt was a comfort to her, and Rebecca gave all her love to the baby. She would sit for hours in the same room with him, neither picking him up nor holding him, because she had no wish to spoil him. Nonetheless, she remained with him. She would always be thankful to Jonathon for giving her their son, something Jonathon could never take from her.

Jonathon found relief from his thoughts in the work at the mine or by riding over the land to check the wells and the growing number of stock. The separation from Rebecca pained him, but he could find no way to repair it. He was too proud to beg, and she was too hurt. It distressed him to see her suffer. Of late, she had become thinner and had lost the open enthusiasm for life that had always radiated from her. She seldom went riding over the land anymore, and she no longer asked him about the progress being made in the mine or in the fields. It was as if she had lost interest in living and was content to stay at home. He could not believe she was happy.

Ben often asked about Rebecca, since she never came to see him anymore. Jonathon usually found himself at a loss to say anything. He had lost all touch with her. They never spoke, except over dinner when other people were present. He no longer knew how she felt, what she did with her time.

Jonathon wanted to reach out to Rebecca. Yet, he wanted to hold back. He was beginning to believe the rift between them was for the best. When he went back to England, the parting would not be so painful if they were no longer living and sharing their lives as husband and wife. But a doubt lingered in his mind. He needed to set things right between them before he left. He couldn't leave her knowing she hated him for what she believed were his plans. How could he approach her? *Should* he approach her? Would it be best if he left her hating him?

December came and a trip to town was planned. Everyone was expected to go, but Rebecca had no intention of accompanying the others. She said nothing until the day came. She knew she could never make the journey. She could not go into town pretending to be Jonathon's wife and then openly occupy a separate bedroom. She did not want to face that moment or take the chance of being alone with him. She also didn't want to see Mark and Alison make their plans to depart. When they made their plans, it was likely Jonathon would make his, too.

On the morning they were to leave, Rebecca stayed in her room until she knew the others were downstairs. Making her way onto the porch, she stopped Alison and handed her cousin a list and some money.

Alison accepted the paper reluctantly. "Are you certain you won't come with us?"

"I am," Rebecca replied with a small smile. "Someone has to remain here to hold the roof down."

Alison nodded. A question was on her lips, but she remained silent and moved down the porch stairs to join Mark.

Jonathon strode out of the house, pulling on his riding gloves. He stopped abruptly when he saw Rebecca standing outside, dressed in a cool summer smock. "You're not coming with us?"

"No. There's no need for me to go."

"But you haven't been into town in months."

"I'll go when I have the need," she replied, avoiding his eyes.

"If it's because *I'm* going, I can remain behind."

"You're going, Jonathon. I'm staying," Rebecca stated firmly. "Good-bye, Jonathon. Have a safe trip." She turned and walked back into the house, followed by the big yellow dog.

Jonathon set his jaw firmly, hesitating before

descending the stairs to his horse. "Are we ready?" he asked Mark and Alison as he mounted.

"I think so," Mark replied, helping Alison into the saddle before casting a look at the door Rebecca had passed through.

"Rebecca has decided not to come," Jonathon said.

Mark shrugged and swung into the saddle. "Let's go then."

They started out, cantering to the end of the plateau, when Mark suddenly snapped his fingers. "My letters. I forgot them on my dresser. You two go on. I'll catch up in a few minutes."

Jonathon nodded as Mark spun his horse around. He did not see the relief reflected on Alison's face.

Mark thundered to a halt before the house, racing up the stairs to Matt's room.

"Mark! What are you doing here?"

"I've come to talk to you."

"Can't it wait until you return from town? Surely, the others are waiting."

"I've told them to go on, that I forgot some letters I wanted to mail."

"But why?"

"Because I have to ask you a question. I know you and Jonathon have had a difference of opinion about something, and Alison and I are afraid it was because of us."

Rebecca held up her hands and turned away with a pained expression. "You can ease your mind, Mark. It's not because of you and Alison. It would have happened sooner or later. Perhaps it's better sooner."

"Becky."

She shook her head. "It's no use, Mark. There's nothing you can say that I haven't already thought." She sighed. "Your brother and I were not married because we loved one another like you and Alison. We were married because I needed a husband and he wanted to be rich."

"But you learned to love each other."

"No. No, we didn't."

"You can't tell me you don't love Jonathon."

Rebecca turned to him. "No, I won't try to tell you that."

"And he loves you. I don't understand."

She closed her eyes and shook her head. "Your brother may love me in a small way, but it's not the kind of love to build a marriage on. He believes he has to return to England, and so he must. I knew when I married him that he would leave me in two years and never return."

"I can't believe he'll leave," Mark insisted. "He *does* love you. He won't leave you."

"Believe what you will, Mark. It's always good to believe the best. In this case, it's not possible for me." He opened his mouth to speak, but she waved him silent. "Go now, Mark. There's nothing more to be said. The three of you will return to England, and I'll remain here. You've made your choice, and I mine."

Mark tried to think of something to say, something that would change her mind. There was nothing. No words could express how helpless he felt. The damage had been done, and he was not the one to repair it. "You'll be all right here alone?" he asked.

"I'm not alone," she replied, bending to pick up her son. "I have Matt, and Matt has me."

Mark's throat contracted as he watched what would be a loving scene under other circumstances. But he knew the truth behind her gesture. He turned quickly and hurried down the stairs to his horse before she could see the tears coming to his eyes.

For seven days, they remained away. Rebecca discovered what a big and lonely place her home could be. In the new year, the house would always be empty. Faced with this prospect, she realized she must find more to occupy her time than just her son. She couldn't shut herself up in the house forever and watch him grow. No, she would have to take over Jonathon's responsibilities. She would have to become the one who checked on the mine, the stock, the fields, the wells, and the dam. She would have to sit at night and balance the books as he now did. She would have to keep a close eye on the bank account, and she would have to make decisions when problems arose.

She was glad she had three good men working with her whom she knew she could trust: Ben, Jeremiah, and Bill Mallory. All three would help her as much as possible to make her job easier. It would be a difficult adjustment to make, but she could do it. She would have to.

There were the hotel, the restaurant, and the docks and warehouses to concern her, too. Considering the distance from her home to town, she wondered if she shouldn't sell her interests there. She wouldn't have time to run back and forth to check on their progress and problems. No, she must give them up.

When the others returned from town, Rebecca had made up her mind to prepare herself for the life and obligations she would soon have to bear alone. Her first step would be to once again become a constant visitor at the tent town. If the miners and their families became aware of her presence once more, they wouldn't feel deserted when Jonathon left.

Jonathon noticed the change in Rebecca immediately. It wasn't the change he wished to see, but he was glad she had begun to take an interest in her surroundings again. He knew the motivation behind her unexpected activity was due to his imminent departure. He recognized her actions as mute acceptance of his intention to leave, and he felt an aching emptiness gnawing at him. Alone in his room, he lay staring at the ceiling, going over and over again the passing of the last two years. Doubts began to grow about the depth of his hate for Arthur Boyd. He had to do something, but what? What could he do? He had to go back, didn't he? His only purpose in coming to Australia had been to return. So he must return. Mustn't he?

By the time Christmas Eve arrived, the heat was insufferable. No rain had fallen during December, and the sky continued to remain clear. The wells began to dry up, and Mark was keeping an anxious eye on the dam. The ground was dehydrating rapidly. Still the sun continued to burn, scorching the grass brown and baking the earth until jagged cracks split the soil.

"I don't like the way everything's been drying up," Ben told Jonathon as he wiped the sweat from his brow. "We're heading for a brush fire sure enough."

"Brush fire?" Jonathon questioned, running his already soaked handkerchief over his face and neck. Even the mine had been invaded by the heat. Most of the men worked bare chested these days.

"It's a sight you'll never want to see," Ben answered shaking his head. "A little spark will do it in this weather. It'll catch on the dry grass and spread for miles in a matter of minutes. I've seen fire burn acre upon acre of land in an hour's time before it just up and quits."

"Isn't there any way of stopping one when it starts?"

"Nope. There won't be any water to fight it with by the time it starts. The only way the fire stops is when it runs across dry river beds or dried-up rock gullies. Natural barriers stop the fire and turn it back on itself."

Jonathon looked at the cloudless sky. "Let's hope it doesn't come to that. Maybe it will rain."

Ben followed his gaze. "No harm in hoping."

The noon bell rang and Jonathon and Ben remained by the entrance of the mine until every man had left, wishing all their workers a good holiday before closing down the operation until after Christmas.

Rebecca and Sarah worked through the day to prepare a Christmas dinner. Despite their efforts to serve a delicious meal, no one ate much. The heat absorbed their appetites.

Eventually, everyone left the table to try to find a private corner when he could escape the heat. Rebecca chose the front porch, accompanied by Dingo. She sat down on the steps and looked out over the plateau. How different this Christmas Eve was compared to last year! Then there had been a big celebration. People had laughed and danced, singing loudly while they ate good food. It had been a happy night. She had been surrounded by happy people. She had been pregnant with Matt and had sat at Jonathon's side throughout the evening, awakening to his gentle touch in the morning and a front porch filled with gifts.

Rebecca patted Dingo and wondered at how time changed so many things. Even her birthday had not been on such a grand scale in November. There had been a cake and presents, but it reminded her more of birthdays spent at Cunningham House than of the gay night she had enjoyed at the mine a year ago.

There would be no more babies, she thought miserably. No more Jonathon. She had no one to blame but herself. She should have thought of the future as well as the present before asking Jonathon Gray to marry her. If only she had. What use were ifs? What was done was done.

The sky above the plateau stretched from horizon to horizon, holding a bright moon and a kaleidoscope of stars. It should have been a beautiful night, a peaceful night, but Rebecca felt no peace inside. She felt only sorrow and loneliness. With a deep sigh, she rose to go into the house.

"You're not leaving already?" Jonathon asked. "It's much nicer out here than in there," he continued, stepping forward from the shadows.

"I didn't know you were there," Rebecca said, wondering frantically how long he had been watching her.

"I didn't want you to know," he replied. "Come, sit down. There's room enough for two on these steps and space to spare for this ugly mongrel." She hesitated. "Even if you don't wish to share my company, I'd very much like to share yours."

Rebecca felt her will melt under the quiet serenity of

the spell he wove, and she slowly sank down to sit tensely beside him. She forced her eyes back to look at the land, waiting for him to speak, fearing the conversation she had been avoiding had come at last.

"It's quite a different Christmas from the one we spent here last year," Jonathon commented.

"Aye. Very different."

"I asked the workers if they wanted another party, but they refused, saying it was too hot. I told them I'd wait until the weather turned cooler."

"I didn't know."

"You didn't ask."

Rebecca flushed and clenched her hands tightly together in her lap. He was right. It was only this month she had begun taking an interest again in the people who worked for them. Even so, she still thought much more about her personal problems than she did about her employees. "I'm sorry," she murmured. "Have you set a date for the celebration?"

"No. I thought sometime in the fall would be best."

She glanced quickly at him. "By the time fall arrives, you'll no longer be here, but I'll see that your word is kept."

Jonathon turned to look at her, frowning slightly as he studied her profile. "I'll still be here when March comes."

"There's no need for you to stay so long," she told him. "You should return with Mark and Alison to your home. It would be better for you to go with them than to go alone."

"You asked me to stay for two years."

"There's no need. I won't be keeping you if you wish to go. You've done what I asked and more, and I thank you for keeping your half of the agreement."

"No more than a thank you?"

Rebecca swallowed and felt her nails dig into the soft flesh of her palms. "What would you have me say?"

"Perhaps that you'll miss me, even a little. I wouldn't like to leave believing you thought ill of me."

"I could never think ill of you, Jonathon."

"Never?"

"No." She rose quickly. "Now if you'll excuse me, I'd like to go in."

He stood, too, his great height seeming much greater to her now. "Becky?"

"Please, Jonathon, don't. I couldn't stand it. Leave and take what you will, but don't ask me to do the impossible. Don't ask me to stand by and calmly discuss your leaving, because I can't. You're the father of my son, and I won't be glad to see you go. But if you feel you must go, then you must. I won't try to stop you and I won't weight you down with tears."

"And if I don't go? If I stay?"

Rebecca drew her breath sharply. "Jonathon, don't. Don't say that unless you mean it."

Hurt pride rebelled within him. As he looked at her, unspoken words burned on his lips. He wanted to cry out at all the doubts, the endless demands running through his mind. He wanted time to stop. He had to think. He needed to reason it out, but time kept slipping away. What was right and what was wrong had been lost to him long ago. His love for Rebecca had cast a dark and overpowering shadow on his plans for vengence. Questions plagued him, and indecision had become his constant companion.

Watching him, Rebecca could see the turmoil he felt. She wanted to help, to reach out to him, but she could not. He was the only one who could make the decision. He was the only one who could decide what was to be. She shook her head. "I cannot live on hope, Jonathon. I have to know."

Jonathon reached out to touch her, but he turned away abruptly as an indistinguishable cry rumbled from his throat.

Rebecca put a hand to her mouth as tears stung her eyes. Every instinct in her told her to go to him, but common sense held her back. If she relented, if she gave in to him, he would come to no decision. They would remain as they were now, suspended in uncertainty. No, she could not go to him. Before she gave into the beating of her heart instead of the reason in her head, she turned and fled to the safety of her room.

36

Work continued as usual after the holiday, leaving the house empty the morning after Christmas, except for Sarah and Matt. Alison went with Mark to the dam, knowing that in two short weeks, they would be on their way to England. Jeremiah rode north to the stock, to check on the amount of grazing land still available to the animals. Rebecca and Jonathon left for the mine at different times each day; Rebecca went to visit the tent town, Jonathon to join Ben in the mine.

It was quiet at the tent town, the heat keeping even the children quiet. Rebecca left after staying only two hours. A light breeze was blowing from the west, the first welcome sign of a change in the weather in months. She took advantage of the coolness and cantered off. She lost herself for an hour among the sounds and smells of the wilderness, watching kangaroos bound through the dry grass and listening to the calls that echoed about her. Soon, a strange smell began to invade the fresh air. Smoke?

Rebecca stopped to look around, searching for a sign of a campfire where someone was cooking a meal. There was no one to be seen, but the smell continued. She turned in the saddle and a gasp tore from her lungs.

A huge cloud was building and growing off to the west, filling the sky and air. A brush fire! It was coming her way. She knew only too well what a fire in a drought could do.

Jonathon and Matt—she had to get to them. She had to warn them. As she swung her horse around, she realized she couldn't reach both of them. At least, not in time. The fire would spread too far and too fast.

Jonathon was safe. He was at the mine. Ben would

293

take care of him and the miners. All the men and their families would be safe in the cavern, and Jonathon would be with them. But Matt. Sarah and Matt were alone. There was no shelter on the open plateau, no protection. Sarah wouldn't know what to do. Rebecca had to reach them! She had to get to them in time!

Only short miles away, Jonathon and Ben stopped work to listen to the murmuring of the miners at the mouth of the cave. Ben hesitated only a moment before dropping his tools to run to the entrance. Jonathon followed him and stopped to stare at the oncoming cloud the ignorant workers were watching.

"It's a brush fire!" Ben exclaimed. All the men spun to look at him, their expressions fearful and unsure. "You men, go down and get your families up here now! Get them inside the mine as deep as you can, and keep your heads down!"

The men ran, no questions asked. Jonathon grabbed Ben's arm. "Becky's down there. Make sure she's safe. I'm going to try to get Matt."

Jonathon turned to run, but Ben stopped him. "Becky's not down there. She left over an hour ago to ride in the bush."

"She what?!"

"She's a smart girl," Ben said. "She'll come back."

"No, she won't. She won't leave Matt. She'll try to get to him." Jonathon pulled away and ran for his horse.

"Where are you going?" Ben called after him. "You can't go out there looking for her. You'll never find her. You'll end up getting yourself killed!"

"I'm going to the house—for Matt and her. If she can get there, she will. I'm going to try to be there, too!"

At the house, Sarah was outside hanging clothes on the line when her son called to her from the stable. Following his excited gesture, she turned to stare at the great cloud hovering in the sky. She had heard of brush fires during the past few weeks. They said they swept the country for miles. If that was what this was, they had to find cover. What if it wasn't? Could it be only a dust storm? She frowned. There wasn't enough wind. "It's a fire! I'll get Matt. We've got to find a place to stay."

"How bad is it?" Alison asked, watching Mark bend to examine the dry ground.

"Bad enough," he answered rising. "We've got enough water in the dam to keep it . . ."

Alison followed his gaze and cried out in alarm. "Mark! It's a brush fire!"

"Are you sure?"

She didn't bother to answer. "We've got to find shelter." She grabbed his hand and they began to run, unaware that, miles away, where Alison had sat watching many brush fires burn, a structure had already caught fire. Cunningham House was falling, burying Richard Cunningham and his dreams.

Jeremiah was the last to see the fire coming. Being far to the north, it was a while after the fire started that the cloud began to rise up on his horizon. A cold chill ran over him as he watched the black cloud grow. He knew what it was. He had seen too many prairie fires not to. He was without shelter, completely in the open. His only chance was to run, and it was a small chance at that. He jerked his horse around and drove his heels into the animal's side.

Rebecca bent low on her horse's neck, urging the animal on as it stretched out, putting distance behind them. It wasn't much further now. Only a few short minutes and she'd be there. She *had* to be there. She had to save Matt!

All of a sudden, she found herself out of the saddle, flying over her mount's neck and hitting the ground. Dazed, the wind knocked from her, she lay for a moment in pain and shock. A tortured cry ripped into her consciousness, and she shook her head to see her horse struggling pitifully, flailing as it lunged again and again to try to gain its feet. The animal had stepped into a hole. Its leg was broken. There was no helping it or herself now. They were both caught.

Staggering to her feet, her leg throbbing painfully under her, Rebecca limped to the panicked animal. Trying to still its struggles with soothing words, she withdrew the shotgun from its boot and backed away.

She cocked the triggers as tears burned her eyes. The animal lurched once more. Sh had to put it out of its misery. She might be able to reach the house yet, but she couldn't leave the animal like this.

The blast of a gun rumbled over the plateau. Jonathon jerked his horse sharply to a halt. Who would be out shooting when there was an inferno burning its way across the horizon? He hesitated, but only briefly, before spurring his horse toward the shot. Whoever it was, they had to be warned. The house was only moments away. There would be time for a quick warning.

Rebecca fell to the ground when she tried to walk, her leg giving out under her weight. She pulled herself to a sitting position, crying out in pain and frustration. Matt! Who was going to help Matt? The cloud was bigger now, blacker, closer. Any moment it would be upon her. It would take her and then Matt. No one could help either of them.

A loud pounding echoed on the ground beneath her. A horse? A horse coming her way? She struggled to her feet again, using the shotgun for support and blinking the tears from her eyes. Jonathon! It was Jonathon!

Plunging to a stop beside her, Jonathon swept her up behind him. "Are you all right?"

"Don't worry over me! We've got to reach Matt!"

He didn't reply but spun his horse around as Rebecca wrapped her arms around him and held on.

The house soon appeared before them. Jonathon was off his horse and running before the animal stopped. "Sarah!" he called, halting in the kitchen. "Sarah!"

Vague noises echoed from the kitchen, and a moment

later the door to the cellar storage area opened. Sarah came out. "We're here. It's the only place I could think of to hide. It has dirt walls."

Jonathon took Matt from her. "And a house on top of it. Come on. Hurry. Becky's outside. We've got to get to cover." Jonathon hustled Sarah and her son out the door, handing Matt up to Rebecca, who had remained on the lathered horse.

Racing across the plateau, Jonathon led them to a group of boulders and rocks.

"Get down on the ground and bury yourselves as close to the rocks as you can," he ordered, helping Rebecca off the horse.

Sarah and her son immediately fell to digging, but Rebecca cast a reluctant gaze at the house. "We'll lose the house."

Jonathon put an arm around her shoulders. "We'll build another," he answered.

Rebecca felt hope ignite in her. But Jonathon looked toward the fire. It had spread to the southwest rapidly and appeared to be coming back from the east.

"There's something wrong," Jonathon murmured. "The fire's coming from the east."

"The fire doesn't spread in any one direction, Jonathon. It burns wherever the land leads it."

He held up his hand to test the wind, hope dawning in his eyes. "It's switched! The wind's switched!" Straining to see through the rapidly gathering smoke, he scanned the horizon where the dam stood. "The wind will blow the fire out. It'll force it to go back on the land it's already burned. We'll be in its path unless . . . if the river and dam stops it, it won't reach the house!" He suddenly remembered his younger brother. "Mark. Where's Mark?"

"He and Alison went to the dam this morning."

Jonathon's jaw set firmly as the smoke began to drift around them. There was no cover in the fields. It was all open land. The only protection would be the dam, inside it, against its solid dirt walls, and in the water it held. For them, on the plateau, it was their only hope, but for Mark and Alison, if they were there, it could be their damnation.

Rebecca began to cough, and Jonathon turned to pull her to the ground. Digging at the hard dirt with his bare hands, he put her against one of the giant boulders and began throwing dirt over her and Matt.

If the fire got through the fields, past the river and the dam, it would go right over them. They wouldn't have much of a chance, but they had to try.

Jonathon buried himself when Rebecca was covered, and settled down to wait. The heat bore down, surrounding them, suffocating them as the smoke burned their nostrils and painful tears were forced from their eyes. Time ceased to exist as the heat increased. Burning ash and smoke penetrated their safety.

Holding his face against his sleeve, Jonathon felt anger pound through his veins. Fire was threatening everything he knew, everything he loved. It was trying to take what he had, what he had built. Soon his anger was burning as hot as the air around him. He lifted his head to look through the smoky dimness. Surely, the fire would have passed them by now if it was coming. Even a delay at the river and dam wouldn't hold back the flames this long.

Impatiently, he heaved himself from the dirt and jumped to his feet, fighting against the smoke to see through to land beyond. His eyes burned and watered as he watched the wisps of smoke. It was neither thick nor constant. It was dispersing, not burning.

Jonathon ran a hand over his eyes and stared out at the plateau where the house stood. It was still there. It was still standing!

He quickly looked toward the fields. That was where the smoke was coming from, but he could see no flames, no fire. The water had stopped it. The dam and river had stopped the fire.

"Becky! Becky, come here."

Forcing her way out from under the dirt covering her, she left Matt to stand beside Jonathon. "What is it?"

she asked.

"Look for yourself."

Rebecca hesitantly turned her eyes to the land, prepared to see nothing but a blackened mass where once there had been green life. But the sight she imagined wasn't there. The house was untouched, the plateau unburned. "It burned itself out," she gasped in disbelief.

"If it hasn't, it will. It can't burn the same land twice," Jonathon agreed smiling down at her. "It's over."

"We're safe?"

"We're safe, Mrs. Gray."

Mrs. Gray? Slowly she raised her eyes to his, uncertainty and fear still lingering inside her. But they quickly gave way to something better, and she threw her arms around her husband.

The battle for their land was over. So was the battle between them. There was no indecision in Jonathon's eyes now. He had found what was important in his life. He had found his home. What he loved didn't lay back in England. It was here!

Jonathon held her tightly, new tears stinging his eyes because of what he had almost lost—and not because of a fire. Hurt pride and seething hate had allowed him to become obsessed with getting vengence, blinding him to everything except one purpose. He had tried to rule his life with his head. He had erected a wall to protect his feelings, forgetting and pushing aside whatever touched his heart. But when his hate turned against him because of the pain he put those he loved through, the wall holding him back weakened. The fire was the instrument that broke down the last barrier.

Jonathon lifted Rebecca's face to his, staring down into her green eyes and wiping away the tears staining her cheeks. Her lips trembled into a smile and told him she understood what he knew. He was going to stay. He was going to stay with his family, in his home in Australia.

37

It wasn't until nightfall when people started to straggle in that Rebecca and Jonathon learned the extent of the damage.

The mine had made it through. Ben and the tent-town families had huddled together inside as the fire raged over the hill, burning the tents.

The range land to the north had remained completely untouched except by the smoke carried on the wind. Jeremiah never saw any fire, but he had traveled a good distance from the stock before there was a recognizable change in the smoke's direction.

Mark and Alison hadn't been as lucky. They sat in the dam with the other farmers while the fire swept up from the southwest, racing across the land toward them until the wind switched direction. When it did, Mark realized their only hope for survival was in releasing the water. He emptied the dam and flooded the fields, stopping the fire from roaring past them onto the plateau. It was on the saved plateau that the workers and their families came to stay, accepting food and drink from Rebecca and Sarah, who had returned to the house with Jonathon soon after the fire burned itself out on the riverbed.

On reaching the house, Ben gathered several men and set out for town. The supplies inside the house wouldn't keep everyone fed for very long.

Sam remained behind to scout the charred land, searching for survivors and checking how far the fire had run. While doing it, he discovered the remains of Cunningham House. Thinking that Richard and Elaine Cunningham might have sought shelter in the Cunningham mine, Sam rode to the mine's devastated tent town to speak with the people there. Neither of the Cunninghams had been seen since the fire had begun. The house had been burned to the ground and the land for miles around it had been swept by the fire. There was no chance Richard or Elaine Cunningham could have survived on the open land. They were presumed dead and buried.

Alison took the news hard, but she threw herself feverishly into helping the workers to keep from dwelling on her lost family. Mark stayed with her as much as possible, and Rebecca and Sarah were at Alison's side constantly.

It was a long, hard first week on the plateau. Supplies were stretched to the limit before Ben and the other men returned from town. It was only days later when Rebecca and Jonathon had to accompany Mark and Alison to meet their ship. The young couple were going to England to make their home.

"I won't say I'm sorry you're not coming with us," Mark told Jonathon as they shook hands on the dock. "I'm glad you've decided to stay."

"As am I," Jonathon agreed as Rebecca came forward to stand beside him.

"We'll miss you, Mark," she told him as he took her hands in his.

"And I you," he agreed. "But not for long. You're still planning on coming to England before the rains, aren't you?"

"We haven't decided on an exact date yet," Jonathon answered. "But we'll be coming. We have to buy the rest of the furniture for the house."

"And we'll be coming to pick it out ourselves," Rebecca smiled.

"If you don't mind, I'll come along and help," Alison suggested.

"I'd like that," Rebecca agreed. "We might even leave the men at home."

The ship's whistle blew, echoing across the harbor as it stood moored at the dock.

"I guess it's good-bye for now then," Mark said kissing Rebecca and shaking Jonathon's hand once more.

Alison kissed Jonathon and turned to Rebecca. "Thank you for everything, Becky. I owe you . . ."

"You owe me nothing," Rebecca interrupted. "Be happy, Alison. That's what counts most."

Mark slipped his hand in Alison's and led her off, moving up the gangplank to stand at the ship's railing. Rebecca and Jonathon remained on the dock to watch the ropes being cast off, waiting there as the ship moved away. It lumbered slowly out of the port, gliding over the blue waters toward the distant horizon.

A feeling of awe swept through Rebecca as she stood beside Jonathon and saw the ship become smaller and smaller. How much their lives had influenced those of others, and how much the land had affected them all! The land had brought them together, the land and what it offered. The land had also kept them together in the end. It was a strange land, this Australia. It could be wicked or good, cruel or kind, hateful or forgiving. It could give richness, or it could leave poverty.

The land hadn't been good to the Cunninghams. It had given them nothing and taken all. It had been the cause of death for Richard Cunningham's wife; it had demanded Richard Cunningham's wealth and affections through his ceaseless efforts to obtain gold. Eventually, it had taken most of his family—and himself.

Yes, it was a hard land, but it had been good to Rebecca and those she loved. It had made her rich, given her a kingdom, and a man to share her kingdom with.

To Jonathon, it had given something to live for, to fight for. It had given him something and someone to love. To Mark it had given Alison and a feeling of achievement and satisfaction. Ben and Jeremiah, wanderers in a big world, had found a home, a place to live, to work and be happy.

Rebecca looked at Jonathon as he watched the ship move out of view. He would stay. She was certain of that now. He would stay and help her continue to make the land grow. He would return to England. but when he did, there would be no malice in his heart as he walked the crowded and busy streets of London. Instead, he would find only relief and happiness there, knowing he had made his place in life. It had taken him a long time to realize that, when he found Australia, he found everything he was seeking. He discovered the truth before it was too late.

Jonathon turned to find Rebecca watching him. He tightened his arm around her shoulders. He would stay. He would be happy. Rebecca would always be at his side to insure he remained that way.

*The towering novel of love and adventure
as vast and romantic
as Australia itself!*

OUTBACK

The bestselling saga by
AARON FLETCHER

Patrick Garrity started life as the bastard son of a female convict. Unwanted and unloved, he was born in shame and raised in the poverty of a Sydney orphanage. Barely out of his teens, he left the brawling city to make a new life for himself in the limitless back country of New South Wales. Alone and hungry, he met the woman who would change his destiny and that of an entire continent.

Innocent in the ways of the Europeans, Mayrah was the native girl Garrity bought to satisfy his passions. Divided by competing cultures, they were nevertheless united by their fierce love of the land—and eventually, each other. Together they carved out an enormous empire in the great Outback, and founded a new generation of Australians who would forever bear the imprint of their pride and passion.

More than 2 million copies in print!

____2611-2   OUTBACK by Aaron Fletcher $4.50US/$5.50CAN